"Few writers are as energetic and prolific as Joyce Carol Oates.... Hers is an intensely truthful, explicitly emotional yet sometimes nightmarishly heightened world.... This book is angry and tough and deeply, viscerally unsettling.... Oates is the most agile and effective of poets, able to pin down a moment while never compromising on pace or atmosphere.... This collection could be used as a master class in the art of pure, suspenseful storytelling."
  —*New York Times*

"Although American fiction offers few distinctive voices at present, there is no mistaking a Joyce Carol Oates story for anyone else's. You could tear off the cover of her latest collection, *Sourland*, and identify these stories from their opening lines alone.... Not just their virtuosity but also their aura of menace make them hers.... We think of Oates, like Poe, as a master of terror, but her real mastery is in almost never depicting a strong emotion in isolation.... Oates makes for a caustic companion in *Sourland*—a fearless experimenter forcing the reader ahead of her at knifepoint."
  —*Los Angeles Times*

"Making sense of life in a cataclysmic inner and outer landscape has been Joyce Carol Oates' obsession for five decades. This evocative new collection shows just how much sense she can make of it now."
  —*Chicago Tribune*

"Innovative, brilliant.... There are sentences that leave a deeply sensuous pleasure in their wake."
  —*San Francisco Chronicle*

"Splendid yet shocking…. Each of the tales does what only Oates can do—which is take us, easily, where we do not wish to go, rushing us headlong toward something cruel and unspeakable, something we don't want to know and are now bound never to forget. Gift or curse, it is Oates' great talent…. These are devastating pieces—made more so by their brevity. For, if there is anything more disturbing than a Joyce Carol Oates novel, it is one of her short stories—with its ability to condense her dark intent to a handful of images that will be forever engraved upon our psyches."

—*Buffalo News*

"Oates is a master of the dark tale—stories of the hunted and the hunter, of violence, trauma, and deep psychic wounds. Brilliant in her disclosure of the workings of minds under threat, Oates also possesses a heightened sense of the body's expressiveness, from a man's gait to the smell of his breath to the strength of his grip to the intensity of his stare. Oates grows more insightful, virtuosic, and audacious in her confrontations with fear, pain, and death. Her latest stories of sexual mayhem, family crisis, and shattered identity are barely contained beasts of narration, snorting, pawing, and pulling against the confines of the page…. This is a trenchant book of 'cruel fairy tales' in which people are severely tested, profoundly punished, and tragically transformed."

—*Booklist* (starred review)

SOURLAND

ALSO BY JOYCE CAROL OATES

SOURLAND

STORIES

JOYCE CAROL OATES

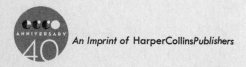

An Imprint of HarperCollinsPublishers

for my husband Charlie Gross

SOURLAND. Copyright © 2010 by The Ontario Review. All rights reserved.
Printed in the United States of America. No part of this book may be used or
reproduced in any manner whatsoever without written permission except in the case
of brief quotations embodied in critical articles and reviews. For information address
HarperCollins Publishers, 10 East 53rd Street, New York, NY 10022.

HarperCollins books may be purchased for educational, business, or sales
promotional use. For information please write: Special Markets Department,
HarperCollins Publishers, 10 East 53rd Street, New York, NY 10022.

A hardcover edition of this book was first published in 2010 by Ecco, an imprint of
HarperCollins Publishers.

FIRST ECCO PAPERBACK EDITION PUBLISHED 2011.

Designed by Mary Austin Speaker
Frontispiece photograph by Kramer O'Neill

Library of Congress Cataloging-in-Publication Data has been applied for.

ISBN 978-0-06-199653-5

11   12   13   14 15   /RRD   10   9   8   7   6   5   4   3   2   1

CONTENTS

I.

II.

III.

ACKNOWLEDGMENTS

Many thanks are due to the editors of the magazines and journals in which, often in slightly different versions, these stories originally appeared.

"Pumpkin-Head" in *The New Yorker*.

"The Story of the Stabbing" in *The Dark End of the Street*, edited by Jonathan Santlofer.

"Babysitter" in *Ellery Queen*; reprinted in *Horror: The Best of the Year 2006*.

"Lost Daddy" in *Playboy*.

"Bonobo Momma" in *Michigan Quarterly Review*; reprinted in *Pushcart Prize XXXIII: Best of the Small Presses 2009*, edited by William Henderson.

"Bitch" in *Boulevard*.

"Amputee" in *Shenandoah*.

"The Beating" in *Conjunctions*.

"Bounty Hunter" in *The Guardian*.

"The Barter" in *Story*.

"Honor Code" in *Ellery Queen*; reprinted in *The Finest Crime and Mystery Novellas of the Year*, edited by Ed Gormand and Martin Greenberg.

"Probate" in *Salmagundi*.

"Donor Organs" in *Michigan Quarterly Review*.

"Death Certificate" in *Boulevard*.

"Uranus" in *Conjunctions*.

"Sourland" in *Boulevard*.

I.

PUMPKIN-HEAD

In late March there'd been a sleet storm through north central New Jersey. Her husband had died several days before. There was no connection, she knew. Except since that time she'd begun to notice at twilight a curious glisten to the air. Often she found herself in the doorway of her house, or outside—not remembering how she'd gotten there. For long minutes she stared seeing how, as colors faded, the glassy light emerged from both the sky and from the Scotch pines surrounding the house. It did not seem to her a natural light and in weak moments she thought *This is the crossing-over time.* She stared not certain what she might be seeing. She felt aroused, vigilant. She felt apprehension. She wondered if the strange glisten to the air had always been there but in her previous, protected life she hadn't noticed it.

This October evening, before the sun had entirely set, headlights turned into the driveway, some distance away at the road. She was startled into wakefulness—at first not sure where she was. Then she realized, Anton Kruppe was dropping by to see her at about this time.

Dropping by he'd said. Or maybe she'd said *Why don't you drop by.*

She couldn't see his face distinctly. He did appear to be driving a pickup truck with indistinct white letters on its side. Out of the driver's seat in the high cab of the truck he climbed down and lurched toward her on the shadowy path—a tall male scarecrow figure with a misshapen Halloween pumpkin for a head.

What a shock! Hadley backed away, not knowing what she was seeing.

The grinning pumpkin-head on a man's shoulders, its leering cutout eyes not lighted from within, like a jack-o'-lantern, but dark, glassy. And the voice issuing through the grinning slash-mouth in heavily accented English:

"Ma'am? Is correct address? You are—lady of the house?"

She laughed, nervously. She supposed she was meant to laugh.

With grating mock-gravity the voice persevered:"You are—resident here, ma'am? I am—welcome here? Yes?"

It was a joke. One of Anton Kruppe's awkward jokes. He'd succeeded in frightening Hadley though probably that hadn't been his intention, probably he'd just meant to make her laugh. It was embarrassing that she'd been genuinely frightened for she had known perfectly well that Anton was coming of course. And who else but Anton Kruppe would show up like this, with a Halloween pumpkin for a head?

Hadley scarcely knew the man. She felt a stab of dismay, that she'd invited him to drop by. Impulsively she'd invited him and of course he'd said *yes.*

At the co-op, Anton was the most eager and courteous of workers. He was the one to joke with customers, and to laugh at his own jokes; he was boyish, vulnerable and touching; his awkward speech was itself a kind of laughter, not fully intelligible yet contagious. For all his clumsiness you could tell that he was an exceptionally intelligent man. Hadley could see that he'd gone to painstaking trouble carving the Halloween pumpkin-head: it was large, bulbous, weirdly veined and striated, twice the size of a normal man's head, with triangular eyes, triangular nose, grinning mouth studded with fang-teeth. Somehow, he'd managed to force the thing over his head—Hadley couldn't quite see how.

"How ingenious, Anton! Did you—carve it yourself?"

This was the sort of inane question you asked Anton Kruppe. For you had to say something, to alleviate the strain of the man's aggressive-doggy eagerness to please, to impress, to make you laugh. Hadley recalled the previous time Anton had dropped by the house to see her, which had been the first time, the previous week; the forced and protracted conversation between them when Anton hadn't seemed to know how to depart, after Hadley had served him coffee and little sandwiches made of multigrain bread; his lurching over her, his spasm of a handshake and his clumsy wet kiss on her cheek that had seemed to sting her, and to thrill her, like the brush of a bat's wings.

"Yes *ma'am*. You think—you will *buy*?"

"That depends, Anton. How much . . ."

"For you, *ma'am*—'no charge'!"

This forced joke, how long would it be kept up, Hadley wondered in exasperation. In middle school, boys like Anton Kruppe were snubbed by their classmates—*Ha ha very funny!*—but once you were an adult, how could you discourage such humor without being rude? Anton was considerably younger than Hadley, as much as ten or twelve years, though looking older than his age, as Hadley looked younger than her age; he'd been born in what was now called Bosnia, brought to the United States by a surviving grandparent, he'd gone to American schools including MIT yet had not become convincingly *American* in all those years.

Trying too hard, Hadley thought. The sign of the foreign-born.

In a kind of anxious triumph, sensing his hostess's exasperation yet determined not to acknowledge it, Anton swung the lurid pumpkin-head down from his shoulders, in his chafed-looking big-knuckled hands. Now Hadley could see that the pumpkin wasn't whole but only two-thirds of a shell—it had been gutted and carved and its back part cut away—the back of what would be, in a human skull, the cranium. So the uncanny pumpkin-head was only a kind of pumpkin-mask set on Anton's shoulders and held in place by hand. Yet so lifelike—as the scarecrow-figure lurched up the walk in her direction the face had appeared alive.

Could have sworn, the eye-sockets had glared merrily at *her*.

"Is good? Is—surprise? 'Happy Halloween'—is right?"

Was it Halloween? Hadley was sure it was not. October thirty-first wasn't for another several days.

"Is for you—Hedley. To set here."

Flush-faced now and smiling in his shyly aggressive manner that was a plea for her, the rich American woman, to laugh at him, and with him; to laugh in the spontaneous way in which Americans laughed together, mysteriously bonded in their crude American humor. On his angular face and in his stiff-wiry hair that receded sharply from his forehead were bits of pumpkin-flesh and seeds at which Anton wiped, surreptitiously, like a boy whose nose is running, wiping at his nose. Hadley thought *If he kisses me he will smell of pumpkin.*

Her husband had died and abandoned her. Now, other men would *drop by* the house.

Anton presented Hadley with the misshapen pumpkin. The damned thing must have weighed fifteen pounds. Almost, it slipped from her hands. Hadley thought it would have served Anton Kruppe right if she'd dropped the pumpkin and it smashed on the brick. No doubt, he'd have offered to clean it up, then.

"Anton, thank you! This is very . . ."

Their hands brushed together. Anton was standing close beside her. He was several inches taller than Hadley though his posture was slouched, his back prematurely rounded. Perhaps there was something wrong with his spine. And he breathed quickly, audibly—as if he'd been running. As if he were about to declare something—then thought better of it.

At the organic food and gardening co-op where Hadley had once shopped frequently, when she'd prepared elaborate meals for herself and her husband, and now only shopped from time to time, tall lanky Anton Kruppe had appeared perhaps a year ago. He'd always been alert and attentive to her—the co-op manager addressed her as Mrs. Schelle. Since late March in her trance of self-absorption that was like a narcotic to her—in fact, to get through the worst of her insomniac nights Hadley had to take sleeping pills which left her dazed and groggy through much of the day—she'd scarcely been aware of Anton Kruppe except as a helpful and persistent presence, a worker who seemed always to be waiting on her. It was just recently that he'd dared to be more direct: asking if he might see her. Asking if he might *drop by* her house after the co-op closed one evening, to bring her several bags of peat moss that were too heavy and cumbersome for Hadley to remove from the trunk of her car by herself. He'd offered to spread the peat moss wherever she wanted it spread.

Hadley had hesitated before saying *yes*. It was true, she was attracted to Anton Kruppe, to a degree. He reminded her of foreign-born classmates in her school, in north Philadelphia; pasty-faced skinny boys with round eyeglasses, tortured ways of speaking as if their tongues were malformed. Hadley had been attracted to them, but she'd never befriended them. Not even the lonely girls had she befriended. And now in weak moments she was grateful for anyone who was kind to her; since her husband's premature death she'd felt eviscerated, worthless. *There is not one person to whom you matter, now. This is the crossing-over.* For long entranced minutes like one in a hypnotic state she found herself listening to a voice not her own yet couched in the cadences of her own most intimate speech. This voice did not accuse her nor did the voice pass judgment on her yet she knew herself judged, contemptible. *Not one person. This is the crossing-over.*

She had signed the paper for her husband's cremation. In her memory distorted and blurred by tears as if undersea her own name had been printed on the contract, beside her husband's name. Signing for

him, she'd signed for herself as well. It was finished for her, all that was
over—the life of the emotions, the ability to feel.

Yet with another part of her mind Hadley remained alert, prudent.
She was not an adventurous woman, still less was she reckless. She had
been married to one man for nearly twenty years, she was childless and
had virtually no family. She had a circle of friends in whom she confided
sparingly—often, it was her closest friends whom she avoided, since
March. Never would she have consented to a stranger *dropping by* her
house except she'd learned that Anton Kruppe was a post-doc fellow in
the prestigious Molecular Biology Institute; he had a Ph.D. from MIT
and he'd taught at Cal Tech; his area of specialization was *microbial genetics*. She'd seen him at a string quartet recital on campus, once. Another
time, walking along the canal towpath, alone. Wearing earphones, head
sharply bowed, his mouth working as if he were arguing with someone
and so lost in concentration his gaze drifted over Hadley unseeing—his
favored co-op customer in cable-knit sweater, wool slacks and boots, a
cap pulled low over her head, invisible to him.

She'd liked it that Anton Kruppe hadn't noticed her, at that moment. That she could observe the young man without his observing her.
Thinking *He's a scientist. He won't see anything that isn't crucial for him to see.*

Now, in her house, Hadley felt a *frisson* of power over her awkward
visitor. He could not have been more than twenty-nine—Hadley was
thirty-nine. She was certain that Anton hadn't known her husband or
even that she'd had a husband, who had died. (Hadley still wore her
engagement and wedding ring of course.) Her power, she thought, lay
in her essential indifference to the man, to his very maleness: his sexuality clumsy as an odd-sized package he was obliged to carry, to proffer
to strangers like herself. He had the malnourished look of one who has
been rebuffed many times yet remains determined. There are men of
surpassing ugliness with whom women fall in love in the mysterious
way of women but Anton Kruppe didn't possess anything like a charis-
matic ugliness; his maleness was of another species altogether. Think-

ing of this, Hadley felt a swell of elation. *If he kisses me tonight he will smell of—garbage.*

Hadley was smiling. She saw how Anton stared at her, as if her smile was for *him*.

She thanked him for the pumpkin another time. Her voice was warm, welcoming. What an "original" gift it was, and so "cleverly" carved.

Anton's face glowed with pleasure. "W-Wait, Hedley!—there is more."

Hedley he called her. At the co-op, *Mrs. Schelle* with an emphasis on the final *e*. Hadley felt no impulse to correct him.

With boyish enthusiasm Anton seized Hadley's hand—her fingers must have been icy, unresponsive—and pulled her with him out to the driveway. In the rear of the pickup was a large pot of what appeared to be cream-colored chrysanthemums, past their prime, and a long narrow cardboard box of produce—gnarly carrots with foot-long untrimmed greens, misshapen peppers and pears, bruised MacIntosh apples the co-op couldn't sell even at reduced prices. And a loaf of multigrain bread that, Anton insisted, had been baked only that morning but hadn't sold and so would be labeled "day-old" the next morning. "In this country there is much ignorant prejudice of 'day-old'—everything has to be 'new'—'perfect shape'—it is a mystery to me why if to 6 P.M. when the co-op closes this bread is good to sell but tomorrow by 8:30 A.M. when the co-op opens—it is 'old.' In the place where we come from, my family and neighbors . . ." Moral vehemence thickened Anton's accent, his breath came ever more audibly.

Hadley would have liked to ask Anton more about his background. He'd lived through a nightmare, she knew. *Ethnic cleansing. Genocide.* Yet, she felt uneasy in his presence. Very likely, it had been a mistake to have invited the eccentric young molecular biologist to drop by her house a second time; she didn't want to mislead him. She was a widow who had caused her husband to be burnt to ashes and was unrepentant, unpunished. Since March declining invitations from friends who had known her and her husband for years. Impatient with their solicitude, their concern for her who did not deserve such concern. *I'm sorry! I don't want to go out. I don't want to leave the house. I'm very tired. I don't sleep any longer. I go to bed and can't sleep and at 1 A.M. I will take a sleeping pill. At 4 A.M. I will take another. Forget me! I am something that is finished.*

Thinking now that possibly she didn't have to invite her awkward visitor into the house, a second time; maybe Anton wouldn't notice her rudeness—wouldn't know enough to interpret it as rudeness. He'd set the mums and the box with the produce onto a white wrought-iron bench near Hadley's front walk and was now leading Hardley around the side of the large sprawling stone-and-timber house as he'd done previously, as if he'd been summoned for this purpose. He'd boasted to Hadley of being "Mister Fix-It"—he was the "Mister Fix-It" of his lab at the Institute—his quick, critical eye took in the broken flagstones in the terrace behind Hadley's house which he'd "repair"—"re-place"— for her, on another visit; with the scrutiny of a professional mason he stooped to examine corroding mortar at the base of the back wall of the house; he examined the warped and lopsided garden gate which he managed to fix with a deft motion of his hands—"Now! It is good as 'new'—eh?"—laughing as if he'd said something unexpectedly witty. Hadley was grateful that Anton had made no mention of the alarming profusion of weeds amid a lush tangle of black-eyed Susans, Russian sage and morning glory vines in her husband's garden that had not been cultivated this year but allowed to grow wild.

"Thank you, Anton! Truly you are—'Mister Fix-It.'"

Hadley spoke with more warmth than she'd intended. It was her social manner—bright, a little blurred, insincere and animated.

There was something admirable—unless there was something daunting, aggressive—about her visitor's energy—that brimmed and thrummed like rising yeast. Hadley would have supposed that after a day presumably spent at the molecular biology lab—work-weeks in such labs could run beyond one hundred hours during crucial experiments—and several hours at the co-op Anton would have been dazed with exhaustion; yet there he was, tireless in his inspection of the exterior of Hadley's house—inspecting windows, locks, dragging aside broken limbs and storm debris. You'd think that Anton Kruppe was an old friend of the family for whom the discovery that one of the floodlights on Hadley's garage had burnt out was something of a *coup*, arousing him to immediate action—"You have a bulb to replace—yes? And a ladder with 'steps'—'step-ladder'—? I will put in—now—before it is too dark."

So adamant, Hadley had no choice but to give in.

And no choice except to invite Anton Kruppe inside, for just a while.

Politely and with regret explaining that she had a dinner engagement, later that evening. But would he come inside, for a drink?

"Hedley yes thank you! I would like—yes so much."

Stammering with gratitude Anton scraped his hiking boots against the welcome mat. The soles were muddy and stuck with leaves. Though Hadley insisted it wasn't necessary Anton removed the boots with a grunt and left them on the front step carefully placed side by side. What large boots they were, like a horse's hooves! The sodden shoelaces trailed out—left, right—in perfect symmetry.

Inside, most of the downstairs rooms were dark. Now it was late October night came quickly. Pleasantly excited, a little nervous, Hadley went about switching on lights. There was a curious intimacy between her and Anton Kruppe, in this matter of switching on lights. Hadley heard her voice warmly uplifted—no idea what she was saying—as her tall lanky guest in his stocking feet—soiled-looking gray wool socks— came to stand at the threshold of the living room—stared into the interior of the long beautifully furnished living room with a shoulder-high stone fireplace at its farther end, book-filled shelves, Chinese carpets on a gleaming hardwood floor. Above the fireplace was a six-by-eight impressionist New England landscape of gorgeous pastel colors that drew the eye to it, as in a vortex.

Excitedly Anton Kruppe asked—was the painting by Cezanne?

"'Cezanne'! Hardly."

Hadley laughed, the question was so naïve. Except for surreal pastel colors and a high degree of abstraction in the rendering of massed tree trunks and foliage, there was little in the Wolf Kahn canvas to suggest the earlier, great artist.

Outside, while Anton changed the floodlight, Hadley had been thinking *I will offer him coffee. That's enough for tonight.* But now that they were out of the October chill and inside the warm house it was a drink—wine—she offered him: a glass of dark red Catena wine, from a bottle originally purchased by her husband. Anton thanked her profusely calling her "Hedley"—a flush of pleasure rose into his odd, angular face. In his wiry hair that was the color of ditch water a small pumpkin seed shone.

Hadley poured herself a half-glass of wine. Her hand shook just slightly. She thought *If I don't offer him a second glass. If I don't ask him to stay.*

Since there was an opened jar of Brazilian nuts on the sideboard, Hadley offered these to Anton, too. A cascade of nuts into a blue-ceramic bowl.

Gratefully Anton drank, and Anton ate. Thirstily, hungrily. Drifting about Hadley's living room peering at her bookshelves, in his gray wool socks. Excitedly he talked—he had so much to say!—reminding Hadley of a chattering bird—a large endearingly gawky bird like an ostrich—long-legged, long-necked, with a beaky face, quick-darting inquisitive eyes. So sharply his hair receded from his forehead, it resembled some sort of garden implement—a hand trowel?—and his upper body, now he'd removed his nylon parka, was bony, concave. Hadley thought *He would be waxy-pale, beneath. A hairless chest. A little potbelly, and spindly legs.*

Hadley laughed. Already she'd drunk half her glass of wine. A warm sensation suffused her throat and in the region of her heart.

Politely Hadley tried to listen—to concentrate—as her eccentric guest chattered rapidly and nervously and with an air of schoolboy enthusiasm. How annoying Anton was! Like many shy people once he began talking he seemed not to know how to stop; he lacked the social sleight of hand of changing the subject; he had no idea how to engage another in conversation. Like a runaway vehicle down a hill he plunged on, head-on, heedless. And yet, there was undeniably something attractive about him.

More incensed now, impassioned—though he seemed to be joking, too—speaking of American politics, American pop culture, "American fundamentist ignorance" about stem-cell research. And how ignorant, more than ninety percent of Americans believed in God—and in the devil.

Hadley frowned at this. Ninety percent? Was this so? It didn't seem plausible that as many people would believe in the devil, as believed in God.

"Yes, yes! To believe in the Christian God is to believe in His enemy—the devil. That is known."

With his newfound vehemence Anton drained his glass of the dark red Catena wine and bluntly asked of his hostess if he might have more?—helping himself at the sideboard to a second, full glass and scooping up another handful of the Brazilian nuts. Hadley wondered if he meant to be rude—or simply didn't know better. "I can't really think," she persisted, "that as many Americans believe in the devil, as believe in God. I'm sure that isn't so. Americans are—we are—a tolerant nation . . ."

How smug this sounded. Hadley paused not knowing what she meant to say. The feral-dark wine had gone quickly to her head.

With a snort of derision Anton said, "'A tolerant nation'—is it? Such 'tolerance' as swallows up and what it cannot, it makes of an enemy."

"'Enemy'? What do you mean?"

"It makes of *war*. First is declared the *enemy*, then the *war*."

Anton laughed harshly, baring his teeth. Chunky yellow teeth they were, and the gums pale-pink. Seeing how Hadley stared at him he said, in a voice heavy with sarcasm, "First there is the 'tolerance'—then, the 'pre-empt strike.'"

Hadley's face flushed with the heat of indignation. This was insulting—it had to be deliberate—Anton Kruppe who'd lived in the United States for much of his life knew very well the history of the Iraq War, how Americans were misled, deceived by the Republican leadership. Of course he knew. She opened her mouth to protest bitterly then thought better of it.

Surreptitiously she glanced at her wristwatch. Only 6:48 P.M.! Her guest had been inside the house less than a half hour but the strain of his visit was such, it seemed much longer.

Still Anton was prowling about, staring. Artifacts from trips Hadley and her husband had taken, over the years—Indonesian pottery, African masks, urns, wall hangings, Chinese wall scrolls and watercolors, beautifully carved wooden figures from Bali. A wall of brightly colored "primitive" paintings from Mexico, Costa Rica, Guatemala. Yet more, the books on Hadley's shelves seemed to intrigue Anton, as if these hundreds of titles acquired years ago, if not decades ago, mostly by Hadley's husband who'd earned both a Ph.D. in European history and a law degree from Columbia University, possessed an immediate, singular significance and were not rather relics of a lost and irretrievable private past.

"You have read all these, Hedley—yes?"

Hadley laughed, embarrassed. No, she had not.

"Then—someone else? All these?"

Hadley laughed again, uncertain. Was Anton Kruppe mocking her? She felt a slight repugnance for the man, who peered at her, as at her art-objects and bookshelves, with an almost hostile intensity; yet she could not help it, so *American* was her nature, so female, she was anxious that he should like her, and admire her—if that could be settled, she would send him away, in triumph.

Remembering the foreign-born children at her schools. In middle school they had seemed pitiful, objects of sympathy, charity, and condescension, if not derision; in high school, overnight it seemed they'd become A-students, star athletes. A *drivenness* to them, the complacent Americans had mistaken initially as weakness.

In soiled wool socks Anton continued to prowl about. Hadley had not invited him to explore her house—had she? His manner was more childlike than aggressive. Hadley supposed that Anton's own living quarters in university-owned housing were minimal, cramped. A row of subsidized faculty housing along the river . . ."Ah! This is—'solar-room'?" They were in a glass-walled room at the rear of the stone house, that had been added to the house by Hadley and her husband; the "solarium," intended to be sun-warmed, was furnished with white wicker furniture, chintz pillows and a white wrought-iron table and chairs as in an outdoor setting. But now the room was darkened and shadowed and the bright festive chintz colors were undistinguishable. Only through the vertical glass panels shone a faint crescent moon, entangled in the tops of tall pines. Anton was admiring yet faintly sneering, taunting:

"Such a beautiful house—it is old, is it?—so big, for one person. You are so very lucky, Hedley. You know this, yes?"

Lucky! Hadley smiled, confused. She tried to see this.

"Yes, I think so. I mean—yes."

"So many houses in this 'village' as it is called—they are so big. For so few people. On each acre of land, it may be one person—the demographics would show. Yes?"

Hadley wasn't sure what Anton Kruppe was saying. A brash sort of merriment shone in his eyes, widened behind the smudged lenses of his wire-rimmed schoolboy glasses.

He asked Hadley how long she'd lived in the house and when she told him since 1988, when she and her husband had moved here, he'd continued smiling, a pained fixed smile, but did not ask about her husband. *He must know, then. Someone at the co-op has told him.*

Bluntly Anton said, "Yes, it is 'luck'—America is the land of 'opportunity'—all that is deserved, is not always granted."

"But it wasn't 'luck'—my husband worked. What we have, he'd earned."

"And you, Hedley? You have 'earned'—also?"

"I—I—I don't take anything for granted. Not any longer."

What sort of reply this was, a stammered resentful rush of words, Hadley had no clear idea. She was uneasy, Anton peered at her closely. It was as if the molecular biologist was trying to determine the meaning of her words by staring at her. A kind of perverse echolocation— was that the word?—the radar-way of bats tossing high-pitched beeps of sound at one another. Except Anton was staring, his desire for the rich American woman came to him through the eyes . . . Hadley saw that the pumpkin seed—unless it was a second seed, or a bit of pumpkin-gristle—glistened in his wiry hair, that looked as if it needed shampooing and would be coarse to the touch. Except she could not risk the intimacy, she felt a reckless impulse to pluck it out.

He would misunderstand. He is such a fool, he would misinterpret.

But if I wanted a lover. A lover for whom I felt no love.

As if Anton had heard these words, his mood changed suddenly. His smile became startled, pained—he was a man for whom pained smiles would have to do. Asking Hadley if there were more repairs for "Mister Fix-It" in her house and Hadley said quickly, "No. No more."

"Your basement—furnace—that, I could check. I am trained—you smile, Hedley, but it is so. To support myself in school—"

Hadley was sure she wasn't smiling. More firmly she thanked Anton and told him she had to leave soon—"I'm meeting friends for dinner in town."

Clearly this was a lie. Hadley could lie only flatly, brazenly. Her voice quavered, she felt his eyes fixed upon her.

Anton took a step closer. "I would come back another day, if needed.

I would be happy to do this, Hedley. You know this—I am your friend Anton—yes?"

"No. I mean—yes. Some other time, maybe."

Hadley meant to lead her awkward guest back out into the living room, into the lighted gallery and foyer near the front door. He followed in her wake muttering to himself—unless he was talking to Hadley, and meant her to hear—to laugh—for it seemed that Anton was laughing, under his breath. His mood was mercurial—as if he'd been hurt, in the midst of having been roused to indignation. He'd drained his second glass of wine and his movements had become jerky, uncoordinated like those of a partially come-to-life scarecrow.

It was then that Anton began to confide in Hadley, in a lowered and agitated voice: the head of his laboratory at the Institute had cheated him—he'd taken discoveries of Anton Kruppe to claim for his own—he'd published a paper in which Anton was cited merely in a list of graduate assistants—and now, when Anton protested, he was exiling Anton from the lab—he refused to speak to Anton at the Institute and had banished him and so Anton had gone to the university president—demanding to be allowed to speak to the president but of course he'd been turned away—came back next morning hoping to speak with the president and when he was told no, demanding then to speak with the provost—and the university attorney—their offices were near-together in the administration building—all of them were in conspiracy together, with the head of the Institute and the head of Anton's laboratory—he knew this!—of course, he was not such a fool, to not know this—he'd become excited and someone called security—campus police arrived and led Anton away protesting—they had threatened to turn him over to township police—to be arrested for "trespassing"—"threatening bodily harm"—Anton had been terrified he'd be deported by Homeland Security—he had not yet an American citizenship—

"You are smiling, Hedley? What is the joke?"

Smiling? During this long breathless disjointed speech Hadley had been staring at Anton Kruppe in astonishment.

"It is amusing to you—yes? That all my work, my effort—I am most hardworking in the lab, our supervisor exploits my good nature—he was always saying 'Anton is the *stoic* among us'—what this means, this flattery of Americans, is how you can be used. To be *used*—that is our purpose, to the Institute. But you must not indicate, that you are *in the know.*" Anton spoke like one whose grievances are so much in excess of his ability to express them, he might have been the bearer of an ancient, racial burden. "And now—after three years—when my findings are cheated from me and I am of no more use—it is time to toss away into the 'Dumpster'—that is good word, good joke, eh?—'Dumpster'—very good American joke—the Institute is saying my contract will not be renewed, for the federal grant is ended. And my supervisor had not ever gotten around to aiding me with my citizenship application, years it has been, of course I have been dial-tory myself—I have been working *so hard* in the lab—yesterday morning it was, the decision came to me by e-mail . . . You—you must not smile, Hedley! That is very—selfish. That is very selfish and very cruel."

The indignant man loomed over Hadley. His angular face wasn't so soft now but hardened with strain. His jaws were clenched like muscles. The trowel-shaped triangle of hair at his hairline was more pronounced and a sweaty-garbagey smell wafted from his heated body. Behind the smudged schoolboy lenses his eyes were deep-socketed, wary. Hadley said nervously, "Maybe you should leave, Anton. I'm expecting friends. I mean . . . they're stopping by, to take me with them. To dinner in town . . ."

Hadley didn't want her agitated visitor to sense how frightened she was of him. Her mistake was in turning away to lead him to the door. Insulting him. His arm looped around her neck, in an instant they were struggling off balance, he caught at her, and kissed her—kissed and bit at her lips, like a suddenly ravenous rodent—both their wineglasses went flying, clattering to the floor—"You like this, Hed-ley! This, you want. For this, you asked me."

He overcame her. She was fighting him, whimpering and trying to scream, trying to draw breath to scream but he'd pushed her down, horribly she was on the floor, pushed down helpless and panicked on the floor of her own house, in terror thinking that Anton was trying to strangle her, then it seemed that he was kissing her, or trying to—in panic she jammed her elbows into his chest, his ribs—his mouth came over hers again—his mouth was wet and ravenous and his teeth closed over her lip, in terror she thought that he would bite off her lip, in a kind of manic elation he was murmuring what sounded like *You like me! You want this!* Grunting with effort he straddled her, his face was flushed with emotion, fury; he brought his knee up between her legs, roughly; their struggle had become purely physical, and desperate, enacted now in near-silence except for their panting breaths. Hadley had no idea what she was doing moving her head from side to side trying to avoid the man's mouth, his sharp yellow teeth, the smell of his agitated breath, the mouth was like that of a great sea leech sucking at her, sucking at her tongue, the back of her head was being struck against the hardwood floor *Oh!—oh—oh* as if he wanted to crack her skull, his fingers were poking and jabbing at her between her legs, in a paroxysm of desperation Hadley managed to squirm out from beneath him, like a panicked animal crawling on hands and knees and almost in that instant she believed that she might escape Anton Kruppe except he had only to lunge after her, seize her ankle in his strong fingers, laughing and climbing over her straddling her again more forcibly this time closing his fingers around her neck so now she knew she could not escape, she knew it was certain, she would die. In a choked voice Anton was saying, "You—want me here! You asked for this. You have no right to laugh at me. You and your 'trustee' husband . . ." In the confusion of the moment Hadley had no idea what Anton was saying. Trustee? Her husband had served on an advisory board for the history department at the university, he'd had no association with the molecular biology institute. She could not have explained this, she had not the strength, or the breath; she felt her assailant's fingers now poking inside her, she cried out in pain and kicked at him squirming beneath him like a creature desperate to escape a predator yet she had time to think almost calmly *This can't be happening. This is wrong.* She seemed to see herself in that instant with a strange stillness and detachment as frequently through her marriage when she'd lain with her husband and made love with her husband and her mind had slipped free and all that was physical, visceral, immediate and not-to-be-halted happening to her was at a little distance, though now tasting the wine on Anton's tongue, the dark-sour-feral wine taste of a man's mouth like her own, he'd lost patience now and was jamming at her with two fingers, three fingers forced up inside the soft flesh between her legs which Hadley knew was loathed by the man, he was furious with her there, disgusted with her there, his hatred was pure and fiery for her there as she begged him *Please don't hurt me Anton, I want to be your friend Anton I will help you.* It wasn't wine she was tasting but blood—he'd bitten her upper lip—on his feet now looming over her—his work-trousers unzipped, disheveled—his shirt loose, blood-splattered—he'd managed to get to his feet disengaging himself from her—their tangle of limbs, torn clothing, tears, saliva—he staggered away to the front door—stiff-legged as a scarecrow come partway to life—and was gone.

She lay very still. Where he'd left her, she lay with a pounding heart, bathed in sweat and the smell of him, her brain stuck blank, oblivious of her surroundings until after several minutes—it may have been as many as ten or fifteen minutes—she realized that she was alone. It had not quite happened to her as she'd believed it would happen, the *crossing-over.*

She managed to get to her feet. She was dazed, sobbing. Some time was required, that she could stand without swaying. Leaning against a chair in the hall, touching the walls. In the opened doorway she stood, staring outside. The front walk was dimly illuminated by a crescent moon overhead. Here was a meager light, a near-to-fading light. She saw that the pumpkin-head had fallen from the step, or had been kicked. On its side it was revealed to be part-shattered, you could see that the back of the cranium was missing. Brains had been scooped out but negligently so that seeds remained, bits of pumpkin-gristle. She stepped outside. Her clothing was torn. Her clothing that was both expensive and tasteful had been torn and was splattered with blood. She wiped at her mouth, that was bleeding. She would run back into the house, she would dial 911. She would report an assault. She would summon help. For badly she required help, she knew that Anton Kruppe would return. Certainly he would return. On the front walk she stood staring toward the road. What she could see of the road in the darkness. On the roadway there were headlights. An unmoving vehicle. It was very dark, a winter-dark had come upon them. She called out, "Hello? Hello? Who is it?" Headlights on the roadway, where his vehicle was parked.

THE STORY OF THE STABBING

Four years old she'd begun to hear in fragments and patches like handfuls of torn clouds the story of the stabbing in Manhattan that was initially her mother's story.

That morning in March 1980 when Mrs. Karr drove to New York City alone. Took the New Jersey Turnpike to the Holland Tunnel exit, entered lower Manhattan and crossed Hudson and Greenwich Streets and at West Street turned north, her usual route when she visited an aunt who lived in a fortress-like building resembling a granite pueblo dwelling on West Twenty-seventh Street—but just below Fourteenth Street traffic began abruptly to slow—the right lane was blocked by construction—a din of air hammers assailed her ears—vehicles were moving in spasmodic jerks—Madeleine braked her 1974 Volvo narrowly avoiding rear-ending a van braking to a stop directly in front of her—a tin-colored vehicle with a corroded rear bumper and a New York license plate whose raised numerals and letters were just barely discernible through layers of dried mud like a palimpsest. Overhead were clouds like wadded tissues, a sepia glaze to the late-winter urban air and a stink of diesel exhaust and Madeleine Karr whose claim it was that she loved Manhattan felt now a distinct unease in stalled traffic amid a cacophony of horns, the masculine aggressiveness of horns, for several blocks she'd been aware of the tin-colored van jolting ahead of her on West Street, passing on the right, switching lanes, braking at the construction blockade but at once lurching forward as if the driver had carelessly—or deliberately—lifted his foot from the brake pedal and in so doing caused his right front fender to brush against a pedestrian in a windbreaker crossing West Street—crossing at the intersection though at a red light, since traffic was stalled—unwisely then in a fit of temper the pedestrian in the windbreaker struck the fender with the flat of his hand—he was a burly man of above average height—Madeleine heard him shouting but not the words, distinctly—might've been *Fuck you!* or even *Fuck you asshole!*—immediately then the van driver leapt out of the van and rushed at the pedestrian—Madeleine blinked in astonishment at this display of masculine contention—Madeleine was expecting to see the men fight together clumsily—aghast then to see the van driver wielding what appeared to be a knife with a considerable blade, maybe six—eight—inches long—so quickly this was happening, Madeleine's brain could not have identified *Knife!*—trapped behind the steering wheel of the Volvo like a child trapped in a nightmare Madeleine witnessed an event, an action, to which her dazzled brain could not readily have identified as *Stabbing! Murder!*—in a rage the man with the knife lashed at the now stunned pedestrian in the windbreaker, who hadn't time to turn away—striking the man on his uplifted arms, striking and tearing the sleeves of the windbreaker, swiping against the man's face, then in a wicked and seemingly practiced pendulum motion slashing the man's throat just below his jaw, right to left, left to right causing blood to spring instantaneously into the air—*A six-foot arc of blood at least* as Madeleine would describe it afterward, horrified—*even as the bleeding man kept walking, staggering forward*. Never had Madeleine Karr witnessed anything so horrible—never would Madeleine Karr forget this savage attack in the unsparing clarity of a morning in late March—the spectacle of a living man *attacked, stabbed, throat slashed* before her eyes and what was most astonishing *He kept walking—trying to walk—until he fell.* The victim wore what appeared to be work clothes— work-boots—he was at least a decade older than his assailant—late thirties, early forties—bare-headed, with steely-gray hair in a crew cut—only seconds before the attack Madeleine had seen the victim visibly seething with indignation—empowered by rage—the sort of rough-hewn man with whom, alone in the city in such circumstances on West Street just below Fourteenth Street, Madeleine Karr would never have dared to lock eyes. Yet now the burly man in the windbreaker was rendered harmless—stricken—sinking to his knees as his assailant leapt back from him—dancer-like, very quick on his feet—though not quick enough (Madeleine had to suppose) to avoid being splattered by his victim's blood. *Fucker! Moth'fukr!*—the van driver mouthed words Madeleine couldn't hear but comprehended. In the righteousness of his fury the driver made no attempt to hide the bloody knife in his hand— in fact he appeared to be brandishing the knife—ran back to his vehicle, climbed inside and slammed shut the door and in virtually the same instant propelled the van forward head-on and lurching—Madeleine heard the protesting shriek of rubber tires against pavement—reckless now the fleeing man aimed the van into a narrow space between another vehicle and the torn-up roadway where construction workers in safety helmets had ceased work to stare—knocking aside a sawhorse, a series of orange traffic cones scattering in the street and bouncing off other vehicles as in a luridly colorful and comic simulation of bowling pins scattered by an immense bowling ball; by this time the stricken man was kneeling on the pavement desperately pressing both hands—these were bare hands, Madeleine could see from a distance of no more than twelve feet—against his ravaged throat in a gesture of childlike poignancy and futility as blood continued to spurt from him *Like water from a hose—horrible!*

In a paralysis of horror Madeleine observed the stricken man now fallen—writhing on the pavement in a bright neon-red pool—still clutching desperately at his throat, as if the pressure of his hands could staunch that powerful jet-stream—vaguely Madeleine was becoming aware of a frantic din of horns—traffic was backed up for blocks on northbound West Street as in a nightmare of mangled and thwarted movement like snarled film. *Help me! help me out of here!*—nothing so mattered to Madeleine Karr as escaping from this nightmare—she was thinking not of the stricken man a short distance from the front bumper of the Volvo—not of his suffering, his terror, his imminent death—she was thinking solely of herself—in raw animal panic yearning only to turn her car around—turn her damned car around, somehow—reverse her course on accursed West Street back to the Holland Tunnel and out of New York City—to the Jersey Turnpike—and so to Princeton from which scarcely ninety minutes before she'd left with such exhilaration, childlike anticipation and defiance *Manhattan is so alive!—Princeton is so embalmed. Nothing ever feels real to me here, this life in disguise as a wife and a mother of no more durability than a figure in papier-mâché. I don't need any of you!*

But that was ninety minutes before. Driving along leafy Harrison Street over the picture-book canal to Route 1 north in blustery skidding patches of winter sunshine.

Through a constricting tunnel—as if she were looking through the wrong end of a telescope—Madeleine became aware of other people—other pedestrians cautiously approaching the dying man—workmen from the construction site—a young patrolman on the run—a second patrolman—there came then a deafening siren—sirens—emergency vehicles approached on a side-street peripheral to Madeleine's vision—now there were figures bent over the fallen man—the fallen man was lifted onto a stretcher, carried away—until at last there was nothing to see but a pool of something brightly red like old-fashioned Technicolor glistening on the pavement in cold March sunshine. *And the nightmare didn't end. The police questioned all the witnesses they could find. They came for me, they took me to the police precinct. For forty minutes they kept me. I had to beg them, to let me use the women's room—I couldn't stop crying—I am not a hysterical person but I couldn't stop crying—of course I wanted to help the police but I couldn't seem to remember what anything had looked like—what the men had looked like—even the "skin color" of the man with the knife—even of the man who'd been stabbed. I told them that I thought the van driver had been dark-skinned—maybe—he was "young"—in his twenties possibly—or maybe older—but not much older—he was wearing a satin kind of jacket like a sports jacket like high school boys wear—I think that's what I saw—I couldn't remember the color of the jacket—maybe it was dark—dark purple?—a kind of shiny material—a cheap shiny material—maybe there was some sort of design on the back of the jacket—Oh I couldn't even remember the color of the van—it was as if my eyes had gone blind—the colors of things had drained from them— I'd seen everything through a tunnel—I thought that the van driver with the knife was dark-skinned but not "black" exactly—but not white—I mean not "Caucasian"—because his hair was—wasn't—his hair didn't seem to be— "Negroid hair"—if that is a way of describing it. And how tall he was, how heavy, the police were asking, I had no idea, I wasn't myself, I was very upset, trying to speak calmly and not hysterically, I have never been hysterical in my life. Because I wanted to help the police find the man with the knife. But I could not describe the van, either. I could not identify the van by its make, or by the year. Of course I could not remember anything of the license plate—I wasn't sure that I'd even seen a license plate—or if I did, it was covered with dirt. The police kept asking me what the men had said to each other, what the pedestrian had said, they kept asking me to describe how he'd hit the fender of the van, and the van driver—the man with the knife—what had he said?—but I couldn't hear—my car windows were up, tight—I couldn't hear. They asked me how long the "altercation" had lasted before the pedestrian was stabbed and I said that the stabbing began right away—then I said maybe it had begun right away— I couldn't be sure—I couldn't be sure of anything—I was hesitant to give a statement—sign my name to a statement—it was as if part of my brain had*

been extinguished—trying to think of it now, I can't—not clearly—I was trying
to explain—apologize—I told them that I was sorry I couldn't help them better, I hoped that other witnesses could help them better and finally they released
me—they were disgusted with me, I think—I didn't blame them—I was feeling weak and sick but all I wanted to do was get back to Princeton, didn't even
telephone anyone just returned to the Holland Tunnel thinking I would never use
that tunnel again, never drive on West Street not ever again.

In that late winter of 1980 when Rhonda was four years old the story
of the stabbing began to be told in the Karr household on Broadmead
Road, Princeton, New Jersey. Many times the story was told and retold
but never in the presence of the Karrs' daughter who was too young and
too sensitive for such a terrifying and ugly story and what was worse, a
story that seemed to be missing an ending. Did the stabbed man die?—he
must have died. Was the killer caught?—he must have been caught. Rhonda
could not ask because Rhonda was supposed not to know what had
happened, or almost happened, to Mommy on that day in Manhattan
when she'd driven in alone as Daddy did not like Mommy to do. Nothing is more evident to a child of even ordinary curiosity and canniness
than a family secret, a "taboo" subject—and Rhonda was not an ordinary child. There she stood barefoot in her nightie in the hall outside
her parents' bedroom where the door was shut against her daring to listen to her parents' lowered, urgent voices inside; silently she came up behind her distraught-sounding mother as Madeleine sat on the edge of a
chair in the kitchen speaking on the phone as so frequently Madeleine
spoke on the phone with her wide circle of friends. The most horrible
thing! A nightmare! It happened so quickly and there was nothing anyone could
do and afterward . . . Glancing around to see Rhonda in the doorway,
startled and murmuring Sorry! No more right now, my daughter is listening.
 Futile to inquire what Mommy was talking about, Rhonda knew.
What had happened that was so upsetting and so ugly that when
Rhonda pouted wanting to know she was told Mommy wasn't hurt,
Mommy is all right—that's all that matters.

And *Not fit for the ears of a sweet little girl like you. No no!*

Very soon after Mrs. Karr began to tell the story of the stabbing on a Manhattan street, Mr. Karr began to tell the story too. Except in Mr. Karr's excitable voice the story of the stabbing was considerably altered for Rhonda's father was not faltering or hesitant like Rhonda's mother but a professor of American studies at the University, a man for whom speech was a sort of instrument, or weapon, to be boldly and not meekly brandished; and so when Mr. Karr appropriated his wife's story it was in a zestful storytelling voice like a TV voice—in fact, Professor Gerald Karr was frequently seen on TV—PBS, Channel 13 in New York City—discussing political issues—bewhiskered, with glinting wire-rimmed glasses and a ruddy flushed face. *Crude racial justice! Counter-lynching!*

Not the horror of the incident was emphasized, in Mr. Karr's telling, but the irony. For the victim, in Mr. Karr's version of the stabbing, was a *Caucasian male* and the delivery-van assailant was a *black male*—or, variously, a *person of color*. Rhonda seemed to know that *Caucasian* meant *white*, though she had no idea why; she had not heard her mother identify *Caucasian, person of color* in her accounts of the stabbing for Mrs. Karr dwelt almost exclusively on her own feelings—her fear, her shock, her dismay and disgust—how eager she'd been to return home to Princeton—she'd said very little about either of the men as if she hadn't seen them really but only just the stabbing *It happened so fast*—*it was just so awful*—*that poor man bleeding like that!*—*and no one could help him. And the man with the knife just*—*drove away* . . . But Mr. Karr who was Rhonda's Daddy and an important professor at the University knew exactly what the story meant for the young black man with the knife—the young *person of color*—was clearly one of *an exploited and disenfranchised class of urban ghetto dwellers rising up against his oppressors crudely striking as he could, class-vengeance, an instinctive "lynching," the white victim is collateral damage in the undeclared and unacknowledged but ongoing class war.* The fact that the delivery-van driver had stabbed—killed?—a pedestrian was unfortunate of course, Mr. Karr conceded—a tragedy of course—but who could blame the assailant who'd been provoked, challenged—hadn't the pedestrian struck his vehicle and threatened him—shouted obscenities at him—a good defense attorney could argue a case for self-defense—the van driver was protecting himself from imminent harm, as anyone in his situation might do. For there is such a phenomenon as *racial instinct, self-protectiveness. Kill that you will not be killed.*

As Mr. Karr was not nearly so hesitant as Mrs. Karr about interpreting the story of the stabbing, in ever more elaborate and persuasive theoretical variants with the passing of time, so Mr. Karr was not nearly so careful as Mrs. Karr about shielding their daughter from the story itself. Of course—Mr. Karr never told Rhonda the story of the stabbing, directly. Rhonda's Daddy would not have done such a thing for though Gerald Karr was what he called *ultra-liberal* he did not truly believe—all the evidence of his intimate personal experience suggested otherwise!—that girls and women should not be protected from as much of life's ugliness as possible, and who was there to protect them but men?—fathers, husbands. Against his conviction that marriage is a bourgeois convention, ludicrous, unenforceable, yet Gerald Karr had entered into such a (legal, moral) relationship with a woman, and he meant to honor that vow. And he would honor that vow, in all the ways he could. So it was, Rhonda's father would not have told her the story of the stabbing and yet by degrees Rhonda came to absorb it for the story of the stabbing was told and retold by Mr. Karr at varying lengths depending upon Mr. Karr's mood and/or the mood of his listeners, who were likely to be university colleagues, or visiting colleagues from other universities. *Let me tell you—this incident that happened to Madeleine—like a fable out of Aesop.* Rhonda was sometimes a bit confused—her father's story of the stabbing shifted in minor ways—West Street became West Broadway, or West Houston—West Twelfth Street at Seventh Avenue—the late-winter season became midsummer—in Mr. Karr's descriptive words *the fetid heat of Manhattan in August.* In a later variant of the story which began to be told sometime after Rhonda's seventh birthday when her father seemed to be no longer living in the large stucco-and-timber house on Broadmead with Rhonda and her mother but elsewhere—for a while in a minimally furnished university-owned faculty residence overlooking Lake Carnegie, later a condominium on Canal Pointe Road, Princeton, still later a stone-and-timber Tudor house on a tree-lined street in Cambridge, Massachusetts—it happened that the story of the stabbing became totally appropriated by Mr. Karr as an experience he'd had himself and had witnessed with his own eyes from his vehicle—not the Volvo but the Toyota station wagon—stalled in traffic less than ten feet from the incident: the delivery van braking to a halt, the pedestrian who'd been crossing against the light—*Caucasian, male, arrogant, in a Burberry trench coat, carrying a briefcase—doomed*—had dared to strike a fender of the van, shout threats and obscenities at the driver and so out of the van the driver had leapt, as Mr. Karr observed with the eyes of a front-line war correspondent—*Dark-skinned young guy with dreadlocks like Medusa, must've been Rastafarian—swift and deadly as a panther*—the knife, the slashing of the pedestrian's throat—a ritual, a ritual killing—sacrifice—in Mr. Karr's version just a single powerful swipe of the knife and again as in a nightmare cinematic replay which Rhonda had seen countless times and had dreamt yet more times there erupted *the incredible six-foot jet of blood even as the stricken man kept walking, trying to walk—to escape* which was the very heart of the story—the revelation toward which all else led.

What other meaning was there? What other meaning was possible?

Rhonda's father shaking his head marveling *Like nothing you could imagine, nothing you'd ever forget, the way the poor bastard kept walking—Jesus!*

That fetid-hot day in Manhattan. Rhonda had been with Daddy in the station wagon. He'd buckled her into the seat beside him for she was a big enough girl now to sit in the front seat and not in the silly baby-seat in the back. And Daddy had braked the station wagon, and Daddy's arm had shot out to protect Rhonda from being thrown forward, and Daddy had protected Rhonda from what was out there on the street, beyond the windshield. Daddy had said *Shut your eyes, Rhonda! Crouch down and hide your face darling* and so Rhonda had.

By the time Rhonda was ten years old and in fifth grade at Princeton Day School Madeleine Karr wasn't any longer quite so cautious about telling the story of the stabbing—or, more frequently, merely alluding to it, since the story of the stabbing had been told numerous times, and most acquaintances of the Karrs knew it, to a degree—within her daughter's presence. Nor did Madeleine recount it in her earlier breathless appalled voice but now more calmly, sadly *This awful thing that happened, that I witnessed, you know—the stabbing? In New York? The other day on the news there was something just like it, or almost . . . Or I still dream about it sometimes. My God! At least Rhonda wasn't with me.*

It seemed now that Madeleine's new friend Drexel Hay—"Drex"— was frequently in their house, and in their lives; soon then, when they were living with Drex in a new house on Winant Drive, on the other side of town, it began to seem to Rhonda that Drex who adored Madeleine had come to believe—almost—that he'd been in the car with her on that March morning; daring to interrupt Madeleine in a pleading voice *But wait, darling!—you've left out the part about . . .* or *Tell them how he looked at you through your windshield, the man with the knife*—or *Now tell them how you've never gone back—never drive into the city except with me. And I drive.*

Sometime around Christmas 1984 Rhonda's mother was at last divorced from Rhonda's father—it was said to be an *amicable parting* though Rhonda was not so sure of that—and then in May 1985 Rhonda's mother became Mrs. Hay—which made Rhonda giggle for *Mrs. Hay* was a comical name somehow. Strange to her, startling and disconcerting, how Drex himself began to tell the story of the stabbing to aghast listeners *This terrible thing happened to my wife a few years ago— before we'd met—*

In Drex's excited narration Madeleine had witnessed a street mugging—a savage senseless murder—a white male pedestrian attacked by a gang of black boys with switchblades—his throat so deeply slashed he'd nearly been decapitated. (In subsequent accounts of the stabbing, gradually it happened that the victim had in fact been decapitated—even as, horribly, he'd tried to run away, staggering forward until he fell.) (But was *decapitation* so easy to accomplish, cutting through the spinal cord?—Rhonda couldn't think so.) The attack had taken place *in broad daylight in front of dozens of witnesses and no one intervened—somewhere downtown, below Houston—unless over by the river, in the meat-packing district—or by the entrance to the Holland Tunnel—or* (maybe) *by the entrance to the Lincoln Tunnel, one of those wide ugly avenues like Eleventh? Twelfth?—not late but after dark.* The victim had tried to fight off his assailants—valiantly, foolishly—as Drex said *The kind of crazy thing I might do myself, if muggers tried to take my wallet from me*—but of course he hadn't a chance—he'd been outnumbered by his punk-assailants— before Madeleine's horrified eyes he'd bled out on the street. *Dozens of witnesses and no one wanted to get involved—not even a license plate number or a description of the killers—just they were "black"—"carried knives"—Poor Madeleine was in such shock, these savages had gotten a good look at her through her windshield—she thought they were "high on drugs"—only a few yards from Madeleine my God if they hadn't been in a rush to escape they'd have killed her for sure—so she couldn't identify them—who the hell would've stopped them? Not the New York cops—they took their good time arriving.*

Drex spoke with assurance and authority and yet—Rhonda didn't think that the stabbing had happened quite like this. So confusing!— for it was so very hard to retain the facts of the story—if they were "facts"—from one time to the next. Each adult was so persuasive— hearing adults speak you couldn't resist nodding your head in agreement or in a wish to agree or to be liked or loved, for agreeing—and so—how was it possible to know what was *real*? Of all the stories of the stabbing Rhonda had heard it was Drex's account that was scariest— Rhonda shivered thinking of her mother being killed—trapped in her car and angry black boys smashing her car windows, dragging her out onto the street stab-stab-stabbing . . . Rhonda felt dazed and dizzy to think that if Mommy had been killed then Rhonda would never have a mother again.

And so Rhonda would not be Drex Hay's *sweet little stepdaughter* he had to speak sharply to, at times; Rhonda would not be living in the brick Colonial on Winant Drive but somewhere else—she didn't want to think where.

Never would Rhonda have met elderly Mrs. Hay with the soft-wrinkled face and eager eyes who was Drex's mother and who came often to the house on Winant Drive with presents for Rhonda—crocheted sweater sets, hand-knit caps with tassels, fluffy-rabbit bedroom slippers which quickly became too small for Rhonda's growing feet. Rhonda was uneasy visiting Grandma Hay in her big old granite house on Hodge Road with its medicinal odors and sharp-barking little black pug Samson; especially Rhonda was uneasy if the elderly woman became excitable and disapproving as often she did when (for instance) the subject of the stabbing in Manhattan came up, as occasionally it did in conversation about other, related matters—urban life, the rising crime rate, deteriorating morals in the last decades of the twentieth century. By this time in all their lives of course everyone had heard the story of the stabbing many times in its many forms, the words had grown smooth like stones fondled by many hands. Rhonda's stepfather Drex had only to run his hands through his thinning rust-colored hair and sigh loudly to signal a shift in the conversation *Remember that time Madeleine was almost murdered in New York City* . . . and Grandma Hay would shiver thrilled and appalled *New York is a cesspool, don't tell me it's been "cleaned up"—you can't clean up filth—those people are animals—you know who I mean—they are all on welfare—they are "crack babies"—society has no idea what to do with them and you dare not talk about it, some fool will call you "racist"—Oh you'd never catch* me *driving into the city in just a car by myself—even when I was younger—what it needs is for a strong mayor—to crack down on these animals—you would wish for God to swipe such animals away with His thumb—would that be a mercy!*

When Grandma Hay hugged her Rhonda tried not to shudder crinkling her nose against the elderly woman's special odor. For Rhonda's mother warned *Don't offend your new "grandma"—just be a good, sweet girl.*

Mr. Karr was living now in Cambridge, Massachusetts, for Mr. Karr was now a professor at Harvard. Rhonda didn't like her father's new house or her father's new young wife nor did Rhonda like Cambridge, Massachusetts, anywhere near as much as Rhonda liked Princeton where she had friends at Princeton Day School and so she sulked and cried when she had to visit with Daddy though she loved Daddy and she liked—tried to like—Daddy's new young wife Brooke who squinted and smiled at Rhonda so hard it looked as if Brooke's face must hurt. Once, it could not have been more than the second or third time she'd met Brooke, Rhonda happened to overhear her father's new young wife telling friends who'd dropped by their house for drinks *This terrible thing that happened to my husband before we were married—on the street in New York City in broad daylight he witnessed a man stabbed to death—the man's throat was slashed, blood sprayed out like for six feet Gerald says it was the most amazing—horrible—thing he'd ever seen—the poor man just kept walking—trying to walk—with both his hands he tried to stop the bleeding—Gerald shouted out his car window—there was more than one of them—the attackers—Gerald never likes to identify them as black—persons of color—and the victim was a white man—I don't think the attackers were ever caught—Gerald opened his car door, and shouted at them—he was risking his life interfering—he's utterly reckless, he has the most amazing courage—the way Gerald describes it, it's like I was there with him—I was in middle school at Katonah Day at the time—just totally unknowing, oblivious—I dream of it sometimes—the stabbing—how close Gerald and I came to never meeting, never falling in love and our entire lives changed like a tragic miracle . . .*

You'd have thought that Mr. Karr would try to stop his silly young wife saying such things that weren't wrong entirely—but certainly weren't right—and Rhonda knew they weren't right—and Rhonda was a witness staring coldly at the chattering woman who was technically speaking her *stepmother* but Mr. Karr seemed scarcely to be listening in another part of the room pouring wine into long-stemmed crystal glasses for his guests and drinking with them savoring the precious red burgundy which appeared to be the center of interest on this occasion for Mr. Karr had been showing his guests the label on the wine bottle which must have been an impressive label judging from their reactions as the wine itself must have been exquisite for all marveled at it. Rhonda saw that her father's whiskers were bristly gray like metal filings, his face was ruddy and puffy about the eyes as if he'd just wakened from a nap—when "entertaining" in his home often Mr. Karr removed his glasses, as he had now—his stone-colored eyes looked strangely naked and lashless—still he exuded an air of well-being, a yeasty heat of satisfaction lifted from his skin. There on a nearby table was Gerald Karr's new book *Democracy in America Imperiled* and beside the book as if it had been casually tossed down was a copy of *The New York Review of Books* in which there was said to be—Rhonda had not seen it—a "highly positive" review of the book. And there, in another corner of the room, the beautiful blond silly young wife exclaiming with widened eyes to a circle of rapt listeners *Ohhh when I think of it my blood runs cold, how foolishly brave Gerald was—how close it was, the two of us would never meet and where would I be right now? This very moment, in all of the universe?*

Rhonda laughed. Rhonda's mouth was a sneer. Rhonda knew better than to draw attention to herself, however—though Daddy loved his *sweet little pretty girl* Daddy could be harsh and hurtful if Daddy was displeased with his *sweet little pretty girl* so Rhonda fixed for herself a very thick sandwich of Swedish rye crisp crackers and French goat cheese to devour in the corner of the room looking out onto a bleak rain-streaked street not wanting to think how Daddy knew, yes Daddy knew but did not care. That was the terrible fact about Daddy—he knew, and did not care. A nasty fat worm had burrowed up inside Daddy making him proud of silly Brooke speaking of him in such a tender voice, and so falsely; the *stepmother* who was so much younger and more beautiful than Rhonda's mother.

✦ ✦ ✦

Here was the strangest thing: when Rhonda was living away from them all, and vastly relieved to be away, but homesick too especially for the drafty old house on Broadmead Road where she'd been a little girl and Mommy and Daddy had loved her so. When Rhonda was a freshman at Stanford hoping to major in molecular biology and she'd returned home for the first time since leaving home—for Thanksgiving—to the house on Winant Drive. And there was a family Thanksgiving a mile away at the Hodge Road house of elderly Mrs. Hay to which numerous people came of whom Rhonda knew only a few—and cared to know only a few—mainly Madeleine and Drex of course—there was the disconcerting appearance of Drex's brother Edgar from Chevy Chase, Maryland—identified as an *identical twin* though the men more resembled just brothers than twins. Edgar Hay was said to be a much wealthier man than Drex—his business was pharmaceuticals, in the D.C. area; Drex's business was something in *investments*, his office was on Route One, West Windsor. The Hay twin-brothers were in their late sixties with similar chalky scalps visible through quills of wetted hair and bulbous noses tinged with red like perpetual embarrassment but Edgar was heavier than Drex by ten or fifteen pounds, Edgar's eyebrows were white-tufted like a satyr's in an old silly painting and maddeningly he laughed approaching Rhonda with extended arms—*Hel-lo! My sweet li'l step-niece happy Turkey-Day!*—brushing his lips dangerously close to Rhonda's startled mouth, a rubbery-damp sensation Rhonda thought like being kissed by a large squirmy worm. (*Call me Ed-gie* he whispered wetly in Rhonda's ear *That's what the pretty girls call me.*) And Madeleine who might have observed this chose to ignore it for Madeleine was already mildly drunk—long before dinner—and poor Drex—sunken-chested, sickly pale and thinner since his heart attack in August in high-altitude Aspen, Colorado, clearly in some way resentful of his "twin" brother—reduced to lame jokes and stammered asides in Edgar's presence. And there was Rhonda restless and miserable wishing she hadn't come back home for Thanksgiving—for she'd have to return again within just a few weeks, for Christmas—yet more dreading the long holiday break—wishing she had something useful to do in this house—she'd volunteered to help in the kitchen but Mrs. Hay's cook and servers clearly did not want her—she'd have liked to hide away somewhere and call her roommate Jessica in Portland, Oregon, but was fearful she might break down on the phone and give away more of her feelings for Jessica than Jessica had seemed to wish to receive from Rhonda just yet . . . And there was Rhonda avoiding the living room where Hay relatives were crowded together jovial and overloud—laughing, drinking and devouring appetizers—as bratty young children related to Rhonda purely through the accident of a marital connection whose names she made no attempt to recall ran giggling through a forest of adult legs. Quickly Rhonda shrank back before her mother sighted her, or the elderly white-haired woman who insisted that Rhonda call her "Grandma"—sulkily making her way along a hall, into the glassed-in room at the rear of the house where Mrs. Hay kept potted plants—orchids, African violets, ferns. Outside, the November air was suffused with moisture. The overcast sky looked like a tin ceiling. A few leaves remained on deciduous trees, scarlet-bright, golden-yellow, riffled by wind and falling and sucked away even as you stared. To Rhonda's dismay there was her stepfather's brother—Drex's twin—wormy-lipped Edgar—engaged in telling a story to a Hay relative, a middle-aged woman with a plump cat-face to whom Drex had introduced Rhonda more than once but whose name Rhonda couldn't recall. Edgar was sprawled on a white wicker sofa with his stocky legs outspread, the woman in a lavender silk pants suit was seated in a matching chair—both were drinking—to her disgust and dismay Rhonda couldn't help but overhear what was unmistakably some crude variant of the story of the stabbing of long ago—narrated in Edgar's voice that managed to suggest a lewd repugnance laced with be-musement, as the cat-faced woman blinked and stared open-mouthed as in a mimicry of exaggerated feminine concern *My brother's crazy wife she'd driven into Manhattan Christ knows why Maddie'd been some kind of hip-pie fem-ist my brother says those days she'd been married to one of the Commie profs at the University here and so, sure enough Maddie runs into trouble, this was before Giuliani cleaned up the city, just what you'd predict the stupid woman runs into something dangerous a gang of Nigra kids jumping a white man right out on the street—in fact it was Fifth Avenue down below the garment district—it was actual Fifth Avenue and it was daylight crazy "Made-line" she calls herself like some snooty dame in a movie came close to getting her throat cut—which was what happened to the poor bastard out on the street—in the paper it said he'd been decapitated, too—and the Nigra kids see our Madeline gawking at them through the windshield of her car you'd think the dumb-ass would've known to get the hell out or crouch down and hide at least*—as Rhonda drew nearer her young heart beating in indignation waiting for her step-father's brother to take notice of her. It was like a clumsy TV scene! It was a scene improbable and distasteful yet a scene from which Rhonda did not mean to flee, just yet. For she'd come here, to Princeton. For she could have gone to her father's house in Cambridge, Massachusetts—of course she'd been invited, Brooke herself had called to invite her, with such forced enthusiasm, such cheery family-feeling, Rhonda had felt a stab of pure loneliness, dread. *There is no one who loves me or wants me. If I cut my throat on the street who would care. Or bleed out in a bathtub or in the shower with the hot water running . . .*

So she'd had a vision of her life, Rhonda thought. Or maybe it was a vision of life itself.

Not that Rhonda would ever cut her throat—of course! Never. That was a vow.

Not trying to disguise her disgust, for what she'd heard in the doorway and for Edgar Hay sprawling fatuous-drunk. The ridiculous multi-course Thanksgiving dinner hadn't yet been brought to the dining room table, scarcely 5:30 P.M. and already Edgar Hay was drunk. Rhonda stood just inside the doorway waiting for Edgar's stabbing-story to come to an end. For maybe this would be the end?—maybe the story of the stabbing would never again be told, in Rhonda's hearing? Rhonda would confront Edgar Hay who'd then gleefully report back to Drex and Madeleine how rude their daughter was—how unattractive, how *ungracious*—for Rhonda was staring, unsmiling—bravely she approached the old man keeping her voice cool, calm, disdainful *O.K then—what happened to the stabbed man? Did he die? Do you know for a fact he died? And what happened to the killer—the killers—the killer with the knife—was anyone ever caught? Was anyone ever punished, is anyone in prison right now?* And Edgar Hay—"Ed-gie"—looked at Rhonda crinkling his pink-flushed face in a lewd wink *How the hell would I know, sweetheart? I wasn't there.*

BABYSITTER

Midday, early spring, sunshine in steel bars flashing on the river, she drove to meet him where he'd summoned her. Wind swept in roiling gusts from the Canadian shore.

Suburban life: appointments! Mornings, afternoons. And then the children's appointments. Dentist, orthodontist. Gynecologist, hair salon, yoga. Architect, community relations forum, library fund-raiser for which she's a committee co-chair, flattered to be invited, yet uneasy. Suburban life: each calendar day is a securely barred window, you shove up the window and grasp the bars, grip the bars tight, these are bars that confine but also protect, what pleasure in shaking them!

My appointments this afternoon, she'd told them. Two o'clock, then three, after the library I must drive downtown.

It was a journey: downtown. Twelve miles south and east on the thunderous expressway.

She drove without haste. She drove like a woman already fatally stricken, resigned. She drove at a wavering speed, in the right lane. Calm as a woman in a dream the outcome of which she already knows though in fact she did not know *What will happen? I will never go through with this—will I?*

She didn't think so. It would be her first time, she hadn't such courage.

Out of the leafy suburbs north of the Midwestern city she drove. Massive vehicles passed on the left, her station wagon shuddered in their wake. The nape of her neck was bare, her pale hair swung in scissor-cut wings about her face. Suburban villages were passing beyond the six-foot chain-link fence above the expressway, barely visible from the highway that seemed to be sucking her into it, by degrees downhill in the direction of the river, what was called, as if it were a self-contained place, City Center.

The air was clamorous, like an argument among strangers you can't quite hear. It was a gusty April, not yet Easter. There was something she meant to remember: Easter. Something about the children. Her skin burned in anticipation of him.

He was her friend, she wished to think. He'd touched her only once. The imprint of his fingers on her forearm was still visible to her, in secret.

The station wagon was a new model, handsome and gleaming and paneled in wood. A sturdy vehicle, in the rear strewn with children's things. Still, gusts of wind rocked it, she gripped the steering wheel tight. Such wind! In their hillside house in Bloomfield Heights that was an old fieldstone Colonial wind whistled in the chimneys, rattled the windows with a furtive sound like something trying to get in. Doors were blown open by the wind, or blown shut with a crash. Oh Mommy! their five-year-old daughter cried. The ghost!

My appointment downtown, she'd told Ismelda who had her cell phone number in any case. *Should anything happen. Should you need me. You can pick up the children at the usual door, at their school. I will be back by five-thirty, I'm sure.*

Five-thirty! This was a statement, a pledge. She wondered should she tell him, as soon as she stepped inside the door.

I can't stay long. I will have to leave by.

It was astonishing to her, how the city began to emerge out of a muddle of wood-frame houses, aged tenements, flat-topped roofs and debris-strewn pavement. Suddenly in the distance, two or three miles ahead, were a number of high-rise buildings, some of them quite impressive. City Center was ahead, a narrow peninsula at the tip of downtown, on the restored riverfront: Renaissance Plaza. She would exit there.

The city had once been a great Midwestern city, before a catastrophic "race riot" in 1967. Since then, the white population had gradually declined, like air escaping from a balloon.

I won't have the courage, I'm not a reckless woman. I will only just talk to him. I will tell him . . .

The next exit was City Center. Last Exit Before Tunnel to Canada. Her heart quickened like the heart of a creature sensing danger though not knowing from which direction danger will spring.

. . . I want you as a friend. Someone in whom I can . . .

She'd driven the children to school that morning, as she did most mornings. Mommy in a bulky car coat. She had been married for nine years. That morning the children had been unusually fretful, tugging at her. Mommy! Mom-*my*! That sound of reproach in a child's voice, your heart is lacerated. It was a summons to her blood, she could not resist. The children adored her, they were insatiable. Perhaps they sensed something. The little girl was in kindergarten, the little boy in second grade. Mommy kiss-kiss! She laughed, she was wounded by their beauty that seemed to her fragile like something tiny that has fallen from its nest, or something that has been expelled from its shell, its protective armor.

She shuddered with the knowledge, Mommy was their protective armor. She was not wearing the bulky car coat now but a coat of soft black cashmere with a blank mink collar, that fell in loose folds about her slender legs.

In the rearview mirror above the windshield her face gleamed pale as a moon. Fine lines at the corners of her eyes not visible in the glass. She smiled, uneasy. For a long time she'd been one of the young wives, one of the younger mothers, now no longer. She thought *I am a beautiful woman, I have a right to be loved.*

Lying beside her heavily sleeping husband, nights in succession for nine years. She could not remember their first time together, it seemed as if they had always known each other, as children perhaps. Her husband was a man who shook hands forcefully, looked you in the eye. A man you could trust. A man you wanted to know. She had seen him look appraisingly at women, she'd seen the way women looked at him. He was careless, there was something imperial about him, he was a six-foot boy, confident of being admired. He was a man who could not love her quite so much as she loved him, he'd admitted this. Even in wounding her, saying such a thing, he seemed to be granting a blessing, tossing gold coins at her.

In all marriages there is the imbalance: one who loves more than the other. One who licks wounds in secret, the rust-taste of blood.

Now she was no longer on the expressway, she was uncertain where to turn. The streets of the City Center were narrow, one-way, congested with delivery trucks. A dying city, why was there so much traffic? She could see the gleaming tower of the hotel that was her destination. She could not possibly get lost in a maze of streets, so close to the hotel! She regretted she hadn't left home earlier. Her pride in not having left home earlier. She had stared at the clock mesmerized, she had held herself back. Then calmly telling Ismelda: I have an appointment, downtown. I will be back by. Her eyes shone like the eyes of one unaccustomed to emotion, taking care not to stammer.

In this season of their marriage, her husband often returned home late. He was an enormously busy man, he had both an assistant and a secretary. He had business luncheons, dinners. He was in New York City, in Chicago, Houston, Los Angeles. Yet he was one of the younger men in his firm, his elders looked upon him with admiration and approval. The children loved Daddy emptying his pockets for them, pennies and nickels, dimes. She was fearful of lying to this man, he might hear the quaver in her voice with indifference.

She had turned the station wagon in to a parking garage. She was beginning to be anxious. She would be late meeting him, she had no idea if he would wait for her. He was not a man accustomed to waiting for women, she supposed. He was not a resident of this city, he came here on business. Though perhaps it wasn't business as her husband might identify it. He appeared to have money, he appeared to be unmarried, not a father. She tried to recall his eyes, if they were brown, if they were dark, she could recall only the impact of his eyes, the heavy lids, the carved-looking face, a singular face, one she'd felt she had recognized, that left her weak to contemplate. She could not have said his middle name: did not know exactly how to spell his surname. (Perhaps—she had to concede this!—she didn't know his actual name.) What he'd said to her, she could not recall except it had made her laugh initially, with a kind of visceral shock, and then it had made her weak. He'd told her he stayed at the new hotel by the river, where there was a heliport. The governor of the state was flown to the city, often. They'd been cadets together out in Colorado.

It was a torment to her, in her agitated state: navigating the damned station wagon, looking for a parking space, turning the clumsy vehicle around tight turns, ascending to the next parking level, and to the next. Was this a joke, a comedy! Was her life a farce, others might observe with scorn! Yet she managed to find a place to park, always you manage somehow. She locked the station wagon, a chill wind blowing at her face, her legs. Tugging at her black cashmere coat, like teasing fingers. Then in the slow clanking elevator descending to street level, ugly graffiti at which she could not look. She was thinking *This is a mistake*

of course. In the hilly suburban village in which she lived there was no
graffiti.

If you don't mind a married woman, she'd joked with him. Her voice
had been bold, wistful. He'd only laughed.

It was a windy walk to the Renaissance Plaza by the river. A fierce
white sun, though half the sky was massed storm clouds. So close to
the great Midwestern lake north of the city, the sky was likely to be
unpredictable, one hour to the next. There was sun, later there might be
sleet, then a warm rain. The Plaza was elevated above the street, there
were numerous steps, revolving doors. There was a symphony hall,
there were restaurants, high-rise apartment buildings, a luxury hotel.
Limousines, airport shuttle buses moving slowly forward. At once she
began to feel more at home, doormen recognized women like her, bell-
boys, security guards. If she was not a guest at the hotel, she resembled
its guests. Good day, ma'am! the uniformed men called to her. They
were dusky-skinned like Ismelda, their smiles flashed white. She was
a beautiful woman, at a distance you saw this. A beautifully sculpted
black coat, black fur collar. Her shoes were expensive, her leather gloves.
She wore dark glasses she'd fumbled to slip onto her face. She carried a
leather handbag, finely stitched. The uniformed doorman smiled at her
as she passed into the revolving door, in the corner of her eye she saw
his smile begin to fade immediately, she felt his scorn for her, she had
to be mistaken.

She could be a guest here certainly! More likely, she was meeting friends for a late lunch. A business lunch, she was a woman who
belonged to numerous committees. Her father served on corporate
boards, he was a trustee of his former university, both her parents were
civic-minded, responsible. Only this once she would be unfaithful to
her husband, and to her children, it would never happen again.

He, the man, was to be in room 2133. She did not think of him as an
individual with a name, she did not think his name to herself, only just
he, him. Without apparent haste or agitation she crossed to the bank of
elevators, sleek glass cubicles that lifted and fell soundlessly through the

immense open space of the hotel's atrium. At midday the hotel lobby was crowded, festive. There was a convention of hairstylists, another of radiologists. There was recorded harp music. There were terraces of Easter lilies, tulips. Potted ferns the size of small trees. A noisily trickling fountain. Like a woman in a spell she stepped into the glass elevator, she was sucked up into the interior of the hotel as if into a vacuum. Still she was thinking *I can turn back at any time.*

How distant her other life seemed to her, where she was Mommy.

That morning the children had behaved strangely, as if sensing her mood. She'd laid her hand against their foreheads that seemed slightly overwarm, damp. The little girl had been fretful, uncooperative while being dressed. The little boy had complained of bad dreams. She would keep them home, she thought. For April, it was such a raw wet windy day. She and Ismelda and the children would make Easter eggs as they'd done the year before. Yet somehow she'd hurried them through breakfast, she'd driven them to school as usual. If they came down with colds, if they had fevers that evening, it would be her fault.

Ismelda had been born in Manila, she belonged to an evangelical sect called the Church of the Risen Christ. In her small room on the third floor of the stone house Ismelda played Christian rock music.

He was to be in room 2133. He'd left a message for her just that morning. Breathless she hurried along the corridor. Underfoot was a thick carpet, rosy as the interior of a lung. The far end of the corridor seemed to dissolve in haze. Closed doors, no movement or sound. On the doorknob of room 2133 was DO NOT DISTURB. Hesitantly she knocked on the door. He would not open it, there was no one inside. She was faint with yearning, dread.

The door opened inward, he was there.

He laughed at her, the expression in her face. He spoke words she couldn't hear. His arms pulled her inside, the door was shut behind her. He wore trousers, a white undershirt. Hair lay in damp dark tendrils on his forehead, like seaweed. The ridge of bone above his eyes was prominent. He was heavier than she recalled, she was trying to speak his name.

. . . my happiness is my children, my husband. My marriage. My family. My happiness is not myself but . . .

It was mid-afternoon, the tall windows were open to the sky. A spangle of sunshine like gold coins against the ceiling. He returned from the bathroom, his face was shadowed. He knelt above her. He straddled her. Their skins slapped wetly together. He laughed into her face, his teeth were bared. She began to plead no, I don't think . . . He was gripping her throat that was so beautiful. His thumbs caressed the arteries beneath her jaw. Beneath her makeup, her skin was wearing through. She began to move in protest, she was a beautiful scaly snake. She was firm-fleshed as a snake, lithe and pained. She was having difficulty breathing. Her eyes were open and stark showing a rim of white above the iris. Her wristwatch and rings had been removed, as before surgery. Her bracelet. On the table beside the bed. She was lost, she had no idea where she was. Her cries were torn from her, like blows. He was not squeezing her throat, only just caressing, forcibly, rhythmically. He was deep inside her, even as his large hands held her throat, he moved deeper, her body had no defense against him. He was unhurried, methodical. He had been a fighter pilot in an earlier lifetime. As a young man he had dropped bombs onto the earth, onto cities. At a distance he had killed. He had not told her this exactly but she knew. He had not done these things by himself, others had performed with him, he was one of many though he'd been alone in the cockpit of his plane as he was alone now inside his skin. His thumbs released their pressure on her arteries, the relief was immediate and enormous. Breath rushed into her lungs, she could have wept with gratitude. The wish to live flooded into her, she adored this man who gave her back her life. In a flat bemused voice he was saying, You like this. You like this. You like this.

Far above her he regarded her. Her hands tried to reach him but could not. Her fingers were weak, her wrists broken. Still he was inside her, she was impaled upon him as upon a hook that pierced her lower body. Now his hands moved onto her torso, her breasts, as if he were a blind man, curious to see her in this way, in the way of touching, sculpting with his fingers. He ran his hands over her, he gripped her breasts as if to test the resiliency of her flesh. Her breasts ached with sensation, the nipples felt raw, as if she'd been nursing, hungry mouths had been feeding from her, tearing at her. She was writhing, darkness opening at the back of her skull. She understood then why she had no name for him, why he had not once spoken her name. When she'd begun to speak his name, at the start of their lovemaking, he'd covered her mouth with the heel of his hand, lightly yet in warning: No.

Beyond the tall windows whose drapes had been pulled back the sky was shot with a vivid chemical light. Below was the river, invisible from where they lay, so chopped by wind you could not have said in which direction it flowed. Her eyeballs shifted upward, a death had come over her brain. She saw only a portion of her lover's face, the glisten of oily sweat on his forehead. Only a portion of the ceiling where shimmering water reflected, live-seeming as microorganisms. How ragged her breath was, short and frayed like cloth that has been ripped! As if she'd been drowning, the man had saved her. No one had brought her to such a place before. He had brought her there as if by chance, negligently. The knowledge was crushing to her.

She heard moans, whimpers. She heard a woman's choked sobs. He laughed at her, there was little tenderness in him.

Still he observed her, curiously. As a pilot might observe the ground far below, at a distance at which everything is in miniature, inconsequential. At such a distance there are no individuals. No cries can be heard. She could not bear it, this distance. She reached for him, he gripped her wrists and brought her arms down, spread outright beside her head, so she was helpless. He moved into her, she began to shout, guttural cries that scraped like gravel against her throat. She was a sinewy snake, every inch of her flesh quivering, her skin a damp scaly glisten. He'd pulled a pillow free of the tangle of bedclothes, it must have been caprice, he must have miscalculated, he lowered the pillow over her sweaty face, her anguished eyes and opened mouth, he was pumping hard between her spread thighs as if there was a fascination in him, what he might do to her, the woman, what was emerging between them in this place. Desperately she pulled at his hands, his wrists that were too thick for her fingers to close about, there were hairs on the backs of his hands, wiry hairs on his wrists, she was blinded by the pillow, she was frantic to breathe. Now her body, in which her soul was mute, dazed, swollen tight against her skin like a balloon blown nearly to bursting, began to struggle for its life. The man held her fixed, she was impaled upon him, a great sinewy snake helpless beneath him, the heavy pillow seemed to enclose her head, she was being suffocated. Tendons stood out in her neck, her arteries swelled. She lost consciousness, in a moment she was gone.

Like companions they lay side by side. Like companions who are strangers, thrown together in the same wreck. For a long time she could not move. Her eyelids fluttered weakly, she could not see. Sensation had obliterated her, in the aftermath of sensation there was nothing. Her heartbeat, that had madly accelerated, was slowed now, almost imperceptible. A match had flared into flame, the flame had touched her, exploded inside her, now the flame was extinguished, her body was numbed, she could barely lift her head. The soles of her bare feet seemed to burn as if she'd been walking on hot sand. She spoke to the man, she was helpless not to speak, hearing with a kind of pitying astonishment the hopeless words in a voice barely audible *I love you*. It was something of a plea, an argument, yet there was no one with whom to argue, the man seemed not to hear as if sparing her.

She lay as if beneath the surface of shallow water. Sun played upon the water, that was warm, unthreatening. She could not drown in this water, it would protect her. She was drifting into a stuporous sleep.

Mommy? Mom-*my*? the little girl was looking for her, though Mommy stood before her, squatted before her, the little girl stared through her, the little boy, the boy whose name she'd forgotten for the moment, he was looking for her, anxious Mommy where are you?—she'd become a wraith, they could not see her. Someone touched her as if accidentally, in his abrupt way the man was rising from the bed, walking away. He was barefoot, he moved with a negligent ease, no more self-conscious than if he were alone in the hotel room. Weakly she spoke to him, he did not seem to hear. She heard faucets, a toilet flushing. At least she forced herself to move. Her limbs that were paralyzed, broken. Something warmly sticky as blood between her thighs, on her belly.

He went away from her, he wanted her gone. While she was in the bathroom running water, the hottest water she could bear staring at her dilated eyes in the steamy mirror, she heard him on a telephone. His easy laugh, the murmur of his voice. A man among men he seemed to her, unknowable.

She left him. He wanted her gone, she understood and so she left him. Hey: he gripped her chin, kissed her mouth as you might kiss the forehead of a plain child. At the elevator she turned back, the door to 2133 had shut. In the rapidly descending glass cubicle she wiped at her eyes, angry fists in her eyes. She had restored the damage to her mascara, her eye makeup, now it was damaged again, a teary ruin. Her body wept for him, a seepage between her legs. She thought I am soiled, fouled. I am a woman who deserves harm.

She left the hotel quickly, the revolving door seemed to sweep her out. She imagined faint muffled laughter in her wake but heard only a doorman invisible to her calling after her in a voice of scornful familiarity *Good evening, ma'am!*

Evening! She wouldn't be home until nearly seven o'clock.

On the expressway, wind buffeted the station wagon. Other vehicles veered in their lanes. She was too distracted to be frightened. Fumbling to call Ismelda on her cell phone but the battery had run low. She was thinking, If the children have been hurt! It was not a rational thought yet she was thinking if The Babysitter had taken them, this was punishment she deserved.

The Babysitter was an abductor and killer of children in the suburbs north of the city, he'd never been identified, arrested. He had taken nine children in all but he had not taken a child in several years, it was believed that he'd moved away, or was in prison, or had died. He was called The Babysitter for his methodical way of bathing the bodies of his small victims after raping and strangling them, positioning them in secluded places like parks, a golf course, a churchyard, he'd taken time to launder and even iron their clothing which he folded neatly and left beside them. Always their arms were crossed over their narrow pale chests, their eyes were shut, in such peaceful positions they resembled mannequins and not children who had died terrible deaths, it was said you could not see the ligature marks on their throats until you knelt beside them. The Babysitter had not abducted a child from the suburb in which she lived for at least a decade and yet she was thinking almost calmly *If he has taken them, I will have to accept it.*

The house was made of fieldstone, mortar, brick that had been painted a thin weathered white. Most of the house had been built in the mid-nineteenth century, on a large tract of land which was now reduced to three acres, the minimum for property owners in the township. She was relieved to see the warmly lit windows through the trees, of course nothing had happened, they were waiting for her to return and that was all. Her husband had a dinner engagement, he wouldn't be back until the children were in bed. Yet relief flooded her, seeing her husband's car wasn't in the garage. She'd had her revenge, then! She would love her husband less desperately now, she knew herself equal to him.

Rich cooking aromas in the kitchen, the sound of a TV, children's uplifted voices and Ismelda calling: Ma'am?—but quickly she slipped away upstairs, before the children could rush at her. She showered as she hadn't in the hotel. She soaped every part of her body, she was giddy with relief. She had a lover! He hadn't given her his number, vaguely he'd promised to call her the following week. No one knew, no one had come to harm, the family was safe. Bruises and red welts had already begun to show on her body as if a coarser skin were pushing through, her husband would never notice.

She hurried downstairs, she was kneeling with the children. Hugging the little girl, the little boy. Mommy? Mom-*my*? In two arms she hugged them, what did they have to show her? Easter eggs? So many? Yes they were beautiful but hadn't Ismelda understood that Mommy wanted her to wait, they would make the eggs together? She spoke sharply to Ismelda at the stove, Ismelda didn't seem to hear, it was a maddening trait of hers, seeming not to hear so her employers had to raise their voices, invariably you sounded like a bully, a fool, raising your voice to a Filipina woman scarcely five feet tall, staring at you with hurt eyes. And the children were clamoring at her, suddenly she wished them gone, all of them gone, banished from her so that she could think of her lover. *I am a murderer* she thought. *I am the one.* Her children crowded her, adoring.

BONOBO MOMMA

That day, I met my "estranged" mother in the lobby of the Carlyle Hotel on Madison Avenue, New York City. It was a few weeks following the last in a series of surgeries to correct a congenital malformation in my spine, and one of the first days when I could walk unassisted for any distance and didn't tire too quickly. This would be the first time I'd seen my mother since Fall Fashion Week nearly two years ago. Since she'd divorced my father when I was eight years old my mother—whose professional name was Adelina—spent most of her time in Paris. At thirty she'd retired from modeling and was now a consultant for one of the couture houses—a much more civilized and rewarding occupation than modeling, she said. For the world is "pitiless" to aging women, even former *Vogue* models.

As soon as I entered the Carlyle Hotel lobby, I recognized Adelina waiting for me on a velvet settee. Quickly she rose to greet me and I was struck another time by the fact that my mother was so *tall*. To say that Adelina was a striking woman is an understatement. The curvature of my spine had stunted my growth and even now, after my last surgery, I more resembled a girl of eleven than thirteen. On the way to the hotel I'd become anxious that my beautiful mother might wince at the sight of me, as sometimes she'd done in the past, but she was smiling happily at me—joyously—her arms opened for an embrace. I felt a jolt of love for her like a kick in the belly that took my breath away and left me faint-headed. *Is that my mother? My—mother?*

Typical of Adelina, for this casual luncheon engagement with her thirteen-year-old daughter she was dressed in such a way— cream-colored coarse-knit coat, very short very tight sheath in a material like silver vinyl, on her long sword-like legs patterned stockings, and on her feet elegantly impractical high-heeled shoes—to cause strangers to glance at her, if not to stare. Her ash-blond hair fell in sculpted layers about her angular face. Hiding her eyes were stylish dark glasses in oversized frames. Bracelets clattered on both her wrists and her long thin fingers glittered with rings. In a hotel like the Carlyle it was not unreasonable for patrons to assume that this glamorous woman was *someone*, though no one outside the fashion world would have re-called her name.

My father too was "famous" in a similar way—he was a painter/ sculptor whose work sold in the "high six figures"—famous in contemporary Manhattan art circles but little-known elsewhere.

"Darling! Look at *you*—such a tall girl—"

My mother's arms were thin but unexpectedly strong. This I recalled from previous embraces, when Adelina's strength caught me by surprise. Surprising too was the flatness of Adelina's chest, her breasts small and resilient as knobs of hard rubber. I loved her special fragrance—a mixture of flowery perfume, luxury soap, something drier and more acrid like hair bleach and cigarette smoke. When she leaned back to look at me her mouth worked as if she were trying not to cry. Adelina had not

been able to visit me in the hospital at the time of my most recent opera-
tion though she'd sent cards and gifts to my room at the Hospital for
Special Surgery overlooking the East River: flowers, candies, luxurious
stuffed animals and books more appropriate for a younger girl. It had
been her plan to fly to New York to see me except an unexpected project
had sent her to Milan instead.

"Your back, darling!—you are all mended, are you?—yet so *thin*."

Before I could draw away Adelina unzipped my jacket, slipped her
hands inside and ran her fingers down my spine in a way that made
me giggle for it was ticklish, and I was embarrassed, and people were
watching us. Over the rims of her designer sunglasses she peered at me
with pearl-colored eyes that seemed dilated, the lashes sticky-black with
mascara. "But—you are very *pretty*. Or would be if—"

Playfully seizing my lank limp no-color brown hair in both her
beringed hands, pulling my hair out beside my face and releasing it.
Her fleshy lips pouted in a way I knew to be distinctly French.

"A haircut, *cherie!* This very day."

Later I would remember that a man had moved away from Adelina
when I'd first entered the lobby. As I'd pushed through the revolving
door and stepped inside I'd had a vague impression of a man in a dark
suit seated beside the striking blond woman on the settee and as this
woman quickly rose to greet me he'd eased away, and was gone.

Afterward I would think *There might be no connection. Much is accident.*

"You're hungry for lunch, I hope? I am famished—*très petit dejeuner*
this morning—'jet lag'—come!"

We were going to eat in the sumptuous hotel restaurant. Adelina
had made a "special reservation."

So many rings on Adelina's fingers, including a large glittery emer-
ald on the third finger of her left hand, there was no room for a wedding band and so there was no clear sign if Adelina had remarried. My
father did not speak of my "estranged" mother, and I would not have
risked upsetting him with childish inquiries. On the phone with me, in
her infrequent calls, my mother was exclamatory and vague about her

personal life and lapsed into breathless French phrases if I dared to ask prying questions.

Not that I was an aggressive child. Even in my desperation I was wary, hesitant. With my S-shaped spine that had caused me to walk oddly, and to hold my head at an awkward angle, and would have coiled back upon itself in ever-tighter contortions except for the corrective surgery, I had always been shy and uncertain. Other girls my age hoped to be perceived as beautiful, sexy, "hot"—I was grateful not to be stared at.

As the maître d' was seating us in the restaurant, it appeared that something was amiss. In a sharp voice Adelina said, "No. I don't like this table. This is not a good table."

It was one of the small tables, for two, a banquette seat against a mirrored wall, close by other diners; one of us would be seated on the banquette seat and the other on the outside, facing in. Adelina didn't want to sit with her back to the room nor did Adelina want to sit facing the room. Nor did Adelina like a table so close to other tables.

The maître d' showed us to another table, also small, but set a little apart from the main dining room; now Adelina objected that the table was too close to the restrooms: "I hate this table!"

By this time other diners were observing us. Embarrassed and unhappy, I stood a few feet away. In her throaty aggrieved voice Adelina was telling the maître d' that she'd made a reservation for a "quiet" table—her daughter had had "major surgery" just recently—what was required was a table for four, that we would not be "cramped." With an expression of strained courtesy the maître d' showed my mother to a table for four, also at the rear of the restaurant, but this table too had something fatally wrong with it, or by now the attention of the other diners had become offensive to Adelina, who seized my hand and huffily pulled me away. In a voice heavy with sarcasm she said, "We will go elsewhere, *monsieur! Merci beaucoup!*"

Outside on Fifth Avenue, traffic was thunderous. My indignant mother pulled me to the curb, to wait for a break in the stream of vehicles before crossing over into the park. She was too impatient to walk to the intersection, to cross at the light. When a taxi passed too slowly, blocking our way, Adelina struck its yellow hood with her fist. "Go on! *Allez!*"

In the park, Adelina lit a cigarette and exhaled bluish smoke in luxurious sighs as if only now could she breathe deeply. Her mood was incensed, invigorated. Her wide dark nostrils widened further, with feeling. Snugly she linked her arm through mine. I was having trouble keeping pace with her but I managed not to wince in pain for I knew how it would annoy her. On the catwalk—*catwalk* had been a word in my vocabulary for as long as I could remember—Adelina had learned to walk in a brisk assured stride no matter how exquisitely impractical her shoes.

"Lift your head, *cherie*. Your chin. You are a pretty girl. Ignore if they stare. Who are *they*!"

With singular contempt Adelina murmured *they*. I had no idea what she was talking about but was eager to agree.

It was a sunny April day. We were headed for the Boathouse Restaurant to which Adelina had taken me in the past. On the paved walk beside a lagoon excited geese and mallards rushed to peck at pieces of bread tossed in their direction, squawking at one another and flapping their wings with murderous intent. Adelina crinkled her nose. "Such a *clatter*! I hate noisy birds."

It was upsetting to Adelina, too, that the waterfowl droppings were everywhere underfoot. How careful one had to be, walking beside the lagoon in such beautiful shoes.

"Not good to feed wild creatures! And not good for the environment. You would think, any idiot would know."

Adelina spoke loudly, to be overheard by individuals tossing bread at the waterfowl.

I was hoping that she wouldn't confront anyone. There was a fiery sort of anger in my mother, that was fearful to me, yet fascinating.

"Excuse me, *cherie*: turn here."

With no warning Adelina gripped my arm tighter, pivoting me to ascend a hilly incline. When I asked Adelina what was wrong she hissed in my ear, "Eyes straight ahead. Ignore if they stare."

I dared not glance back over my shoulder to see who or what was there.

Because of her enormously busy professional life that involved frequent travel to Europe, Adelina had relinquished custody of me to my father at the time of their divorce. It had been a "tortured" decision, she'd said. But "for the best, for all." She had never heard of the private girl's school in Manhattan to which my father was sending me and alluded to it with an air of reproach and suspicion for everyone knew, as Adelina said, that my father was "stingy—*perfide*." Now when she questioned me about the school—teachers, courses, classmates—I sensed that she wasn't really listening as she responded with murmurs of *Eh? Yes? Go on!* Several times she turned to glare at someone who'd passed us saying sharply, "Yes? Is there some problem? Do I know you?"

To me she said, frowning, "Just look straight ahead, darling! Ignore them."

Truly I did not know if people were watching us—either my mother or me—but it would not have surprised me. Adelina dressed like one who expects attention, yet seemed sincere in rebuffing it. Especially repugnant to her were the openly aggressive, sexual stares of men, who made a show of stopping dead on the path to watch Adelina walk by. As a child with a body that had been deformed until recently, I'd become accustomed to people glancing at me in pity, or children staring at me in curiosity, or revulsion; but now with my repaired spine that allowed me to walk more or less normally, I did not see that I merited much attention. Yet on the pathway to the Boathouse my mother paused to confront an older woman who was walking a miniature schnauzer, and who had in fact been staring at both Adelina and me, saying in a voice heavy with sarcasm, "Excuse me, *madame?* My daughter would appreciate not to be stared at. *Merci!*"

Inside the Boathouse, on this sunny April day, many diners were awaiting tables. The restaurant took no phone reservations. There was a crowd, spilling over from the bar. Adelina raised her voice to give her name to the hostess and was told that we would have a forty-minute wait for a table overlooking the lagoon. Other tables were more readily available but Adelina wanted a table on the water: "This is a special occasion. My daughter's first day out, after major surgery."

The hostess cast me a glance of sympathy. But a table on the lagoon was still a forty-minute wait.

My disappointed mother was provided with a plastic device like a remote control that was promised to light up and "vibrate" when our table was ready. Adelina pushed her way to the bar and ordered a drink— "Bloody Mary for me, Virgin Mary for my daughter."

The word *virgin* was embarrassing to me. I had never heard it in association with a drink and had to wonder if my capricious mother had invented it on the spot.

In the crowded Boathouse, we waited. Adelina managed to capture a stool at the bar, and pulled me close beside her as in a windstorm. We were jostled by strangers in a continuous stream into and out of the dining area. Sipping her bloodred drink, so similar in appearance to mine which turned out to be mere tomato juice, my mother inquired about my surgery, and about the surgeon; she seemed genuinely interested in my physical therapy sessions, which involved strenuous swimming; another time she explained why she hadn't been able to fly to New York to visit me in the hospital, and hoped that I understood. (I did! Of course.) "My life is not so fixed, *cherie*. Not like your father so settled out there on the island."

My father owned two residences: a brownstone on West Eighty-ninth Street and, at Montauk Point at the easternmost end of Long Island, a rambling old shingleboard house. It was at Montauk Point that my father had his studio, overlooking the ocean. The brownstone, which was where I lived most of the time, was maintained by a house-keeper. My father preferred Montauk Point though he tried to get into the city at least once a week. Frequently on weekends I was brought out to Montauk Point—by hired car—but it was a long, exhausting journey that left me writhing with back pain, and when I was there, my father spent most of the time in his studio or visiting with artist friends. It was not true, as Adelina implied, that my father neglected me, but it was true that we didn't see much of each other during the school year. As an artist/bachelor of some fame my father was eagerly sought as a dinner guest and many of his evenings both at Montauk Point and in the city were spent with dealers and collectors. Yet he'd visited me each day while I'd been in the hospital. We'd had serious talks about subjects that faded from my memory afterward—art, religion?—whether God "existed" or was a "universal symbol"—whether there was "death" from the perspective of "the infinite universe." In my hospital bed when I'd been dazed and delirious from painkillers it was wonderful how my father's figure melted and eased into my dreams with me, so that I was never lonely. Afterward my father revealed that when I'd been sleeping he had sketched me—in charcoal—in the mode of Edvard Munch's "The Sick Child"—but the drawings were disappointing, he'd destroyed them.

My father was much older than my mother. One day I would learn that my father was eighteen years older than my mother, which seemed to me such a vast span of time, there was something obscene about it. My father loved me very much, he said. Still, I saw that he'd begun to lose interest in me once my corkscrew spine had been repaired, and I was released from the hospital: my medical condition had been a problem to be solved, like one of my father's enormous canvases or sculptures, and once such a problem was solved, his imagination detached from it.

I could understand this, of course. I understood that, apart from my physical ailments, I could not be a very interesting subject to any adult. It was a secret plan of mine to capture the attention of both my father and my mother in my life to come. I would be something unexpected, and I would excel: as an archaeologist, an Olympic swimmer, a poet. A neurosurgeon . . .

✦   ✦   ✦

At the Boathouse bar, my mother fell into conversation with a man with sleek oiled hair and a handsome fox face; this man ignored me, as if I did not exist. When I returned from using the restroom, I saw the fox-faced man was leaving, and my mother was slipping a folded piece of paper into her oversized handbag. The color was up in Adelina's cheeks. She had a way of brushing her ash-blond hair from her face that reminded me of the most popular girls at my school who exuded at all times an air of urgency, expectation. "*Cherie*, you are all right? You are looking pale, I think." This was a gentle admonition. Quickly I told Adelina that I was fine. For some minutes a middle-aged couple a few feet away had been watching my mother, and whispering together, and when the woman at last approached my mother to ask if she was an actress—"Someone on TV, your face is so familiar"—I steeled myself for Adelina's rage, but unexpectedly she laughed and said no, she'd never been an actress, but she had been a model and maybe that was where they'd seen her face, on a *Vogue* cover. "Not for a while, though! I'm afraid." Nonetheless the woman was impressed and asked Adelina to sign a paper napkin for her, which Adelina did, with a gracious flourish.

More than a half hour had passed, and we were still waiting to be seated for lunch. Adelina went to speak with the harried young hostess who told her there might be a table opening in another ten-fifteen minutes. "The wand will light up, ma'am, when your table is ready. You don't have to check with me." Adelina said, "No? When I see other people being seated, who came after us?" The hostess denied that this was so. Adelina indignantly returned to the bar. She ordered a second Bloody Mary and drank it thirstily. "She thinks that I'm not aware of what she's doing," my mother said. "But I'm very aware. I'm expected to slip her a twenty, I suppose. I hate that!" Abruptly then my mother decided that we were leaving. She paid the bar bill and pulled me outside with her; in a trash can she disposed of the plastic wand. Again she snugly linked her arm through mine. The Bloody Marys had warmed her, a pleasant yeasty-perfumy odor lifted from her body. The silver-vinyl sheath, which was a kind of tunic covering her legs to her mid-thighs, made a shivery sound as she moved. "Never let anyone insult you, darling. Verbal abuse is as vicious as physical abuse." She paused, her mouth working as if she had more to say but dared not. In the Boathouse she'd removed her dark glasses and shoved them into her handbag and now her pearly-gray eyes were exposed to daylight, beautiful glistening eyes just faintly bloodshot, tinged with yellow like old ivory.

"*Cherie*, your shoulder! Your left, you carry it lower than the other. Are you aware?"

Quickly I shook my head *no*.

"You don't want to appear hunchbacked. What was he— *Quasimodo*—A terrible thing for a girl. Here—"

Briskly like a physical therapist Adelina gripped my wrists and pulled them over my head, to stretch me. I was made to stand on my toes, like a ballerina.

Adelina scolded: "I don't like how people look at you. With pity, that is a kind of scorn. I hate that!"

Her mouth was wide, fleshy. Her forehead was low. Her features seemed somehow in the wrong proportions and yet the effect of my mother was a singular kind of beauty, it was not possible to look away from her. At about the time of their divorce my father had painted a sequence of portraits titled *Bonobo Momma* which was his best-known work as it was his most controversial: enormous unfinished canvases with raw, primitive figures of monkey-like humanoid females. It was possible to see my beautiful mother in these simian figures with their wide fleshy mouths, low brows, breasts like dugs, swollen and flushed female genitalia. When I was older I would stare at the notorious *Bonobo Momma* in the Museum of Modern Art and I would realize that the female figure most closely resembling Adelina was unnervingly sexual, with large hands, feet, genitalia. This was a rapacious creature to inspire awe in the merely human viewer.

I would see that there was erotic power greater than beauty. My father had paid homage to that, in my mother. Perhaps it was his loathing of her, that had allowed him to see her clearly.

Approaching us on the path was a striking young woman—walking
with two elegant borzoi dogs—dark glasses masking half her face—
in tight designer jeans crisscrossed with zippers like stitches—a tight
sweater of some bright material like crinkled plastic. The girl's hair was
a shimmering chestnut-red ponytail that fell to her hips. Adelina stared
with grudging admiration as the girl passed us without a glance.

"That's a distinctive look."

We walked on. I was becoming dazed, light-headed. Adelina mused:
"On the catwalk, it isn't beauty that matters. Anyone can be beautiful. Mere beauty is boring, an emptiness. Your father knew that, at
least. With so much else he did not know, at least he knew that. It's the
walk—the authority. A great model announces 'Here I am—there is
only me.'"

Shyly I said, "'There is only I.'"

"What?"

"'There is only I.' You said 'me.'"

"What on earth are you talking about? Am I supposed to know?"

My mother laughed, perplexed. She seemed to be having difficulty
keeping me in focus.

I'd meant to speak in a playful manner with Adelina, as I often did
with adults who intimidated me and towered over me. It was a way of
seeming younger than I was. But Adelina interpreted most remarks lit-
erally. Jokes fell flat with her, unless she made them herself, punctuated
with her sharp barking laughter.

Adelina hailed a taxi, to take us to Tavern on the Green.

The driver, swarthy-skinned, with a short-trimmed goatee, was
speaking on a cell phone in a lowered voice, in a language unknown
to us. At the same time, the taxi's radio was on, a barrage of noisy advertising. Adelina said, "Driver? Please turn off that deafening radio,
will you?"

With measured slowness as if he hadn't quite heard her, the driver
turned off his radio. Into the cell phone he muttered an expletive in an
indecipherable language.

Sharply Adelina said, "Driver? I'd prefer that you didn't speak on the phone while you're driving. If you don't mind."

In the rearview mirror the driver's eyes fixed us with scarcely concealed contempt.

"Your cell phone, please. Will you turn it off. There's a law against taxi drivers using their cell phones while they have fares, you must know that. It's dangerous. I hate it. I wouldn't want to report you to the taxi authority."

The driver mumbled something indistinct. Adelina said, "It's rude to mumble, *monsieur*. You can let us off here."

"Ma'am?"

"Don't pretend to be stupider than you are, *monsieur*! You understand English perfectly well. I see your name here, and I'm taking down your license number. Open this damned door. Immediately."

The taxi braked to a stop. I was thrown forward against the scummy plastic partition that separated us from the furious driver. Pain like an electric shock, fleeting and bright, throbbed in my spine. Adelina and the swarthy-skinned driver exchanged curses as Adelina yanked me out of the taxi and slammed the door, and the taxi sped away.

"Yes, I will report him! Illegal immigrant—I wouldn't be surprised."

We were stranded inside the park, on one of the drives traversing the park from Fifth Avenue to Central Park West. We had some distance to walk to Tavern on the Green and I was feeling light-headed, concerned that I wasn't going to make it. But when Adelina asked me if I was all right, quickly I told her that I was fine.

"Frankly, darling, you don't look 'fine.' You look sick. What on earth is your father thinking, entrusting you with a *housekeeper*?"

I wanted to protest, I loved Serena. A sudden panic came over me that Adelina might have the authority to fire her, and I would have no one.

"Darling, if you could walk straighter. This shoulder!—*try*. I hate to see people looking at my daughter in *pity*."

Adelina shook her head in disgust. Her ash-blond hair stirred in the wind, stiffly. At the base of her throat was a delicate hollow I had not seen before. The bizarre thought came to me, I could insert my fingers into this hollow. I could push down, using all of my weight. My mother's brittle skeleton would shatter.

"—what? What are you saying, darling?"

I was trying to protest something. Trying to explain. As in a dream in which the right words won't come. Not ten feet from us stood a disheveled man with a livid boiled-beet face. He too was muttering to himself—or maybe to us—grinning and showing an expanse of obscenely pink gum. Adelina was oblivious of him. He'd begun to follow us, lurching and flapping his arms as if in mockery of my gorgeous mother.

Adelina chided: "You shouldn't have come out today, darling. If you're not really mended. I could have come to see you, we could have planned that. We could have met at a restaurant on the West Side."

Briskly Adelina was signaling for another taxi, standing in the street. She was wearing her dark-tinted glasses now. Her manner was urgent, dramatic. A taxi braked to a stop, the driver was an older man, darker-skinned than the other driver, more deferential. Adelina opened the rear door, pushed me inside, leaned into the window to instruct the driver: "Please take my daughter home. She'll tell you the address. She's just thirteen, she has had major surgery and needs to get home, right away. Make sure she gets to the actual door, will you? You can wait in the street and watch her. Here"—thrusting a bill at the driver, which must have been a large bill for the man took it from Adelina's fingers with a terse smile of thanks.

Awkwardly Adelina stooped to kiss my cheek. She was juggling her designer handbag and a freshly lit cigarette, breathing her flamy-sweet breath into my face. "Darling, goodbye! Take a nap when you get home. You look ghastly. I'll call you. I'm here until Thursday. Au-voir!"

The taxi sprang forward. On the curb my mother stood blowing kisses after us. In the rearview mirror the driver's narrowed eyes shifted to my face.

A jarring ride through the park! Now I was alone, unobserved. I wiped at my eyes. Through the smudged window beside me flowed a stream of strangers on the sidewalk—all that I knew in my life that would be permanent, and my own.

BITCH

It was a bitch. The summer was jinxed. Her father died on her birthday which was July 1. Then, things got worse. Though before that, things had not been exactly good. There were clouded memories. There had been a fear of entering the hospital. Her father had joked that hospitals are dangerous places, people die in hospitals. Her father had believed that hospitals are to be avoided at all costs. The air of hospitals is a petri dish of teeming microorganisms. Her father had rarely stepped into hospitals in his former life. Her father had had to be taken by ambulance to this hospital. Her father had not returned from the hospital. Her father had seemed to know he would not return from the hospital. Her father began to call her Poppy in the hospital. Each time she entered the hospital with dread. Each time she entered his room shivering with dread. Why are hospitals refrigerated? You don't want to ask this question. Each time she entered his room, if he was awake, if he was awake and in his bed and able to see her, he would say Is that you, Poppy? He would squint and smile eagerly and say Is that you, Poppy? Her name was not Poppy. Poppy was not a name much like her actual name though it was rare, it had become rare, for anyone to call her by that name, either. She wondered if Poppy had been her baby name, and she'd forgotten. This thought frightened her so she tried not to think it. Nor could she ask her father Who is Poppy? Before the ambulance and the hospital and the elevator to the eighth floor which had become her life things had not been exactly good and yet not-good in a way of meaning not-bad, considering. You might have said not-good in the way of meaning pretty-good, considering. She wished now that that simple happy time would return but it wasn't likely. She was visiting her father in the hospital because she was the daughter. The two of them were marooned alone together as in a lifeboat. Somehow, suddenly this had happened. There had been a family at one time, there were other relatives living now but the father did not wish to see anyone else. The father could not bear complications in his life. He had been an aggressive man in his former life but he had had to surrender his life as a man, now he would endure the life of the body. And so they were a father and a daughter alone together as in a lifeboat in the midst of the ocean. They had to shout at each other to be heard over the rushing winds and the slosh of six-foot waves. The hospital air was teeming with microorganisms poised to devour them. These were sharks too small to be detected by the human eye but obviously they were there. Disinfectant could keep them at bay but not for very long. The smell of disinfectant had seeped into her hair and could not be washed out. The smell of disinfectant had seeped into her clothing, her skin, even her fingernails. Beneath her fingernails, a sharp smell of disinfectant as if she'd been scratching her own skin, or scalp. No one would ever kiss her mouth again. No one would ever draw close to her again. What a joke! The summer was jinxed. The entire year would be jinxed. The preceding year, seen in retrospect, must have been jinxed. Though she had not known then, for she had believed that the not-so-good present was a "phase," a "stage," some sort of "transition." Until the hospital, much can be interpreted as "transition." She hadn't known that her father had loved her. That was a surprise! She hadn't known that her father had taken much notice of her. As a girl she had loved her father but eventually she'd given up, as we do when our love is not returned. Though possibly she'd been mistaken. Oh, it was a bitch! It was a bad joke. She was a bitch to think such thoughts at such a time. Though it was a comfort in this, that she was a bitch who deserved bad luck and not a nice person who deserved better. There had been a previous life involving her but in the hospital at her father's bedside she could not recall this life very clearly. Perhaps it had involved someone else, in fact. Perhaps her family had been other people. *Through a glass darkly* came to her. She was envious of those other people she had not known. The nurses on the eighth floor knew her. Some of them, the nice ones, smiled encouragingly. Some of them smiled in pity. Some of them did not smile but glanced quickly away. Some of them ducked into supply closets. The attendants who spoke little English knew her. Everywhere were hospital workers who had no idea who she was yet knew her. Each time she entered the hospital with an eager dread. She shivered with an eager dread. The hospital was refrigerated in summer. You had to wear heavy clothing. You had to wear warm stockings. You had to clench your hands into fists and squeeze them beneath your armpits for warmth. She stepped out of the elevator on the eighth floor with her eager dread. She pushed through the doors of the cardiac unit with her eager dread. She was bringing flowers, or a basket of fruit. She was bringing the local newspaper which she would read to her father. Yet, she entered his room with her eager dread never knowing what she would encounter. For each time, her father was a smaller man in the ever-larger bed. Each time, her father's eyes were sunk more deeply in their ever-larger sockets. Each time, something was missing from the room. Her father's wristwatch that had been on the bedside table. Her father's fuzzy bedroom slippers that had been neatly positioned on the floor beside the bed. Her father's reading glasses were taken from him, who would want a dying old man's reading glasses! Her father's dentures were taken from him, who would want a dying old man's dentures! Tears glistened on her father's sunken cheeks. His collapsed mouth was frantic. She was his only hope. Her voice became excited. A nurse warned of calling security. You can't accuse theft. You had better not accuse theft. You had better have evidence for theft. He was saying, You are my only hope. You will live on. I will live in you, my only hope. My beautiful daughter. Only you. She was terrified by such words. She began to tremble, such words. There was a roaring of wind, a terrible sloshing of waves. She wanted to scream at him, I'm not the one! Don't count on me. No one had said she was beautiful in a long time. No one had kissed her mouth in a long time. Her father looked at her with love—but what is love, in a dying old man! What is love, in a deranged old man! On the eve of her father's death, the missing dentures turned up. "Turned up" was the explanation. Yet her father died with a collapsed mouth, for it was too late for dentures. She was wakened from a stuporous sleep by a ringing phone. She who was his daughter who'd been claiming to be insomniac and sleep deprived yet she'd been wakened from a stuporous sleep to be informed by a woman's voice that her father had passed away and she must come to the hospital as quickly as possible to make arrangements for the disposal of the body and to clear out the room. Now the summer stretched ahead like an asphalt parking lot to the horizon. *Through a glass darkly* rang in her head. She had no idea why. Though she'd been warned, there was the shock of entering an empty room. There was the shock of the stripped bed, the bare mattress. There was the shock of an overpowering smell of disinfectant. It was her task to clear this room of her father's things. She was capable of this task, she thought. Her father's dentures were given to her. Her father's dentures had "turned up." Later she might wonder if these dentures were in fact her father's dentures but at the time she had not doubted that this was a happy ending. Later she would doubt for there was no way of knowing, really. She took care to wrap the dentures in tissue paper, though her hands were trembling. She was terrified of dropping the dentures onto the floor and breaking them. She was her father's only hope. She believed that she was equal to the task except she was distracted by something murmurous. It sounded like an anxious Is that you, Poppy? But she couldn't be sure.

AMPUTEE

You're wondering how we meet. People like us.

"Excuse me?"—near closing time at the library & suddenly he's looming over me. His manner is friendly-anxious & his eyes behind steel-rimmed glasses are dark & shining like globules of oil. He smells of wettish wool, something chalky & acrid. He's a neatly dressed man in his late thirties whom I have seen previously in the library, at a little distance. Or maybe I have seen him elsewhere in Barnegat. His breathing is oddly quickened & shallow as if he's just run up a steep flight of stairs with a question only *Jane Erdley*   *Circulation* can answer.

In fact *Jane Erdley* has been observing this person for the past hour—he's tall, lanky-limbed & self-conscious—as if he's ill at ease in his body—there's a glare in his clean-shaven face, a look of intense excitement, yet dread—for the past hour, or more, he's been sitting at the long polished-pine table in the periodicals & reference room across the foyer, covertly glancing over at me while reading, or pretending to read, a copy of *Scientific American*.

"Excuse me?"

"Yes?"

"I have a, a question—"

"Yes?"

Vaguely I remember—in the way a near-forgotten dream is recalled not by an act of will but unwittingly—that I'd first glimpsed this man shortly after the New Year. He'd worn a dark woolen overcoat—another time, a hooded windbreaker—now it's late winter he's wearing a tweed herringbone sport coat frayed at the elbows, black corduroy trousers & white dress shirt open at the throat. He might be as old as fifty, or as young as thirty-five—his thick dark hair is threaded with filaments of gray & receding unevenly from his forehead.

On the previous occasions I'd sighted him in the library, he'd been watching me, too. But not so fixedly that I took note of him.

For others stare at me, often. Mostly men, though not exclusively men. Rarely do I take note, any longer.

When I was younger, yes. When I was a girl. But no longer.

Today has been an odd, ominous day. Icy pelting rain & few people came to the library & abruptly then by late afternoon the sky above the Atlantic Ocean cleared & now at dusk there is an eerily beautiful blue-violet tinge to the eastern sky outside the Barnegat library's big bay window a quarter-mile from the shore & somehow it has happened, who knows why at this moment, the man in the herringbone coat has decided to break the silence between us.

"There is a writer—'Triptree'—"

"'Tiptree.'"

"'Tiptree.' That's the name?"

"'James Tiptree, Jr.'—in fact, Tiptree was a woman."

"A woman! I guess I'd heard that—yes."

How eager, his eyes! Behind the steel-rimmed glasses a terrible hunger in those eyes.

In this way we meet. In this way we talk. There's both excitement between us & a strange sort of ease—a sense that we know each other already, & are re-meeting—reviving our feeling for each other. Later I will learn that Tyrell premeditated this exchange for some time. *Tiptree* is just a pretext for our meeting—of course. Any reader interested in Tiptree would know that "James Tiptree, Jr." is the pseudonym of a female science-fiction writer of the 1950s, of considerable distinction— but Tyrell's question is a shrewd one since as it happens I am the only librarian in the small Barnegat library who has actually read the few Tiptree books on our shelves & can discuss Tiptree's stories with him as I check out other patrons at the circulation desk.

In the Barnegat Public Library where I've worked—in *Circulation*, in *Reference*, in *Children & Young Adults*—for the past two years, since graduating from library school, it's common that visitors pause to speak with me like this; it's common that they hope to establish some sort of bond with me, which I find repellent. With what absurd sobriety do people regard *Jane Erdley*—with what *respect* they speak to her—as if the youngest librarian on the Barnegat staff were composed of the most delicate crystal & not flesh, blood & bones, or afflicted by some hideous disease which causes the victim to waste away before your eyes & wasn't a reasonably attractive & healthy young woman of twenty-six with long curly rust-colored hair, hazel-green eyes and skin flawed only by tiny tear-sized scars at my hairline—ninety-seven pounds, five-foot-three— small hard biceps & sculpted shoulder muscles just visible through my muslin blouses, silk shirts open at the throat & loose-crocheted tops. You might expect me to wear trousers like the other female librarians but I prefer skirts; from vintage clothing stores I've assembled a small but striking wardrobe of velvet, satin, lace dresses & shawls & in winter I am sure to wear stylish leather shoe-boots. In warm weather, quite short skirts: & why not?

Deliberately I'm not looking at the man in the frayed herringbone coat leaning his elbows on the counter as we speak together of the mysterious & entertaining fiction of *James Tiptree, Jr.* I've become so accustomed to checking out books—a mindless task like most of my librarian duties & therefore pleasant & soothing—that I can manage a conversation with one library patron while serving another—though sensing how this man is staring at me, turning a small object in his fingers—car keys?—compulsively, like dice; I can sense his unease, that my attention is divided—I'm withholding from him my fullest attention—when he has surprised himself with his boldness in speaking to me, at last. Clearly this is a reserved man—not shy perhaps but secretive, wary—the kind of person of whom it's said he is *a very private person*—& now he's feeling both reckless & helpless—resentful of the other library patrons who are taking up my time.

That sick-drowning look in the man's eyes—it would be embarrassing of me to acknowledge.

This is one who wants me. Badly.

When he walks away I don't glance after him—I am very busy checking out books. I assume that he has exited the library but no— there he is in the front lobby a few minutes later, peering into glass display cases at papier-mâché dinosaurs made by grade school children, best-selling gardening books & romance novels.

How strange! Or maybe not so strange.

He isn't looking back at me. He's determined not to look. But finally he weakens, he can't resist, a sidelong glance which I give no indication of having seen.

Don't look at me. Try not to look at me.

Go away. Go home. You disgust me!

Much disgusts me. For a long time I was encouraged to count myself *blessed,* for of course *it could have been much worse,* but in recent years, no.

Since graduating from library school at Rutgers. Since having to surrender my life as a student, a privileged sort of person in a university setting in which, though never numerous, others like myself were not

uncommon; that large & varied sub-species of *the disabled* of which I am
but a single specimen & by no means the most extreme.

Wanting to say to the somber faces & staring eyes *Save your God
damned pity for the truly piteous. Not me.*

This I resent: though I could be trained to drive a motor vehicle—
with mechanical adjustments for my disability, of course—I'm forbidden by the Motor Vehicle Department of the State of New Jersey which
will not grant me a driver's license. How ridiculous this is, & unjust!—
when any idiot with two legs & half a brain can get a license in New
Jersey. And so I'm dependent upon accepting rides with co-workers or
taking the shore bus.

For the first several months of my employment at Barnegat I rode
with one of the other librarians, who also lives on Shore Island, three
miles to the north. Until one day it became abundantly clear that
this woman was too curious about me. Too *interested* in me. So now
I take the shore bus. Now I ride with predominately dark-skinned
commuters—African-American, Hispanic—most of them nannies,
cleaning women & day-laborers of various kinds. This is something of
a scandal at the library—something of which my co-workers speak rue-
fully behind my back—*Why won't Jane let us help her? If only Jane would
let us help her!* To their faces I am not at all unfriendly; in fact I'm very
friendly, when I wish. But the bus stop is less than a block from the
library. The trip itself is less than three miles, from my (rented) apartment (duplex, ground-floor) on Shore Island to Barnegat; if you continue south from Barnegat it's another three miles to Lake View, & so
along the Jersey shore—densely populated in the summer, sparsely
populated in the winter—forty-three miles to Atlantic City.

Yes I've taken the bus to Atlantic City since moving to the Jersey
shore.

Yes I've gone alone.

My family disapproves *of course.* My mother in particular who is
anxious & angry about her cripple-daughter *of course.*

Why on earth would you take public transportation when you could ride with a friend, she asks.

Not a friend, I tell her. A co-worker.

A *co-worker*, then! But why live alone on the Jersey shore when you could live in Highland Park, with us.

(Highland Park is a very nice middle-class suburb of New Brunswick not far from the sprawling campus of Rutgers University where my father teaches engineering.)

Because I do what I want to do. And not what you want me to do.

My mother & I are not close. And so I would not tell her how fascinated I am by others' fascination with me. How I love the eyes of strangers moving onto me startled, shocked—by chance, at first—then with deliberation—making of me an object of sympathy, or pity; an object of revulsion. *Love making you feel guilty for having two normal legs, feet. For being abled, not disabled. Staring at my face fixing your eyes on my eyes to indicate how pointedly you are not looking away nor are you glancing down at my lower body to see what is missing in me that makes me irremediably different from you who are whole & blessed of God.*

Now at the rear of the darkened library he's waiting.

In the parking lot, near *Library Staff Parking Only*—he's waiting.

Later he will say *I tried to go away. But I couldn't.*

He will say *Do you know why, Jane? Why I couldn't go away?*

By 6:20 P.M. the parking lot behind the library is empty except for a single vehicle, a station wagon, which must be his. In no hurry I have prepared to leave. For I know he'll be there: already between us the bond is established, should I wish to acknowledge it.

Like an actress preparing to step out onto a stage & uncertain of the script—uncertain what will be said to her. By this time the sky has darkened. The clouds are thickening. There is a wan melancholy beauty remaining in the sky in the heavy massed clouds like a watercolor wash of Winslow Homer, shading into night & oblivion. On the pavement are swaths of snow pockmarked with the grime of the long Jersey winter but at this hour, imperfections are scarcely visible. I am wearing a long military-looking dark wool coat swinging loose & unbuttoned— a chic, expensive designer coat purchased at an after-Christmas sale at the East Shore Mall—my face is stony & composed & in fact I am very uneasy—I am very excited—pushing open the rear door that bears on the outside the admonition *No Admittance—Library Staff Only*—& at once the man in the herringbone coat steps forward to take hold of the door & pull it farther open, as if I required assistance. In a thrilled voice saying, "May I help you, Ms. Erdley? Let me get this door."

"Thank you—but no. I can manage the door myself."

"Then—let me carry this bag for you."

"No. I can carry this bag myself."

On my crutches I'm strong, capable—swinging my *Step Up!* legs like a girl-athlete in a gym. On my crutches I exude an air of such headlong & relentless competence, your instinct would be to jump out of my way.

No I tell him. And again *No*. Almost I'm laughing—the sound of my laughter is startling, high-pitched—a laughter like breaking glass—it's astonishing to me, this sudden sexual boldness in the man in the tweed coat & white shirt who'd been so polite, earnest & proper, inside the library. No one is close by—no one is a witness—he can loom over me, taller than I am by several inches—he can coerce me with his height & the authority of his maleness. Very deliberately & tenderly he appropriates my leather bag—slips the strap from my shoulder and onto his own.

"Yes. This is very heavy. I can carry this."

I can't tug at the shoulder bag—I don't want to get into a struggle with the man. We're walking together awkwardly—as if neither of us has a sure footing—the sidewalk is wet, icy—my crutches are impediments, obstacles—my crutches are weapons, of a kind, & make me laugh, so ugly & clumsy & this man isn't sure how to appropriate me, armed as I am with both crutches & prosthetic lower limbs that clearly fascinate him even as they frighten him—I can't help but laugh at the situation, & at him—he's trying to laugh, too—but agitated, embarrassed—daring to grip my arm at the elbow as if to steady me.

"Ms. Erdley—maybe I should carry you? This pavement is all ice . . ."

"No. You can't carry me."

"Yes. I think I should."

"No. Don't be ridiculous."

"Where is your car?"

"I don't have a car."

"You don't have a car?"

"I said no. Now leave me alone, please."

"But—how are you getting home?"

"How do you know I'm going home?"

"Wherever you're going, then—how will you get there?"

"The way I got here."

"Ms. Erdley—how is that?"

"I think that's my business."

"Just tell me—how? You're not walking home, are you?"

"And what if I am?"

"Well—are you?"

"No. I am not walking home."

"Then—where are you going?"

"I'm taking the bus."

"The bus! No—I'll drive you."

"How do you know where I live?"

"I'll drive you."

How we meet, people like us.

He tells me his name: *Tyrell Beckmann.*

He knows my name: *Jane Erdley.*

He was born in Barnegat Sound, thirty-seven years ago this month. Moved away for all of his adult life & just recently moved back for "family & business reasons."

He has a wife, two young daughters.

Matter-of-factly enunciating *Wife, two young daughters* in the stoic way of one acknowledging an act of God.

A miracle. Or a natural disaster.

Solemnly he confides in me: "After my father died last fall the family put pressure on me to return to Barnegat—to work with my brothers in the family business—'Beckmann & Sons'—I'd rather not discuss it, Jane! In February I enrolled in a computer course at the community college—anything that's unknown to me, I'm drawn to like a magnet. Also it's a good excuse for getting out of the house in the evening. Until I came into the library. Until I saw you."

His breath is steaming in the cold air. Shrewdly he has shifted the heavy shoulder bag to his right side so that I can't tug it away from him, & he can walk close beside me unimpeded.

Here is a surprise: the man's long-legged stride is a match for me on my crutches. Despite my so-called *disability* I normally walk a little too fast for other people especially women in impractical footwear— it makes me smile to hear them plead laughingly *Jane! For heaven's sake wait*—but Tyrell Beckmann keeps pace with me, easily. Though he doesn't seem very coordinated—as if one of his legs were shorter than the other, or one of his knees pained him. His head bobs as he walks, like the head of a large predator bird. His forehead is creased with the intensity of his thoughts & the corners of his mouth have a downward turn except when something surprises him & he smiles a quick startled boyish smile.

Already I take pride in thinking *I will make this man smile! I have the power.*

As we walk, Tyrell does most of the talking. Like a man long deprived of speech he tells me how as a boy he took out books from the Barnegat library—how he loved the children's room, & read virtually every book on the shelves. He tells me about the writers he'd read since boyhood & most admired—Ray Bradbury, Rudyard Kipling, Jack

London (*The Call of the Wild*), Isaac Asimov, Philip K. Dick—then in high school Henry David Thoreau, Jorge Luis Borges, Italo Calvino, Dostoyevsky—the Dostoyevsky of *Notes from the Underground* & not the massive sprawling novels. As a "mystic-minded" adolescent he fell under the spell of the Upanishads & the Vedantists—the belief that the individual is one with the universe. As a young man in his twenties he read Søren Kierkegaard & Edmund Husserl & at Union Theological Seminary—where he'd enrolled with the vague intention of becoming some sort of Protestant-existentialist minister—he fell under the spell of the theologian Paul Tillich who'd once been on the faculty there & whose influence prevailed decades later.

Tillich was a Christian, he says, for whom Christianity wasn't an *encoded* religion but *living, vital.* So too Tyrell is a Christian in principle though he finds it difficult to believe in either Jesus Christ or in God.

" 'By their fruits shall ye know them, not by their roots.' "

These beautiful words! I wonder if they are from the Bible—the Old Testament, or the New.

I ask Tyrell do these words mean it's what people *do* that matters, & not what people *are*, or in what state they are *born*; & Tyrell squeezes my hand, awkwardly & eagerly as my fingers grip the crutch—"Yes, Jane. That is exactly what that means."

He has called me *Jane*. His hand lingers on mine, as if to steady me, or himself.

By this time it's beyond dusk—nearly nighttime. We didn't walk to the bus stop but as if by mutual consent we made our way behind the library parking lot along a path through tall rushes & dune grass & spindly wild rose & descended to the wide hard-crusted beach where a harsh wet wind whips at our faces & clothing. Here is the Atlantic Ocean—moving walls of jagged slate-colored waves—exactly the waves painted by Winslow Homer so precisely & obsessively, farther north along the Maine shore—in these waves a ferocious wish to sweep over us, to devour us.

Tyrell sees that I am shivering. Tyrell leans close to me, his arm around my shoulders. How clumsy we are, walking together! A man, a girl, a pair of crutches.

I ask him why he'd dropped out of the seminary & he says he was in despair, badly he'd wanted to be a "man of God"—to help others—while believing neither in God nor in others—& at last he realized that his desperation was to help himself—& so he quit. Living alone then in a single room on 113th Street, New York City—he'd broken off with his family in Barnegat Sound—went for days sometimes without speaking to anyone—took night courses at Columbia—found solace in his secular courses, psychology & linguistics—did research into the "secret language of twins"—the "social construction of twinness" & the "psychic ontology of twins"—its reception in the world.

"In some primitive cultures, twins are sacred. In others, twins are demonic and must be destroyed."

"Why is that?"

"Why? No one knows why."

From the subject of twins Tyrell shifts to the subject of the Hebrew Bible he'd studied—"deconstructed"—in the seminary; the compendium of writings—crude, inspired, primitive, surpassingly beautiful & terrifying—of an ancient people possessed by the idea that they are the chosen of God & hence their fate is God's fate for them & never mere accident lacking in meaning.

"Essentially there are two ontologies: the accidental & the necessary. In the one, we are free. In the other, we are fated."

"Are we! You sound very sure of yourself."

"Don't laugh at me, Jane! Please."

"But why are you telling me these things? I don't even know you."

"Of course you know me, Jane."

"No!"

"And you know why I'm telling you these things, Jane."

"Why?"

"Because we are twins, Jane."

"Twins! Don't be ridiculous."

The man's calmness frightens me. His matter-of-fact speech. Though the wind is whipping at our faces, making our eyes tear. I want to think *He's mad. This is madness.*

"Twins: in our souls. You know that."

"I don't know any such thing."

"Yes. You know that, Jane. It's clearer to me than any mystic identity of oneness in the universe. Just—us. We are oneness."

"Oneness! That's so—"

I want to say *ridiculous, mad.* Instead, my voice trails off. I'm overcome by a fit of shivering & Tyrell grips my arm at the elbow, his fingers strong through the fabric of my coat.

Oblivious of our surroundings we've been hiking on the winter beach—a mile? Two miles? We turn back & retrace our steps in the hard-crusted sand.

The man's heavy footprints, my smaller footprints & the slash-like prints made by my crutches.

No one could identify us, studying these prints. No one could guess at us.

The winter beach is littered with storm debris. Python-sized strips of brine, swaths of frozen & crusted ocean froth resembling spittle, or semen. Through a tear in the cloud-mass is a pale glaring moon like a mad eye winking.

The next time he asks, I will say *Yes. You may carry me.*

No one can understand how we are perfect together.
My stumps, fitted into the shallows at the base of his thighs.
My pale-pink skin, the most secret skin of my stumps, so soft, a man touching this skin exclaims as if he has been scalded. Oh! My God.

How do such things happen you ask & the answer is *Quickly!*

◆   ◆   ◆

Those weeks of late-winter, early spring at the Jersey shore at Barne-gat. Those weeks when Tyrell Beckmann entered my life. For there was no way to prevent him.

Saying *Jane you are perfect. I adore you.*

Saying I *was born imperfect—"damaged." There is something wrong with my body, no one can see except me.*

It was so: Tyrell inhabited his body as if at an awkward distance from it. As if he had difficulty coordinating the motions of his legs as he walked & his arms that hung stiffly at his sides. Almost you might think *Here is a man in the wrong body.*

Confiding in me as I lay in his arms fitted into his body like a key in a lock.

So often in those weeks Tyrell came to me at the library, once I asked him where was his wife? & he said his wife was at home & in the mild-est way of taunting I asked didn't she wonder where he was on those evenings he was with me & he said she would suppose he was at the community college & I said oh but not every night!—& not so late on those nights—& it was then he said in a voice of male smugness: "She doesn't want to know."

Hearing this I felt a small stab of pleasure. Resenting as always the very syllable *wife* & certainly any thought of Tyrell's wife until seeing now that this man was the prince of his household, very likely—the marriage, the family life, was centered upon *him.*

In any love-relationship there is the stronger person, & there is the weaker. There is the one who loves, & the one who is loved.

Loved, & therefore feared.

As often as he could come to me, he came. Arriving a half hour before the library closed. Or breathless & flush-faced arriving a scant five minutes before closing time. Sometimes Tyrell came directly from *work*—as he called it, without wishing to elaborate—as if the subject of his *work* in a family-owned local business was painful to him— & wore a sport coat or a suit, white shirt & necktie & black dress shoes like any professional man; at other times he wore corduroy trousers, the herringbone-tweed coat with leather elbow-patches, salt-stained running shoes.

Never did I look for the man. Never did I betray surprise or even (evident) pleasure glancing up & seeing the man looming over me with his tense tight smile, at the circulation desk.

There is the *hunter*, and there is the *hunted*.

Power resides not in the *hunter*—as you might think—but in the *hunted*.

In his hand a book as a prop. A book as a pretext. A book to be checked out of the Barnegat Public Library by the librarian at the circulation desk.

"Jane! Hello."

It was not forbidden that Tyrell call me *Jane*. Many of the library patrons knew me & called me *Jane*.

It was not forbidden that Tyrell smile at me. Every patron known to me at the library was likely to smile at me.

It was forbidden that Tyrell touch me in public. Not even a handshake. Not even a brushing of his fingers against mine when I handed him back his plastic library card. Nor did I allow Tyrell to stare at me, in that way of his that was raw, ravenous. I had a horror of others knowing of us, or guessing. I had a horror of being *talked-of, whispered-about*.

Though it gave me a childish pleasure to lie in my bed in the early morning—amid my bedclothes tousled & rumpled from the man's perspiring body of the previous night—& languidly to think yes probably others had noticed Tyrell lingering in my vicinity, or waiting for me when the library closed; very likely, some had seen us walking together on the deserted winter beach. *Jane Erdley & that man—that tall man who comes into the library so much & is always hovering over her.* The other librarians on the staff who are so sharp-eyed & our supervisor Mr. McCarren whose particular project *Jane Erdley* has been.

We are committed to hiring the disabled here, Ms. Erdley. This was the Barnegat mandate long before it was a directive of the State of New Jersey.

Oh thank you! Mr. McCarren that is so—kind.

I did not like it that others might wonder of us & gossip but I did like it that Tyrell revealed so plainly in his face the desire he felt for me. I liked it that the older, married man should be so reckless, desperate.

It pleased me perversely to think that he was the prince of his household. He was a man of thirty-seven who retained the youth & cruel naivete of a man a decade younger, or more—& so his maleness, his sexuality, withheld from the woman who was his wife, would aggrieve her. Not a syllable of reproach would pass the wife's lips—so I imagined!—yet her hurt, her woundedness, her anxiety would be considerable. It is natural that a husband hold his wife in disdain, for she is his possession, available to him & known to him utterly as *Jane Erdley* would never be fully known.

Oh God! So beautiful.

Beneath the red plaid flannel skirt flared & short as a schoolgirl's—beneath the schoolgirl white-woolen stockings worn with shiny red ankle-high boots—the (expensive, clumsy) prosthetic limbs: pink-plastic, with aluminum trim, lewd & ludicrous & to remove these, to unbuckle these, the man's fingers trembling & the man's face heated with desire, or dread—the first stage of the act of love—the act of sex-love—that will bind us, close as twins.

"Has there been any other—? Any other who—like this?"

"No. No one."

"Am I the first?"

"Yes. The first."

Seeing the look in the man's face, the adoration in the man's eyes I burst into laughter, it was not a malicious laughter but a child's laughter of delight & playfulness & tears spilled from my eyes—a rarity for *Jane Erdley* does not cry even stricken with phantom-pain in her lower limbs—& I kissed the man hard on the lips as I had never kissed anyone in my life & I said, "Yes you are the first & you will always be the first."

Throbbing veins & nerve-endings in the stumps. The stumps of what had once been my legs, my thighs—years ago in my old, lost life. Spidery red veins, thicker blue arteries deep inside the flesh. Where the stumps break off—where the *amputation* occurred—about six inches below the fine-curly-red-haired V of my groin—there is a delicious shiny near-transparent skin, an utterly poreless skin, onion-skin-thin, an infant's skin; in wonderment you would want to stroke this skin, & lick it with your tongue yet in fact this skin isn't only just soft but strangely sturdy, resilient—a kind of cuticle, a protective outer layer as of something shimmering & unspeakable.

"And you, Jane—you will always be my first."

On Shore Island in his station wagon he kissed me. That first night shyly asking permission & several nights in succession I told him *No— that isn't a good idea* & at last as he persisted I said *Well—all right. But just once* for the man knew that I would say *Yes* finally, from the first he'd known.

On Shore Island in my (small, sparely furnished) apartment he first kissed me *there.* Undressed me & unbuckled the plastic legs & kissed me many times *there.*

On Shore Island overlooking marshland: six-foot rushes that swayed & thrashed in the wind, a brackish odor of rotting things & at dawn a crazed choir of gulls, crows, marsh birds shrieking in derision, or in warning.

Kissing & sucking. For long delirious minutes that became half hours, & hours. Shivering & moaning & kissing/sucking the stumps, the soft infant-skin at the end of the stumps, so excited I could feel the blood rush into his penis, in my hand his penis was a kind of stump, immediately erect & smallish then filling out with blood leech-like filling with blood & hardening with blood & at last a hard yearning stump with a blunt blind soft head that seemed wondrous to me, so vulnerable & beautiful—a ludicrous thing, yet beautiful—as the stumps that are all that remain of my girl-legs are ludicrous, ugly & yet to this man's eyes beautiful, as I am beautiful—the female torso, the upper limbs, the spread-open thighs, stump-thighs, & the openness between the thighs, moist & slash-like in the flesh, thrumming with heat & life & yearning—*I will love you forever, there is no one like you my darling Jane you are so beautiful, my darling! Love love love love you*—& in his delirium he seemed not to comprehend how I did not claim to love *him*.

For to be loved is to bask in your power, like a coiled snake sunning itself on a rock.

To love is weakness. This weakness must be overcome.

"I first saw you with some other women. I think they were your colleagues. The other librarians. You were walking into town"—this would be a distance of only a few blocks, on Holland Street leading into Barnegat Avenue where there is a very good inexpensive restaurant named *Wheatsheaf*—"you were laughing, & so beautiful—the braces just visible beneath your skirt shining, your crutches—the other women were just—so—ordinary—plain & heavy-footed—they were just *walking*. All the light was on you, & you were *flying*. Your beautiful shimmering-red hair, your beautiful face, all the light was on you & you seemed almost to be seeing me—taking note of me, & smiling—at *me!*—you passed by so close on the sidewalk, I could have reached out & touched you . . . I felt faint, I stared after you, I had never seen anyone like you—beside you all other women are maimed, their legs are clumsy, their feet are ugly. I could have reached out & touched you . . ."

"Why didn't you touch me?"

I laugh in his arms. I am very happy. In the man's arms, my thigh-stumps lifted to fit in that special place. He is caressing, kissing, the pit of my belly. My tiny slant-eye belly button. With his tongue. & my shoulder tucked into the crook of his arm. So snugly we fit together, like tree-roots that have grown together. & this not over a period of years but at once, all but overnight as by a miracle.

"Because one touch would not have been enough for me. That's why."

✦   ✦   ✦

At the Jersey shore spring is slow to arrive. Still in early April there are dark-glowering days spitting icy rain. Fierce swirling snowflakes & ice-pellets—flotillas of snow-clouds like gigantic clipper ships blown overhead—yet by degrees with the passing of days even the storm-sky begins to remain light later & later—until at last at 6 P.M.—the library's closing time, weekdays—the sky above the ocean, visible through the broad bay window at the front of the library, was no longer dark. "Jane! Your friend is waiting at the front desk."

"My friend? My friend—who?"

My face flushed hot with blood. My eyes welled with tears of distress. So it must have been known to them, casually known to the other librarians, that crippled *Jane Erdley* had a *friend*; that the tall, taciturn slightly older man who came frequently to the library was Jane Erdley's special *friend*.

This was a day I was working at the rear of the library doing book orders on a computer. Another librarian had taken over the circulation desk.

"He—isn't my friend. He's a relative—a cousin—a distant cousin—he lives over in Barnegat Sound."

I did not meet the woman's eye. My voice was husky, wavering.

Though I was smiling, or trying to smile. A flash of a smile lighting up my face, in defiance of pity, sympathy. *Whatever you are offering me, I am not in need of.*

On this windy April day I was wearing a pleated skirt made of cream-colored wool flannel, that resembled a high school cheerleader's skirt, & I was wearing a crimson satin blouse with a V-neckline glittering with thin gold chains & small crystal beads, & if you dared to lean over, to peer at my legs, or what was meant to represent my "legs," you would see the twin prostheses, shiny plastic artificial legs & steel pins & on my (small) feet eyelet stockings & black patent leather "ballerina slippers."

My crutches were nearby. My crutches have a look of having been flung gaily aside, as of little consequence.

"Well. He seems very nice—gentlemanly. He's obviously very fond of you."

The woman spoke in a voice of mild reproach. A chill passed over me. *She knows! They all know, & are disgusted.*

This was clear to me, suddenly. & there was no pleasure in it, only a shared disgust, dismay.

& so that evening I told Tyrell I did not want to see him anymore, I thought it was best for us not to see each other after this night. In his station wagon he was driving us along the ocean highway to Shore Island & gripping the steering wheel tight in his left hand so the knuckles glared white & with his other hand he held my left hand & spread his fingers wide grasping my upper thigh, that was my "stump"—the living flesh that abutted the plastic prostheses, so strangely—compulsively he was squeezing the pleats of my skirt & the tip of his middle finger pressed against the pit of my belly; it was past 6:30 P.M. but not yet dusk, the eastern sky above the ocean was streaked with horizontal strips of clouds of the color of bruised rotted fruit & quietly I told him I did not think that this was a good idea—"seeing each other the way we do"— I told him that people were beginning to talk of us in Barnegat— & eventually, his family would find out—his wife . . .

My voice trailed off. I knew that I had upset him & knew that he could not turn to face me while he was driving, to protest.

Yet: without speaking Tyrell pulled the station wagon off the highway & turned onto a gravel service road—the abruptness of his behavior was exciting to me, & unnerving—behind us traffic streamed on the highway but this was a desolate place amid stunted trees & sand dunes & scattered trash & out of sight of the highway Tyrell braked the station wagon & turned to me & his shadowed face was anguish & his hands were on me roughly & in desperation—his mouth on mine, his tongue in my mouth hungry & strangely cool & I held him in my arms in triumph feeling the strength of my biceps & my shoulders flow into the man, though I could not match the man in physical strength yet he would have to acknowledge the strength & the suppleness of my body & he said, "Don't say such things, Jane—I love you so much, Jane, there is no one but you. There is no one"—pulling at my clothing, at the pleated skirt & now his hands were on the prosthetic limbs fumbling to detach them from my thigh-stumps & he was moaning—trembling—he was desperate with love for me & behind the rain-splotched windshield of the vehicle that same waxy-pale moon now a diminished quarter-moon, winking.

No one Jane but you.
Nothing but this.

In the night he cries out in his sleep. He thrashes, he shivers, he shudders & I am frightened of his sudden strength, if he tries to defend himself against a dream-assailant. From his throat issue loud crude animal cries, like nothing I have heard from him before. With some difficulty I manage to wake him & he's uncertain of where he is & agitated & by degrees becomes calmer & finally laughs—he has turned on the bedside lamp, he has fumbled to find a cigarette in a trouser pocket—saying he'd had a nightmare. Some "ridiculous" creature with sharp teeth & a stunted head like a crocodile was trying to eat him—devour him.

I ask him if he often has nightmares & he laughs irritably saying who knows or gives a damn—"Dreams are debris to be forgotten."

Later: "I dreamt that we were both dead. But very happy. You said *Maybe we will never be born.*"

Then in early April, I saw him.

In the East Shore Mall, I saw him.

Suddenly then & with no preparation, Tyrell Beckmann & his family.

On their strong, whole legs. As in the central open atrium of the Mall I approached these strangers & saw how one of them, the male, the *husband & father*, materialized into Tyrell who was my lover—this was a shock!—this was an ugly surprise—yet I did not falter unless for a half-second, a heartbeat & immediately then I had recovered & on my crutches gripped beneath my arms like paddles or wings & my useless but showy plastic legs swinging I flew past them—swift as an arrow *Jane Erdley* can move, at such times propelled by adrenaline like a wounded creature.

His face. A startled blur as I flew past on my crutches staring straight ahead & ignoring him. Tyrell, the wife, the two daughters—within seconds I was past them. The younger of the two girls sucked at her fingers murmuring to her mother *Ohhh what happened to that lady—oh did it hurt!*

Beside her an older sister, ten or eleven, fleshier & resembling the mother crinkled up her face & rudely stared after me.

Ohhh is she crippled? Is she missing her legs? Ohhh that's ugly.

But already I was past, unseeing. And not a backward glance.

Immediately I left the Mall. Immediately retreating to lick my wounds & to prevent further humiliation & on the bus back to Shore Island my brain in a frenzy replayed the scene. Helpless & furious replaying the scene like one digging at a raw wound with a fingernail.

I did not choose to linger on my guilty lover's face. For in that moment it was clear that Tyrell Beckmann *was not my lover*. The man's allegiance was to his family—the wife, the daughters. In his shocked face & alarmed eyes there was no discernible love for Jane Erdley only just startled recognition & a cowardly terror of being found out, exposed. Instead, I concentrated on the wife—I did not know the wife's name, Tyrell had not told me—a woman in her late thirties or perhaps older—solid-bodied, husky—brown hair of no discernible style brushed back from her face round as a moon—fleshy cheeks, flushed with color—staring eyes though veiled, unlike her rude daughter—not a striking woman but you could see she'd been attractive when younger, with slackening jowls, a fatty chin—a look of *competence, capability* about her & yet some slight worry, anxiety—a tiredness in the fleshy-female body—a no-longer-young mother harried by two children of whom the

younger was fretting & dragging at her arm & her husband—her prince
of a husband—walking a few feet ahead of his family in corduroy slacks,
pullover sweater, running shoes frowning as he leafed through a glossy
brochure advertising some sort of expensive electrical appliance. In the
positioning of wife/mother—husband/father—you could see the dy-
namics of their family & the thought came to me, as consolation *She is
wary of losing him. Of course she is anxious, & she is resentful. As she ages, her
prince of a husband will remain young.*

What I saw was: the woman's eyes glancing onto me, dropping to
my lower body & to the artificial limbs—taking in my crutches, & the
dexterity with which I manipulated the crutches—you could see that
I'd been doing this a long time & had learned to propel myself forward
with a kind of defiant ease—& the woman's eyes that were smallish,
piggish, with scanty brown lashes—narrowed in disdain or revulsion
just perceptibly & in those eyes not a glimmer of sympathy for me as for
one like herself who has been afflicted with grievous bodily harm, this
woman who was Mrs. Tyrell Beckmann did not wish to acknowledge
There but for the grace of God am I.

That arrow, shot into my heart.

And what would you like for Christmas, little girl? Tell Santa!

Very little of this I remember. I never dream of it since I don't
remember.

How at the age of eleven my legs above the knees were amputated
& taken from me & I would not run again nor even walk except with
crutches flailing & falling & both missing legs alive with pain like invisible flame. How it was Daddy's fault for Daddy had been drinking at
the Fourth of July picnic & afterward driving to the traffic circle for a
bag of ice & six-packs of cold beer & his favorite child Jane-Jane in the
passenger's seat beside him & in the confusing dimness of dusk & headlights on the highway there was a head-on collision with a truck whose
headlights were blinding or maybe it was just that Daddy fell asleep

at the wheel, drunk-Daddy's eyelids were drooping & drunk-Daddy's mouth drooping & in an instant the vehicles careened together & the front of Daddy's car was smashed flat like a snub nose.

I was pried from the wreckage. So it was said. I have no memory of this.

Mostly my face was spared. Except for glass-cuts, bruises & welts but the skin itself was not torn off nor the face-bones smashed. As if God meant to mock: a pretty-girl face on a broken body.

Many of the bones of my body were broken, fractured or sprained but the spinal column was spared, & the skull. All of the parts of my body were great lurid bruises orange & purple like rotted fruit. Both my legs, both my feet & my knees were smashed. There were few bones remaining intact. The calf of my right leg was sheared off. Much of my blood was lost. Transfusions kept me alive. Yet, I had died. It was said that my heart ceased beating more than once. In surgery for six hours & the heart will cease beating after such trauma. Six hours surgery but this made little difference. The leg-bones were lost. The muscle-flesh had been torn away. The surgeon would operate above the knees. The stumps were made to be the same size. The nerve-endings were cauterized. By the age of twelve I'd been fitted with *prostheses—prosthetic legs—* but these were clumsy & hateful & I could not manage them at first—it would require many weeks & months—it would require years—before I would acquire the skill to use these plastic legs in the way that I do now provoking relatives & friends of our family to say within my hearing as if such words were a gift to the tragic cripple-girl *Isn't Jane wonderful! Isn't Jane brave! Isn't Jane a miracle.*

My father was very shamed. My father too was injured but he did not lose his legs nor any of his limbs though he would never walk fully upright again & without pain. His ribs were broken & chest muscles lacerated & he could not lie in bed but required a special chair of soft leather with moveable parts that could be lowered & raised & yet often he would scream in pain like a stricken animal. He took painkillers & he continued to drink. He could not look upon me. His shame was so great he could not look upon the prosthetic legs with the perky name *Step Up!* & he could not bear to hear my crutches against the hardwood floor. It was my mother & my aunt who drove me to the rehab clinic at Robert Wood Johnson so many months. After my father was gone from us at Christmastime we drove to the Fair Hills Mall which is the largest shopping mall in all of New Jersey & there we shopped for presents & when I was tired we stopped to rest & looked at the Christmas tree lights & animated figures & there was Santa Claus on his throne, I was too old & my eyes ringed with the fatigue of an old child but in my *Step Up!* artificial legs, braces, & crutches, I was small for my age, never would I catch up with other children my age as I would not return to school with my class but would remain a year behind forever. At this time I was almost thirteen but so small I might have been eleven, or ten. Inside his fluffy fake-beard Santa smiled at me as my mother urged me forward. "My little girl is a brave little girl Santa isn't she! Her name is Jane."

"Well—Jane! Hel-lo little girl how are you!"

"Jane is very well, Santa. Jane is doing very well."

Santa's eyes narrowed in concern. Santa's cheeks blushed beneath the silly white whiskers, you could see. Santa was compelled to ask, "And what would you like for Christmas this year, Jane?" as Santa asked all the children who came to sit on his knee. I felt the man stiffen, I felt the man steel himself, what words little cripple-Jane might utter. & my mother gripping me, my arm, as if I were a doll who might topple over without Mommy holding tight & smiling as if nothing was more natural than to bring a twelve-year-old legless dispirited child to Santa Claus at the Fair Hills Mall & await her answer to Santa's question.

I was not a young child even then. I felt sorry for Santa. In a scratchy broken little doll-voice saying, "For Christmas I would like Cowgirl Barbie."

Whether my father was made to go away or whether my father went away of his own volition was not clear. He would move to another state,

Minnesota. Some time later he would move to Wyoming. He would *drink himself to death* as it was said by my mother & my mother's family grim with satisfaction.

My mother said it was a blessing he had gone, & I was blessed of God & one day I would understand.

"Why should I believe that?" I asked her.

I was an angry-mouthed girl. I have learned to hide this.

"Because"—my mother chose her words with care, fixing her eyes on my face as if there was no other part of me that could be looked-at, without revulsion—"if God didn't love Jane very much, He would have smote her down when he took her poor legs. He had that opportunity, & He let it pass."

The man who is Mr. Erdley who has been my father for many years, who is a professor of engineering at Rutgers New Brunswick, is my stepfather. It is expected of me to say that *I love my stepfather as I had loved Daddy long ago* but this is not true & I do not say it.

At the library at the circulation desk was another librarian & through that long day I remained in the rear at a computer typing in book orders & I did not think of him—of Tyrell—I would not think of him—& when he came into the library rushed & breathless in the late afternoon, as I had expected he would come, I did not see him nor was *Jane Erdley* anywhere in his sight. That weekend he had called me—he had left phone messages which I had not answered. He'd sent emails which I deleted without reading. *He has betrayed me. There is no love between us. There is nothing*—these words chill & hard & resolute as polished stones were a consolation to me. & then through a doorway I saw him, abruptly there was Tyrell, leaning on my crutches I stood very still & calm & observed him—the man who was my lover & who so claimed to love me, yet had been appalled by the sight of me in the Mall; my lover who had been terrified of me, that I would expose him to his wife & rude staring daughters.

At last, he saw me. In his face a look of anguish—I felt the force of his love, & his regret—quickly I drew back, & hid from him.

Thinking *Maybe it isn't over yet. Not yet.*

When I left the library that evening—not with the others but at 6:25 P.M. there was Tyrell waiting at the rear & seeing me approach the door quickly he came forward & pulled the door open as I pushed it & in a lowered voice though there was no one within earshot he said, "Jane, may I carry you?—just to my station wagon let me carry you," & this time I did not say *No.*

In his arms I feel airy, guiltless. My arm around his neck, my stump-thighs borne aloft in his embrace. The crutches he leaves behind, leaning against the rear wall of the library. In the car he settles me, buckles me into the seat belt & returns to the crutches & positions them beneath his arms—Tyrell is several inches taller than I am, & so the crutches are short for him—he is clumsy & funny using them—"walking"—he has not the knack of swinging his body, his legs as if they were useless, life-less. But he is very funny—we are both laughing—breathless & giddy like drunken lovers.

At the station wagon Tyrell shoves the crutches into the backseat with a clatter—he seizes my shoulders, seizes my head, my face framed in his hands & he kisses me—his kisses are hungry, predatory—he begs me to forgive him & exulting in my power which is the most exquisite sexual power I tell the man *Yes maybe. This time.*

Our naked bodies. The man's body is heavier & thicker than you would think. His chest is nearly hairless, & the hairs a very pale brown, almost invisible. His man-breasts are flat but the nipples are small & hard as pits. On his back, like an outline of wings, are whorls of hair. At his waist, a ring of excess flesh. With what passion the man licks, kisses, sucks at my thigh-stumps, that end above my knees; very excited, aroused, the man lifts my stumps onto his shoulders & presses his hot

hungry face between them. What he does to me with his lips, teeth &
tongue is near-unbearable to me, in a delirium I murmur his name, I cry
out his name, I am utterly helpless, lost. In orgasm the man is rocked as
by a sudden powerful wave yet within minutes he has begun again licking, kissing, sucking at the thigh-stumps *Love love love you there is no one
like you & there is nothing   like this.*

It is not true as Tyrell believes, that no man ever carried me in his
arms as Tyrell has.

In Atlantic City, this occurred. But only once, when I was new to
Barnegat & lonely & reckless one weekend.

The man was a stranger—of course—& the name I gave him was
not my true name nor did he know where I lived or how I was em-
ployed though I saw in his watering eyes that unmistakable look of sick-
helpless love. For without my *Step Up!* legs I am petite as a child, I weigh
so little a man of below average height & strength can lift me & carry
me in his arms. & nothing further came of this. So little do I recall, I
could not tell you the name of the glittering casino & hotel where we
met, in a lounge near the blackjack tables. It was a meeting I entered into
of my own volition but with much doubt & distaste & abruptly then I
ended it without telling the man, fled from a women's restroom & back
to Barnegat, on the bus.

As I said, he did not know my name. Had he wished to find me, he
could not.

He will leave her, he says. His wife.

He speaks bravely, recklessly. You would believe that he speaks
sincerely.

He wants to live with me, he says. He loves me, he thinks that we
should live together . . .

His words are stunning to me, unreal. My heart begins to beat
quick, hard & erratically. Calmly I say to him—my voice is light, lightly
teasing—"You loved her when you married her—you can't deny

that"—& Tyrell protests, "No. I don't think so" & I say, cruelly, "What do you mean—you 'don't think so'—not only did you marry your wife, you had two children with her. You must love her," & he says, speaking slowly, grimly, "I was lonely when we met—I was desperate to be 'normal'—Courtney was somehow *there*—she wanted a more permanent relationship & I didn't want to hurt her—There is so little between us now, only the children, household matters, problems—the minutiae of life. Nothing like what I feel for you. Nothing like what binds us together. Courtney is a good decent woman & of so little interest to me, I have difficulty listening to her—her flat whining hurt voice—even when we were newly married we didn't 'have sex' often—& never, now—we've become old people—prematurely old—only the children & the household keep us together—a kind of adhesive—adhesive tape, soiled & frayed—we're like people of the 1950s—that feels like us, when you see a movie of that era, or photographs—the men wearing hats, fedoras—the men so determined to be *mature*—the women wearing hats, gloves—stockings—'girdles'—the photography in black & white, not color. What infuriates me is how Courtney complains of me, to the children—she speaks of me in the third person to them, so that I can overhear—she says, 'Does Daddy love us? Daddy never tells us that he loves us'—" his voice going shrill, mocking; a voice of such masculine derision, for a moment I am silenced; for a moment pricked with guilt, sympathy for the contemptible unloved female.

Then recovering I say, in my lightly teasing voice, "So—what do you tell this poor woman?" & Tyrell says, "I tell her—'Courtney, why should that matter? Why the hell should that matter so much?'"

He pauses, breathing quickly. In his eyes a look of utter exasperation, righteousness.

"It only proves that I was living a mistake, Jane. It proves that I don't know why I did anything before I met you."

Courtney! The name makes me smile, in scorn. A pretentious name, for a plain dull unloved woman.

◆ ◆ ◆

After lovemaking that exhausts us, strains our hearts & chafes our skin—my most sensitive skin, the insides of my stump-thighs, & the soft pale cottony flesh of my breasts—sinking then into sleep, open-mouthed, quivering. The man breathes heavily, deeply—his face close up appears contorted—his forehead creased & lines in his cheeks like erosion in earth—his skin is a rough hot parchment-like skin—clammy with sweat, exuding a sharp pungent smell—by degrees I feel myself weakening *I don't want to love this man, I am not able to love any man.* Still awkwardly my thigh-stumps are spread & fitted to the man's thighs, & his arms around me are still tight, uncomfortably tight, as he sinks into a jagged twitchy sleep where I can't follow except the love that passes between us—I think it is *love*—as in a single thrumming artery—whose thought is *We are twins. In our souls. We are joined together at the heart.*

In the morning, he was gone.

Very early in the morning, before dawn. While I lay dazed & groggy in sleep & he lowered his weight onto the bed beside me, stroking my hair, my naked shoulders & back saying he has to leave & he will call me—he will see me that evening—he will try to see me—there is so much happening in his life, a series of crises—"You are the central crisis of my life, Jane!—but you are not the only crisis"—& on his strong legs he goes away & for an hour or more I lie unmoving like a child trapped in a wreck—waiting to determine *Am I alive? Or—am I dead?* Rousing myself then & reaching for my *Step Up!* legs & my crutches & maneuvering myself into the day & at Barnegat library there is *Jane Erdley* reliable & professional as usual—in a lime-green velvet vintage dress, with a tinkling glass-bead necklace—her *Step Up!* legs stylishly encased in ivory eyelet stockings & her demure plastic feet in black patent leather Mary Janes. Yet sternly instructing myself through this long day—as for much of my life following the accident when drunk-Daddy fell asleep at the wheel—*Look, Jane: you are alone. You will always be alone.*

No one will love you, & no one will desire you. And if there is love, & desire, it will be a sickness in the other, that will revolt you.

Monday night following Easter Sunday when he had to be with his family—a large family gathering at his parents' house on the Sound—& there seems to have been some stress at this gathering— he doesn't speak of it, & I will not ask—he is morose, brooding—by the smell of his breath I understand that he has been drinking before he came to the library for me—complaining how his body hadn't ever "fitted" him right—his left leg especially is "wrong-angled"—only with me, his darling Jane, does his body *fit right*; suddenly he confides in me, there was a girl in his grammar school, in fact in kindergarten he'd first seen her, she'd had to use crutches—children's crutches—& when she was older, a wheelchair—bright steel braces on her legs which were her legs but withered, wasted-away—yet she'd been so pretty—& smart— her name was *Wendy—Wendy Hauserman*—he'd been fascinated by this girl whose family moved away from Barnegat when they were in sixth grade & later when he was thirteen at summer camp in the Poconos there was the wife of the camp director—a tall blond beautiful woman with a sullen face, wide mouth & gray eyes & rarely smiled—said to be "Swedish"—her hair long & straight & so pale it looked white in certain lights—at dusk, & by firelight—her name was *Brigit* & she was missing a leg—her left leg, below the knee—half her leg had been amputated after a skiing accident—yet she lay in the sunshine in a bikini on an outcropping of shale, her pale skin oiled & her eyes hidden behind dark glasses & sometimes Brigit wore her prosthetic limb, & sometimes not; sometimes Brigit smiled at the boy-campers, & sometimes not.

"Then—when I first met you . . . I mean, when I first saw you—on the sidewalk, with your colleagues—I thought . . ."

Holding my breath & trying not to stiffen in the man's embrace. He has been stroking my breasts, my stomach, my thighs idly, as if not aware of what he's doing; since Easter dinner at his family's house, he has been in a strange unsettled mood; he has smoked several cigarettes,

he has not asked if he can smoke in my apartment & I have not told him
Please no! The smell of smoke makes me nauseated & numbly I listen to him
revert to the familiar account of how he'd first seen me, he has told me
this several times in virtually the same words, I am listening in dismay,
in disgust & impatience & when he prepares to leave my apartment at
midnight I tell him:

"Maybe—please—you should not come back."

He goes away, he is gone.
He doesn't call me. He calls.
He sends me a letter, Federal Express. A plain white envelope, a
folded sheet of plain white paper.

> *Dear Jane I love you!!! Only you.*
> *I will make you know this. I believe you know this.*

He returns to my apartment. He knocks at the door. His is a special
knock, a kind of code. I have not answered his phone messages or his
frantic emails & so he has driven to Shore Island & stands at my door
& I have no choice but to admit him. On my crutches—I open the
door. He is unshaven, his white shirt is rumpled & his eyes behind the
(crooked) steel-rimmed glasses are ringed in fatigue. In triumph he says,
"I left her. It's over. I told her, I couldn't continue to live with her, I'm in
love with another woman."

The room is darkened, we grope for each other like blind persons.

"I can change my life, Jane. The externals of my life. If I can be here
with you."

In bed he fits my stumps to his shoulders. He is hot-skinned, trembling. He is rough, agitated—he hurts me, without knowing. His cries
are like his nightmare-cries, he'd dismissed so lightly. I feel the jump of
his seed inside me, the juice of the man, his most secret life. He is not a
young man & yet every cell in his body yearns to impregnate me, the female; what remains of me, the stump-torso, legless & open to the male,

vulnerable as a wound. "We could die together. I want to die with you. The two of us together, as in the womb. As if we haven't been born yet."

Tangled in the bedclothes we fall asleep. In the night I'm wakened by his breathing, his harsh breathing & the mutterings of his sleep. I kiss his mouth, his breath is heated, moist & sour-smelling. I suck at his breath like a giant cat. His jaws are covered in silvery stubble. Beneath my groping fingers, his penis stirs. The stump-penis, soft & limp as a slug. I rub one of my stumps against it, the sensation is electric—the nerve-endings are not dead, or cauterized, only dormant, awaiting this touch.

We could die together. I want to die with you. It would have been better—the two of us not yet born.

That weekend in Atlantic City at the Trump Casino—where I've come alone, by bus. Friday night entering the vast glittering-humming casino & feeling eyes move upon me idly at first, & then—some of them—snagging. In a pool of fish I am a curious-shaped fish—I am a "wounded" specimen. Yet making my way swiftly through the Friday evening crowds—to the blackjack tables—here, my senses are alert—here, I feel a tug of *hope*—for the occasion I am wearing one of my velvet dresses—luscious dark crimson with a sharp V-neck & a scalloped hemline, lifted at the front to expose the knee—the knees—the steel-gleaming *Step Up!* knees—& my shoulder-length hair brushed & glossy & pinned back with tortoiseshell combs like a schoolgirl of another era long-ago & romantic & as a novelty—to set me apart from *Jane Erdley   Circulation*—my skin is powdered geisha-white—my mouth is a damp crimson rose, or wound—in mirrors on the casino floor I've glimpsed my reflection, I am repelled by my reflection & fascinated thinking *Oh is that me? Would Daddy recognize his Jane-Jane, now?* I love the way strangers stare at me—the way they step aside, clear a path for me as I fly by them—there is respect for me, a young woman alone, on a Friday night, in Atlantic City, decked out in sleek white arm-support plastic crutches & prosthetic legs—respect & repugnance in about equal measure but at the blackjack table I am a serious gambler—I am totally absorbed in the action—the blackjack dealer (male, mid-thirties, sharp-eyed) is stiff with me, stiff-smiling & avoiding my eye—as if warning me off but I am oblivious—I am not drunk, but I am oblivious—I pay no heed to others observing me—I have just two chips remaining, of five—each chip is worth fifty dollars—in less than an hour I have lost three hundred fifty dollars. At a nearby table a man has been watching me intently—his face is a blur—their faces are always blurs—his hair is a blur of sandy-white—though my impression is, his face is not old— I love the sensation of eyes crawling onto me like ants—unlike ants, these eyes can be shaken off—I can make my way past them defiant & graceful on my crutches—if I am patient at the blackjack table there will be one who will approach me carrying his drink in his hand, his chips in his other hand loose & jangling like coins & he will wait for the opportunity to slip in beside me at the blackjack table guessing it might be time for this rueful cripple-girl-gambler—who appears to be alone in the Trump Casino, 10 P.M. Friday night—to ask to borrow a chip— a chip, or two—to regain my losses—smiling to think how *losses* sounds like *kisses*—& bring a cheery smile to my face—such smiles flare up like a sudden struck match here in the glittery gaudy casino—the blurred-faced man is drawing closer, he is an older man yet not an *old man* & he is somber & sympathetic beside me now observing the blackjack cards from my perspective, observing my set-aside crutches, my lifeless but showy *Step Up!* legs in black patterned stockings all but hidden by the table & seeing the uplifted card & the flash of its numerals & if it's a loss, very likely it is a loss, the girl-gambler will wince, suck at her crimson lips & wipe at her eyes & this is the strategic moment for the gentleman to lean a little closer & to say, just audibly above the hum & buzz of the casino—"Excuse me?"

II.

THE BEATING

S till alive! from the doorway of the intensive care unit I can see my father in his bed swaddled in white like a comatose infant, and he is still alive.

So long I've been away. So long I've traveled, and so far.

Yet nothing seems to have changed in my absence. My mother and two other visitors are standing beside my father's bed, their backs to me. From their demeanor you can deduce that my father is still "unresponsive" after the morning's surgery to reduce swelling in his brain; he is unmoving except in random twitches and shudders; he is breathing—arduously, noisily—by way of a machine; his every heart-beat is being monitored on a screen above his bed; on this screen as on a TV screen an erratic scribble is being written, accompanied by an electronic beeping that reminds me of the cheeping of baby chicks.

Grotesquely my father's wounded head has been swathed in white gauze exposing a single bruised eye like a peephole someone has cruelly defaced so you can't see in.

Earlier that day my mother had asked me to leave, there wasn't room for me at my father's bedside. Descending then three floors to the first floor of Sparta Memorial Hospital where there was a small visitor's lounge adjacent to a small cafeteria beneath dim-flickering fluorescent lights. Such a depressing place! Such chill, such smells! This was July 1959. That long ago, you have to smile—I don't blame you, I would smile in your place—to think that people like us took ourselves so seriously. You think *But you're all going to die, why does it matter exactly when?* Yet this was the time, and this was the place, when my father was still alive.

Madelyn! heard the news about your father, what a terrible thing, what a shock how is he?

Madelyn! tell us all you can remember, all that you must have seen?

Hadn't changed my clothes since my father had been brought to the hospital two and a half days before. Slept in the clothes I'd been wearing at the time of the beating, Rangers T-shirt, khaki shorts, sneakers without socks, we'd been visiting my grandmother earlier that afternoon and we'd dropped by the Sparta Blues Festival on the river on our way home, and after that, a detour, as my father called it, to his office on East Capitol Street, and now my clothes were rumpled and smelly for I'd slept in them sprawled on top of my bed without the energy to undress and anxious to be prepared should someone from the hospital call in the night, if my mother came to wake me *Hurry! get up! they want us at the hospital, your father may be dying.* This terrible call had not yet come and yet every breath I drew was a preparation for it, I was fourteen years old and found myself in one of those cruel fairy tales in which a daughter must perform certain rituals and tests without question, that her father will be allowed to live. And when we were at my father's bedside in the chill of the ICU where your fingernails turned blue without your noticing, and you could fall asleep on your feet like a zombie, and begin to crumple to the floor without your noticing, it could not happen that the terrible call would come waking us from our exhausted sleep for already we were awake and we were at the hospital. Softly my mother spoke my father's name: *Harvey? Harvey? I love you.* And in an urgent undertone I said: *Daddy? Daddy? It's Madelyn.* For to say *I love you* was not possible. For so desperately I loved my father, to have spoken such words *I love you* was not possible. I could not have explained why, there were no words to explain why. Seeing me you'd have thought, *A sulky girl, when she should be a good girl.* My mother who was ordinarily very alert to my moods and to my "personal appearance" hadn't seemed to notice that I'd been sleeping in my clothes and smelled of my body for having washed only my sticky hands and rubbed a washcloth over my feverish face, my red-rimmed pig eyes. (Those pig eyes in the mirror, I could not bear to see. Brimming with hot-guilt tears that spilled and burned like acid.) In the past two and a half days I hadn't been able to sit down at any table to eat and had not been able to eat much as a consequence but I made certain that I brushed my teeth until my gums bled for I could not bear the sensation of anything between my teeth.

Who was it? they'd asked. *Who did this to your father?*

Try to remember if you saw. Must've seen.

Hospital rules for ICU differed from rules for the rest of the hospital: no more than three visitors at a time were allowed at a patient's bedside. And so when my father's older brother and his wife came to see my father, my mother asked me to leave. Of course this was a reasonable request. Of course I was not angry at my mother, or my relatives. Yet quickly I walked away, avoiding the friendly smiles of the ICU nurses who'd come to recognize me and my family *Don't look at me! Please don't smile at me! You don't know me! Leave me alone.* I took the stairs down to the foyer, not the elevator. I dreaded being trapped inside an elevator with strangers, still more I dreaded encountering someone who recognized me as Harvey Fleet's daughter who would take my hand in sympathy or hug me, and I would push rudely away, my face would break and turn ugly with tears glistening like snot.

◆ ◆ ◆

How small the Sparta Hospital was, in 1959! Yet no one then seemed to have known.

Such silly people. It's easy to laugh at us.

The very air exuded a spent, sepia cast as if faded by time like an old Polaroid photograph. Though the hospital was air-conditioned, cold as a refrigerator, yet there was a just-perceptible odor of stale urine, fecal matter, rot beneath the sharper odor of disinfectant. Visitors to the hospital and hospital staff appeared stiff and clumsy as mannequin figures in a painting by Edward Hopper. Voices were overly shrill and emphatic as TV voices and if there was laughter it was not convincing laughter but reminded me of canned TV laughter. Of course I was one of those figures myself, a solitary girl of fourteen in rumpled clothes sitting at a table, at the edge of the cafeteria. My eyes stung with fatigue, my head ached, and there was a sour, dark taste at the back of my mouth. Badly I did not want to be in this place but had nowhere else to go, for if I left the hospital, and went home, my father might die, and I would not be at his bedside. I'd brought a library book with me but couldn't concentrate, how insubstantial were printed words, passages of type in a book of dog-eared pages, I could think only of my father trapped in his hospital bed in the intensive care unit, unconscious, made to breathe in anguished gasps by a machine, his ravaged head and face swathed in white gauze and a single bruised and bloodshot eye exposed. . . . And I thought of how I had found him lying on the floor of his office on East Capitol Street. Thinking at first that he had lost his balance somehow and fallen, struck his head on the sharp edge of the desk, for he was bleeding from a head wound, and he was bleeding from injuries to his face. He was whimpering and moaning through clenched teeth. The door to my father's office had been left open and so I stood in the doorway for an astonished moment uncertain what it was I was seeing. Before I had time to be frightened the thought came to me *Daddy would not want me to see him like this. He would not want anyone to see him like this.*

I began to see how memory pools might accumulate in such places as this cafeteria and in waiting rooms through the hospital. In corners, in the shadows. Beneath tables like mine. These memory pools made the worn tile floor damp, sticky, discolored as by mildew. And maybe there were actual tears, soaked into the floor. I felt a shiver of dread: you could not walk anywhere in such a place without the anguished memories of strangers sticking to your shoes. Their dread of what was to come in their lives, what ruptures, what unspeakable losses. Early that morning my father had undergone emergency surgery to reduce pressure on his brain, into which burst blood vessels had been bleeding since he'd suffered "blunt force trauma" to the head. Yet my father was but one of how many thousands of patients who'd been hospitalized at Sparta Memorial Hospital over the years. . . . One day with precise scientific instruments certain of these memories might be exhumed, I thought. Like organic matter identified from the stains of long ago. And so there might be a future time when these thoughts that so tormented me now would be calmly recalled; when all this, in which I was trapped—the hospital, the visitors' lounge, the slow-ticking afternoon in July 1959—would be past.

He lived! He did live, he survived.

He died. "Passed away." There was nothing to be done.

Yet at this time, I was safe from such knowledge. At this time, my father, Harvey Fleet, was still alive.

"Madelyn?"

Vaguely I had been aware of someone approaching my table, coming up behind me, as frequently individuals were making their way past in this crowded space, and I had been aware of someone pausing, looming over me. I looked up in expectation of seeing one of my male relatives but instead I saw a man whom I didn't recognize at first, with a two days' growth of beard on his jaws, amber-tinted sunglasses, and thick disheveled graying hair that seemed to rise like a geyser at the crown of his head. "Madelyn Fleet. It is you." The surprise was that this man was my seventh-grade math teacher, Mr. Carmichael, whom I had not seen in more than two years and then only in our school building. The way in which Mr. Carmichael had intoned *Madelyn Fleet* was his teacherly teasing way, which I remembered. I had to remember too, with a quick stab of emotion, that I'd been in love with Mr. Carmichael, in secret, when I was twelve years old.

Now I was fourteen, and much changed. In my former teacher's eyes this change was being registered.

Smiling down at me, Mr. Carmichael was smoking a cigarette for in 1959 it was not forbidden to smoke cigarettes in a hospital, even in most hospital rooms. How strange it was to see my seventh-grade math teacher unshaven as none of his students had ever seen him, and his hair that had always been trimmed short now grown long, curling languidly behind his ears, and threaded with silvery gray wires. It was a warmly humid midsummer and so Mr. Carmichael had rolled up his shirtsleeves to his elbows; the cuffs hung free, at a rakish angle. The front of Mr. Carmichael's shirt was damp with perspiration and looked as if it hadn't been changed in days. From such signs I understood that Mr. Carmichael too was an anxious visitor to Sparta Memorial Hospital, yet even in his state of distraction and dread he was smiling at me, and his eyes behind the tinted lenses of his glasses were alert and intense in a way I did not remember from when I'd been his student. When he inquired what I was reading I had no choice but to show him the cover of the book, which was a novel by H. G. Wells that elicited from Mr. Carmichael a remark meant to be clever and knowing, for at our school Mr. Carmichael—whose first name we giggled to see was Luther—had a reputation for being clever and knowing if also, at times, sarcastic, sardonic, and inscrutable; a teacher who graded harshly, at times; for which reason, while some girl students admired Mr. Carmichael and strove to please him, most of our classmates were uncomfortable in his classes, and disliked him. Even boys who laughed at Mr. Carmichael's jokes did not wholly trust him, for he could turn on you, if you were not cautious. There were rumors about Mr. Carmichael being complained of by the parents of certain students and perhaps by certain of his fellow teachers and vaguely last year I'd heard that

Mr. Carmichael no longer taught at the school. . . . As if he could hear my thoughts and wished to commandeer them, Mr. Carmichael leaned over me, saying, in a lowered voice, that he thought he'd recognized me as I crossed the lobby and came here to sit, he'd thought it might be me—"Or some older sister of little Madelyn Fleet"—but he wasn't sure that he could trust his eyes—"You've gotten taller, Madelyn. And you carry yourself—differently." In embarrassed confusion I laughed, leaning away from him; my face throbbed with blood; I was overwhelmed by such attention, and did not know how to reply. There was nowhere to look except at Mr. Carmichael's flushed and roughened face, and his eyes so warmly intent upon me beyond the smudged lenses of his sunglasses. Mr. Carmichael's breath smelled of—was it whiskey?—a sweetish-sour odor with which I was long familiar, for all my male relatives drank whiskey at times, and certainly my father drank whiskey. It had not been the case during my year of seventh-grade math that Mr. Carmichael had singled me out for any particular attention, or praise; I could not have claimed that Mr. Carmichael had ever really looked at me, as an individual; though I'd been one of five or six reliable students who'd usually received high grades, I hadn't been an outstanding math student, only a doggedly diligent good-girl student. Nor had I been one of the popular and flirtatious girls in our class who'd had no trouble attracting Mr. Carmichael's attention. Yet now he was asking, "Why are you here in this depressing place, Madelyn? I hope it isn't a family emergency. . . ." He did not seem to be teasing but spoke sincerely, with sympathy; lightly his hand rested on my shoulder, to comfort. I was frightened now for such sympathy left me weak, defenseless; I did not want to cry; in my bedroom I'd cried until my eyes were reddened and swollen like blisters but I had not cried in front of anyone except my mother. It would be held against Harvey Fleet's daughter that she was "cold"—"snotty"— stiffening in her relatives' embraces and shrinking from their kisses with a look of disdain. Yet how could I bring myself to say to Mr. Carmichael, *My father is upstairs in the intensive care unit, he had surgery this morning to reduce swelling in his brain, he has not regained consciousness after a terrible beating.* . . . Quickly I told Mr. Carmichael that my mother had come to see a friend in the hospital who'd had minor surgery and I'd been with them for a while then became restless, couldn't breathe, came downstairs to read my novel but couldn't concentrate, and now I was thinking of going home. (For suddenly it came to me; I could leave this hateful place, I could go home without my mother.) Mr. Carmichael said he'd had enough of the hospital too. More than enough. He'd drive me home, Mr. Carmichael said now, nudging my ponytail, and I laughed, saying thank you but I could take a city bus, or I could walk. (In the heat, the three-mile walk would be punishing. My mother would be astonished and would not know if she should be apologetic or disgusted with me.) Mr. Carmichael squinted down at me through his sunglasses, saying in his brisk-bemused-teacher voice that his car was out back: "C'mon, Madelyn. I'll drive you home."

How was it possible to say *no?*

"This is a little detour, kid. Our secret."

It was dusk. We were late returning home. Yet we were driving east along the river, back toward Sparta. If we'd been headed home, as we were expected, my father would have been driving us west. The air at dusk was humid and porous as gauze and through the Cadillac's lowered windows warm air rushed that smelled of something overripe like rotted fruit and beneath, a fainter, sour smell of rotted fish.

It was a festive time of evening! I was very happy. On the river there were ghostly white sailboats and power-driven boats that glittered with lights against the darkening, choppy water and on shore, in the park where the blues festival was being held, there were steadier lights like flames.

A detour. Our secret. These mysterious pronouncements of my father's were usually made in a playful voice that carried an unmistakable warning: do as I say, without acknowledging that I have said it.

By these words I was given to understand that my father didn't want my mother to know we'd gone back into the city. I liked it that there were such understandings between my father and me, which excluded my mother.

On the evening of the beating that was never to be explained, for which no "assailant" or "assailants" would ever be charged, my father was distracted and appeared to be in a hurry. We'd left the blues festival abruptly for he'd said that we had to get home and now, not ten minutes later, he was headed for downtown Sparta and his office on East Capitol Street. Gripped between his legs was a bottle of ale he'd brought with him from the festival. The dashboard of the car gleamed and glittered with so many dials, switches, controls you'd have thought you were in the cockpit of a fighter plane.

The car was my father's newest: a showy 1959 cream-colored Cadillac Eldorado with Spanish red leather interior, a chrome grille like shark's teeth, swooping tail fins and flaring taillights. A massive vehicle twenty feet in length, like a yacht it glided past ordinary traffic seemingly without effort. Within the family it was believed that Harvey Fleet had acquired this car from one of his gambler friends in Sparta in need of quick cash but my father typically offered no explanations, he'd only just driven the Cadillac home: "Look out in the driveway. Anybody want a ride?"

My father was like that: impulsive, unpredictable. He was a man of secrets and he was generous when he wanted to be generous and not so generous when he didn't want to be. He owned properties in Sparta and vicinity, mostly rentals, and recently he'd become a developer, with partners, of a new shopping center north of the city. Business was the center of my father's life. Yet you could not gain entry into that life by asking him about his work, for when relatives asked him such questions he would say, with a disarming smile, "Can't complain." Or, "Holding my own." He would not elaborate. He had as little interest in boasting of successes as he had in acknowledging failures. If a question was too personal or pointed he would say, "Hell, that's business"—as if his business affairs were too trivial to speak of. Yet you knew that what Harvey Fleet meant was *None of your damned business.*

We had stayed at the blues festival for less than an hour and during that time I'd seen how my father, in his trademark white cotton shirt (no tie, open at the collar) and seersucker trousers (melon colored, for summer), and canvas shoes (white), moved easily among the crowd shaking hands with people who were strangers to me; being greeted by the musicians, most of whom were black men (young, middle-aged, elderly) eager to shake Harvey Fleet's hand for Harvey Fleet was one of the sponsors of the festival—"A friend to blues and jazz music." (Was this so? At home, my father never listened to music of any kind, never even watched television.) In Sparta, my father had many friends: local politicians, the chief of police, the district attorney, county officials. On a wall of his office were framed caricatures of Sparta personalities, including Harvey Fleet, crude but clever line drawings by a cartoonist for the *Sparta Herald* who'd exaggerated my father's vulpine good looks, his thick dark hair springing from a low forehead, his fistlike jaw and his trademark smile so wide and emphatic it looked riveted in place. Years later I would see on TV the 1946 film *The Postman Always Rings Twice* with flawlessly blond Lana Turner and darkly handsome John Garfield and it would be a shock to me, how closely my father had resembled Garfield when he'd been young. At the blues festival to the sexy-seductive strains of "Stormy Weather"—"Mood Indigo"—"Sleepy Time Gal"— I'd seen how my father was acquainted with women who were strangers to me, some of them very attractive, and I thought, *My father has his secret life, which none of us can know.*

I wondered if it was better that way, our not knowing.

Though you couldn't question him about his past, my father sometimes spoke of his youthful nomadic adventures: he'd quit school at fifteen and gone to work on a Great Lakes freighter bearing iron ore from Duluth to Buffalo; he'd hitchhiked out west, worked in Washington State, and in Alaska, where he'd worked on salmon fishing boats. His own father, Jonas Fleet, who'd died before I was born, had been exhausted and broken by the age of fifty, having worked in a Lackawanna steel mill; my father was determined not to emulate him; he said,

"There's better use for a man's lungs than to be coated with steel filings." In the army, in World War II, he'd been stationed in Italy, and the names of Italian regions and towns—*Tuscany, Brescia, Vicenza, Parma*—rolled off his tongue like an exotic sort of music, which meant little to his listeners. Of these long-ago adventures he'd had before he returned home to Sparta he spoke in a tone of wistfulness and pride; he'd made it through the war without being seriously wounded or "drove crazy" and of ugly memories he did not speak, at least not to us.

He laughed often. He liked to laugh. There were some in our family who distrusted my father's laughter, which made them uneasy. Why is Harv laughing? Is Harv laughing at us? You understood that there was a prevailing joke to which my father's joking alluded, but it was a private joke not accessible to others. "The only laugh that matters is the last laugh," my father said. "And that isn't guaranteed."

"Wait here in the car. Read your book. I'll be a few minutes. Don't come looking for me."

My father had parked at the rear of the Brewer Building, on a back street not far from the river. Buildings on the other side of this street had been razed and lay in heaps of rubble behind a ten-foot fence posted NO TRESPASSING: DANGER and a half block beyond was a wharf at which battered-looking fishing boats were docked. This was not the Sparta Yacht Club marina several miles to the east on the Black River, where my father kept his Chris-Craft powerboat; this was the old Sparta waterfront downtown. On Sundays the area was nearly deserted except for a few taverns and riverside restaurants; except for East Capitol, there was little traffic. Seagulls flew overhead and the air was pierced by their sharp cries; river smells—briny water, rotted pilings, dead fish—made my nostrils pinch. These were mostly pleasurable smells, and I liked being here. From time to time my father brought me with him to his office where his secretary Charlotte smiled to see me: "Madelyn, hello. Come to help us out today?"

The Brewer Building, owned by a real estate broker friend of my father, was the tallest building in the neighborhood and impressive with a smooth-shiny facade like polished marble. Inside was a foyer with a barbershop, a smoke shop, and a newsstand, all of which would be closed on Sunday. Only dimly could you see the stately mosaic figures on the foyer ceiling meant to suggest Egyptian pyramids, ancient hieroglyphics. There was an elevator with an elaborate grillwork door. Yet at the rear and sides of the Brewer Building you saw only weatherworn dark brick; the facade was what a *facade* meant—just a showy front. Especially from the rear, the building looked shabby. On each floor were ugly fire escapes. Some of the windows were cracked and opaque with grime. My father's office on the eighth floor overlooking East Capitol Street and in the near distance the gleaming spire of St. Mary's Roman Catholic Church was nothing like these. Years ago when my father had told me to wait in the car for him I'd disobeyed him, gone inside, and dared to take the elevator to the tenth, top floor of the building; on the tenth floor, I'd dared to climb a brief flight of steps and pushed open a door marked NO ADMITTANCE: ROOF and stepped outside on a shimmering-hot tar roof. So high! A sensation of vertigo overcame me, a sense of being physically drawn to the edge of the roof where the parapet was no more than two feet high; in halting steps I made my way to the edge; my eyes blinked in amazement, at this height I could see the S-curve of the Black River, boats on the river, more tall buildings than I would have imagined in Sparta, rooftops, church spires, chimneys. Airplanes droning high overhead, pigeons and seagulls. Everywhere were bird droppings, white crusted like concrete. How exhausting the wind, and hypnotizing. It was both exhilarating to me and frightening that no one knew where I was. If someone were to glimpse me from a window in another tall building, he would not know who I was; he would not care. When I turned back to the heavy door a chilling thought struck me—*Now the door will be shut and locked against you.*

The door wasn't locked. I'd been eleven at the time. I did not tell my father that I'd dared to walk on the roof of the Brewer Building that day and I never walked on the roof again.

Don't come looking for me, my father had said. I would wait for him in the car, reading my book. I'd opened the passenger's door so that I could sit sideways, with my legs dangling. Close by the river where there were no buildings obscuring the setting sun it was still light enough for me to read and I had only the vaguest awareness of my surroundings. In the near distance waves lapped against the wharf and from farther away came muffled sounds of music. At the periphery of my vision I might have been aware of another car turning onto the street behind the Brewer Building and parking a short distance away but this awareness was scarcely conscious and failed to register. *Did you see—anyone? Must've seen! Try to remember.* I was captivated by H. G. Wells's *The Time Machine,* which was the first of Wells's *Seven Scientific Romances* that I'd discovered in the public library. I was captivated by the brashness of the Time Traveller—flinging himself onto the "saddle" of his homemade time machine into not the near future but the distant future, with none of the provisions you would take on an overnight camping trip. You could foresee that the unnamed Time Traveller would return from his journey to the year 802,701, since he was telling his one story, but the way would not be easy for he'd discovered that humankind had evolved into two distinct subspecies: the "graceful children" of the Upper World and the "obscene, nocturnal Things" that dwelled like humanoid spiders underground. In much of my reading at this time in my early adolescence there was a terrible logic: something virulent and vengeful prepared to rise up in the night, beneath us as we slept, like an animated earthquake, to punish us. Why we were to be punished was not explained. Punishment was something that happened, and could not be averted. Punishment suggests a crime: but what is the crime? *Born bad,* it was said of some people. *Born bad,* it was said even of some individuals in Sparta. Yet I could not understand how an infant could be *born bad,* for no infant in my experience could plausibly be described in such a way.

Out on the river, men's voices lifted in shouts of laughter, muffled by a motor's roar. The sun was starting to set; I was losing the light at last.

I left the car and took up a position nearer the river, leaning against a great cracked slab of concrete. If at this time the vehicle that might—or might not—have been parked behind the Brewer Building was driven away—if someone had hurriedly exited the building, gone to the car, and driven away—I had no awareness of it. I was in no position to see. *Didn't see. Don't know. Leave me alone!*

Another powerboat passed by, trailing drunken laughter. Vaguely it seemed to me that my name had been called—*Madelyn! Madelyn!* At the blues festival there had been several boys whom I knew from school, older boys at the high school, they'd called to me *Madelyn! Madelyn Fleet!* But I'd only just waved to them, I'd been standing with my father listening to a black jazz quartet playing "I Can't Give You Anything But Love, Baby." Now I seemed to hear my name in a faint, failing voice, my father's voice, but unlike my father's voice as I had ever heard it. Quickly I closed *The Time Machine*, and returned to the car.

My father had been inside the building for more than a half hour, I thought. A ripple of pain pulsed in my eyes. How garish the Cadillac Eldorado looked, the cream-colored luxury car with Spanish red leather interior, parked amid rubble. I tossed *The Time Machine* onto the passenger's seat and entered the building, into dim, humid heat and despite the heat I began to shiver. There was the elevator in the foyer: I could not bring myself to take it up to the eighth floor. What if the power failed, what if I was stuck between floors? Instead I took the stairs. Only dimly was the stairwell lighted by naked lightbulbs at each landing. The heat in the stairwell was stifling and by the time I reached the eighth floor I was panting and sweating. My Rangers T-shirt clung to my sticky skin. My hair stuck to the nape of my neck. On the eighth floor I struggled with the heavy door and another time the cruel taunt came to me *Now the door will be locked against you, this is your punishment.* But another time the door wasn't locked against me, I ran down the corridor to my father's office where the door was open. . . .

At first I thought that my father had fallen somehow, struck his head against the sharp edge of a desk. He was bleeding from a head wound and from cuts to his face. His white cotton shirt was dappled with blood, and torn. His melon-colored seersucker trousers were dappled with blood, and torn. One of his sporty white shoes had been wrenched off. He was conscious, trying to sit up. I could hear his terrible labored breathing and his grunting with the effort of maneuvering himself into a sitting position. "Daddy—," I called, and ran to him, and his glassy eyes fixed on me without seeming to recognize me: "Get away, get out of here"—"Don't touch me." Drawers had been yanked out of his desk and out of the green filing cabinet against the wall. There was a sharp, rank animal sweat of panic, male sweat. And a prevailing smell of cigarette smoke. By the time my father managed to stand shakily, he was calling me "Madelyn"—"honey." He assured me he was all right—"Nothing to worry about, honey." He was wiping at his dazed and bloody face with the front of his ruined shirt. When I asked him what had happened, had someone hurt him, he seemed not to hear. I asked if I should call an ambulance or the police and quickly he said *no*. In his stricken and disheveled state my father hovered over me. I could feel the heat of his skin. He was trying to explain through swollen lips that someone whose face he hadn't seen had forced his way into the office and tried to rob him, he had not seen who it was because he'd been attacked from behind. Yet then my father said whoever it was had been waiting for him in his office when he'd unlocked the door, surprised him with a blow to the head. And maybe there was more than one of them, he hadn't seen. I asked him what had been taken from the office and he said nothing had been taken because he'd surprised the thieves. I asked him if I should call the police and he said, with an angry laugh: "Didn't I say no police?"

Now he would wash up, he said. As if his injuries could be washed away! Like a drunken man he leaned heavily on me, making his way to the men's restroom outside in the corridor. "Stay out here. I'll be all right. Don't look so scared, your old man isn't going to die." My father spoke disdainfully, dripping blood. And in the restroom he remained for what seemed like a long time. I could hear water rushing from faucets, a groaning of aged pipes. I heard a toilet flush several times. I stood at the door calling, *Daddy? Daddy?* in a plaintive voice until he staggered back out. His face was washed, his hair dampened though not combed; he'd removed the torn and bloodstained shirt, and was in his sleeveless undershirt of ribbed cotton, which was also bloodstained. Fistfuls of wiry dark hair bristled on his chest, covering his forearms like pelt. He was walking lopsided because he'd left his left shoe back in his office, where I fetched it for him. I also shut the door, and locked it. Afterward I would realize that my father hadn't seemed to be afraid that his assailant or assailants would return, and do more injury to him. He'd seemed to know that his daughter wasn't endangered. The beating was finished, and would not be repeated.

To my amazement my father insisted upon returning to the car and driving home. "I can handle this. My head is clear." Though he was obviously weak, dazed, swaying on his feet. Though his eyes seemed to be swerving out of focus even as he spoke to me in such emphatic terms. So we took the elevator down to the foyer, and returned to the cream-colored Cadillac Eldorado parked so conspicuously behind the building. In the west the sun resembled a lurid red egg yolk bleeding into banks of dark thunderhead clouds. I was reminded of the "huge red-hot dome of the sun" the Time Traveller had encountered hundreds of millions of years in the future, swollen to one-tenth of the sky. Once in the car, my father tried to behave as if nothing had happened. He was muttering to himself, giving himself instructions. The fingers of his right hand were strangely swollen; I had to insert the ignition key and turn it for him. By this time I'd begun to cry. I was trembling badly, my bladder pinched with a panicked need to pee. Another time I asked my father if we shouldn't call an ambulance or the police and another time he said *no*—"No police." This seemed strange to me, for my father was friendly with the chief of police and with other men on the Sparta police force. Yet it seemed to infuriate him, the prospect of summoning police. Another time I asked him if he'd seen who had beaten him and another time he said Goddamn no, he hadn't seen. Strange it seemed to me that my father's anger was directed at me, not at whoever had hurt him.

"They jumped me from behind. They were waiting inside. I never saw their faces. It was over before it began."

And, "Might've been just one person. All I know is, he was white."

On Route 31 headed east, the cream-colored Cadillac drifted out of its lane. My father had forgotten to switch on the headlights. He winced with pain, his injured head and face had to be throbbing with pain. At the hospital it would be revealed that he'd suffered a concussion, several of his ribs were cracked, his right wrist and fingers sprained. Teeth had loosened in his jaws, deep cuts would leave scars in both his eyebrows. He'd been beaten with something like a tire iron, and he'd been kicked when he'd fallen. In our wake on the river road the horns of other vehicles sounded in reproach. I begged my father to pull over to the side before we had an accident and at last he did, after a mile or two. He was too dazed and exhausted to keep going. On the littered shoulder of the highway the cream-colored Caddie limped to an ignoble stop. Traffic passed us by. My father slumped over the steering wheel like an avalanche suddenly released, a stream of bright blood trickling down his neck. I scrambled out of the car to stand at the edge of the highway waving frantically until at last a Sparta police cruiser appeared. "Help us! Help my father! Don't let him die."

The cry that came from me was brute, animal. I had never heard such a cry before and would not have believed that it had issued from me.

Madelyn, tell us what you know.

Anything you can remember, Madelyn. If you saw a car anywhere near. If you saw someone. In the street behind the building. Entering the building. If your father mentioned anyone. Before your father passed out, all that he said to you. Whatever he said to you. Tell us.

In July 1959. That wild ride into the countryside, when my father was still alive.

Mr. Carmichael asked me where I lived and I told him. Then he said we were taking the long way round, a little ride out into the country, how'd I like that; and I said yes, I loved the country, loved riding in a car with the windows rolled down and the radio on loud. *Love love love you, Mr. Carmichael,* shutting my eyes to be kissed. Giggling to think if he sniffed at my armpits—! But Mr. Carmichael looked as if he'd been sleeping in his clothes too.

He hadn't forced me to drink, I would say afterward. None of what happened he'd forced me to do.

Exiting the hospital by the rear revolving door. Inside, the sickish refrigerated air and outside, hot-humid-sticky midsummer sunshine. "Know what a hospital is, Madelyn?—a petri dish breeding germs. Have to get the hell out, sometimes. Save your own life."

I think it was then—on our way to the parking lot—I asked Mr. Carmichael if someone in his family was in the hospital, and Mr. Carmichael, rummaging for his car keys in his trouser pocket, took no more notice of my question than in our seventh-grade class he'd taken notice of certain students who were not his favorites, waving their hands in the air to ask silly questions.

Repeating in a brisk staccato voice tugging at my ponytail:

"Save—your—own—goddamn—*life.*"

Mr. Carmichael's 1955 Dodge station wagon had faded to a dull tin color and was stippled with rust like crude lace. The front bumper was secured by ingenious twists of wire. I might have thought that it was strange, my former math teacher Mr. Carmichael was driving such a vehicle, very different from any vehicle my father, Harvey Fleet, would have driven. Mr. Carmichael was clapping his hands as you'd clap your hands to hurry a clumsy child, or a dog: "Got to keep moving. Like the shark, perpetual motion or it drowns. Chop-chop, Maddie!" Exuberantly Mr. Carmichael gathered up clothes, empty beer bottles, a single shoe out of the front passenger's seat of the station wagon, tossed out into the already messy rear.

Out of Sparta we drove west along the Black River. On the radio,

pop music blared, interrupted by loud jocular advertisements from a local radio station. Though I had told Mr. Carmichael where I lived, it did
not seem that Mr. Carmichael had heard, or he'd forgotten. He was in
very good spirits. It is unusual to see a man, an adult man, in such good
spirits. The front windows of the station wagon were rolled down and
wind in crazed gusts whipped at our heads. In the gauzy-humid sunshine the wide choppy river glittered like a snake's scales. In Sparta you
are always driving along the river, for the river intersects the city: you
are driving on Route 31 East, or you are driving on Route 31 West;
you are driving on Route 31A West, or you are driving on Route 31A
East. Yet the river seemed always different, and sometimes it did not
look familiar. That day there was a massive freighter on the river, ugly
and ungainly as a dinosaur. Far away downtown were high-rise buildings and one of these was the Brewer Building but it was lost in haze.
At Sentry Street beside the railroad trestle bridge a train was passing
thunderous and deafening. Mr. Carmichael shouted to be heard over
the noise but his words were blown away. It did not seem to matter if
I replied to Mr. Carmichael or not. From the side, Mr. Carmichael did
not resemble anyone I had ever seen. A faint doubt came to me, *was
this Luther Carmichael? My seventh-grade math teacher?* This man's
face was flushed as if he'd been running in the heat. His skin looked
as if it had been scraped by sandpaper. His silvery brown beard was
poking through like tiny quills. The thought came to me *If he brushes
his face against my face* . . . I laughed, and squirmed as if I was being tickled. By now the train had passed, Mr. Carmichael glanced sidelong at
me, smiling. "Something funny, Maddie?" His smile was quick and loose
and crinkled his face like a soft rag. More clearly I could see how the
tinted lenses of Mr. Carmichael's glasses were smudged, and his eyes
beyond, staring. My hair was streaming in the wind, I had to blink tears
from my eyes. How reckless I felt, and how happy: I was sitting as I'd
never have dared to sit in my father's cream-colored Cadillac Eldorado
with the Spanish red-leather seats, my left leg lifted, the heel of my

sneaker on the seat nudging the base of my left buttock. I saw how Mr. Carmichael's gaze moved over my leg—the tanned smooth skin with fine brown hairs, the muscled calf and sudden milky white of my upper thigh.

"Open the glove compartment, Maddie. See what's inside."

Fumbling to remove from the glove compartment a quart bottle of amber liquid: whiskey. Mr. Carmichael instructed me to unscrew the top and take a drink and quickly I shook my head no, shyly I shook my head no, and Mr. Carmichael nudged me in the ribs with his elbow, winking: "Yes, you'd better, Maddie. Kills germs on contact and where we came from—" Mr. Carmichael shuddered, as if suddenly cold.

It is death he is taking me from, I thought. I had never loved anyone so much.

With a gesture of impatience Mr. Carmichael took the bottle from me, and drank. Fascinated I watched, the greedy movements of his mouth, his throat. Mr. Carmichael handed the bottle back to me with another nudge in the ribs and so—must've been, I lifted the bottle to my mouth, and drank cautiously. Searing-hot liquid flooded my mouth, down my throat like flames. My eyes leaked tears as I tried not to succumb to a spasm of coughing.

Here is a secret Mr. Carmichael was never to know: I knew where he lived, on Old Mill Road beyond the Sparta city limits. I knew for, with the cunning of a twelve-year-old girl in love with her seventh-grade math teacher, I had looked up "Carmichael"—"Luther Carmichael"— in the Sparta telephone directory. More than once I had bicycled past Mr. Carmichael's house, which was approximately four miles from my house, a considerable distance. But I had done this, in secret. And I'd forgotten more or less, until now. On a mailbox at the end of a long driveway was the name CARMICHAEL. And the name CARMICHAEL, in black letters shiny as tar, seemed to me astonishing. So suddenly, so openly—CARMICHAEL. It had seemed to me a very special name. In secret I'd written it out, how many times. And sometimes with only my finger, tracing the letters on a smooth desktop. On the Old Mill

Road where Mr. Carmichael lived with his family—for it was known, Mr. Carmichael had a wife and young children—I dared to bicycle past the end of his driveway, and once dared to turn into the driveway, hurriedly turning back when it seemed to me that someone had appeared at the house.

In math class when Mr. Carmichael handed back our test papers marked in red ink, though Mr. Carmichael spoke my name in a friendly way and may even have smiled at me I did not smile in return, I kept my eyes lowered out of superstition and dread for the red number at the top of the paper was my fate for that day: my grade. You would not have guessed, surely Mr. Carmichael would not have guessed, which of the seventh-grade girls was most desperately in love with him.

So long ago! You have to smile, to think that people like us took ourselves, and one another, so seriously.

And so on Old Mill Road beyond the Sparta city limits it wasn't surprising to me when Mr. Carmichael turned the station wagon onto the bumpy cinder drive leading back to his house. I knew, this was where we were headed. And there was the mailbox with CARMICHAEL in black letters on the sides, stuffed with newspapers—this wasn't surprising to me. (So Mr. Carmichael hadn't been bringing in his mail, reading the local paper. Which was why he hadn't seen the front-page news of Harvey Fleet's "savage" beating.) "Won't stay long, Maddie," Mr. Carmichael was saying, "—unless we change our minds, and we do." The sweet warm sensation of the whiskey in my throat had radiated downward like sunshine into my belly, into my bowels, and below between my legs and my response to this was breathy laughter. Out of excitement—or anxiety—I was asking Mr. Carmichael silly questions, for instance, did he own horses?—(no, he did not own horses)—did he know a Herkimer County judge who was a friend of my father's, who lived on Old Mill Road?—(yes, Mr. Carmichael knew the man, but not well). Surprising to see how much shabbier—sadder—Mr. Carmichael's house looked now than it had two years before, when I'd dared to bicycle partway up the driveway. The large front lawn had become a field of tall grasses and wildflowers and the cinder driveway was badly rutted. The house that looked ugly but dignified from the road looked, up close, only just ugly; a squat two-story block-shaped cobblestone with a steep-slanted slate roof, the kind of house (I bit my lower lip to stop from bursting into a fit of giggling at the thought) in which, in a fairy tale, a troll would live. "Glad to see you're laughing, Maddie," Mr. Carmichael said. "Damn lot better than crying."

Mr. Carmichael parked the Dodge station wagon close beside the house. In the backyard was a children's swing set among tall grasses. Cicadas were shrieking out of the trees. Close up the cobblestones were misshapen rocks that looked as if they'd been dredged up out of the earth with dirt still clinging to them. The back screen door was ajar as if someone in the house had rushed out without taking time to close it. One of the first-floor windows had been shoved open to the very top and a yellow-print muslin curtain had been sucked out by the wind, wanly fluttering now. The thought came to me *He is living alone here. There is no wife now.* With the cruelty of a fourteen-year-old female I felt a stab of satisfaction as if I'd known my math teacher's wife, a youngish blond woman glimpsed by me only at a distance, years ago; a figure of idly jealous speculation on the part of certain of Mr. Carmichael's girl students, in fact a total stranger to us. That Mr. Carmichael had young children was of absolutely no interest to us. "Won't stay long," Mr. Carmichael repeated, nudging me between the shoulder blades, urging me into the house, "but damn we are thirsty."

It was true. I'd been drinking from the quart bottle out of the glove compartment and I was very thirsty now, my throat on fire.

All going to die. Why's it matter exactly when.

This raw and unimpeachable logic emerges like granite outcroppings in a grassy field, at such moments. You will remember all your life.

"Welcome! 'Ecce homo.'" Inside it looked as if a whirlwind had rushed through the downstairs rooms of Mr. Carmichael's house. In the kitchen the linoleum stuck to my feet like flypaper. In grayish water in the sink stacks of dirty dishes were soaking. Every square inch of countertop was in use, even the top of the stove with filth-encrusted burners; in the hot stale air was a strong odor of something rancid. Flies buzzed and swooped. Mr. Carmichael seemed scarcely to notice, exuberantly opening the refrigerator door: "*Voilà*! cold beer! Not a moment to spare." He grabbed a dark brown bottle, opened it, and drank thirstily and offered it to me but I could not force myself to take more than a cautious little sip. I hated the taste of beer, and the smell. I asked Mr. Carmichael if there was a Coke in the refrigerator and he said no, sorry, there was not: "Only just beer. Made from malted barley, hops—nutrients. Not chemical crap to corrode your pretty teen teeth." I saw Mr. Carmichael's eyes on me, his smile that looked just slightly asymmetrical as if one side of his mouth was higher than the other. Impossible to gauge if this smile was on your side or not on your side, I remembered from seventh grade: yet how badly you yearned for that smile. "C'mere. Something to show you"—lightly Mr. Carmichael slipped his arm around my shoulders and led me into a dining room with a high ceiling of elaborate moldings and a crystal chandelier of surprising delicacy and beauty, covered in cobwebs. This was the room with the opened window through which the yellow-print curtain had been sucked and here too flies buzzed and swooped. Around a large mahogany dining table were numerous chairs pulled up close as if no one sat here any longer, except at one end; the table was covered with books, magazines, old newspapers, stacks of what appeared to be financial records, bills, and receipts. On sheets of paper were geometrical figures, some of them conjoined with humanoid figures (both female and male, with peanut heads and exaggerated genitals), which I pretended not to see. Idly I opened a massive book—*Asimov's Chronology of the World*. It came to me then: a memory of how Mr. Carmichael had puzzled our class one day "demonstrating infinity" on the blackboard. With surprising precision he'd drawn a circle, and halved it; this half circle, he'd halved; this quarter circle, he'd halved; this eighth of a circle, he'd halved; as he struck the blackboard with his stick of chalk, addressing us in a jocular voice, as if, though this was mathematics of a kind, it was also very funny, by quick degrees the figure on the blackboard became too small to be seen even by those of us seated in the first row of desks; yet Mr. Carmichael continued, in a flurry of staccato chalk strikes, until the chalk shattered in his fingers and fell to the floor where in a playful gesture he kicked it. No one laughed.

" 'Infinity.' *Ex nihilo nihil fit.*"

It wasn't clear what Mr. Carmichael wanted to show me. He'd wandered into the living room, sprawled heavily on a badly worn corduroy sofa, tapping at the cushion beside him in a gesture you might make to encourage a child to join you, or a dog. Tentatively I sat on the sofa, but not quite where Mr. Carmichael wanted me to sit.

This room was not nearly so cluttered as the other rooms. You could see that Mr. Carmichael often sprawled here at his end of the sofa, which had settled beneath his weight. Close by was a small TV with rabbit ears on a portable stand and beside it a hi-fi record player, with long-playing records in a horizontal file, Beethoven's Symphony No. 7, a piano quintet by Mozart, a piano sonata by Schubert. . . . These were only names to me, we never heard classical music in our household; eagerly I asked Mr. Carmichael if he would play one of his records?—but Mr. Carmichael said, "Fuck 'Mr. Carmichael.' You'd like to, eh?" Seeing the shock and hurt in my face quickly Mr. Carmichael laughed, and in a tender voice said: "Anyway, call me 'Luther.' No 'Mr. Carmichael' here."

Mr. Carmichael passed the icy-cold beer bottle to me, and I managed to swallow a mouthful without choking. Hesitantly I tried the name: " 'Luther.' " Biting my lower lip to keep from laughing, for wasn't "Luther" a comic-strip name?—then I did begin to cough, and a trickle of beer ran down inside my left nostril that I wiped away on my hand, hoping Mr. Carmichael wouldn't notice.

Another time I wanted to ask Mr. Carmichael who he'd been visiting at the hospital, and where his family was, but didn't dare. Against a wall was an upright piano with stacks of books and sheet music on its top. I could image a girl of my age sitting there, dutifully playing her scales. The living room looked out upon the vast front yard now overgrown with tall grasses and yellow and white wildflowers. The walls were covered in faded once-elegant wallpaper and in this room too was sculpted molding in the ceiling. On the coffee table near the sofa were ashtrays heaped with butts and ashes. I resolved, if Mr. Carmichael lit another cigarette, I would ask if I could have a "drag" from it as girls were always doing with older boys they hoped to impress. Mr. Carmichael took back the beer bottle from me and drank again thirstily and asked me which year of high school I would be in, in the fall, and I told him that I was just starting high school: I would be in tenth grade. "That sounds young," Mr. Carmichael said, frowning. "I thought you were older."

To this I had no ready reply. I wondered if I should apologize.

"You were my student years ago, not recently. How's it happen you're just going into tenth grade?"

Our math teacher's displeasure showed itself in a quick furrow of Mr. Carmichael's forehead and a crinkling of his nose as if he were smelling something bad—and who was to blame? He asked if I had a boyfriend and when I said no, the bad-smell look deepened. Stammering, I said, "People say—I have an 'old' soul. Like maybe—I've lived many times before."

This desperate nonsense came to me out of nowhere: it was something my grandmother had told me when I'd been a little girl, to make me feel important, I suppose, or to make herself feel important.

Still frowning, Mr. Carmichael said suddenly, "The Stoics had the right goddamn idea. If I was born a long time ago, that's what I was—'Stoic.' Y'know who the Stoics were? No? Philosophers who lived a long time ago. Marcus Aurelius—name ring a bell? 'In all that you say or do recall that the power of exiting this life is yours at any time.'"

"You mean—kill yourself?" I laughed uncertainly. This didn't sound so good.

Mr. Carmichael was in a brooding mood so I asked him if he thought there might be memory pools that collected in certain places like the hospital, the way puddles collect after rain; in places where peo-

ple have had to wait, and have been worried, and frightened; if there
were places where you left your trace, without knowing it. Mr. Carmichael seemed to consider this. At least, he did not snort in derision.
He said, " 'Memory pools.' Why not. Like ghosts. Everywhere, the air is
charged with ghosts. Hospitals have got to be the worst, teeming with
ghosts like germs. Can't hardly draw a deep breath, you suck in a ghost."
Mr. Carmichael made a sneezing-comical noise that set us both laughing. "Could be, I am a ghost. You're a sweet trusting girl, coming here
with a ghost. Or maybe you're a ghost yourself—joke's on me. Some
future time like the next century there'll be explorers looking back to
now, to 1959—what's called 'lookback time'—y'know what 'lookback
time' is? No?" Mr. Carmichael's teacherly manner emerged, though as
he spoke he tapped my wrist with his forefinger. " 'Lookback time' is
what you'd call an astronomical figure of speech. It means, if you gaze
up into the night sky—and you have the look of a girl eager to learn
the constellations—what you see isn't what is there. What you see is
only just light—'starlight.' The actual star has moved on, or is extinct.
What you are looking into is 'lookback time'—the distant past. It's only
an ignorant—innocent—eye that thinks it is looking at an actual star.
If our sun exploded, and disappeared, here on earth we wouldn't know
the grim news for eight minutes." Now Mr. Carmichael was circling my
wrist with his thumb and forefinger, gently tugging at me to come closer
to him on the sofa. "Eight minutes is a hell of a long time, to not know
that you are dead."

I shuddered. Then I laughed, this was meant to be funny.

Somehow, we began arm wrestling. Before I knew it, with a gleeful
chortle, Mr. Carmichael had kicked off his moccasins, worn without
socks, slouched down on the sofa, and lifted me above him, to strad-
dle his stomach. "Giddyup, li'l horsie! Giddyup." My khaki shorts rode
up my thighs, Mr. Carmichael's belt buckle chafed my skin. Beneath
the Rangers T-shirt he ran his hard quick hands, where my skin was
clammy-damp; he took hold of my small, bare breasts, squeezing and
kneading, running his thumbs across the nipples, and I slapped at him,

shrieking in protest. Suddenly then Mr. Carmichael rolled me over onto the sofa, pinned me with his forearms, and gripped my thighs, between my legs he brought his hot, rock-hard face, his sucking mouth, against the damp crotch of my shorts and my panties inside my shorts, an act so astonishing to me, I could not believe that it was happening. Like a big dog Mr. Carmichael was growling, sucking, and nipping at me. "Lie still. Be still. You'll like this. L'il bitch god*damn*." Wildly I'd begun to laugh, I kicked frantically at him, scrambled out of his grasp on my hands and knees—on the floor now, on a carpet littered with pizza crusts, dumped ashtrays, and empty beer bottles. Cursing me now, Mr. Carmichael grabbed hold of my ankle and pinned me again, mashing his mouth against mine, his mouth and angry teeth tearing at my lips as if to pry them open. By this time I'd become panicked, terrified. No boy or man had ever kissed me like this, or touched me like this, so roughly—"Why'd you come here with me? What did you think this was—seventh grade? You're a hell of a lot older than you let on. Hot li'l bitch." With each syllable of *hot l'il bitch* Mr. Carmichael struck the back of my head against the carpet, his fingers closed around my throat. Fumbling, he tried to insert his knee between my thighs, he pressed the palm of his hand hard against my mouth to quiet me, I struggled, desperate to free myself like a fish impaled on a hook desperate to free itself at any cost, I would have torn open my flesh to be free of Mr. Carmichael's weight on me. Now he lurched above me, grunted and fumbled, unzipped his trousers, I had a glimpse of his thick engorged penis being rammed against my thighs, another time Mr. Carmichael grunted, and shuddered, and fell heavily on me; for a long stunned moment we lay unmoving; then he allowed me to extricate myself from him, to crawl away whimpering.

Somehow next I was in a bathroom, and I was vomiting into a sink. Must've been, Mr. Carmichael had led me here. In this sweltering-hot little room, which was very dirty—shower stall, toilet, linoleum floor— I ran water from both faucets to wash away my vomit, desperate to wash all evidence away. I could not bring myself to look into the mirror above the sink, I knew my mouth was swollen, my face burned and throbbed. On the front of my T-shirt were coin-sized splotches of blood. (Was my nose bleeding? Always in school I'd been in terror of my nose suddenly beginning to bleed, and the stares of my classmates.) With shaking hands I washed away the sticky semen on my thighs, which was colorless and odorless. Outside the bathroom Mr. Carmichael was saying, in an encouraging voice: "You'll be fine, Maddie. We'll take you back. We should leave soon." Yet the thought came to me *He could kill me now. He is thinking this. When I come out of here. No one will know.* But when I opened the bathroom door Mr. Carmichael was nowhere in sight. I heard him in the kitchen, he was speaking on the phone, pleading, and then silence, the harsh laughter, and the slamming down of a telephone receiver. A man's raw aggrieved voice—"Fuck it. What's the difference. . . ."

When Mr. Carmichael came for me, his mood had shifted yet again. In the kitchen he too had been washing up: his flushed face was made to appear affable, his disheveled hair had been dampened. His badly soiled sport shirt was tucked into his trousers, and his trousers were zipped up. The moccasins were back on his feet. It was with a genial-teacher smile that Mr. Carmichael greeted me: "Madelyn! Time to head back, I said we wouldn't stay long."

In the Dodge station wagon, in late-afternoon traffic on Route 31 East, Mr. Carmichael lapsed into silence. He'd forgotten about driving me home, there was no question but that we were returning to Sparta Memorial Hospital. From time to time Mr. Carmichael glanced anxiously at me as I huddled far from him in the passenger's seat, trying to stop my nose from bleeding by pinching the nostrils and tilting my head back. So distracted and disoriented was Mr. Carmichael, as we passed beneath the railroad trestle bridge, he nearly sideswiped a pickup truck in the left-hand lane of the highway; behind the wheel of the pickup was a contractor friend of my father's. He saw me, and he saw Mr. Carmichael at the wheel beside me, not knowing who Mr. Carmichael was but knowing that it was very wrong for a fourteen-year-old girl to be with him, this flush-faced adult man in his mid- or late thirties. I thought, *He sees us, he knows.* With the inexorable logic of a dream it would happen then: my father's friend would telephone my mother that evening, that very night Luther Carmichael would be arrested in the cobblestone house on Old Mill Road. Mr. Carmichael would be dismissed from his teaching position because of me, of what he'd done to me; because of this—having been seen with me, in the Dodge station wagon this afternoon. And now, telling this story, I remember: Mr. Carmichael hadn't yet been dismissed from his teaching job, as I'd said. All that lay ahead of him. The remainder of his foreshortened life lay ahead of him. He would be arrested, he would be charged with sexual assault of a minor, providing alcohol to a minor; he would be charged with the forcible abduction of a minor, and with kidnapping. He would be charged with keeping me in his house against my will. Some of these charges would be dropped but still Luther Carmichael would kill himself in the ugly cobblestone house on Old Mill Road, hanging from a makeshift noose slung over a rafter in the smelly earthen-floored cellar.

All this had not happened yet. There was no way to accurately foretell it. All I knew was, I had to return to my father's bedside. I was desperate to return to my father's bedside. Before Mr. Carmichael brought the station wagon to a full stop in the parking lot, I had jumped out, I was making my way into the chill of the hospital that never changes, taking the stairs two at a time to the intensive care unit on the fourth floor, avoiding the elevator out of a morbid fear that, at this crucial time, the elevator might stall between floors, now breathless from the stairs and my heart pounding in my chest as if it might burst—

Still alive! From the doorway of the intensive care unit I can see my father in his bed swaddled in white like a comatose infant, and he is still alive.

BOUNTY HUNTER

*I*s there a soul I have to wonder. Look inside myself like leaning over the rim of an old stone well and the danger is, you might lose your balance and fall and there is no water inside to break your fall. *Hello? Hello? Anybody there?* Old stone well with a broken hand pump, I'm thinking of. That well was old when I was a kid. My grandfather's farm that's just "acreage" now north of Herkimer waiting to be sold, how many years. Nobody wants to live in the country now, we've all moved to town.

It's a fact: there's fewer people living in the country in this century than fifty years ago. New houses and a shopping mall going up south of Herkimer and along the highway halfway to Sparta. The new Church of the Risen Christ like a great shining ark rising out of the moldered earth, sailing the waves of the righteous as our pastor says. From the outside the prow of the ark is a beacon of light, inside there is a dazzle of shining surfaces, pinewood pews in long curving rows too many to count and in the balcony more pews rising farther than you can see. At the front of the ark is a great floating gold cross illuminated in light. Each service, three thousand individuals worship here. The Church of the Risen Christ is the fastest-growing church in all the Adirondack region. Started in a storefront in downtown Herkimer, now there's people coming from as far away as Utica, Rome, Watertown, Potsdam. Our tabernacle choir is on cable TV each Sunday morning. What is beautiful is the congregation singing hymns. Nobody laughs at my voice here. My voice is wavering as a girl's but gains strength from the voices close about me, I am not so self-conscious here. Shut your eyes in the Church of the Risen Christ you could be any of these.

In this pew with strangers but we are all children of God. Feeling my heart quicken because this is a secret time for me. My husband is not a churchgoer. I have not yet brought the girls, they would be restless and it makes me angry to see restless children at church. *Is there a soul* is a question I ask myself when I am alone, I am afraid of my thoughts when I am alone. One Sunday I asked Reverend Loomis and he gripped my hand in both his hands smiling he saying *Who is it who asks this question, Diane? Who is it looks through your eyes that are such beautiful eyes?* My face flushed like sunburn. My eyes filled with tears. It was after the service, so many of us anxious to speak with Reverend Loomis and waiting in the aisle for him to take our hands, ask our names and repeat our names as a blessing. So many of us and most of us are women wishing to "seek counsel" with our pastor but Reverend Rob Loomis's time is limited. His special smile for women like me, oh God I hope it isn't pity.

A wife and mother, not yet thirty-five. Yet not young. You feel it at the waist, a bulge of flesh. Turning, and in the mirror a ridge of fat at the small of the back, a crease beneath my chin, I felt so hurt!—betrayed!—until the girls, until I got pregnant, I'd been lean like a boy. *Is there a soul* because if there is and I am lacking a soul, just this body going to fat, I am not like other people but a freak. But if there is a soul and there is one inside me waiting to emerge into the light this is a thing that scares me more.

So what my cousin Michie Dungarve would say. *Who gives a damn, why's it a big deal.* Michie who'd been in the navy and then apprenticed to a bail bondsman/bounty hunter up in Watertown, it would be said of him he was a cold-blooded killer without a soul and Michie conceded that was probably a fact.

In the Church of the Risen Christ, three thousand of us lift our voices in a joyful noise to the Lord and to His Only Begotten Son that Jesus will drive out the devils from us and dwell in our hearts forevermore and I know this to be true. *Rock of ages* we are singing *cleft for me let me hide myself in thee* we are singing. I feel the waves buoying our ark, I feel how we are lifted like the gold cross floating in air. Reverend Loomis teaches us to laugh at sin, laugh away Satan for he is helpless in the face of Jesus. There is not a thing to regret nor even to remember once Jesus is in your heart. Like a light so bright and blinding why'd you even make an effort to see. I tell myself *Jesus understands, He was in my heart even then.*

When I was DeeDee Kinzie. That long ago.

This thing that happened when we were kids living out north of Herkimer. The Rapids it was called, where we lived that wasn't a town but had a post office and a volunteer fire company that shared the building. We went to school at Rapids Elementary then at Rapids Junior-Senior High. My cousin Michie Dungarve who was two years older than me but just one year ahead of me in school. These guys he hung out with in eighth grade, Steve Hauser and Dan Burney. And me. This thing that happened.

Like a sudden storm, like lightning striking. You can be standing on a porch watching the rain out of a boiling-dark sky like my mother's older sister Elsie smoking a cigarette and there's a flash of something like fire and a booming noise so loud it near-about knocked her over, lightning had struck the porch post and splinters shot into the side of her face like buckshot. Happened that fast, my aunt would tell that story the rest of her life thanking God, He had spared her blindness, or worse.

This thing that happened. Except I guess it had to be something we made happen. Not like a lightning storm that's an act of God out of the empty sky.

This single time I was granted an appointment with Reverend Loomis asking why you would call some terrible thing an act of God, for isn't everything that happens an act of God. And Reverend Loomis gives me this frowning smile saying an "act of God" means a great cataclysm beyond any mortal to control. And I say yes, Reverend. But why.

There is something dogged about me, I know. Seeing how our pastor smiled harder at me, that I was a challenge to his kindly nature. I was trying not to stammer saying what I meant is, if God did not wish a terrible thing to happen, why'd He let it happen?

Reverend Loomis spoke calmly and carefully as you would speak to a child. Saying we can't demand such questions of God, he grants us freedom of will to sin or not to sin. Freedom of will to take sin into our hearts or cast it from us. You don't need theology to know this, Mrs. Schmidt!

I felt the man's warmth touch my heart that has such a chill upon it like an old spell.

But needing to say, I wasn't speaking of myself but of this boy that something happened to. When we were children out in the Rapids.

My voice cracked then. For why'd I say that: *children*. We were not young children, none of us. And why say the Rapids. Reverend Loomis has family in Watertown, he would scarcely know rural Herkimer County.

Somehow I was talking fast. I was nervous, and I was anxious, and I was missing my painkillers, that keep my heart from racing and sweat from prickling in my armpits. Saying I don't understand, Reverend. See, I don't understand!

Reverend said let us pray together, Diane. Then you will understand. Reverend smiled and touched my arm. His smile is a flash of white flame, each night following I will sink into sleep into that white flame.

My cousin Michie said it's good to have a little evil in you, people know not to fuck with you. Like a vaccination where they put germs in you, to make your blood stronger.

This swampy woods off the logging road. A thing that scares me is snakes. When we were kids, tramping through the woods back of our houses and after a heavy rainfall or the thaw in spring there'd be sheets of water in the woods, the creeks overflowing, the ditches, even the ravine and afterward a deposit of mud, silt, storm debris. Snakes in the swampy woods and some of them water moccasins. Four feet long and thick as a man's leg. I never saw one of these but knew of them. Copperheads are smaller snakes but poisonous, too. Even garter snakes and grass snakes in just our backyard, in our woodpile in the garage, I'd be terrified of. There was this story of what happened to a ten-year-old boy a cousin of Dan Burney he was tramping in the woods with his dog and the dog waded into a pond and started swimming and something in the water attacked it, the dog was howling and yipping and the boy waded in to rescue it and turned out to be water moccasins, they came swarming out of the cattails and rushes and attacked the boy, sank their fangs in his legs, pulled him down and sank their fangs in his belly, his chest, his face thrashing and swarming at their prey and he screamed for help but nobody could hear him, his heart stopped there in the swamp.

Pressed my hands over my ears. I was feeling sick just to hear this. Begging the guys to stop it, I didn't want to hear it, I didn't believe them but the guys just laughed at me.

The boy we hurt, his name was Arvin and he was Michie's age or older but in special ed. not in eighth grade. In special ed. that was taught by a man teacher, in a corner of the school building by the shop/vocational arts, students who couldn't read like the rest of us or couldn't talk right or had things wrong with them you could see, like in their eyes, in their faces, or maybe they'd be very fat or very thin and had trouble walking, or had ways of acting that were signs of their strangeness like laughing too much or twitching their shoulders or shrinking away when you saw them. On the school bus, they sat together at the front, near the driver. That way, they'd be protected.

Arvin Huehner, 14. The name in the newspaper.

We were surprised, the way the name was spelled. You just called them *Hugh-ners*, the family.

Arvin was taller than Michie and his friends but bony-thin, with rounded shoulders and something wrong with his chest: "pigeon-breasted" it was called, he'd been excused from gym classes and swimming. His shoulder blades curved forward as if he'd been stooped over too long and couldn't straighten his back. His neck was at an angle like he was leaning away from himself. His face was pasty-pale and hairless like something skinned. His lips were rubbery and loose. His teeth were crooked and stained and his eyes were weak behind thick lenses and he had a high-pitched whiny voice you'd hear sometimes when he was scolding his younger brother and sisters who rode the bus with us, in mimicry of an adult Arvin would cry, "Bad! *Bad!*"

When I saw Arvin Huehner my eyes seemed to sting. Quickly I looked away. The thought came to me *There is someone like myself.*

(Why this was, I don't know! There was nothing of DeeDee Kinzie in Arvin Huehner, or in any of the special ed. kids.)

Michie said, There's the freak.

In a freak, there is something that draws the eye. You resent it, having to look.

My cousin Michie was thirteen, when I was eleven. Michie wasn't tall but solid-built for a boy his age. He had a wedge-shaped face, a heavy jaw. You could see how he would grow into a heavy man like the older Dungarves. But his cheeks were soft and smooth-looking and had a natural flush like sunburn. His eyes were bright and shrewd. Already in junior high, Michie Dungarve was "sexy" in the eyes of older girls. He hated school and cut classes when he could. He had a posse he called it, guys who hung out with him. When he was younger Michie used to paint stripes on his face like an Indian, red clay to give him a wild scary look. On a leather thong around his neck he wore an animal jawbone and a black turkey vulture feather. In the family Michie was known for his mule-stubbornness. Aged two, his mother said, he'd dig in his heels in the ground, even an adult man could hardly budge him.

I was DeeDee, short for Diane. I was the only girl.

Why it happened I was with them, it had to do with where we lived. Red Rock Road, that ran along Red Rock Creek from Rapids to Route 14 which was a state highway. Red Rock Road was just two miles, not a through road so you'd wind up at the old logging site where the woods look ravaged even now. It's mostly wild woods and fields and a big swampy marsh where only rushes and cattails grow and there's a terrible smelly black muck through late summer. There were six houses on this road and naturally you got to know the kids if they were your age and took the bus to school. The Dungarves lived next-door to us, my mother was all the time over visiting her sister Elsie, or Elsie was at our house, and when he'd been younger, Michie sometimes came with her. There was a path through the field to the Dungarves' house. My cousin Michie was only two years older than me but when you're a child two years is a long span of time and always I wanted Michie to like me.

Showing off for Michie, to get Michie's attention. My aunt Elsie would tease me.

At school, Michie would protect me. Not because he liked me but because I was his cousin. Fuck with DeeDee Kinzie, you'd be fucking with Michie Dungarve.

I hated girls! Mostly, girls hated me.

I wore clothes like the guys. Jeans, zip-up parkas, shirts pulled over shirts. My chest was flat as a guy's chest. My hips were lean as a guy's. Where my legs came together there was a frizz of pale brown hair, it wouldn't be for another two years or so that hairs began to grow in my armpits and on my muscled legs sharp as tiny thorns. My face was small and oliveish-pale and my eyes deep-set like shiny black glass.

I had a mouth on me, my mother said. She stopped slapping that mouth by the time I was eleven. She'd learned.

Water moccasins. Slow-moving and mud-colored in the stagnant swamp water. I'd be wading in the swamp and see the snake-shapes start toward me beneath the surface of the black water, a faint ripple all you'd see, oh God I could not move my legs I could not scream for help the snakes swimming toward me surrounding me in a circle rushing at me to sink their fangs into me . . .

How many times I dreamt this, it makes me sick to think. At school I asked a teacher why'd God make poison snakes and she answered some bullshit answer like they do and I had to pretend to believe it, like I always did.

Tell Nose Pick c'mere, Michie said to me.

Nose Pick was one of the names they called Arvin. On account of him always picking at his nose, his mouth, his ears like he had terrible itches all over. Arvin had a way of watching the rest of us, kind of smiling at us, laughing if we did something meant to be funny, wanting to be with us except most of the time, at school, if we were outside on the school grounds, he couldn't: there was a yellow line painted on the pavement dividing one part of the paved ground from the rest and the special ed. students were not allowed to cross this yellow line or vice versa. This was a school rule. You could figure that it protected some of the special ed. kids from being teased or tormented but also it was meant to protect other kids from being teased or tormented by the special ed. kids who were bigger and older and kind of unpredictable in their behavior. Arvin Huehner was between these, you could say. He'd be picked on by the guys but, tall and kind of bossy like he was, Arvin sometimes picked on younger kids himself. That high-pitched nasal voice scolding *Bad!*

The Hugh-ners as they were called lived on Red Rock Road in a house that was just a basement, you could see the basement windows and part of the first floor that resembled a skeleton, just boards and planks where rooms would be, except work stopped on the house years ago and never started again. There was no outside to the Hugh-ners' house only just raw planks and strips of something like canvas that became ripped and flapped in the wind. This house, that people called an eyesore, and were contemptuous of, was about a mile from where we lived, and the Dungarves lived, toward the dead end of the Red Rock Road. The older Hugh-ners were said to be "normal" but the children were all special ed. Arvin had only younger sisters and a brother, no older relative to protect him.

Hey Arvin, I said, Michie wants you to come with us.

Arvin narrowed his eyes at me not trusting me exactly. This was in April, a day that smelled of wet earth. Warm when the sun came out and chilly when the sun went in. Arvin was wearing a parka that was an ugly mustard color and corduroy trousers that fitted his legs narrow as pencils. That Arvin would believe my cousin Michie and his friends would want him to join them, that Arvin was so stupid hardened my heart against him. *Why'd you think you could be their friend* I wanted to laugh in his face.

Arvin adjusted his glasses on his nose, blinking at me. He was licking his loose rubbery lips excited and scared.

O.K. c'mon, I told Arvin.

We weren't taking the school bus after school. There was a way we hiked home along the railroad embankment then along the creek for maybe a mile.

So Arvin trotted with us like a scrawny dog. Along the railroad embankment and into a thicket of trees and there was the edge of the swamp and the ravine you had to cross over some fallen logs. Below was a marshy ditch thick with rushes and cattails and water that smelled like sewage, that was high after some days of rain. Below were bullfrogs croaking so loud and hoarse, you can't believe the noise is coming from something so small. The guys threw rocks at the frogs but the frogs were too quick for them. Turtles sunning on logs, they'd slip off and disappear at the sound of a voice.

A surprise how a turtle can see you and hear you and maybe feel your footsteps at a distance. How a creature with such a thick clumsy shell can move so fast, to save its life.

Michie told Arvin go climb down into the ravine where there was something glinting in the mud, looked like a car hood ornament. Arvin began to whimper saying he didn't want to, his mother would be angry if he came back muddy. And maybe then Michie or one of the other guys pushed him. Or maybe Arvin decided to climb down. We told Arvin we'd be friends with him, he could come home with us. So he climbed into the ravine which was maybe thirty feet deep, slipping and sliding in the mud. I said to Michie what if there are water moccasins in that water and Michie just laughed. Arvin managed to get hold of the hood ornament but his feet were sinking in mud. He began to cry, he was stuck in the mud. The guys were laughing and yelling down at Arvin it was quicksand he'd gotten into. He was red-faced and snivelling and his glasses were crooked on his nose. I saw a swirl of something in the water just a few yards from where Arvin was struggling. I saw the ripples, I saw the rubbery-thick black snakes just below the surface of the water. We were waiting for Arvin to be sucked into the quicksand. Like in a TV movie where a man was trapped in quicksand in a jungle, you watched as the quicksand sucked him down, the lower part of his face disappeared into the mud, his mouth, then his terrified eyes, then he was gone, the quicksand shut above his head only just frothy bubbles.

In the movie, monkeys were flying through the trees overhead and chattering and shrieking. At the top of the ravine, the guys were laughing at Arvin. I said, Hey we better pull him up. Laughing like the guys but getting scared. I didn't say anything about the snakes because the guys would only laugh at me. I wasn't sure I had seen snakes, maybe it was just wind blowing the rushes.

Arvin was trying to grab hold of some vines, to pull himself up. His legs were sunk in mud to his knees. He was crying, bawling like a calf.

A calf bawls for its mother, just a few hours old and already its lungs are strong enough it can bellow. But a human scream is thin and weak and can crack if you're afraid. Arvin was bawling like a calf, bawling with no words, like he'd forgotten what words were. Michie and Steve were tossing stones and mud-chunks at him. Dan Burney dragged a heavy rock to the edge of the ravine, let it drop and roll down the slope at Arvin but missing him. There was a broken tree limb shaped like a spear, I threw. The spear fell short of Arvin where he'd fallen in the mud and was bleeding from a cut on his forehead, he was bawling but not so loud as before. The guys got into seeing who could hit Arvin with the most stones. The biggest rocks. The sky was darkening like something begun to boil. It happens that fast, east of Lake Ontario. There came a harder wind, and rain like warm spit. We backed off and left Arvin in the ravine.

Hiked through the woods to Red Rock Road, and to our houses. Michie, Steve, Dan. And DeeDee who was me.

Two years later in ninth grade my name would be Diane. I had a close girlfriend through high school who called me Di. And Frank calls me Di sometimes. Nobody calls me DeeDee now, if I heard this name I would freeze.

It was years later my cousin Michie was arrested for what he did to a girl named Sheryl Ricks over at Alcott. Michie denied it at first saying it must've been some other guy, Sheryl was seeing other guys not only him. The rumor was, Sheryl was pregnant with Michie Dungarve's baby but that turned out to be false, the Niagara County coroner reported.

When you die every fact of your body can be exposed. Not just are you pregnant but have you ever been pregnant. Have you ever had a baby. Are there "bruises and lacerations" in the vaginal area, meaning have you been raped. Or maybe not raped but you've had sex. Once you are dead they can know everything about you.

By the time of Sheryl we were out of school. Michie was twenty-two. What he'd done was beat his girlfriend then twist her head with both his hands so that the vertebrae in her neck broke. In his bare hands. Michie was that angry and that strong. He'd been in the navy for two years and the family was proud of him then he tested positive for amphetamines and was discharged "less than honorable" and came back to Herkimer where his family was living then. Then there was a few months he worked for a bail bondsman up at Watertown and was apprenticed to a licensed bounty hunter which was work he liked, he said. His name wasn't Michie now but Mitch.

Mitchell Dungarve is my cousin's actual name. In the papers and on TV it would be *Mitchell Dungarve, 22.*

Mitch would tell anyone who asked him, Sheryl Ricks had it coming. She'd known it, too, which was why she'd tried to run from him in the parking lot. Mitch told the *Herkimer Journal* reporter he'd kind of wanted to see what it was like killing somebody, anyway. Since he'd been a kid, he was curious. And in the navy, he'd never seen "combat." The reporter said, well—what was it like? and Mitch said it happened so damn fast like a fire flaring up almost he hadn't felt anything at all.

Mitch said it isn't that big a deal killing somebody who deserves it except for all that comes afterward. People make so much of it, Jesus! That's what he hadn't guessed, how his life would be fucked up afterward.

It was his freedom he missed. Worse than in the navy, once you get arrested. Fuck Sheryl, she had it coming.

Cold-blooded murderer lacking a soul it was said of Mitch Dungarve but anybody who knew Mitch, his family and relatives, his close friends, knew Mitch wasn't all that different from anybody else.

What had happened to Arvin Huehner was different, it never got beyond what was reported in the papers. A "special education" student at the Rapids school had a "fatal accident" coming home from school. He'd tried to cross a deep ravine on some rotted logs but fell and injured himself on rocks below, fractured his skull and died. Arvin had been a clumsy boy even his family conceded. They could not understand why he hadn't come home from school on the bus as he always did. It was revealed that, that day, the special ed. teacher had had to discipline Arvin for harassing a girl in their class, and Arvin had been upset about that and hadn't wanted to ride the bus home. There was no witness to what had happened to Arvin but Sheryl Ricks was a different situation, plenty of people had seen Mitch Dungarve with her at a tavern in Alcott the night she'd died.

In the prison at Attica, Mitch gave interviews. He said he was not afraid to die, he'd done what needed to be done and that was all. His lawyer told him show remorse but that was bullshit, he would not.

He never spoke of Arvin Huehner, never told our names, that we were involved. It came to me one day, he'd forgotten.

The ravine and the logging road in the woods have not changed much in twenty years. I drove out once, to investigate. We'd all moved into town by then. I was married and had my girls by then. What is strange is how much of Red Rock Road is abandoned now, houses collapsed in tall weeds and scrub trees and the Huehner house, what there was of it, hardly visible from the road. Some people live in our old house but the Dungarves' house next-door is boarded up. Properties like my grandfather's old farm are overgrown like jungles. The big interstate I-81 cuts a swath through the countryside north of Rapids so there's heavy traffic only just a mile or so from the ravine but not even an exit at Rapids.

Arvin was found in the ravine the next day, after seven hours of searching it was said.

Everybody in the special ed. class was asked about him. And kids on the bus. The driver was questioned, why hadn't he waited for Arvin, or gone to look for him. Arvin's teacher was questioned, and made to look bad in the paper. Even the school principal. Arvin's sister and brothers riding the school bus had not seemed to miss him. Acted like they hadn't noticed Arvin wasn't there.

Some of us, who lived on Red Rock Road, were asked if we'd seen Arvin after school, where he'd gone, and we said no we had not seen Arvin Hugh-ner, he wasn't in our classes and wasn't our friend and nobody we knew had much to do with him or with any of the Hugh-ners.

That poor boy not right in the head was how people spoke of Arvin afterward. Like my mother, and my aunt Elsie. *You'd think his parents would keep a closer watch, a retarded boy like that wandering and getting lost.*

In Herkimer where I live now, I see Steve and Dan sometimes. I see their families at the mall. Steve married a girl I knew from school, they have two children at least. I think they live on Buell Road, Steve works for a contractor. Dan Burney was in the navy with Michie, got sent overseas and when he came back he got married and later divorced and he works at the stone quarry where my husband Frank Schmidt is foreman. Dan is grown to three hundred pounds muscle-and-fat and shaves his head so his head and face look swollen like something made of hard rubber. Dan lives with his mother who has some wasting disease like Parkinson's.

We see each other at Kroger's, or Eckerd's, or at the mall. There's a glaze over our eyes when we meet. Steve Hauser, Dan Burney. If they tried to call me DeeDee, I'd tell them no: I am Diane. But they don't call me any name at all. We talk together trying to remember why we know each other. The guys always ask about Mitch but there's nothing to say about Mitch, he will spend the rest of his life in "death row" at Attica. The death penalty in New York State is lethal injection but no one has been executed for a long time.

Steve Hauser and Dan Burney and me, there's a nagging feeling between us. But we don't know what.

We ask about one another's families. Dan takes his mother to the Church of the Risen Christ some Sundays, helps the old woman with her walker. Dan doesn't always sit in the pew with her but waits out in the parking lot, smoking. He's a big man but soft and vague in the eyes. Sometimes he will push into the pew beside his mother. I see Dan

Burney, I smile and wave and Dan will wave back. I wonder if Dan sings with the rest of us! The way some men sing under their breath like they don't want anyone but Jesus to hear.

I have two daughters: Kyra who will be in seventh grade next year and Tamara who will be in fourth.

Their eyes! The most beautiful eyes. When I tell Steve Hauser and Dan Burney about my family I tell them my daughters are getting to be big girls but I don't tell them how beautiful my daughters are, it's hard for me to speak of it. The other day Frank said, You see those girls, you know why you were born.

Out of nowhere Frank said this. It isn't like him, or any of us to speak in such a way. But I'm hoping it is that simple, what Frank said. All I'd needed to do to be saved was have my babies, that is my purpose on earth. You would not need a soul for that!

A feeling used to come to me sometimes, a true life is being lived somewhere, but I am not in that life. Since having my babies, I don't feel this way. It's a stronger feeling even than Jesus in my heart.

Because you can backslide and lose Jesus. But you can never lose the fact you have given birth.

Strange that it's water moccasins I dream of, that I never saw. I never dream of Arvin Huehner. I dream of myself in the swamp and the snakes and the quicksand but I never dream of Arvin Huehner and there is probably nobody who knows that name Huehner where we live now.

I saw the hood ornament on a four-wheel-drive pickup, a long time ago. I think it was the same kind.

Things that scare me are any kind of snakes. Even a picture of a snake, a feeling like faintness comes over me. Also the shadows of clouds passing on the ground. In the countryside you can see these shadows miles away on the hills, it takes your breath away watching them move so fast. Sunshine and green fields and the swift shadow rolling toward you taking away the green. I think *The valley of the shadow of death*.

Another thing that scares me: mammograms and pelvic exams. Pap smears. My legs tremble so, though I have given birth from my body yet I am frightened of the sharp instruments. I am frightened of the doctor seeing into me. For one day it will be revealed *You have tested positive for cancer, Mrs. Schmidt. Your punishment was deferred but will now begin.*

And I am afraid of my own anger sometimes. Wanting to smash things, precious things to me like the girls' faces when they are stubborn and mouth off at me. Kyra is the worst, the way her eyes slide over me in scorn. Beautiful eyes so liquidy-brown and their faces are beautiful yet I could grab these faces and squeeze until the bones broke. My husband says, God damn it, Diane, keep it down, you should see yourself, Jesus. Frank starts toward me and I back off, fast. Frank could break my face in his hand if I hurt the girls so this is O.K., this is good. I'm grateful for that.

I asked Reverend Loomis what is the root of anger, why I am angry sometimes at my family I love, and Reverend Loomis said it is a test put to me. Every day and every hour of my life is a test, will Satan triumph, or Our Lord. Diane, it's that simple!

Soon as I heard those words, I was comforted.

After you leave school, there are people you'd been seeing every day of your life you never see again. Even relatives.

Last time I saw my cousin Michie close up, I guess he'd been Mitch by then, it was at the 7-Eleven out on the highway and I was only just married then and not more than a few weeks' pregnant which I hoped Mitch would not know. It was after 10 P.M., I was going for milk and cereal and cigarettes and Mitch was going for beer and cigarettes and there was no one else in the lot, the pavement was wet with snow. By then Mitch had been discharged from the navy and was back but not living with his family. It was rumored that Mitch was dealing in drugs. Also Mitch was said to be apprentice to a bounty hunter in Watertown. You had to have a license to be a bounty hunter, you were allowed to carry a concealed weapon. Mitch was wearing his hair long and tied in a pigtail and his jaws were covered in whiskers and in the midst of these whiskers he was smiling at me. Heat lifting from his skin and I could see the swell of his eyeballs moist and quivering like gasoline somebody might hold a match to, it would explode into flame.

He'd just jumped down from his pickup. Every vehicle I see, my eyes slide over the hood, I can't stop myself looking for a shiny hood ornament, Mitch was driving a four-wheel pickup like a jeep, with no ornament on the hood. Smiling at me with just his teeth saying, Hey there, DeeDee, like there was something between us and it wasn't that we were blood kin. I was smiling at Mitch quick and breathless which was my way around guys like Mitch, I felt this faintness come over me thinking *He has a knife he carries, he can kill me any time.* And my cousin's hands were big-knuckled, and scarred. It was six months before he'd kill his girlfriend Sheryl Ricks at Alcott but there was no sign of that now. Seeing he'd scared me Mitch was in a teasing mood pushing close to me, laughing like there was some joke between us, I smelled beer on his breath, he's saying, How're you doing, DeeDee, you and Frank, and I said, trying to keep my voice even, not stepping back from Mitch like he was daring me, We're doing really well, Mitch. But I'm not DeeDee these days.

THE BARTER

1.

Let something of mine be taken from me! Let Father be returned to us.

So the son David Rainey, thirteen years old, who prided himself on not-believing-in-God, prayed.

2.

In the medical center whose higher floors were frequently shrouded in mist, in the men's lavatory in the eighth-floor cardiac unit, he hid away to cry. What he hated about crying was his face shattering into pieces like a pane of struck glass. His eyes turned to liquid. His ridiculous nose ran. In a fury he tore off a long strip of toilet paper in which to blow it. A Möbius strip, unending. In despair thinking *I hate them all!* For it seemed to him that all of the family, not only his stricken father, had betrayed him.

His father would be nine days in the cardiac unit. On the first interminable day, David entered the lavatory to hide and realized too late he wasn't alone. Somebody was in one of the stalls, sobbing. A helpless muffled sound as if the invisible person (a boy David's age?) was jamming his knuckles against his mouth.

Quickly, David retreated. He was in dread of meeting another so like himself.

3 .

The father was down, the Rainey family was stricken.

For years they'd been Meems and Dadda, Kit-Kit, the Goat, Pike, and Billy-o. They were Granmum Geranium, Auntie Bean, and Uncle Ike. (True, Pike and Billy-o had left home. Uncle Ike wasn't married any longer to Dadda's sister Bean.) These were their secret family names in the big old red-brick Colonial on Upchurch Street on the highest hill of the hilly city. David, who was the Goat, knew the secret names were sort of silly, but he hadn't realized how sad-silly until Dadda was admitted to the medical center as "Mr. Rainey" (which was how the staff on the fifth floor referred to him, often as if he weren't even present) or "Marcus J. Rainey" (which was imprinted on the stiff paper bracelet around his left wrist, along with a computer number). And suddenly there was Mother who'd been Meems for so long, a pretty, freckle-faced, flurried woman with corn-silk hair and a laugh like a tickle in her throat, that made you laugh with her, now overnight a wooden-faced not-young woman with bulgy eyes, rat's-nest hair, and a misbuttoned black cashmere coat.

Kit-Kit, the vigilant daughter, sixteen years old, scolded in an undertone as three Raineys ascended in an elevator to the eighth floor. "*Mother*. Your *coat*." "What?" Mother blinked as if she'd become hard of hearing. Kit-Kit growled, "Your *coat*." Still, Mother was confused. Her face visibly heated. "What—about my coat?" "The buttons!" Kit-Kit, exasperated, deftly rebuttoned the coat herself. There!

Kit-Kit's true name was Katherine. No one called her Kathy.

David, the Goat, the youngest Rainey child, observed his mother and sister from a corner of the elevator. There were two or three strangers between himself and the stunned-looking woman and the tall girl who was breathing with an open mouth, so he might not be identified as belonging with them. Did all the Raineys resemble one another? Not the Goat! He was thinking how pointless to rebutton their mother's coat since they were headed for Father's hospital room where the coat would be unbuttoned and removed anyway.

Nobody's thinking clearly any longer except me, David thought grimly.

4 .

The night before, he'd been working on geometry problems in his bedroom after he'd been supposed to turn off his lights at 11 P.M. weekdays. Then he'd gone to bed and was wakened, it seemed, almost immediately, by his mother's panicked cry outside his door, and from that moment onward the world's surfaces had become tilted and slip sliding. Always he would be hearing *Help! Help us!* in a woman's terrified voice he'd hardly identified as belonging to his mother. *Something has happened to my husband!*

(And that, too, was strange to his ears: *My husband.*)

So Mr. Rainey who'd been Dadda, the children's father, was taken away by ambulance in the night. Now the Raineys had to know themselves unprotected by God or by the general good fortune they'd taken for granted. As Kit-Kit told David, swiping at her nose with a look of somber disbelief, "I guess anything can happen to us now. *Anything.*"

5 .

The father hadn't died, though he'd been near unconscious and on an oxygen machine, three hours in the emergency room and eleven hours in intensive care and then transferred to room 833, a private room where at last anxious relatives could visit him, cautioned not to crowd around his bed and not to tire him. The diagnosis was not a heart attack exactly but severe atrial fibrillation, with a possibility of blood clots in the heart and elsewhere.

It isn't him, I don't know him. Who is it? Amid the tense whispery talk it was the Raineys' youngest son who held back, shyly staring at his father in the cranked-up hospital bed. Overnight the father had become strangely sunken chested and feeble lying there in a hospital gown through which his graying chest hair faintly glowered, only fifty-one years old (but, thought David, fifty-one *is* old) yet stricken as if with a sledgehammer. Into his bruised right forearm two IV tubes were running, attached to clear-liquid sacs on poles beside the bed; around his upper left arm a blood-pressure cuff was tightly wrapped, and this cuff was timed to take readings every few minutes with a peculiar whirring sound. (The patient's vital signs, as they were called—heartbeat, blood pressure, heartbeat, blood pressure, heartbeat, blood pressure—were indicated on a monitor in his room and in a nurses' station: if one of the readings dipped or soared too much, an emergency alarm would be sounded and help would come running.) When it was David's turn to speak with his father, he didn't know what to say as the pale, squinting man in the bed smiled at him, fumbling for his hand, icy cold the man's fingers, poor Dadda—as if this stranger was Dadda or could ever have been. "Davy, don't worry—I'm a little under the weather—all these drugs they're pumping into me—" his father was saying, insisting, as if there weren't a reason for the powerful drugs or for his being in this strange place, and David smiled anxiously and nodded, having to lean close to hear his father's voice. For overnight the change was upon Mr. Rainey, you could see it, and you could smell it—"don't worry, I'll be home soon, I promise. Things will be as before. I love you"—this, David couldn't be certain he'd heard, his face crinkling suddenly like a baby's, and this was the signal for his mother to embrace him, or to try, as if he weren't thirteen years old—but the Goat was quick to sidestep her, mumbling words that might have been *See you later!* or *Leave me alone.*

They let him go. Knowing he wouldn't go far. To a men's lavatory on the floor. To hide, to cry.

It was like he'd been tricked. And he didn't know who to blame.

6.

The Goat, or Little Goat, was so called because as a very small child he'd scampered up stairs before he could walk, on hands and knees like a frisky kid. Meems and Dadda laughed at him in delight and clapped. *Look at that baby billy goat climbing the mountain!* The Goat was proud of his talent, wouldn't have known that such talent was only just showing off for the family. And long after he'd ceased scampering up stairs in the big old red-brick house on Upchurch Street, he'd be known within the family as the Goat, as his sister was Kit-Kit, and his brothers were Pike and Billy-o. *And none of this sad, silly stuff mattered in the slightest in the real world.*

7.

That night kneeling bare-kneed on the hardwood floor in a corner of his bedroom. *Let something of mine be taken!* He was breathless and fearful as if God in whom he didn't believe might be in the very room with him. *Let my father be returned to us.*

It would be a simple trade, barter. It would be a secret transaction. None of the others would know. Not even Father.

For it was a fact: all was changed now. Even if his father's heartbeat could be returned to normal. Even if there were no clots sifting through his blood to strike him dead like bullets. Even if the house on Upchurch Street that looked now as if winds had blown through the rooms, where the phone was forever ringing, returned to normal. His father had promised things would be *as before* but David no longer believed his father. For nothing could be *as before*. He was angry that they'd think him so young, and credulous, to believe such a lie.

It was like a theorem in his geometry text. It was irrefutable. There is no *before* without *after*.

In the dark he went to his desk, switched on a lamp, and took up his geometry compass. He stabbed the sharp point into the palm of his left hand and pressed, grunting with the surprise of the pain. The skin was punctured and blood oozed grudgingly out. His upper lip was beaded with sweat. *Push it all the way through, like a spike.*

The compass slipped through his fingers and fell to the floor gleaming faintly with blood.

Coward.

8 .

"The Cheetah"—so David called the boy, in secret.

This was the person, David believed, who'd been crying in the men's lavatory the first day of the Raineys' vigil at the medical center.

He was a slender, handsome, foreign-looking boy of about fourteen whose father, too, was a heart patient in the cardiac unit. In room 837, two doors from 833. David began noticing him on the second day. After that, he couldn't not notice him. The boy was "foreign" though dressed like an American teenager in jeans, T-shirt, expensive running shoes. He spoke English with no evident accent (that David could overhear) though his relatives, crowded into room 837, spoke a language David couldn't recognize, or heavily accented English the medical staff had trouble understanding. Maybe they were Middle Eastern? Turks, Lebanese, Arabs? Or were they Pakistanis? Or—Portuguese? Their language was rapid, harsh, and sometimes sibilant, teasingly familiar to David (from TV?) yet mysterious. In David's suburban school there were few ethnic or minority students and most of these were Asian-Americans. The Cheetah was black haired, olive skinned, with distinctive features that reminded David of a cat's, and he was catlike in his movements, restless, inclined to impatience. Sometimes he appeared stricken with grief; at other times he looked sulky, even bored. He and David often saw each other in the eighth-floor corridor, in the visitors' lounge, just stepping out of an elevator, with relatives, or alone, eyes turned downward. The Cheetah was taller than David by several inches, about five foot five. He only vaguely acknowledged David, with a glance, though David was certain he recognized him. The Cheetah was the most striking boy of his age that David had ever seen up close.

His father has been struck down, too. Maybe dying.

The Cheetah's father lay as if near comatose in his bed, breathing oxygen from a plastic tube. His dark-skinned face was ravaged though probably, David thought, he wasn't any older than David's own father. He looked like a big man who'd lost weight suddenly, like a partly deflated balloon. His room was the most frequently visited in the corridor, and many of these visitors brought young children with them. The nursing staff repeatedly asked them not to speak so loudly, to watch their children more closely, to "be considerate" of other patients. Always, they obeyed at once; yet shortly afterward, others arrived, and there was more commotion. Mr. Rainey complained that the "foreign" family stayed past 11 P.M. sometimes and woke him on their way out. David would have liked to inquire what nationality they were, what their name was, but didn't want to appear curious.

There was another boy, older than the Cheetah, about seventeen, who came to visit the patient in room 837 less frequently. They were obviously brothers, the one a taller, heavier version of the other. The older boy, whom David came to call "the Hawk," was handsome, too; his nose was prominent, beak-like—like a hawk's. His black hair had been severely trimmed to a buzz cut. The Hawk was a swaggering high school kid in a black Pearl Jam T-shirt, ratty designer jeans, a gold stud glittering in his left earlobe. He, too, was taking his father's hospitalization hard, you could see that, but he was more readily bored than the Cheetah and prowled about the cardiac unit talking to the West Indian orderlies and nurses' aides. When the brothers were together, the Hawk was clearly dominant. He talked, and the Cheetah listened. It was easy to imagine their childhood: the older brother bossing the younger. David's brothers, too, were older than he was, but so much older (Pete by ten years, Billy by six) they'd been protective of him rather than bullying, though mostly they hadn't had time for him. Seeing the way the

Cheetah glanced at the Hawk, alert and even admiring, David felt a stab of envy.

The Hawk took no notice of David but the Cheetah was different, at least some of the time. One night at 10 P.M., when David was sent to get fruit juice for his father, there was the Cheetah on a similar errand. Their gazes locked for an awkward moment. David might have mumbled, "Hi," and the Cheetah might have mumbled something inaudible in passing.

That night in his dream he was Little Goat! He and the Cheetah were in kindergarten together. Playing on the slide and on the swings. They'd climbed, clambered up a steep staircase. A feeling of overwhelming happiness spread through David.

For the first time since the ambulance had come for his father, taking away Dadda to die amid strangers, David was able to sleep through to morning.

9.

The puncture wound in his hand had come to nothing; he *was* a coward. His father wasn't improving and until Mr. Rainey was stronger, the cardiologist couldn't "proceed." A voice taunted him, the God-in-whom-he-didn't-believe. *What would you give up to bring your father home?*

His eyesight? The vision in one eye? His hearing? What about an arm? Which arm? His right? What about a leg? And what of his "future"—would he give that up? Never play any game again: softball, soccer, basketball? Would he give up his trombone? His friends? His high grades? His special feeling for math? His soul?

A sacrifice must be made. But what?

Around the house he was a sleepwalker-zombie; it wouldn't be a surprise if an accident happened. Turning an ankle on the stairs and falling. Shutting a car door on his hand. All of them were distracted and not themselves. Mother on the telephone, Mother walking slowly through the rooms she seemed not to recognize. There was nothing for them to talk about except the father's condition, yet there was so little for them to say of it that they hadn't already said. Through this, the God-voice taunted the Raineys' youngest son, the coward.

What would you give up? give up? give up?

He did return to school for a morning. There was a midterm test in solid geometry he didn't want to miss. He made certain he failed, hoping his teacher wouldn't be suspicious. He got enough answers wrong so he calculated his numerical grade was about 55%, a letter grade of F.

Maybe that would help?

10.

On the fourth morning Mr. Rainey was strong enough to endure a heart-probe procedure, and afterward Mrs. Rainey was crying, clutching at their hands. "It's all right! The doctor said there were *no blood clots*."

11.

Yet the father's arrhythmia didn't respond to medication as the cardiologist expected. There was the probability that, if Mr. Rainey was removed from his intravenous medication, the atrial fibrillation would return. For that was the rhythm which his fifty-one-year-old heart, like a suddenly deranged clock, had taken on. So they might try electric shock.

Admittedly this was a more extreme procedure with some element of risk.

How much "element of risk" the Raineys wanted to know.

The cardiologist's reply was lengthy, tactful, and, in the end, vague. For each heart patient is a unique problem, each heartbeat a unique beat, and any general anesthetic is a trauma to the brain.

"And to the heart?" Mrs. Rainey asked.

"Well, yes." The cardiologist cleared his throat.

12.

David wondered if the Cheetah had noticed: room 833 and room 837 were mirror-rooms.

Each was private and of the same proportions, bathroom to the rear, a single window. In each, as you approached, you could see a gowned man in bed, attached to intravenous sacs on poles. In each, you often saw visitors sitting or standing around the bed. Each room exuded the possibility of the *empty bed*.

After a few days, David began to worry not just that he'd return to room 833 and see his father's bed empty, but he'd return to see the bed empty in room 837, too. That would mean he'd never see the Cheetah again. For the Cheetah's father did seem sicker than David's father. He was still breathing oxygen through a tube in his nose. There was more often a curtain drawn around his bed. Rarely did the Cheetah's father sit up to talk with visitors or watch TV as David's father had done since the second evening, and not once had David seen the Cheetah's father walking in the corridor as David's father did, slowly but gamely, twice a day, with one of the West Indian orderlies, hauling his two jingly IV poles and his blood-pressure paraphernalia with him. ("Like a cyborg.") Once, when David was prowling the corridor, he passed the open door of 837 and happened to see the patient being prepared by two orderlies for a trip on a gurney, lifted stiffly out of his bed like a dead weight. There was the Cheetah at the foot of the bed, and there was the plump, anxious-looking woman David supposed was the Cheetah's mother. David circled the floor, and when he returned to his corridor, there was the ravaged man, barely conscious, being wheeled to an elevator; in his wake, the Cheetah and his mother followed slowly, gripping each other's hand. David would have liked to say, "If it's the blood-clot test, it isn't too bad. My dad had it and he's okay. Good luck!" Of course, he said nothing.

Yet the Cheetah glanced at him in passing, a swift sidelong look of fear, hurt, anger, and an obscure shame.

13.

He wasn't spying on the brothers. Yet it happened he saw them everywhere.

In the parking garage, for instance. By what coincidence did Mrs. Rainey park one morning, on level B, close by the "foreign" family's car? Both cars were large, new-model luxury cars, but the Raineys' was mud splattered and its chrome fixtures dimmed as if in mourning while the other family's car gleamed and glittered as if it had been driven directly out of a dealer's showroom.

The Hawk was driving. In the harsh early sunshine he looked older than seventeen. He drove with a slight edge of impatience, pulling into the parking space and braking almost simultaneously. Beside him was his mother; in the backseat were an elderly white-haired woman, a young girl, and the Cheetah slouched and sullen, a baseball cap pulled down over his forehead. David looked quickly away.

"Those people," Mrs. Rainey sighed. "Either they all look alike, or they're everywhere."

14.

On the morning of the sixth day the father began to cry, whispering he'd failed them. The children were sent out of the room. The cardiologist came to explain the electric-shock procedure in such clinical detail, Mrs. Rainey began to faint—"Oh, God. An electric shock to his *heart.*"

15.

That night, David opened his window wanting the ache and hurt of cold. Damp sleeting rain like needles. *What would you give up? What would you give?* Quietly he went downstairs in his pajamas, barefoot. Stepped outside into the harsh cold air. His head, which had felt fevered, like a burning lightbulb, was immediately wet, and it wasn't much but it felt good.

How long he wandered about in the sleety rain, on the driveway, in the grass, tilting his head back, exposing his throat, he wouldn't know. Lost track of time. Thinking *This might be the last night I have a father.*

16.

Next morning, his head ached, his eyes were running, and his nose—
"Oh, Davy. You've given yourself a cold." Somehow, his mother knew,
scolding him, but kissing him, pressing him against her so he hadn't any
choice but, gently, to push away.

Mother was saying in her new, wondering voice, "The life we live in
our bodies, it's so strange, isn't it? You don't ever think how you got *in*.
But you come to think obsessively how you'll be getting *out*."

Later, when they were preparing to leave for the medical center, she
laid her hand on David's arm in that way he'd come to dread. "Your father loves you very much, honey. You know that."

David nodded, yes.

"He told me. He's thinking of you. All the time. He wants you to
know that. I hope you do."

"Okay, Mom."

Desperate to escape, but where to escape *to*?

17.

Like puppets on a string! That was what the Raineys had become.

Even Mr. Rainey in his cranked-up bed, listening to the beat-beat-
beat of his crazed heart.

For no sooner did they arrive in room 833 than they were informed
by the head nurse that the electric-shock procedure was postponed
until the next morning. When Mr. Rainey's vital signs might be more
stable.

"Hell," said Mr. Rainey, managing a ghastly-ashy smile, "I'm set to
go right *now*."

18.

"Hey-*hey*!"

A sharp little cry not meant for him. As the flat stone came skittering and skidding across the icy pavement.

Behind the medical center, adjacent to the parking garage, there was a construction site and in the foreground, an unused, slightly littered space.

It was truly chance! David hadn't followed the brothers here, hadn't had any idea they might be here at all. He'd fled the eighth-floor corridor and the stifling air of room 833 where even the numerous fresh-cut flowers exuded an odor of dread. He hadn't taken time even to put on his jacket, desperate to flee.

And there, in early winter sunlight were the brothers kicking a stone like a hockey puck between them. It was an idle, desultory game. A cigarette slanted from a corner of the Hawk's fleshy mouth. The Cheetah, languid and sulky-seeming, wore a gray baseball jacket. During the night the sleet had turned to snow; there was a light dusting on the ground and ice patches on the pavement. The brothers communicated with each other in grunts of challenge or derision. The Hawk was the louder and the more skilled at the impromptu game. "Hey-*hey*!"—he kicked the flat stone so hard it ricocheted and caught his brother on the ankle; the Cheetah winced, then laughed. David was uncertain whether he should acknowledge watching the brothers or pretend not to see them; he continued along the edge of the pavement as if he had a destination and wasn't just walking to kill time, as the brothers were playing their aimless game to kill time. Out of the corner of his eye he saw the younger brother run to catch the skidding stone with his foot and give it a sidelong kick. There came the stone as if by magic, skittering in David's direction, so with a clumsy, eager kick he sent it spinning back toward the Cheetah, and with a haughty nod the Cheetah both acknowledged David's charitable gesture and dismissed it, sending the stone flying back toward his brother with renewed zest—"Hey-hey-*hey*!"

Elated, David walked on. The brothers continued their rough play behind him; he didn't give them a second glance.

19.

Tomorrow morning?

Something would be decided.

David's mother urged him and his sister to return to school for the afternoon at least. "Some semblance of a normal life"—but neither David nor his sister wanted a normal life right now. Their older brothers Pete and Billy were grimly waiting, too.

In the mirror-room 837, the Cheetah's father seemed little changed. The door was only partway closed, as if in the patient's stuporous state privacy made little difference. David passed on an errand, hoping he wouldn't be seen by anyone inside, and he wasn't.

The patient continued sleeping as before and several visitors were sitting about watching TV.

Entering the men's lavatory which he'd come to know in too much detail. And there at a sink, washing his hands, was the boy he'd remember for the rest of his life as the Cheetah.

Loud splashing water from the faucet, and anger in the very sound. The boy's eyelids looked inflamed as if with fever.

David halted just inside the door. He swallowed, embarrassed. The Cheetah was watching him in the mirror. David tried to show no emotion though a shock ran through him as if he'd carelessly touched an electric wire.

For the first time, the Cheetah smiled. His lips smiled. He was watching David in the mirror. "Somebody in your family sick, eh?" His voice was low and hoarse, almost inaudible.

David said, swallowing again, "Yes. My father."

The Cheetah nodded, drying his hands on a paper towel. "My father, too."

David said, "Something happened to my dad in the middle of the night. He hadn't ever had any heart trouble before. He couldn't breathe, his heart was racing. My mom called an ambulance. That was last week. They said, in the emergency room, my dad's heartbeat was two hundred twenty beats a minute."

"Je-sus." The Cheetah whistled, as if impressed. "I've been seeing you around here, it's shitty, eh? Y'want to go out back for a smoke?"

"—smoke?"

"Just hang out, then. Get out of this shitty place."

David smiled uncertainly. He heard himself say, "Okay."

On his way out of the lavatory the Cheetah cuffed David lightly on the shoulder as a big cat might, in play. He winked at David and drawled, showing the tip of his tongue between his lips. "O-*kay*. Out *back*."

When David left the lavatory, the Cheetah was nowhere in sight.

He returned to 833; his parents were expecting him. It was almost 6 P.M. when an orderly brought his dad a special-diet supper. He wasn't certain whether he was supposed to meet the Cheetah outside immediately, or another time. He kept glancing at the doorway when someone passed by. The network news came on TV. Every night that he'd been strong enough to sit up, Mr. Rainey watched the news. David's mother propped pillows behind him. He'd become one of those patients bent upon "cheering up" visitors. He was saying to David, "—should be in school, Davy, shouldn't you? Don't want to fall behind and I'm going to be fine in a day or two, you'll see." David said "I can't fall behind, Dad, it's like a Möbius strip. Anyway, it's after school now. See?—it's *dark*." He pointed toward the window at the rear of the room as if his father required proof. But his father was laughing, a dry, mirthless laugh, the remark about the Möbius strip was so clever. David reached for his jacket, laid over the back of a chair. His mother called after him but he didn't hear. He'd let forty minutes pass; he was in a desperate hurry.

20.

Where the brothers had been playing their rough game earlier that day, there were patches of ice treacherous underfoot. A boy who might've been the Cheetah signaled to David from the far side of the open space, near the parking garage. He walked rapidly away, turned, and beckoned to David mysteriously. They'd entered the parking garage at the rear. This was level A, now mostly deserted. The Cheetah was smoking a cigarette and trailing smoke over his shoulder, exhaling through his teeth. He held out a pack of cigarettes and David was about to stammer, "Thanks, but—I don't—" when he understood that he must accept the cigarette from his friend and learn to smoke it. He laughed, excited at the prospect. His hand reached out and the Cheetah's hooded eyes flashed and in that instant David was grabbed from behind, and his arms yanked painfully back. Someone had been waiting behind one of the posts. A tall, strong boy, of course it was the Cheetah's brother. David was too surprised to cry for help. He might have thought this was part of a game. He heard his cracked voice, "What?—what—" Already a flurry of hard blows like horses' hooves struck his chest, his stomach, his thighs. He fell, or was pushed. Sprawled on the gritty pavement. The Hawk stooped over him, his breath in short steaming pants. He punched and kicked him and spat in his face and the Cheetah, making a high, whimpering sound like a malicious child, stooped over him too, striking him with his fists, not so hard or with so much fury as his brother.

The beating was quick and cruel and could not have lasted more than two minutes. The Hawk kicked him in the groin, cursing, "Fucker! Little *fag*!" The Cheetah drew his foot back for another kick but changed his mind. He pulled his brother, "Hey, no more." He called the older boy by a name David couldn't recognize, a name whose syllables were foreign, but in fact David heard little, the terrible fiery pain in his groin, his eyes misted over in shock, there was a roaring like a waterfall in his ears. Yet he would always remember the Cheetah hesitating. He would see the Cheetah *not-kick*. That glisten of fierce happiness in the Hawk's face David would never forget; it would be one of the great riddles of his life even as he would cherish the gift of the Cheetah's withheld kick. For both brothers might have kicked and kicked, leaving him limp, broken, bleeding; they might have kicked him to death for that was within their power, yet they had not. The younger boy panted, "Hey, no *more*. C'mon."

The brothers walked swiftly away. David lay where he'd fallen. He was alone, dazed. Never such pain as the pain between his legs, yet he seemed to know it would pass, he wouldn't die, wouldn't even be crippled. Afterward he would realize that the brothers had deliberately spared his face. He wasn't bleeding, he'd have no visible marks.

Always, he'd be grateful for this.

HONOR CODE

1.

Seems like forever I was in love with my cousin Sonny Brandt, who was incarcerated in the Chautauqua County Youth Facility outside Chautauqua Falls, New York, from the age of sixteen to the age of twenty-one on a charge of manslaughter. You could say that my life as a girl was before-Sonny and after-Sonny. Before-*manslaughter* and after-*manslaughter*.

That word! One day it came into our lives.

Like *incarceration*. Another word that, once it comes into your life, the life of your family, is permanent.

No one says "incarcerate" except people who have to do with the prison system. "Manslaughter" is a word you hear more frequently, though most people, I think, don't know what it means.

"Manslaughter."

Those years I whispered this word aloud. Murmured this word like a precious obscenity. I loved the vibration in my jaws, my teeth clenched tight. "Man-slaughter." I felt the thrill of what Sonny had done, or what people claimed Sonny had done, reverberating in those syllables not to be spoken aloud in the presence of any of the relatives.

"Manslaughter" was more powerful than even "murder" for there was "man" and there was "slaughter" and the two jammed together were like music: the opening chord of an electric guitar, so deafening you feel it deep in the groin.

What Sonny did to a man who'd hurt my mother happened in December 1981, when I was eleven. A few years later my mother's older sister Agnes arranged for me to attend a private girls' school in Amherst, New York, where one day in music class our teacher happened to mention the title of a composition for piano—*Slaughter on Tenth Avenue*—and in that instant my jaw must have dropped, for a girl pointed at me, and laughed.

"Mickey is so weird isn't she!"

"Mickey is so funny."

"Mickey is funny-weird."

At the Amherst Academy for Girls I'd learned to laugh with my tormentors who were also my friends. Somehow I was special to them, like a handicapped dancer or athlete, you had to laugh at me yet with a look of tender exasperation. When I couldn't come up with a witty rejoinder, I made a face like a TV comedian. Any laughter generated by Mickey Stecke was going to be intentional.

"Hurry! No time to dawdle! This is an emergency."

It was Hurricane Charley in September 1980 that broke up our household in Herkimer, New York, and caused us to flee like wartime refugees. So Momma would say. That terrible time when within twenty-four hours every river, creek, and ditch in Herkimer County overflowed its banks and Bob Gleason's little shingleboard house on Half Moon Creek where we'd been living got flooded out: "Near-about swept away and all of us drowned."

Momma's voice quavered when she spoke of Hurricane Charley and all she'd had to leave behind but in fact she'd made her decision to leave Herkimer and Bob Gleason before the storm hit. Must've made up her mind watching TV weather news. This confused time in our lives when we'd been living with a man who was my brother Lyle's father, who was spending time away from the house after he and Momma had quarreled, and every time the phone rang it was Bob Gleason wanting to speak with Momma, and Momma was anxious about Bob Gleason returning, so one night she ran into Lyle's and my room excited saying there were "hurricane warnings" on TV for Herkimer County, we'd have to "evacuate" to save our lives. Already Momma was dragging a suitcase down from the attic. "You two! Help me with these damn bags." Momma had a way of keeping fear out of her voice by sounding as if she was scolding or teasing. It became a game to see how quickly we could pack Momma's old Chevy Impala in the driveway. Momma had just the one suitcase that was large, bulky, sand-colored, with not only buckles to snap shut but cord belts to fasten. She had cardboard boxes, bags from the grocery store, armloads of loose clothes carried to the car on hangers and dumped into the back. Already it was raining, hard.

Our destination was my aunt Georgia's house in Ransomville, three hundred miles to the west in the foothills of the Chautauqua Mountains, we'd last visited two summers ago.

I asked Momma if Aunt Georgia knew we were coming. Momma said sharply of course she knew. "Who you think I been on the phone with, all hours of the night? *Him?*"

Momma spoke contemptuously. I was to know who *him* was without her needing to explain.

When a man was over with, in Momma's life, immediately he became *him.* Whatever name he'd had, she'd once uttered in a soft-sliding voice, would not be spoken ever again.

*   *   *

"Pray to God, He will spare us."

It was a frantic drive on mostly country roads littered with fallen tree limbs. From time to time we encountered other vehicles, moving slowly, headlights shimmering in rain. Ditches were overflowing with mud-water and at every narrow bridge Momma had to slow our car to a crawl, whispering to herself. Where it was light enough we could see the terrifying sight of water rushing just a few inches below the bridge yet each time we were spared, the bridge wasn't washed away and all of us drowned. To drown out the noise of the wind, Momma played Johnny Cash tapes, loud. Johnny Cash was Momma's favorite singer, like her own daddy, she claimed, lost to her since she was twelve years old. In the backseat in a bed of wet, rumpled clothes Lyle fell asleep whimpering but I kept Momma company every mile of the way. Every hour of that night. I was Aimée then, not Mickey. I wasn't sorry to leave the shingleboard house on Half Moon Creek that was run-down and smelled of kerosene because Lyle's daddy was not my daddy and in Bob Gleason's eyes I could see no warmth for me, only for Lyle. Where my own daddy was, I had no idea. If my own daddy was alive, I had no idea. I had learned not to ask Momma who would say in disdain, "Him? Gone." From Momma I knew that a man could not be trusted except for a certain period of time and when that time was ending you had to act quickly before it was too late.

Through the night, the rain continued. In the morning there was no sunrise only a gradual lightening so you could begin to see the shapes of things along the road: mostly trees. Then I saw a shivery ray of light above the sawtooth mountains we were headed for, the sun flattened out sideways like a broken egg yolk, a smear of red-orange. "Momma, look!" And a while later Momma drove across the suspension bridge above the Chautauqua River at Ransomville and when at midpoint on the bridge we passed the sign CHAUTAUQUA COUNTY she began crying suddenly.

"No one can hurt us now."

◆ ◆ ◆

These words that came to be confused in my memory with Johnny
Cash's manly voice. *No one can hurt us now* the words to a song of surpassing beauty and hope that was interrupted by applause and whistles
from a vast anonymous audience. *No one can hurt us now* soothing as a
lullaby, you drift into sleep believing it must be true.

My aunt Georgia Brandt lived in a ramshackle farmhouse at the
edge of Ransomville. Of the original one hundred acres, only two or
three remained in the family. Georgia was not a farm woman but a cafeteria worker at the local hospital. She was a soft-fleshed fattish woman
in her late thirties, six years older than my mother, a widow who'd lost
her trucker husband in a disastrous accident on the New York Thruway
when her oldest child was in high school and her youngest, Sonny, was
five months old. Aunt Georgia had a way of hugging so vehemently it
took the breath out of you. Her kisses were like swipes with a coarse
damp sponge. She smelled of baking powder biscuits and cigarette
smoke. To keep from crying when she was in an emotional state Aunt
Georgia blurted out clumsy remarks meant to amuse, that had the sting
of insults. First thing she said to Momma when we came into her house
after our all-night drive was: "Jesus, Dev'a! Don't you and those kids
look like something the cat dragged out of the rain!"

If Sonny happened to overhear one of his mother's awkward at-
tempts at humor he was apt to call out, "Don't listen to Ma's bullshit,
she's drunk."

Aunt Georgia was a hive of fretful energy, humming and singing to
herself like a radio left on in an empty room. She watched late-night
TV, smoking while she knitted, did needlepoint, sewed quilts—"crazy
quilts" were her specialty. Some of these she sold through a women's
crafts co-op at a local mall, others she gave away. After her husband's fiery death she'd converted to evangelical Christianity and sang in a nasal,
wavering voice in the choir of the Ransomville Church of the Apostles.
She was brimming with prayer like a cup filled to the top, threatening

to spill. Even Sonny, at mealtimes, bowed his lips over his plate, clasped his restless hands and mumbled *Bless us O Lord and these thy gifts which we are about to receive through Christ-our-Lord AMEN.* My aunt Georgia was the second-oldest of the McClaren girls who'd grown up in Ransomville and had always been the heaviest. Devra was the youngest, prettiest, and thinnest—"Look at you," Georgia protested, "one of those 'an-rex-icks' you see on TV." In an upscale suburb of Cleveland, Ohio, lived the oldest McClaren sister, my aunt Agnes who was famous among the relatives for being "rich" and "stingy"—"snooty"—"cold-hearted." Agnes was the sole McClaren in any generation to have gone to college, acquiring a master's degree from the State University at Buffalo in something called developmental psychology; she'd married a well-to-do businessman whom few in the family had ever met. Agnes disapproved of her sisters' lives for being "messy"—"out of control"—and never returned to the Chautauqua Valley to visit. Nor did she encourage visits to Cleveland though she'd taken an interest, Momma reported, in me: "Aggie thinks you might take after her, you like books better than people."

I did not like books better than people. I was nothing like my aunt Agnes.

I hated Momma's brash way of talking, that my cousin Sonny Brandt might overhear.

First glimpse I had of Sonny that morning, he came outside in the rain to help us unload the car, insisted on carrying most of the things himself—"Y'all get inside, I can handle it." Sonny was just fifteen but looked and behaved years older. Next, Sonny gave up his room for Lyle and me: "It's nice'n cozy, see. Right over the furnace." The Brandts' house was so large, uninsulated, most of the second floor had to be shut up from November to April; the furnace was coal-burning, in a dank, earthen-floored cellar, and gave off wan gusts of heat through vents clogged with dust. Sonny was always doing some kindness like that, helping you with something you hadn't realized you needed help with. He was a tall, lanky-lean boy with pale ghost-blue eyes, said to resemble his dead father's. His eyebrows ran together over the bridge of his nose.

Already at fifteen he'd begun to wear out his forehead with frowning: one of those old-young people, could be male or female, Momma said, who take on too much worry early in life because others who are older don't take on enough.

Like his mother, Sonny was always busy. You could hear him humming and singing to himself, anywhere in the house. He slept now in a drafty room under the eaves, at the top of the stairs, and his footsteps on the stairs were thunderous. He had a way of flying down the stairs taking steps three or four at a time, slapping the wall with his left hand to keep his balance. He could run upstairs, too, in almost the same way. It was a sight to behold like an acrobat on TV but Aunt Georgia wasn't amused calling to him he was going to break his damn neck or worse yet the damn stairs. Sonny laughed, "Hey Ma: chill out."

Sonny was in tenth grade at Ransomville High but frequently out of school working part-time or pickup jobs (grocery bagger, snow removal, farmhand) or helping around the house where things were forever breaking down. The previous summer, Sonny had painted the front of the house and most of what you could see of the sides from the road but the color Georgia selected was an impractical cream-ivory that looked thin as whitewash on the rough boards and would have required a second coat. Sonny gave up, overwhelmed. If he'd had any brains, he said, he would've worked those weeks for a painting contractor, at least he'd have been paid.

Momma teased Sonny for being a "natural-born Good Samaritan" and Sonny said, scowling: "Natural-born asshole, you mean."

Lyle and I were crazy for our cousin like puppies yearning for attention, any kind of attention: teasing, swift hard tickles beneath the arms, attacks from behind. Sonny never hurt us, or rarely. He was sometimes clumsy, but never cruel. He was just under six feet, built like a whippet with shoulders and arms hard-muscled from outdoor work. His hair was the color of damp wheat and sprang straight from his head. By fifteen he had to shave every other day. His skin was often blemished and he wore grungy old jeans, T-shirts, sweatshirts yet girls called him on the phone after school, giggling and shameless. If Georgia happened to answer she spoke sharply, "No. My son is *not available.*" Sonny basked in the attention but couldn't be troubled to call any girls back. Still Georgia complained, "All that boy has got to do is get some silly girl pregnant. Wind up married, a daddy at sixteen."

A flush rose in Sonny's face if he happened to overhear. He hated to be teased about girls, or sex. Anything to do with sex.

"Chill out, Mom. Or I'm out of here."

One day, Sonny changed my name: he'd had enough of "Aimée," he said. Especially the way my mother wanted it pronounced: "Aim-ée."

" 'Mickey' kicks ass, see? 'Aimée' gets her ass kicked."

It was so! Clear as a column of numbers added up.

Sonny called Lyle "Big Boy." (Which was a sweet kind of teasing, since Lyle was small for his age at six.) Sometimes, Sonny called my brother "Lyle-y" if the mood between them was more serious.

Sonny had a formal way of addressing adults, you couldn't judge was respectful or mocking. He could provoke my aunt Georgia by referring to her as "ma'am" in the politest voice. In town, adults were "ma'am"—"sir"—"mister"—"missus." (Behind their backs, Sonny might have other, funnier names for them.) But he took care to call Momma "Aunt Devra" both to her face and to others. To Lyle and me he'd say, "Your Momma," in a serious voice. The way his eyes shrank from Momma, even when she was trying to joke with him, which was often, you could see he didn't know how to speak to her. Much of the time, he didn't speak. Though he did favors for Momma, constantly. Climbing up onto the roof to repair a drip in Momma's bedroom, changing a flat tire on Momma's car, taking a day off from school to drive Momma to Chautauqua Falls seventy miles away. (Sonny had a driver's permit which allowed him to drive any vehicle so long as a licensed driver was with him. What Momma was doing in Chautauqua Falls wasn't for us to know. She would claim she "had business" which might mean she was interviewing for a job, looking for a new place to live or contacting a friend. So much of Momma's life was secret, her own children wouldn't know what she'd been planning until she sprang the surprise on us like something on daytime TV.) When Momma tried to thank Sonny for some kindness of his he'd squirm with embarrassment and scowl, mumbling *O.K., Aunt Devra* or *Well, hell* and make his escape, fast. Momma hid her exasperation beneath praise, telling Georgia her son was the shyest boy—"For somebody growing up to look like Sonny is going to look."

Georgia said defiantly, "I hope to God he stays that way."

A few months in Ransomville, we'd begun to forget Herkimer. The shingleboard house on Half Moon Creek we'd almost come to believe, as Momma said, had been flooded and swept away by Hurricane Charley. The glowering man who wasn't my daddy and had no wish to pretend he was. Now I was Mickey and not Aimée, I behaved with more confidence. I became brash, reckless. I infuriated my aunt and my mother by careening around the house at high speed, taking the stairs from the second floor two and three at a time, slapping my hand against the wall for balance. (Unlike Sonny, I sometimes missed a step and fell, hard. Skidding down the remainder of the stairs to lie in a crumpled heap at the bottom. The pain made me whimper but embarrassment was worse, if anyone happened to have noticed.) Another roughhouse game if you could call it a game was running and sliding along the hall on my aunt's "throw rugs"; Lyle imitated me, in a shrieking version of bumper cars. When Momma was home she scolded and slapped at me—"Aimée! You're too old for such behavior"—but more and more, Momma wasn't home.

Aunt Georgia's was the kind of household where a single bathroom had to suffice for everyone and the hot water heater was quickly depleted. The kind of household where a shower, a bath, was an occasion. I hid in wait to catch a glimpse of Sonny hurrying into the bathroom barefoot, bare-chested and in beltless trousers, pajama bottoms, or white Jockey shorts dingy from many launderings, quick to shut the door behind him and latch it. Slyly I would draw near to hear him whistling inside as he ran water from the rusty old faucets, flushed the toilet, showered. I drew Lyle into teasing Sonny with me, rapping on the bathroom door when Sonny was inside, managing to jiggle the latch-lock open and reaching inside to switch off the light, to provoke our cousin into shouting, "Put that light back on! God *damn!*" More daring, we crept into the steamy bathroom when Sonny was showering, pushed aside the shower curtain so that I could spray Sonny with shaving cream from his aerosol can, all the while shrieking with laughter like a cat being killed. Nothing was more hilarious than Sonny flailing at us, streaming water, trying to grab the shaving cream can out of my hand. Once or twice I caught a glimpse of Sonny's penis swinging loose, limp and seeming not much longer than his longest finger, innocent-looking as a red rubber toy between his narrow hips. In his rage, Sonny wouldn't trouble to wrap a towel around his waist. The sight of my cousin's penis did not upset or alarm me. If I'd been asked I might have said *Anything that is Sonny's, anything to do with Sonny, could never cause me harm.*

Furious and flushed with indignation, Sonny lunged from the dripping shower stall to shove Lyle and me out of the bathroom with his wet hands, and shut the door behind us, hard.

"Damn brats!"

Of course, Sonny would exact his revenge. If not immediately, in time. Somewhere, somehow. We would not know when. We trembled in anticipation, not knowing when.

It would be years before I glimpsed another penis on another young male. And more years before I saw an erect penis. In my naïveté taking for granted that adult men looked like my boy cousin surprised naked in the shower. In my naïveté taking for granted that, like my protective boy cousin, no man would truly wish to harm me.

That environment my aunt Agnes would say, after Sonny was arrested. *Those people, that way of life* my aunt would speak in disgust as if any sensible person would agree with her. And I would want to protest

It wasn't like that! I would want to say *I loved them, we were happy there, you don't understand.*

"If I could trust you, Dev'a. My mind would be more at peace."

It was difficult to interpret my aunt Georgia's tone of voice when she spoke like this to Momma. She didn't seem to be scolding or sarcastic. She didn't sound reproachful. She laughed, and she sighed. (Fattish people sighed a lot, I knew. Like they were made of rubber pumped up like a balloon and when they felt sad, air leaked out more noticeably than it did with thinner people.) The way Momma murmured in reply as if she was too much in a hurry to be angry, "Georgia, you can trust me! I'm an adult woman," I understood my aunt and Momma had had this conversation before and that, on her way out of the house, Momma would pause to kiss Georgia's cheek, squeeze her hand and say, in her taunting-teasing way, "And you can mind your own business, Georgia. Any time you want us out, we're out."

This hurt my aunt, I knew. (It hurt me, overhearing. Momma was so careless in her words slashing like blades.) So Georgia would say no she didn't mean that, didn't want that, Momma had to know she didn't want that.

Through the winter and into January 1981, Momma sold perfume in a department store at the mall. Then, Momma was "hostess" in a restaurant owned by a new friend of hers. Then, Momma was "receptionist" at Herlihy's Realtors whose glaring yellow and black signs were everywhere in Chautauqua County, and Mr. Herlihy (who drove a showy bronze-blond Porsche) was Momma's new friend.

It seemed that every few days, a new friend called Momma. Male voices asking to speak with "Devra Stecke" but Momma wasn't usually home. Some of the men left names and telephone numbers, others did not. Some of the men my aunt Georgia knew, or claimed to know, others she did not. This was an "old pattern" repeating itself, Georgia said. Complaining to anyone who would listen how her younger sister who'd already had such turmoil in her personal life was "growing apart" from her—"growing estranged"—"secretive"—and this was a signal of trouble to come.

Sonny roiled his mother by saying, in the way you'd explain something to a slow-witted child, "Ma, the fact is: Aunt Devra has got her own life. Aunt Devra ain't *you*."

The plan had been that Momma, Lyle, and I would live with my aunt Georgia only for as long as Momma needed to get a job in Ransomville, find a decent place for us to live, but months passed, and Momma was too busy to think about moving, and Georgia assured her there was no hurry about moving out, there was plenty of room in the house. My aunt's daughters were grown, married, separated or divorced, and dropped by the house with their noisy children at all times, especially when they wanted favors from their mother, but Georgia liked the feel of a family living together day to day. "Like, when you wake up in the morning, you know who you'll be making breakfast for. Who you can rely upon."

It began to be that Momma "worked late" several nights a week at Herlihy Realtors. Or maybe, after the office closed, Momma had other engagements. (Swimming laps at the Y? Taking a course in computers at the community college? Meeting with friends at the County Line Café?) If Momma wasn't back home by 7 P.M. we could expect a hurried call telling us not to wait supper for her, and not to keep food warm in the oven for her. Maybe Momma would be home by midnight, maybe later. (Once, our school bus headed for town passed Momma's car on the road, headed home at 7:45 A.M. I shrank from the window trying not to notice and wondered if my little brother at the front of the bus was trying not to notice, too.) In winter months when we came home from school, ran up the snowy driveway to the old farmhouse so weirdly, thinly painted looking in twilight like a ghost-house, sometimes only our aunt Georgia would be home to call out, "Hi, kids!" Georgia would be changed from her cafeteria uniform into sweatpants and pullover sweater, in stocking feet padding about the kitchen preparing supper (Georgia's specialties were hot-spice chili with ground chuck, spaghetti and meatballs, tuna-cheese-rice casserole with a glaze of potato chip crumbs); or, having lost track of the time, sitting in her recliner in the living room watching late-afternoon TV soaps, smoking Marlboros and rapidly sewing, without needing to watch her fingers, one of her crazy quilts—"Look at this! How it came to be so big, I don't know. Damn thing has a mind of its own."

Georgia tried to teach me quilting, but I hadn't enough patience to sit still. Since I'd become Mickey, not Aimée, seemed like tiny red ants were crawling over me, couldn't stay in one place for more than a few minutes. Momma said it would be good for me to learn some practical skill, but why'd I want to learn quilting, when Momma hadn't the slightest interest in it herself?

Georgia Brandt's quilts were famous locally. She'd made quilts for every relative of hers, neighbors, friends, friends-of-friends. For people she scarcely knew but admired. Georgia's most spectacular quilts sold for two hundred dollars at the women's co-op. She was modest about her skills ("I'm like the momma cat that's had so many kittens, she's lost count") and scowled like Sonny if you tried to compliment her. It was difficult to describe one of Georgia's quilts for if your first impression was that the quilt was beautiful, the closer you looked the more doubtful you became. For there was no way to see the quilt in its entirety, only just in parts, square by square. And the squares did not match, did not form a "pattern." Or anyway not a "pattern" you could see. Not only did Georgia use mismatched colors and prints but every kind of fabrics: cotton, wool, satin, silk, taffeta, velvet, lace. Some quilts glittered with sequins or seed pearls scattered like constellations in the sky. Georgia said she could see a quilt in her mind's eye taking form as she sewed it better than she could see a quilt when it was spread out on the floor. A "crazy" quilt grew by some mysterious logic, moving through Georgia's fingers, grew and grew until finally it stopped growing.

People asked my aunt how she knew when a quilt was finished and Georgia said, "Hell, I don't ever know. I just stop."

＊ ＊ ＊

May 1981 my cousin Sonny turned sixteen: bought a car, quit high school, got a job with a tree service crew.

Aunt Georgia had begged him not to quit school, but Sonny wouldn't listen. He'd had enough of sitting at desks, playing like he was a young kid when he wasn't, in his heart. The tree service job paid almost twice what he'd been making working part-time and he was proud to hand over half of his earnings to Georgia.

Georgia wept, but took the money. Sonny would do what he wanted to do, like her deceased husband. "Now I got to pray you don't kill yourself, too." We picked up the way Georgia's voice dipped on *you*.

Sonny, the youngest member of the tree service crew, soon became the daredevil. The one to volunteer to climb one hundred feet wielding a chain saw when others held back. The one to work in dangerous conditions. The one to be depended upon to finish a job even in pelting rain, without complaining. He liked the grudging admiration of the other men some of whom became his friends and some of whom hated his guts for being the good-looking brash kid who clambered into trees listening to rock music on his Walkman and was still fearless as most of them had been fearless at one time, if no longer. "Hey Brandt: you up for this?" It was a thrill to hear the foreman yelling at him, singling him out for attention.

Sure, Sonny wore safety gloves, goggles, work boots with reinforced toes. Sure, Sonny insisted to Georgia and to Momma, he never took chances and didn't let the damn foreman "exploit" him. Yet somehow his hands became covered in nicks, scratches, scars. His face looked perpetually sunburnt. His backbone ached, his muscles ached, his pale-blue eyes were often threaded with blood and his head rang with the deafening whine of saws that, on the job, penetrated his so-called ear protectors. Away from a work site, Sonny still twitched with vibrations running through his lean body like electric charges. One evening he came home limping, and Georgia made him take off his shoe and sock to reveal a big toenail the hue of a rotted plum, swollen with blood from beneath. Momma cried, "Oh, sweetie! We're going to take you to a doctor."

Sonny waved her off with a scowl. Like hell he was going to a doctor for something so trivial.

Drinking, the men were apt to get into fights. With men they met in bars, or with one another. Sonny was an accidental witness to an incident that might have turned fatal: one of his buddies slammed another man (who'd allegedly insulted him) against a brick wall so hard his head made a cracking sound before his legs buckled beneath him and he fell, unconscious. (No one called an ambulance. No one called police. Eventually, the fallen man was roused to a kind of consciousness and taken home by his friends.) On the job, Sonny tried to keep out of the way of the meanest men, who'd been working for the tree service too many years, yet once, in the heat of midsummer, one of these men took exception to a remark of Sonny's, or a way in which, hoping to deflect sarcasm with a grin, Sonny responded, and before he could raise his arms to protect himself he was being hit, pummeled, knocked off his feet. His assailant cursed him, kicked him with steel-toed boots and had to be pulled away from him by others who seemed to think that the incident was amusing. Sonny was shocked, thought of quitting, but how'd he quit, where'd he work and make as much money as he made with the crew, so he reported back next morning limping, favoring his right leg that was badly bruised from being kicked, a nasty cut beneath his left eye, face still swollen but Sonny shrugged it off saying, as he'd said to his mother and his aunt Devra, "No big deal, O.K.?"

We began to notice, Sonny was getting mean. He was short-tempered with his mother, even with his aunt Devra. The kinds of silly jokes Lyle and I had played with him only a few months before just seemed to annoy Sonny now. One evening Lyle crept up on Sonny sprawled on the sofa, drinking a beer and clicking through TV stations with the remote control, and Sonny told him, "Fuck off." His voice was flat and tired. He wasn't smiling. His jaws were bristling with dark stubble and his T-shirt was stained with sweat. Whatever was on TV, he stared at without seeming to see. Compulsively he poked and prodded a tooth in his lower jaw, that seemed to be loose.

Poor Lyle! My brother crept away wounded. He would never approach Sonny again in such a way.

I knew better than to tease Sonny in such a mood for he didn't seem to like me much any longer, either. *I hate you! I don't love you. Fall out of some damn tree and break your damn neck, see if I give a damn.*

These brash-Mickey words I whispered aloud, barefoot on the stairs a few yards away. Where I could watch my boy cousin through the doorway, slumped on the sofa poking at a tooth in his lower jaw.

In the fall, Momma had her hair trimmed in a feathery cut that floated around her face and made her eyes, warm liquidy brown, look enlarged. She was living her secret life that left her moody and distracted vehemently shaking her head when the phone rang and it was for her and whoever wanted to speak with her left no name and number only just the terse message *She'll know who it is, tell her call back.*

She was still working at Herlihy Realtors. Unless she'd quit the job at Herlihy Realtors. Maybe she'd been fired by Mr. Herlihy? Or she'd quit and Mr. Herlihy had talked her into returning but then after an exchange she'd been fired, or she'd quit for a second, final time? Maybe there'd been a scene of Momma and her employer Mr. Herlihy in the office after hours when everyone else had departed, when the front lights of HERLIHY REALTORS had been switched off, and Momma was upset, Momma swiped at her eyes that were beginning to streak with mascara, Momma turned to walk away but Mr. Herlihy grabbed her shoulder, spun her back to face him and struck her with the flat of his hand in her pretty crimson mouth that had opened in protest.

And maybe there'd been a confused scene of Momma desperately pushing through the rear exit of Herlihy Realtors, blood streaming from a two-inch gash in her lower lip, Momma running and stumbling in high-heeled shoes to get to her car before the man pursuing her, panting and excited, could catch up with her.

Maybe this man had pleaded *Devra! Jesus I'm so sorry! You know I didn't mean it.*

Or maybe this man had said, furiously, snatching again at Momma's shoulder *Don't you walk away from me, bitch! Don't you turn your back on me.*

It was 9:50 P.M., a weekday night in December 1981. Aunt Georgia picked up the ringing phone already pissed at whoever was calling at this hour of the evening (knowing the call wouldn't be for her but for her sister Devra who'd been hiding away in her room for the past several days refusing to talk to anyone even Georgia, even through the door, or her son Sonny who'd been out late every night that week) and a voice was notifying her that it was the Chautauqua County sheriff's office for Mrs. Georgia Brandt informing her that her sixteen-year-old son, Sean, Jr., resident of 2881 Summit Hill Road, was in custody at headquarters on a charge of aggravated assault. It seemed that Sonny had confronted Mr. Herlihy of Herlihy Realtors in the parking lot behind his office earlier that evening, they'd begun arguing and Sonny had struck Herlihy with a tire iron, beating him unconscious. Georgia was being asked to come to headquarters as soon as possible.

Aunt Georgia was stunned as if she'd been struck by a tire iron herself. She'd had to ask the caller to repeat what he'd said. She would tell us afterward how her knees had gone weak as water, she'd broken into a cold sweat in that instant groping for somewhere to sit before she fainted. She would say afterward, over the years, how that call was the second terrible call to come to her on that very phone: "Like lightning striking twice, the same place. Like God was playing a joke on me He hadn't already struck such a blow, and didn't owe me another."

Sonny would say *Well, hell.*

Sonny would swipe his hand across his twitchy face, he'd have to agree *Some kind of joke, like. How things turn out.*

Cupping a hand to his ear, his left ear where the hearing had been impaired following a beating (fellow inmates at the detention center? guards?) he refused to speak of, refused to allow Georgia to report saying *You want them to kill me, next time? Chill out, Ma.*

Each time we saw him, he was less Sonny and more somebody else we didn't know. In the orange jumpsuit printed in black CHAU CO DE-TENTION on the back, drooping from his shoulders and the trouser legs so long, he'd had to roll up the cuffs. The guards called him kid. There was a feeling, we'd wished to think, that people liked him, Sonny wasn't any natural-born killer type, not a mean bone in that boy's body my aunt Georgia pleaded to anyone who'd listen. If only Mr. Herlihy hadn't died.

I only just hate that man worse, God forgive me.

Georgia made us come with her to church. Not Momma (you couldn't get Momma to step inside that holy-roller Church of the Apostles, Momma proclaimed) but Lyle and me. *Pray for your cousin Sonny, may Jesus spare us all.*

I wrote to Sonny, saying how I missed him. How we all missed him. We missed him *so!* But Sonny never answered, not once.

Aunt Georgia said Sonny meant to answer, but was busy. You wouldn't believe how they keep them busy at that damn place.

Momma said maybe Sonny didn't "write so good." Maybe Sonny hadn't paid much attention at school when writing was taught, maybe that was it. So he wouldn't want to show how like a little kid he'd write, that other people might laugh at.

Laugh at Sonny! I was shocked at such a thought. I could not believe that Momma would say such a thing.

Still, I loved Sonny. My heart was broken like some cheap plastic thing, that cracks when you just drop it on the floor.

2 .

"Aimée."

Mrs. Peale's voice was low and urgent. My heart kicked in my chest.

I saw a look in the woman's eyes warning *Take care! You are a very reckless girl.* Later, more calmly I would realize that Mrs. Peale could not have been thinking such a thought for Mrs. Peale could not have known why the dean of students had asked her to pass along the pink slip to me, discreetly folded in two and pressed into my hand at the end of music class.

My trembling hand. My guilty hand. My tomboy-with-bitten-fingernails-hand.

It was a rainy afternoon in October 1986. I was sixteen, a junior at the Amherst Academy for Girls. I had been a student here, a boarder, since September 1984. Yet I did not feel "at home" here. I did not feel comfortable here. I had made a decision the previous day and this summons from the dean of students was in response to that decision I could not now revoke though possibly it was a mistake though I did not regret having made it, even if it would turn out to be a mistake. All day I'd dreaded this summons from the dean. In my fantasies of exposure and embarrassment I'd imagined that my name would be sounded over the school's loudspeaker system in one of those jarring announcements made from time to time during the school day but in fact the summons, now that it had arrived, was handwritten, terse:

> Aimée Stecke
> Come promtly to my office end of 5th period.
> M. V. Chawdrey, Dean of Students

This was funny! *Promtly.*

My first instinct was to crumple the note in my hand and shove it into a pocket of my blazer before anyone saw it, but a bolder instinct caused me to laugh, and saunter toward the door with other girls as if nothing was wrong. I showed the note to Brooke Glover whom I always wanted to make laugh, or smile, or take notice of me in some distinctive way, but my bravado fell flat when Brooke, who'd wanted to leave the room with other friends, only frowned at the dean's note with a look of baffled impatience, like one forced to contemplate an obscure cartoon.

That Dean Chawdrey had misspelled *promptly* made no impression on Brooke for whom spelling was a casual matter. She'd misunderstood my motive in showing her the note, made a gesture of sympathy with her mouth, murmured, "Poor you," and turned away.

Now I did crumple the incriminating note and shove it into my pocket. My face pounded with blood. A terrible buzzing had begun in my head like the sound of flies cocooned inside a wall in winter. I left Mrs. Peale's classroom hurriedly, looking at no one.

Well, hell.

To get you out of that environment. Away from those people, that way of life. My aunt Agnes had come for me, to save me. Her expression had been frowning and fastidious as if she smelled something nasty but was too well-mannered to acknowledge it. Aunt Agnes refused to discuss Sonny with Georgia, though Sonny was her nephew. She refused to hear what Momma had to say about the situation. Yes it was tragic, it was very sad, but Agnes had come to Ransomville to rescue me. She would arrange for me to attend a girls' boarding school in a Buffalo suburb, a "prestigious" private school she knew of since her college roommate had graduated from the Amherst Academy and was now an alumni officer. She would arrange for me to transfer from Ransomville High School as quickly as possible. At the time, I was fourteen. I was ready to leave Ransomville. Momma had accused her oldest sister *You want to steal my daughter! You never had a baby of your own* but Agnes refused to be drawn into a quarrel nor would I quarrel with my mother who'd been drinking and who when she drank said wild hurtful stupid things you did not wish to hear let alone dignify by replying *Momma you're drunk, leave me alone. Haven't you hurt us all enough now leave us alone.*

At this time Sonny was gone from Ransomville. There was shame and hurt in his wake. There was no happiness in the old farmhouse on Summit Hill Road. No happiness without Sonny in that house he'd started to paint a luminous cream-ivory that glowered at dusk. Sonny was "incarcerated" in the ugly barracks of the Chautauqua County Youth facility north of Chautauqua Falls and he would not be discharged from that facility until his twenty-first birthday at which time he would be released on probationary terms. I had not seen Sonny in some time. I still wrote to Sonny, mostly I sent him cards meant to cheer him up, but I had not seen Sonny in some time and from my aunt Georgia the news I heard of Sonny was not good. *Like he doesn't know me sometimes. Doesn't want me to touch him. Like my son is gone and somebody I don't know has taken his place.*

When Sonny was first arrested, after Mr. Herlihy was hospitalized in critical condition, the charge was aggravated assault. He'd told police that he had only been defending himself, that Herlihy had rushed at him, attacked him. He had never denied that he'd struck Herlihy with the tire iron. But when Herlihy died after eleven days on life support without regaining consciousness the charge was raised to second-degree murder and Chautauqua County prosecutors moved to try Sonny as an adult facing a possible sentence of life imprisonment.

At this time, we'd had to leave my aunt's house. Momma had had to move us to live in a run-down furnished apartment in town for she and Georgia could not speak to each other in the old way any longer, all that was finished. Always there was the shadow of what Sonny had done for Momma's sake, that Georgia could not bear. There was no way to undo it, Momma acknowledged. Her voice quavered when she uttered Sonny's name. Her eyes were swollen and reddened from weeping. When Georgia screamed at her in loathing, Momma could not defend herself. She spoke with the police. She spoke with the prosecutors and with the judge hearing Sonny's case. She pleaded on Sonny's behalf. She blamed herself for what he'd done. (She had not asked him to intervene with Mr. Herlihy, Momma insisted. Though she had allowed him to see her bruised face, her cut lip. She'd told him how frightened she was of Herlihy, the threats he'd made.) Momma testified that her nephew had acted out of emotion, to protect her; he'd had no personal motive for approaching Herlihy. He had never seen, never spoken with Herlihy before that evening. Sonny was a boy who'd grown up too fast, Momma said. He'd quit school to work and help support his family. He'd taken on the responsibilities of an adult man and so he'd acted to protect a member of his family, as an adult man would do. Others testified on Sonny's behalf as well. Authorities were persuaded to believe that the killing was a "tragic accident" and Sonny was allowed to plead guilty to voluntary manslaughter as a minor, not as an adult, which meant incarceration in a youth facility and not in a nightmare maximum security prison like Attica.

Lucky bastard it was said of Sonny in some quarters. His tree service buddies seemed to feel he'd gotten off lightly: less than five years for breaking a man's head with a tire iron when not so long ago in Chautauqua County, as in any county in New York State, the kid might've been sentenced to die in the electric chair.

At the Amherst Academy where I was one of a half-dozen scholarship students out of approximately three hundred girls, I would speak only guardedly of my family back in Ransomville. Now my mother had married a man I scarcely knew. Now my aunt Georgia had sold the farmhouse and was living with one of her married daughters. In this place where talk was obsessively of boys I would not confess *I'm in love with my cousin who is five years older than me. My cousin who killed a man when he was sixteen.* Never would I break suddenly into tears to the astonishment of my friends *I am so lonely here where I want to be happy, where I am meant to be happy because my life has been saved.*

Three days of rain and the grounds of the Amherst Academy for Girls were sodden and treacherous underfoot as quicksand. Where there were paths across lawns and not paved walks hay had been strewn for us to tramp on. Soon most of the lovely-smelling hay became sodden too, and oozed mud of a hue and texture like diarrhea and this terrible muck we were scolded for tracking into buildings, classrooms. We were made to kick off our boots just inside the doors and in our stocking feet we skidded about on the polished floors like deranged children, squealing with laughter.

I was Mickey, skidding about. My laughter was shrill and breathless even when a husky girl athlete, a star on the field hockey team, collided with me hard enough to knock me down.

"Mickey, hey! Didn't see you there."

I had friends at the Amherst Academy, I could count on the fingers of both hands. Sometimes, in that hazy penumbra between sleep and wakefulness, in my bed in the residence hall, I named these friends as if defying Momma. *See! I can live away from you. I can live different from you.* Some of the girls at the Academy did not board in the residence hall but lived in the vicinity, in large, beautiful homes to which I was sometimes invited for dinner and to sleep over. And at Thanksgiving, even for a few days at Christmas. After my first year at the Academy, my grades were high enough for me to receive a tuition scholarship so now my aunt Agnes paid just my room, board, expenses. It was strange to me, that my aunt seemed to care for me. That my aunt came from Cleveland to Amherst to visit with me. That my aunt was eager to meet my roommates, my friends. That my aunt did not ask about Momma, or Lyle. My aunt did not ask about Georgia, or Sonny. Not a word about Sonny! *You are the one I take pride in, Aimée. The only one.*

Aunt Agnes was a slender quivery woman in her early forties. She did not much resemble her younger sisters in her appearance or in her manner of speaking. Her face was thin, heated, vivacious. Her teeth were small, like a child's teeth, and looked crowded in her mouth that was always smiling, or about to smile. Where Momma would have been awkward and defensive meeting my teachers, having to say quickly that she "never was very good" at school, my aunt smiled and shook hands and was perfectly at ease.

At the Academy, it may have been assumed by girls who didn't know me that Agnes was my mother.

Even those girls to whom I'd introduced my aunt seemed to hear me wrong and would speak afterward of "your mother": "Your mother looks just like you, Mickey"—"Your mother is really nice."

My mother is a beautiful woman, nothing like me. My mother is a slut.

My first few months at the Academy, I'd been homesick and angry and took the stairs to the dining hall two or three at a time slapping my hand against the wall for balance not giving a damn if I slipped, fell and broke my neck. I'd glowered, glared. I was so shy I'd have liked to shrivel into a ball like an inchworm in the hot sun yet there I was waving my fist of a hand, eager to be called upon.

I was Mickey not Aimée. Fuck Aimée!

I tried out for the track team but ran too fast, couldn't hold back and so became winded, panting through my mouth. Staggering with sharp pains in my side. I helped other girls with their papers though such help was forbidden by the honor code we'd solemnly vowed to uphold. I said outrageous things, scandalizing my roommate Anne-Marie Krimble confiding in her that I didn't have a father like everyone else: "I was conceived in a test tube."

Anne-Marie's mouth dropped softly. She stared at me in disbelief. "Mickey, you were not."

"*In vitro* it's called. My mother's 'egg' was siphoned from her and mixed with sperm from a 'donor male,' shaken in a test tube the way you shake a cocktail."

"Mickey, that did not happen! That is gross."

Anne-Marie had taken a step back from me, uncertainly. I was laughing in the way my cousin Sonny Brandt used to laugh, once he'd gotten us to believe something far-fetched. "*In vivo*, that's you: born in an actual body. But not me."

Tales quickly spread of Mickey Stecke who said the most outrageous things. But mostly funny, to make her friends laugh.

"These are very serious charges, Aimée."

Aimée. In the Dean's flat, nasal voice, the pretentious name sounded like accusation.

Dean Chawdrey was peering at me over the tops of her rimless bifocal glasses. In her hand she held the neatly typed letter I'd sent to her the previous day. I was sitting in a chair facing her across the span of her desk, in my damp rumpled raincoat. I heard myself murmur almost inaudibly, "Yes ma'am."

"You saw, you say, 'someone cheating' last week at midterms. Who is this 'someone,' Aimée? You will have to tell me."

M. V. Chawdrey was a frowning woman in her early fifties, as solidly fleshy as my aunt Georgia but her skin wasn't warmly rosy like my aunt's skin but had a look of something drained, that would be cold to the touch. Her mouth was small, bite-sized. Her eyes were distrustful. It was rare that an adult allowed dislike to show so transparently in her face.

"Aimée? Their names."

I sat miserable and mute. I could see the faces of the girls, some of whom were my friends, or would have believed themselves my friends as I would have liked to think of them as my friends. I could see even the expressions on their faces, but I could not name them.

Of course, I'd known beforehand that I could not. Yet I'd had to report them. It was the phenomenon of cheating I'd had to report, that was so upsetting.

At the Amherst Academy much was made of the tradition of the honor code. Every student signed a pledge to uphold this "sacred trust"—"priceless legacy." The honor code was a distinction, we were repeatedly told, that set the Amherst Academy apart from most private schools and all public schools. On the final page of each exam and paper you were required to say *I hereby confirm that this work submitted under my name is wholly and uniquely my own.* You signed and dated this. But the honor code was more than only just not cheating, you were pledged also to report others' cheating, and that was the dilemma.

Punishments for cheating ranged from probation, suspension from school, outright expulsion. Punishments for failing to report cheating were identical.

Who would know, who could prove. You have only to say nothing.

I knew this, of course. But I was angry and disgusted, too. If I did not want to cheat, I would be at a disadvantage when so many others were cheating. My heart beat in childish indignation *It isn't fair!* It wasn't just incidental cheating, a girl glancing over at another girl's exam paper, two girls whispering together at the back of a room. Not just the usual help girls gave one another, proofreading papers, pointing out obvious mistakes. This was systematic cheating, blatant cheating. Especially in science classes taught by an affable distracted man named Werth where notes and even pages ripped from textbooks were smuggled into the exam room, and grades were uniformly A's and B's. In English and history it had become commonplace for students to plagiarize by photocopying material from the periodicals library at the University of Buffalo that was within walking distance of the Amherst Academy. Our teachers seemed not to know, unless they'd given up caring. It was easier to give high grades. It was easier to avoid confrontations. "Well, Mickey: I know I can trust you," Mrs. Peale had said once, mysteriously. The emphasis on *you* had felt like a nudge in the ribs, painful though meant to be affectionate.

My first few months at the Academy, eager to be liked, I'd helped girls with homework and papers but I'd never actually written any part of any paper. I'd wanted to think of what I did as a kind of teaching. *This isn't cheating. This is helping.* Uneasily I remembered how at freshman orientation questions had been put to the Dean of Students about the honor code, those questions Dean Chawdrey had answered year following year with her so-serious expression *Yes it is as much a violation of the honor code to fail to report cheating as to cheat. Yes!* A ripple of dismay had passed through the gathering of first-year students and their parents, crowded into pine pews in the school chapel. Aunt Agnes had accompanied me and now she murmured in my ear *Remember what that woman is saying, Aimée. She is absolutely right.*

I felt a stab of guilt, thinking of my aunt. Agnes had such hopes for me, her "favorite" niece! She wanted to be proud of me. She wanted to think that her effort on my behalf was not in vain. I seemed to know that what I was doing would hurt Agnes, as it would hurt me.

For nights I'd lain awake in a misery of indecision wondering what to do. In Ransomville, nothing like this could ever have happened. In Ransomville public schools there was no "honor code" and in fact there hadn't been much cheating, that I had known of. Few students continued on to college, high grades were not an issue. Here, I'd come to think, in my anxiety, that our teachers had to know of the widespread cheating and were amused that girls like me, who never cheated, were too cowardly to come forward.

The irony was, I wasn't so moral—so "good"—that I couldn't cheat like the others. And more cleverly than the others. But something in me resisted the impulse to follow the others who were crass and careless in their cheating. *I am not one of you. I am superior to you.* Finally, I'd written to the dean of students a brief letter of only a few sentences and I'd mailed the letter in a stamped envelope. Even as I wrote the letter I understood that I was making a mistake and yet I'd had no choice.

I thought of my cousin Sonny whom I loved. Whom I had not now seen in years. My boy cousin who'd been beaten in the youth facility yet refused to report the beatings out of what code of honor or fear of reprisal, I didn't know. I thought of Sonny who'd killed a man out of another sort of honor, to protect my mother. Sonny had not needed to think, he'd only acted. He had traded his life for Momma's, by that action. But he'd had no choice.

Dean Chawdrey persisted, "*Who* was cheating, Aimée? You've done the right thing to report it but now you must tell me who the girl is."

The girl! I wanted to laugh in the dean's face, that she should imagine only one cheater at midterms.

I mumbled, ". . . can't."

"What do you mean, 'can't'? Or 'won't'?"

I sat silent, clasping my hands in my lap. Mickey Stecke had bitten fingernails, cuticles ridged with blood. One of my roommates had tried to manicure my nails, painted them passionflower purple, as a kind of joke, I'd supposed. Remnants of the nail polish could still be detected if you looked closely enough.

"What was your motive, then, Aimée, for writing to me? To report that 'someone was cheating' at midterms but to be purposefully vague about who? I've looked into your schedule. Perhaps I can assume that the alleged 'cheating' occurred during Mr. Werth's biology midterm, last Friday morning? Is this so?"

Yes. It was so. By my sick, guilty look, Dean Chawdrey understood my meaning.

"I hope, Aimée, that there is merit to this? I hope that you are not making a false report, Aimée, to revenge yourself upon a friend?"

I was shocked. I shook my head. "No . . ."

"Or is there more than one girl? More than one of your 'friends' involved?"

I opened my mouth to speak, but could not. The buzzing in my head had become frantic. I wondered if a blood vessel in my brain might burst. I was frightened recalling how my aunt Georgia had described finding an elderly relative seated in a chair in his home, in front of his TV, dead of a cerebral hemorrhage, blood "leaking" out of one ear.

"Aimée, will you look at me, please! It is very rude, your way of behaving. By this time, you must certainly know better."

Through the buzzing in my head I heard the Dean chide me for my "mysterious subterfuge." Wondering at my "motive" in writing to her. If I refused to be more forthcoming, how was the Academy's honor code upheld? "I wonder if, in your mutinous way, you are not making a mockery of our tradition. This, perhaps, was your intention all along."

At this, I tried to protest. My voice was shocked, hushed. In classes, as Mickey Stecke, I was a girl whose shyness erupted into bursts of speech and animation. I was smart, and I was funny. My teachers liked me, I think. I was brash and witty and willing to be laughed at, but not rebellious or hostile; no one would have called me "mutinous"; I did not challenge the authority of my teachers for I required them desperately, I adored my teachers who were all I had to "grade" me, to define me to myself and my aunt Agnes. Dean Chawdrey should have been one of these adult figures, yet somehow she was not, she saw through my flimsy pose as my cousin Sonny had once laughed at me in a Hallowe'en costume flung together out of Aunt Georgia's cast-off fabrics *What in hell're you s'posed to be, kid?*

Dean Chawdrey had dropped my letter onto her desk, with a look of distaste. It lay between us now, as evidence.

"I've looked into your record, 'Aimée Stecke.' You are a trustee scholar, your full tuition is paid by the Academy. Your grades are quite good. Your teachers' reports are, on the whole, favorable. If there is one recurring assessment, it is 'immature for her age.' Are you aware of this, Aimée?"

I shook my head, no. But I knew that it was so.

"Tell me, Aimée. Since coming to our school, have you encountered any previous instances of 'cheating'?"

I shook my head, yes. "But I . . ."

" 'But'?"

". . . didn't think it was so important. I mean, so many girls were cheating, not such serious cheating as lately, so I'd thought . . ."

" 'So *many*'? 'So *many girls*'? What are you saying, Aimée?"

An angry flush lifted into the Dean's fleshy face. I tried to explain but my voice trailed off miserably. So stared-at, by an adult who clearly disliked me, I seemed to have lost my powers of even fumbling speech. Thoughts came disjointed to me as to one tramping across a field of mud half-conscious that her boots are sinking ever more deeply into the mud, being actively sucked into the mud, not mud but quicksand and it's too late to turn back.

"But why then, Aimée, did you decide just the other day to come forward? If it has been so long, so many instances of 'cheating', and you'd been indifferent?"

"Because . . ." I swallowed hard, not knowing where this was leading. ". . . I'd signed the pledge. To uphold the . . ."

"To uphold the honor code, Aimée. Yes. Otherwise you would not have been permitted to remain at the Academy. But the honor code is a contract binding you to report cheating at all times, and obviously you have not done that." Dean Chawdrey's small prim mouth was creasing into a smile.

I was sitting very still as if paralyzed. I was listening to the buzzing in my head. Remembering how, in the late winter of our first year of living with my aunt Georgia, Lyle and I had heard a low, almost inaudible buzzing in the plasterboard wall in our room. Above the furnace vent where, if you pressed your ear against it, you could hear what sounded like voices at a distance. My brother had thought it might be tiny people inside. I'd thought it had something to do with telephone wires. It was a warm dreamy sound. It was mixed in with our warm cozy room above the furnace, that Sonny had given up for us. Then one day Aunt Georgia told us with a look of amused disgust that the sound in the wall was only flies—"Damn flies nest in there, hatch their damn eggs then start coming out with the first warm weather." And so it had happened one day a large black fly appeared on a windowpane, then another fly appeared on the ceiling, and another, and another until one balmy March morning the wall above the furnace vent was covered in a glittering net of flies so groggy they were slow to escape death from the red plastic swatter wielded in my aunt's deft hand.

"You were one of them, Aimée. Weren't you."

This wasn't a question but a statement. There was no way to defend myself except to shake my head, no. Dean Chawdrey said in the way of a lawyer summing up a case, "How would you know, otherwise? And until now, for some quaint reason, you haven't come forward as you'd pledged you would do. What you've alleged, because it's unprovable, is dangerously akin to slander. Mr. Werth will have to be informed. His integrity has been impugned, too."

I said, faltering, "But, Dean Chawdrey—"

"The only person who has reported cheating at midterms is you, Aimée," Dean Chawdrey paused, to let that sink in. "Naturally, we have to wonder at your involvement. Do you claim that, since coming to the Amherst Academy, you have never participated in 'cheating'?—in any infraction of the honor code?"

It was as if Dean Chawdrey was shining a flashlight into my heart. I had no defense. I heard myself stammer a confession.

". . . sometimes, a few times, freshman year, I helped other girls with their term papers. I guess I helped my roommates earlier this fall, with . . . But I never . . ."

" 'Never'—what?"

I lowered my head in shame, trying not to cry. I could not comprehend what had gone wrong yet I felt the justice of it. Honor was a venomous snake that, if you were reckless enough to lift by its tail, was naturally going to whip around and bite you.

The rest of the visit passed in a blur. Dean Chawdrey did all the talking. You could see that the woman was skilled in what she was doing, other girls had sat in the chair in which I was sitting and had been severely talked-to, many times in the past. Behind the rimless bifocals, Dean Chawdrey's eyes like watery jelly may have glittered in triumph. Her flat, nasal voice may have trembled with barely restrained exhilaration but it was restrained, and would remain restrained. I heard myself informed that I would be placed on "academic probation" for the remainder of the term. I would be summoned to appear before the disciplinary committee. More immediately, Dean Chawdrey would notify the headmistress of the Academy about my allegations and the confession I'd "voluntarily made" to her, and the headmistress would want to speak with me and with a parent or legal guardian, before I could be "reinstated" as a student. The buzzing was subsiding in my head, I knew the visit was ending. The terrible danger was past now that the worst that could happen had happened. I saw Dean Chawdrey's mouth moving but heard nothing more of her words. Behind the woman's large head an oblong-shaped leaden window glared with the sullen rain-light of October. It was no secret that the Dean of Students wore a wig that fitted her head like a helmet: the color of a wren's wet feathers, shinily synthetic, bizarrely "bouffant." Her right hand lay flat on my letter, that incriminating piece of evidence, as if to prevent me from snatching it away if I tried. I gathered my things, and stood. I must have moved abruptly, Dean Chawdrey drew back. I tried to smile. I had seen Momma smiling in a trance of oblivion not knowing where she was, what had been done to her or for her sake. I seemed to be explaining something to Dean Chawdrey but she did not understand: "It was a test, wasn't it—'promtly.' To see if I would say something. The misspelling. 'Promptly.' " Dean Chawdrey was staring at me in alarm, with no idea what I meant. I turned and ran from the room. In the outer office, the Dean's secretary spoke sharply to me. Under my breath I murmured *Get the fuck away*. In my stocking feet (I'd had to kick off my muddy boots in the vestibule of the administration building, all this while I'd been facing the Dean like a child in dingy white woollen socks) I ran down a flight of stairs, located my fallen boots covered in mud and bits of hay and kicked my feet back into them. I ran outside into the rain, across a patch of hay-strewn muddy lawn that sucked at my feet with a lewd energy. Somehow, it had become dusk. The edges of things were dissolving like wet tissue. A harsh wind blowing east from Lake Erie tasted of snow to come that night but for the moment it continued to rain as it had rained for days. *Raveling-out* was my word for this time of day, after classes, before supper. Neither day nor night. I thought of my aunt Georgia in the days before her son had been taken from her humming to herself as she'd unraveled knitting, cast-off sweaters, afghans, energetically winding a ball of used yarn around her hand. My aunt would use the yarn again, nothing in her household was discarded or lost. I would pack my things while the other girls were in the dining hall. What I wished to take with me of my things, my clothes, a few books to read on the bus, not textbooks but paperbacks, and my notebooks, my journal to which I trusted the myriad small secrets of my life in full knowledge that such secrets were of no more worth than the paper, the very ballpoint ink, that contained them. In a flash of inspiration I saw that I would leave a message of farewell on the pillow of my neatly made bed for my roommates and I would leave the residence hall by a rear door and no one would see me. I would never see them again, I thought. Aloud I said, preparing the words I would write: "I will never see any of you again."

No time to dawdle! This is an emergency.

I had money for a bus ticket, even a train ticket. I had money to escape.

This was money scrupulously saved from the allowances my aunt Agnes sent me to cover "expenses" at the Amherst Academy. And money from Momma, five-, ten-, twenty-dollar bills enclosed as if impulsively in jokey greeting cards. *Lyle & I say hello & love & we miss you. Your MOMMA.* I'd hardened my heart against my mother but I'd kept the money she sent me, secreted away in a bureau drawer for just such an emergency.

It was my cousin Sonny I wanted to see. Somehow, I'd become desperate to see him. Not my aunt Agnes who loved me, not my mother who claimed to love me. Only Sonny whom I hadn't seen in almost five years and who never replied to my letters and cards. I'd been told that in September, when he'd turned twenty-one, Sonny had been released into a probationary work program and was living in a halfway house in Chautauqua Falls. Momma had sent me the address and telephone number of Seneca House, as the place was called, saying she hadn't had time to see Sonny yet but she meant to take the trip, soon. Sonny's work was something outdoor like tree service, highway construction—"That boy was always so good with his hands."

Momma was the kind of woman who could say such a thing in utter unconsciousness of what it might mean to another person. And if you'd indicate how you felt, Momma would stare in perplexity and hurt. *Why, Aimée. You don't get that sarcastic mouth from your mother.*

The Greyhound bus that passed through Chautauqua Falls didn't leave until the next morning so I hid away, wrapped in my raincoat with the hood lowered over my face, in a corner of the bus station. This night unlike any other night of my life until then passed in a delirium of partial sleep like a film in which all color has faded and sound has been reduced to mysterious distortions like waves in water. In the morning it was revealed that a gritty snow had fallen through the night, glittery-white like scattered mica that melted in sunshine as the bus lumbered into the hilly countryside north and east of Buffalo. Repeatedly I checked the address I had for Sonny: 337 Seneca. I hadn't yet written to Sonny at this address, discouraged by his long silence. It was sad to think that it was probably so, as my mother had said, Sonny's writing skills were crude and childlike and he'd have been embarrassed to write to me. I had the telephone number for the halfway house but hadn't had the courage to call.

My fear was that Sonny wouldn't want to see me. There was a rift between Momma and the Brandts, I didn't fully understand but knew that I had to share Momma's guilt for what she'd caused to happen in Sonny's life.

I stored my suitcase and duffel bag in a locker in the Chautauqua Falls bus station. I located Seneca Street and walked a mile or so to the half-way house address through an inner city neighborhood of pawnshops, bail-bond services, cheap hotels, taverns and pizzerias and X-rated video stores. In the raw cold sunlight everything seemed heightened, exposed. I felt the eyes of strangers on me, and walked quickly, looking straight ahead. Seneca House turned out to be a three-story clapboard house painted a startling mustard yellow. Next door was Chautauqua County Family Welfare Services and across the street a Goodwill outlet and a storefront church, New Assembly of God. I rang the doorbell at Seneca House and after several minutes a heavy-set Hispanic woman in her thirties answered the door. I said that I was a cousin of Sonny Brandt and hoped that I could see him and the woman asked if I meant Sean Brandt and I said yes, he was my cousin.

The woman told me that Sean was working, and wouldn't be back until six. "There's rules about visitors upstairs. You can't go upstairs." She must have assumed I was lying, I wasn't a relative of Sonny's but a girlfriend. My face pounded with blood.

"How old'r you?"

"Eighteen."

"You got I.D.?"

The woman was slyly teasing, not exactly hostile. I wondered if there was a law about minors visiting residents of Seneca House without adult supervision. In my rumpled raincoat, looking exhausted and dazed from my journey, speaking in a faltering voice, I must have looked not even sixteen. I saw, just off the squalid lobby in which we were standing, a visitors' room, or lounge, with a few vinyl chairs and Formica-topped tables, wanting badly to ask if I could wait for Sonny there, for it wasn't yet 4 P.M. The woman repeated again, with a cruel smile, "There's no visitors upstairs, see. That's for your protection."

I went away, and walked aimlessly. Outside a Sunoco station, I used a pay phone to call the latest telephone number I had for my mother in Ransomville, but no one answered and when a recording clicked on, a man's voice, I hung up quickly. My latest stepfather! I could not remember his name.

I knew that I should call my aunt Agnes. I knew that, by now, the Amherst Academy would have contacted her. And she would be upset, and anxious for me. And she would know how mistaken she'd been, to put her faith in me. Her "favorite niece" who'd betrayed her trust.

"Fact is, I'm Devra's daughter. That can't change."

The weirdest thing: I had a strong impulse to speak with my brother. Lyle was eleven now, a sixth grader at Ransomville Middle School, almost a stranger to me. We had Sonny in common, we'd loved our cousin Sonny in the old farmhouse on Summit Hill Road. Lyle would remember, maybe things I couldn't remember. I called the school to ask if "Lyle Stecke" was a student there (though I knew that he was a student there) and after some confusion I was told yes, and I said that I was a relative of Lyle's but I did not have a message for him. By this time the receptionist to whom I was speaking had begun to be suspicious so I hung up, quickly.

I walked slowly back to the mustard-yellow clapboard house with the handpainted sign SENECA HOUSE. It was nearing 6 P.M. I was very hungry, I hadn't wanted to spend money on food and had had the vague hope that Sonny and I might have dinner together. I thought that I would wait for my cousin on the street, to avoid the Hispanic woman who suspected me of being Sonny's girlfriend. At 6:20 P.M., a battered-looking bus marked CHAUTAUQUA COUNTY YOUTH SERVICES pulled up to the curb in a miasma of exhaust and ten, twelve, fifteen men disembarked. All were young, some appeared to be hardly more than boys. All were wearing work clothes, work boots, grimy-looking caps. Nearly all were smoking. A fattish disheveled young man with sand-colored skin and a scruffy goatee, several young black and Hispanic men, a muscled, slow-moving young Caucasian with a burnt-looking skin, in filth-stiffened work clothes, a baseball cap pulled down low on his forehead . . . The men passed by me talking and laughing loudly, a few of them glancing in my direction, but taking no special notice of me, as I stared at them unable to see Sonny among them, confused and uncertain. Waiting for Sonny, I'd become increasingly anxious. For soon it would be dark and I was in a city I didn't know and would have to find a place for the night unless I called Momma and in desperation told her where I was, and why.

I had no choice but to follow the men into the residence. I saw that the young man in the filthy work clothes and baseball cap was Sonny, moving tiredly among the others, staring at the cracked linoleum floor. His jaws were unshaven. His hands were very dirty. I called to him, "Sonny? Hey, it's Mickey."

He hadn't heard. One of the young black men, eyeing me with a smile, poked at Sonny to alert him to me. When he turned, the sight of him was a shock. His face had thickened, coarsened. The burnt-looking skin was a patchwork of blemishes and acne scars. I could recognize the pale blue eyes, but the eyes were hardened in suspicion. I'd expected that Sonny might smile at me, even laugh at the sight of me, in surprise; I'd expected that he would come to me, to hug me. But this man held back, squinting. There was something wrong about his gaze. I saw to my horror that his left eye seemed to have veered off to the side as if something had caught its attention while his right eye stared straight at me. His lips drew back from his teeth, that were discolored and crooked. "Dev'a? Are you—Dev'a?"

Devra! Sonny was mistaking me for Momma.

I told him no, I was Mickey. His cousin Mickey, didn't he remember me?

I tried to laugh. This had to be funny. This had to be a joke. This had to be Sonny's old sense of humor. But he wasn't smiling, he continued to stare at me with his one good eye. The lines in his forehead had sharpened to creases. His nose was broad at the bridge as if it had been broken and flattened. However old you might guess this man to be, you would not have guessed twenty-one.

"Did you come to see me? Nobody comes to see me."

Sonny spoke slowly, as if he had to choose his words with care, and yet his words were slightly slurred, like speech heard underwater. He'd been injured, I thought. His brain had been injured in a beating. But I came forward, to take hold of one of Sonny's hands, so much larger than my own. Sonny loomed above me, six feet tall but somewhat slump-shouldered, his head pitched slightly forward in the perpetual effort of trying to hear what was being said to him. "I'm Devra's daughter, Sonny. Remember, 'Aimée'? I was just a little girl when we came to live with you and Aunt Georgia. You changed my name to 'Mickey.' 'Mickey kicks ass,' you said. You—"

Sonny jerked his hand from mine, as if my fingers had burnt him. He might have heard something of what I'd said, but wasn't sure how to interpret it. From what I could see of his hair, beneath the grimy cap, it had been shaved close, military-style, at the sides and back. His skin looked stitched-together, of mismatched fabrics like one of Georgia's crazy quilts. His face shriveled suddenly in the effort not to cry. "You lied to me, Aunt Dev'a. That wasn't the man, the man that I hurt, it was somebody else wasn't it! Some other man you'd been married to. You lied to me, I was told you lied to me, Aunt Dev'a, why'd you lie to me?

I hurt the wrong man, you lied to me." Sonny spoke in the aggrieved voice of a child, pushing at me, not hard, but enough to force me to step backward. I was astonished at what he'd said. Though I'd heard something like this from my aunt Georgia, who'd had more than a suspicion that the man who'd actually hurt my mother had been Bob Gleason, not Herlihy. I couldn't make sense of this, I couldn't allow myself to think of it now. I was trying to smile, to laugh, in the old way, as if Sonny's confusion was only teasing and in another moment he'd wink and nudge at me and we'd laugh together. I said, "Do you still like pizza, Sonny? We can have pizza for dinner. I have money." Sonny said, " 'Piz-za,' " enunciating the word in two distinct syllables. His face shriveled and he clenched his fists as if he was considering breaking my face. A middle-aged black man who wore a laminated I.D. badge appeared beside us, laying a restraining hand on Sonny's arm. "Hold on there, Sean. Take it slow, man." I told this man who I was, I'd come to see my cousin, and the man explained to Sonny who listened doubtfully, staring at me. "I'm Mickey. You remember, your cousin Mickey. That's me." I spoke eagerly, hopefully. The filmy look in Sonny's good eye seemed suddenly to clear. " 'Mickey.' That's you. Well, hell." Sonny's lips parted in a slow smile that seemed about to reverse itself at any moment. I said, "I'll get the pizza. I'll bring it back here. I'll get us some Cokes, we can eat right there." I meant the lounge area, where there was a table we could use. On the wall beyond, a mosaic of crudely fashioned bright yellow sunflowers in shards of tile that looked handmade.

I hurried outside. The fresh air was a shock after the stale smokey air of Seneca House. Up the block was Dino's Pizza. I went inside and ordered a large pizza as if it was the most natural thing in the world for me to do. Years ago, in the old farmhouse on Summit Hill Road, Sonny had brought home pizzas for us on evenings Georgia hadn't wanted to cook, our favorite was cheese with pepperoni and Italian sausage, tomatoes, no onions or olives. Lyle and I would drink soda pop, Georgia and Sonny and Momma, if she was home, beer. I wondered if beer was allowed in Seneca House and I thought probably not, I hoped not. I hoped that Sonny would be waiting for me in the lounge, that he hadn't forgotten me and gone upstairs where I couldn't follow. The guy behind the counter was about twenty, olive-skinned, dark-eyed, hair straggling to his shoulders. Half his face creased in a smile. "You don't look like anyone from here."

"What?"

"You don't look like anyone from here but maybe I know you?"

I'd been pretending to be looking through my wallet, to see how much money I had. I laughed, feeling blood rush into my face. But it was a pleasant sensation, like the feel of hot sun on bare skin, before it begins to burn.

III.

PROBATE

"Excuse me?"

It was the third day of her new life. This life was diminished as in the aftermath of brain surgery executed with a meat cleaver yet she meant to do all that was required of her and to do it alone, and capably, and without complaint.

She was in Trenton, New Jersey. Whatever this terrible place was—the rear entrance of a massive granite building, a parking lot partly under construction and edged with a mean, despoiled crust of ice like Styrofoam—and the winter morning very cold, wet and windy with the smell of the oily Delaware River a half-mile away—she was struck by the fact that it appeared to be an *actual place* and not one of those ominous but imprecise nightmare-places of the troubled sleep of her new life.

In a brave voice she said, a little louder: "Excuse me?—I'm sorry to trouble you but is this the rear entrance to Probate Court?"

The girl peered at Adrienne suspiciously. She had a blunt bold fist of a face. Her eyes were tarry-black, insolent. She was about eighteen years old and she was wearing an absurd *faux*-fox-fur jacket. In her arms she held a raggedy bundle—a very small baby—she'd been rocking, and cooing to, with a distracted air. For a full minute or more she'd been openly observing Adrienne shakily approach the rear of the courthouse along a makeshift walk of planks and treacherous icy pavement as if fascinated by the older woman's over-precise cautious-careful steps—*Does she think that I am drunk? Drugged? Is she concerned that I will slip and fall? Is she waiting for me to slip and fall?*—but now that Adrienne stood before her, in need of assistance, the girl blinked as if she hadn't seen Adrienne until this moment, and had no idea what her question meant.

"'Probate court'—it's a division of the county court—I think. Do you know if I can use this entrance?—or do I have to walk all the way around to the front?" Adrienne's numb mouth spoke calmly. In the widow's voice one can detect not only the dazedness of the brain-injured but a profound disbelief that one is still alive, allowed to exist. Her eyes that resembled blood-specked fish eggs scooped from a fish's gravid belly were sparkly-bright and alert fixed on the girl's face.

A powerful sleeping pill called Doleur, she'd taken sometime after 2:30 A.M. the previous night. In anticipation of all that she'd be required to do today, and now she was dazed, groggy; her head felt as if it were stuffed with cotton batting, in her ears was a high-pitched ringing that was easy to confuse with sirens wailing on Trenton streets. She was thinking of how in her previous life—only just visible to her now on the far side of an abyss, and retreating—that life that had been hers until three days before when her husband of thirty-two years had died unexpectedly—she'd been a diligent and responsible person. She remembered that person. She *must be* that person. In preparation for this journey to the Mercer County Courthouse she'd lain in bed that morning rigid and unmoving rehearsing the journey with the manic thoroughness of a deranged actress in an unfathomable and catastrophic play.

She hadn't anticipated getting lost, however. In a maze of one-way streets, detour signs and signs warning NO TURNS. Much of the corroded inner city of Trenton appeared to be under construction as in the aftermath of a geological cataclysm. There were barricaded streets, deafening jackhammers. Because of excavation in the courthouse parking lot, the grinding of earthmoving machines, and more barricades, Adrienne had had to park a considerable distance from the courthouse; she'd had a terrible time finding the courthouse itself which was farther east on State Street than she would have imagined, in a run-down neighborhood of empty storefronts, bail bondsmen's offices and pawnshops. This, the county courthouse!

"'Pro-brate court'"—the girl in the *faux*-fur jacket spoke in a drawling skeptical voice—"that's like to do with 'pro-bration'?"

"'Pro-bate.'" Adrienne spoke cautiously not wanting to offend the girl by seeming to correct her pronunciation. "It has to do with wills. Not probation but civil court. It's a kind of court within the court, I think. The county court, I mean . . ."

In her anxiety she was giving too much information. This too was a symptom of her new life—an over-eagerness to explain to strangers, to apologize. *I know I have no right to be here—to exist. I know that I am of no more worth than a piece of trash. Forgive me!*

The girl continued to stare at her, skeptically. Or maybe—Adrienne wanted to think this—the girl's expression meant only that she was interested, curious. Her nose was flattened as if someone had jammed the palm of his hand against it and her small mouth was an animated crimson wound. She was both sleazy and glamorous in her fox-colored fur jacket opened to display a fleshy turnip-shaped body in a sequined purple sweater, lime-green stretch pants and *faux*-leather boots with miniature tassels. Her skin resembled sandpaper, blotched and blemished despite a heavy coating of makeup. Her brass-colored hair had been corn-rowed and sprang out asymmetrically about her head like frantic thoughts." 'Wills'—like, when somebody's dead? Died? And you find out what they left you?" The girl gazed at Adrienne with repelled respect.

"Well, yes. Something like that."

Find out what they left you. This chilling phrase flashed in the air like a knife blade.

The girl gave the baby-bundle in her arms a fierce little shake, furrowing her forehead in thought. She was the kind of harassed young mother whose cooing is indistinguishable from chiding and whose smiles could turn savage in an instant. "Ma'am, I guess it'd be inside—what d'you callit court. If I was you I'd take this-way-in and see if they let you through. Assholes got all kinds of 'restrictions' and 'penalties' but it's real far to the front and the damn sidewalk is all broke. *I* came that way." Abruptly now there was a bond between them, of grievance. The girl was eager to complain to Adrienne about the "shitty treatment" she'd gotten at the courthouse when she'd brought her grandma to Family Services the previous month, how "nasty mean" they'd been treated and how, this morning, she had business of her own in the courthouse: "See, I'm what's called—*sup-pena'd.* Y'know what that is?" Adrienne said yes, she thought she knew.

As the girl spoke vehemently, Adrienne happened to notice something astonishing and disturbing: about twelve feet behind the girl was a stroller pushed almost out of sight between the blank granite wall of the courthouse and a parked van marked MERCER CO. DETENTION and in this stroller was what appeared to be another child, no more than two years old.

"Oh! Is that your child?"

"Huh? Where?"

"In that stroller, there. Isn't that a—child?"

" 'Child'—what's that? Might be just some rags-like, or some bags or somethin', stuck there."

But this was a joke—was it? The girl laughed a little wildly.

"Ma'am, you are right. Sure is a 'child.' You want her?"

Seeing the startled look in Adrienne's face, the girl brayed with laughter. Her notched-looking teeth were bared in a wide smile. Adrienne tried to fall in with the joke, which didn't seem to her funny. She said, "She's very"—desperately trying to think of an appropriate and plausible word—"sweet-looking, pretty. . . ."

"Ma'am, thanks! You sure you don't want her?"

"Well, I—"

"Just kiddin, ma'am. That's my sweet li'l Lilith, she'd been a preemie would you b'lieve?—now she's real healthy. And you're right, she's pretty. She *is*."

Two small children! The harried young mother had brought two small children with her to the courthouse on this miserable winter morning. The wind was bitter cold and smelled of creosote, across the ravaged parking lot sporadic hissing outbursts of rain mixed with sleet raced like machine-gun fire. Adrienne had the vague impression—the vague, uneasy impression—she didn't want to stare openly—that there was something just subtly wrong with the toddler in the stroller, something stunted, deformed. The small face that should have been pretty was in fact too narrow, or asymmetrical; the eyes were lopsided, unfocused. As Adrienne stared the little girl began to whimper faintly and to make a halfhearted effort to fret against the restraint of a blanket wrapped tightly about her torso pinning her arms inside.

Yet the thought came to Adrienne, in rebuke *No matter how miserable she is, yet she has them.*

How miserable that girl's soul, yet she is not alone.

Adrienne and her husband Tracy had had no children. Why this was, Adrienne hadn't quite known. No decision had been made except elliptically, by omission.

Or maybe one of them had made a decision, and had neglected to inform the other.

In an aggrieved voice the girl was saying, " 'Pro-bration'—that's just inside here. I know 'County Pro-bation'—that's the first floor. Half my family goes there—*I* ain't, yet." She laughed, as if this were a witticism. Adrienne didn't quite get the joke, if it was a joke. "Ma'am, see, they got all these 'departments'—'county services'—in this place. Some days, there's so many people going through security you have to stand outdoors—in the cold—nobody gives a damn how the public is inconven'ced. My poor grandma and me, when we came back in January, there was just one fuckin elevator workin—three fuckin elevators were broke!—so we stand there waitin like a hour for the elevator 'cause my grandma couldn't walk the stairs all the way to Family Court on the sixth floor. I never saw any 'probrate court' but there's 'parole'—there's 'county pros'cutor'—on the third floor—I'm s'posed to check in there. 'Pros'cution witnesses'—they're waiting for me, I guess. They got my name. I was served a *sup-pena*. There's some of them—'pros'cution lawyers'—who know me by name and by my face. So if I go inside, and if they see me—I'm fucked. Except"—the girl paused, with a look of crude cunning, leaning close to Adrienne to speak in confidence—"I got to get a crucial message to somebody, that's on the second floor—that's 'criminal court'—if they brought him over from men's detention like they were s'post to, 8 A.M. this morning. His name is Edro—Edro Hodge. You'd be seeing his picture in the papers, if you live around here—there's been some things about him, independent of him and his family—that's to say, *me*. Some things about 'material witnesses'—what the fuck that is. These shitheads that like disappeared. So who'd they blame?—Edro. Could be when you see him, he's cuffed and his ankles shackled. Like some crazed bull they got him, to keep him 'secured.' Edro has got tats on his left cheek and back of his neck and up and down his arms and his hair is tied back in a rat-tail unless the lawyer made him cut it for the judge. They treat you like shit once they get you. This ain't Family Court! He'd be in one of those freaky orange coveralls that says Mercer County Men's Detention. The hope is to mock and ridicule a man, to break him. But Edro ain't gonna be broke that easy." The girl smiled, baring tea-colored notched teeth, then her smile grew wistful, and then stricken. "Oh Jesus!—I got to get a message to Edro—

it's urgent, ma'am. Please ma'am—you look like a kind lady—say you will help us?"

"'Help you'—how?"

Adrienne felt a sense of dread as the girl clutched at a sleeve of her black cashmere coat. It might have been a TV scene—a movie scene—the girl's heavily made-up face thrust at Adrienne's face. A sweetish-stale odor wafted from her—a smell of desperation, urgency—cigarettes, chewing gum, hair oil, soiled baby diapers. Her eyes widened: "*I don't better go anywhere near him or on any floor they'd see me*—'cause I am a 'prosecution witness'—it's warned of me, I could be arrested like Edro. *Obsuction of justis—givin a false statement to police. Interferin with*—whatever shit it is, they call it. Bastards get you to say what they want you to say—you don't hardly know what shit you are saying but it's *taped*. Then you're fucked if you try to take it back." Adrienne stared in astonishment as the girl flung open the *faux*-fur jacket and tugged at the waist of her purple sweater lifting it to reveal the flaccid flesh of her midriff that was covered in bruises the hue of rotted bananas; now Adrienne saw that the girl's forehead was bruised as well, what she'd believed to be skin eruptions were in fact welts. Obviously, "Edro" had beat the hell out of her, she was lucky to be standing. In an anguished rush of words she said, "Yes ma'am, I turned Edro in—I mean, I caused Edro to be turned in—I freaked and ran into the street near-about naked and some damn neighbor called 911—'domestic violence'—'aggravated assault' is what they'd arrested Edro for the other time—that time, *I* wasn't to blame—it's just some bullshit 'cause they want Edro for the 'material witness' shit—what happened to them, who knows? This time, see, we'd both been drinking—I was scared—I never make a sound judgment when I am scared—the cops asked me who'd been beating on me so I told them—my nose was near-about broke and all this blood on my front—and my front-clothes torn—I told them it was Edro hurting Lilith and the baby I was scared of but he'd never hurt *them*—they are his own blood he knows for a fact, he has vowed he would never hurt *them*.

In my right mind I realized this. But that wasn't right away. Ma'am, see, I have got to get this message to Edro before they take him in to the judge. His damn fuck lawyer told him to plead 'guilty.' They always tell you plead 'guilty'—makes it easy for *them*. They are such shitheads— 'Office of the Public Defender.' You wear out your ass waiting for them in those chairs, nobody gives a fuck how long you wait. Also this is the 'second offense'—'domestic violence'—other things Edro did, the cops hold against him—they have a grudge against the Hodge family Edro says and give them a fucking hard time all they can. One thing he has got to know—*Leisha is not going to swear any statement against him.* If you could tell him this, ma'am—or pass him some note, I could write for you . . ."

Through the girl's torrent of words a crude melancholy narrative emerged like a wounded animal, limping—Adrienne saw clearly. She felt a stab of sympathy for the poor battered girl but her better judgment urged her caution. *Take care! Don't be foolish, Adrienne! Don't get involved.*

Adrienne shivered. Her husband's voice, close in her ear.

Tracy was not one to *get involved*. Tracy was one for *caution*.

"I wish that I could help you," Adrienne said, "but I—I'm already late for—"

"You got some paper, ma'am? Somethin to write with? All you'd need to hand him is some little thing—it could just say like *Leisha has retracted*—or, just *L. has retracted*. He'd know right-away what that meant."

"I—I'm sorry. I wouldn't have time to—"

"Ma'am, fuck that! Ma'am, sure you *do*."

So forcibly Leisha spoke, so glittery her tarry-black eyes, Adrienne found herself meekly providing the girl with a page torn from an address book, and a pen. Leisha scribbled a message onto the scrap of paper while Adrienne glanced anxiously about.

The rear entrance to the courthouse was about twenty feet away. A steady stream of people were entering, mostly individuals. Some were uniformed law enforcement officers. No one took note of Adrienne and the girl in the *faux*-fur coat.

"You can't miss Edro Hodge, ma'am—left side of his face has this like Apache tattoo, and his hair in a rat-tail. And Edro has got these *eyes*, ma'am—you will know him when you see him when it's like he *sees* you down to the roots of your shoes."

Roots of your shoes. These eyes. Adrienne wanted to laugh, this was so absurd. This was so ridiculous, reckless. Leisha pressed the folded note into Adrienne's fingers and Adrienne was about to take it then drew back as if she'd touched a snake. *No no don't get involved. Not ever.* Quickly she backed away from the staring girl saying she was sorry, very sorry, she couldn't help her—"I'm late for Probate Court! Please understand."

Adrienne turned, fled. Adrienne walked quickly in her soft-leather boots, desperate not to slip on the icy pavement. At the courthouse entrance a uniformed police officer gestured to Adrienne, to step ahead of him. Maybe he was thinking she hadn't enough strength to push the revolving door. Was she so ghastly-pale, did she carry herself so precariously? The girl was shouting after her, pleading—"Ma'am wait—ma'am damn you—*ma'am!*"

"Ma'am? Step along, please."

Blindly Adrienne made her halting way through the security checkpoint. What a clamorous place this was, and unheated—overhead a high gray-tinctured ceiling, underfoot an aged and very dirty marble floor. Most of the others shuffling in the line were dark-skinned. Most wore work clothes, or were carelessly or poorly dressed, with sullen or expressionless faces. Adrienne stepped aside to allow a stout middle-aged black woman with an elderly mother to precede her but a security guard intervened speaking sharply: "Ma'am—put your things down here. Step along, ma'am."

Trying not to think *Because I am white. I am the minority here.*

It was so: the only other Caucasian in view was a sheriff's deputy stationed in the inner lobby.

She was not a racist. Yet her hammering heart rebuked her—*Now you are helpless, they have you.*

Her husband had been an academic, a historian. His field of specialization had been twentieth-century European history, after World War I. Like a time traveler he'd moved deftly from the present into the past—from the past into the present—though he had lived with horrors, he'd seemed to Adrienne curiously untouched by his discoveries, intellectually engaged rather more than emotionally engaged. A historian is a kind of scientist, he'd believed. A historian collects and analyzes data, he must take care not to impose his personal beliefs, his theories of history, upon this data. Adrienne had once entered Tracy's study when he was assembling a book-length manuscript to send to his editor at Harvard University Press—chapters and loose pages were scattered across his desk and table and she'd had a fleeting glimpse of photographs he'd hidden from her—scenes of Nazi death-camps? Holocaust survivors?—she'd asked what these were and Tracy had said, "You don't want to know, Adrienne."

Adrienne had protested, but not strongly. Essentially he'd been right—she had not wanted to know.

How concerned for her Tracy would be, if he could see her here, alone. For why on earth was she *here*.

Never had they spoken of *death-duties*. The subject had never arisen—for why should it have arisen? Tracy had not expected to die, not for a long time. He'd been a "fit" man—he exercised, he ate and drank sparingly, he was steeped in the sort of health-knowledge common to people of his education and class. *Knowing is a form of immortality. Ignorance is the only weakness, and that can be prevented.*

So it had seemed to them. Now Adrienne had lost faith, she'd been staggered, stunned. Her husband's knowledge had not saved him. No more than a house of ordinary dimensions could withstand a hurricane or an earthquake.

"Ma'am—remove your coat, please. And your boots. Step along."

Adrienne did as she was told. She placed her things in trays on the conveyer belt to pass through the X-ray machine, as at an airport. Yet there was a harshness here, an air of suspicion on the part of the security staff, she had not experienced while traveling on either domestic or foreign flights. She was told to open her handbag for inspection, in addition to placing it in the tray; as she struggled to open her husband's heavy leather briefcase, which contained several folders of legal documents, some of these documents fell to the floor. Awkwardly Adrienne stooped, her face warm with embarrassment, and reached for the papers. "Ma'am? You needin some help?" A male guard with skin the color of burnt cork stooped to help her retrieve the papers which had scattered on the damp, dirty floor amid the feet of strangers. How had this happened—these were precious documents! One was a notarized IRS form for the previous year, another was the death certificate issued for *Tracy Emmet Myer* on stiff gray-green paper resembling the paper used for U.S. currency and stamped with the New Jersey State seal. Somehow, there was Adrienne's husband's wallet being handed to her—and his wristwatch—which Adrienne had removed from the hospital room after his death and must have placed inside the briefcase without remembering she'd done so. The wallet was unnervingly light, flat—all the bills, credit cards and other items must have been taken from it— and the wristwatch had a broken face as if it had been stepped on. "This yours, too?"—the guard held out to Adrienne a scrap of paper upon which she saw scribbled handwriting—barely legible except for the oversized schoolgirl signature LEISHA.

Leisha! The aggressive girl in the *faux*-fur jacket and corn-rowed hair had somehow succeeded in thrusting the note to her lover into Adrienne's briefcase—how was this possible? Adrienne remembered clearly having refused it, and walking quickly away.

Numbly she took the note from the guard, and the other items, and returned them to the briefcase. Her face throbbed with heat, she was aware of strangers staring at her. How quickly it had happened, Adrienne Myer had become that person, very often a woman, an older woman, who in public places draws the pitying or annoyed stares of others because she has dropped something, or has forgotten something, or has lost something, or has come to the wrong address and is *holding up the line* . . . She was fumbling now to put on her boots, and her coat. And where was her glove, had she dropped a glove . . . The deputy overseeing the checkpoint, a lieutenant, with a dim roughened skin that wasn't nearly so Caucasian as Adrienne had imagined from a short distance, had come over to see what was wrong. Politely he said, "Ma'am? Where you headed—sur'gate?" When Adrienne stared blankly at him he said: "Office of the Sur'gate? Probate Court?" Bemusedly his eyes moved over her: the black cashmere coat that fell to midcalf, expensive but hastily misbuttoned, the expensive leather boots defaced by salt as by graffiti. "Probate is fifth floor, ma'am. Elevators through that doorway."

Is it so obvious, Adrienne wondered. *Where I am headed, and why.*

She thanked the officer. She moved on. She was carrying her handbag and briefcase against her chest, like a refugee; trying not to think that she might have left something behind on the foyer floor—a crucial document—now scuffed and tattered underfoot—someone in the security line or one of the courthouse staff might have pilfered from her. She was not a racist, she was *not a white racist* yet she had to acknowledge that the color of her skin singled her out as one of the oppressors of the dark-skinned peoples of the world, that was a fact of history, and of fate; nowhere more evident than here in Trenton, the decaying and depopulated capital city of the State of New Jersey. The widow is one who comes swiftly to the knowledge *Whatever harm comes to you, you deserve. For you are still alive.*

Not when he'd died—she had been too shocked, too stunned to comprehend that he had died, at that moment—but earlier—on the third or fourth day of his hospitalization—when she'd hurried to her husband's room on the fifth floor of the hospital—"Telemetry"—and had seen an empty bed, a stripped mattress, no human figure in the bed, no surrounding machines—the thought struck her like a knife-blow *He has died, they have taken him away*—in that instant the floor had swung up toward her face, the floor had somehow come loose and swung up as she'd lost her footing, her balance, blood rushed out of her brain leaving her faint, helpless, utterly weak, broken and weeping—a nurse's aide had prevented her from falling—"Mrs. Myer! Your husband has been moved just down the hall"—in an instant her life had ended, yet in the next instant her life had been restored to her; all that would happen to her from now on, she understood, would be random, wayward and capricious.

Now it has begun, now there is nothing to stop it.

The elevators were very slow-moving, crowded. Here too Adrienne was made to feel self-conscious, uneasy. After waiting for several minutes she decided to take the stairs. But what a surprise—these were not ordinary functional stairs but an old-fashioned staircase of carved mahogany, broad and sweeping, baronial; clearly the staircase belonged to an older part of the courthouse. Climbing the curving stairs, gripping the railing, Adrienne found herself staring into a shaft, like a deep pit; the courthouse appeared to be hollow at its core, as if receding in time. Adrienne paused to catch her breath, leaning against the railing, gazing down into the pit-like shaft. She thought *This is a temptation for those who are not strong. Or for those who are strong. To end it now.*

How close she was, to losing her balance, falling . . . She'd begun to perspire with anxiety, inside her warm clothing.

Since the first day of her husband's hospitalization—now just nine days ago—she'd been subject to such flurries of anxiety, dread. She had brought her husband to the ER for he was suffering from an erratic heartbeat and a pronounced shortness of breath; his face was flushed, mottled; his eyes were unnaturally dilated. In the ER he'd been "stabilized"—he'd been kept overnight for cardiac tests—moved from the ER not into the general hospital population but to the seventh floor—"Telemetry"—which Adrienne had not wanted to see was adjacent to "Intensive Care"; from that point onward her life became a sequence of linked yet seemingly disjointed episodes accelerated as in a slapstick silent film in which she might have been observed with pitying eyes, like a rat in a maze, compelled to repeat the same futile actions compulsively, unvaryingly, driving her car to the hospital and parking her car, hurriedly entering the hospital and crossing the wide lobby whose floor smelled of fresh disinfectant and taking one of the elevators to Telemetry, fifth floor, exiting the elevator and hurrying along the corridor to her husband's room—steeling herself for what she might see, or not see, as she approached the doorway—as she approached the bed, and the white-clad figure reclining, or sitting up, in the bed—

On the curving baronial stairs Adrienne became light-headed. A woman with toffee-colored skin clutched at her arm, deftly. "Ma'am? You havin some kind of faint?" Adrienne murmured no, no she was fine, though her lips had gone numb, blood had rushed out of her face. The woman gripped her arm and helped her on the stairs. *She knows where I am headed* Adrienne thought.

On the next floor, Adrienne had to make her way through a long line of individuals filing into a vast assembly room. Here were far more light-skinned men and women than she'd seen in any other part of the courthouse, most of them well dressed and all of them wearing jurors' badges; how plausible it would appear to a neutral observer, that Adrienne Myer had been summoned to the Mercer County Courthouse this morning for *jury duty*; she felt a stab of envy for these individuals, a powerful wish to be one of them, that her reason for being here was so impersonal, so banal and so easily resolved.

On the next floor—was this the third, or the fourth?—Adrienne found herself in another crowded corridor—here was the *Office of the Public Defender*. On a long wooden bench against a wall festooned with warnings—NO SMOKING—NO FOOD OR DRINK IN THE COURTROOM—DO NOT BRING CONTRABAND INTO THE COURTHOUSE—were seated a number of mostly young men, under the eye of several Mercer County sheriff's deputies; all but two of the young men were dark-skinned, and all were wearing lurid-orange jumpsuits marked MERCER CO. MENS DETENTION. All were shackled at the wrists and ankles, like beasts.

Adrienne tried not to stare seeing one of the white men close by, slouching on the bench; he had a sharp hawkish face disfigured by an aggressively ugly tattoo jagged like lightning bolts; his rat-colored hair was pulled back into a tail—a rat-tail? Was this—what was the name—Ezra, Edro?—Edro Hodge?—the person whom Leisha had been desperate to contact? Hodge's eyes were heavy-lidded, drooping; he gave an impression of being oblivious of his surroundings, if not contemptuous. Adrienne slipped past not wanting to attract his attention.

One floor up—two floors?—at last, Probate Court: the Office of the Surrogate.

"Ma'am—here."

Before Adrienne was allowed into the waiting room of the Office of the Surrogate she was required to show a photo I.D—fumbling for her wallet which contained her driver's license, but where was her wallet?—had someone taken her wallet, in the confusion downstairs?—in a panic locating her U.S. passport in the briefcase at which a woman deputy stared suspiciously—"This *you*, ma'am? Don't look much like *you*."

The photo was several years old, Adrienne said. Though having to acknowledge that the woman in the photo, lightly smiling, with a smooth, unlined forehead and hopeful eyes, bore little resemblance to the woman she was now.

"This is my name, though—'Adrienne Myer.' My husband's name is—was—Myer."

How unconvincing this sounded! The very syllables—*Adrienne Myer*—had become nonsensical, mocking.

For if once she'd been married to a man named *Myer*, the man named *Myer* no longer existed; where did that leave *Adrienne Myer*?

Nonetheless, Adrienne was allowed to take a seat. The air in the waiting room was steam-heated, stale. Here was a vast space larger even than the jurors' assembly room on the lower floor—a high-ceilinged room in sepia tones like an old daguerreotype, with high narrow windows that seemed to look out over nothing—unless the glass had become scummy and opaque with grime. Adrienne was nervously conscious of rows—rows!—of uncomfortable vinyl chairs crowded with people—their expressions ranged from melancholy to exhausted, anxious to resigned. At the rear of the waiting room the farther wall appeared to have dissolved into sepia shadow—the waiting room stretched on forever. Blindly Adrienne was seated clutching at her things—handbag, briefcase—she'd removed her black cashmere coat in this stifling heat—a glove had fallen to the floor, she retrieved with some effort—she'd been gripping her things so tightly, the bones of her hands ached. She was thinking *All these people have died! So many of us.*

But this was wrong of course. Everyone in the waiting room was alive. *She* was alive.

"I am—alive."

Alive. It was such a curious boastful word! It was such a *tentative* word, simply to utter it was to invite derision.

She was thinking how, on what was to be the very last day of her husband's life, with no knowledge of what was imminent she and her husband had made plans for his discharge from the hospital in two days. They'd read the *New York Times* together. Tracy had insisted on Adrienne bringing him his laptop and so he'd worked—he was determined to examine the copyedited manuscript of a lengthy article he'd written for the *Journal of 20th-Century European History*—though complaining of his eyes "tearing up" and his vision being "blurred." He'd eaten the lukewarm lunch, or part of it—until he'd begun to feel nauseated and asked Adrienne to take it away. They'd quarreled—almost—over whether Adrienne should call Tracy's parents, to deflect their coming to visit him—an arduous trip for them, from northern Minnesota—since he was being discharged so soon, and was "recovered, or nearly"—Adrienne had thought that Tracy should see his parents, who were concerned about him; Tracy had thought otherwise, now that he was "feeling fine." The hospital allowed visitors until 9 P.M. but Adrienne left at 7 P.M. since Tracy had become tired suddenly and wanted to sleep—Adrienne was exhausted also—maintaining her cheery hospital manner was a strain, like carrying heavy unwieldy bundles from place to place and nowhere to set them down, until at last you drop them—let them fall—she'd managed to drive home and was in bed by 9:20 P.M.

and at 12:50 A.M. she'd been wakened as in a cartoon of crude night-mare cruelty by a ringing phone and in her dazed sleep she'd thought *That is not for me. That is not for me* even as, groping for the phone, she'd known that of course the ringing phone was for her, she'd known that the ringing phone had to be for her and she'd known, or guessed, what the call was.

Mrs. Myer? Your husband is in critical condition, please come to the hospital immediately.

"Mrs. Myer? Come with me, please."

Time had passed: an hour? Two hours? Adrienne was being led briskly along a corridor to the Office of the Surrogate. The name on the door was D. CAPGRASS. Her heart beat quickly. She'd stood so swiftly, blood had rushed from her head. *Don't let me faint. Not here, not now. Not this weakness, now.* It had become confused in the widow's mind—such fantasies are exacerbated in steam-heated waiting rooms, in hard-backed vinyl chairs—that her obligation in Surrogate Court was an obligation to her deceased husband, and not to herself; it was her husband's estate that was to be deliberated, the estate of which she, the surviving spouse, was the executrix. *If this can be completed. Then . . .* Adrienne's thoughts trailed off, she had no idea what came beyond *Then.*

Crematorium is not the polite term. *Funeral home* is the preferred term.

There she'd made arrangements, paid with their joint credit card.

Tracy Emmet Myer was a co-owner of this card. *Tracy Emmet Myer* was paying for his own cremation.

Ashes to ashes, dusk to dusk. The nonsense jingle ran through the widow's brain brazen and jeering as the cries of a jaybird in the trees close outside her bedroom windows, that woke her so rudely from her sedative sleep.

"Mrs. Myer. Please will you sign these consent forms"—a middle-aged bald-headed man with eyeglasses that fitted his face crookedly and stitch-like creases in his forehead was addressing her with somber formality. Without hesitating—eagerly—Adrienne signed several documents—"waivers"—without taking time to read them. How she hoped to placate this frowning gentleman—an officer of the Mercer County Surrogate's court. "And now, you will please provide these required documents, which I hope you've remembered to bring"—frowning as the widow foolishly fumbled removing folders from a briefcase—the deceased husband's birth certificate, and her own birth certificate; their marriage certificate . . .

Quickly Adrienne handed over the marriage certificate. She could not bear to see what was printed on it and, long ago, gaily and giddily signed by her husband and her.

"And your husband's death certificate, Mrs. Myer?"

Your husband's death certificate. What an eccentric form of speech—*Your husband's.* As if the deceased husband yet owned "his" death certificate.

Your husband's body. Your husband's remains.

Adrienne fumbled to hand over the odd-sized document. Though it had been newly issued and was scarcely twenty-four hours old yet it was creased and mud-smeared as if someone had stepped on it. Adrienne murmured an apology but Capgrass silenced her with an impatient wave of his fingers.

"This will do, Mrs. Myer. Thank you."

With a pencil-thin flashlight the Probate Court official examined the death certificate—was this infrared light?—and the ornamental gilt State of New Jersey seal. The document must have been satisfactory since he stamped it with the smaller gilt seal of the Surrogate's Office which bore, for some reason, quaintly and curiously, the just-perceptibly raised figure of a horse's head, or a chess knight in profile.

"Oh—why is that? This seal—why does it have a horse's head on it?" Adrienne laughed nervously.

"It is the Court's seal, Mrs. Myer." Capgrass paused, as if the widow's question was embarrassing, a violation of protocol. "May I see—? Have you brought—?"

"Of course! Of course."

As the primary beneficiary and executrix of her late husband's estate Adrienne was required to provide photo I.D.s of herself and her husband—she'd brought drivers' licenses, passports—as well as IRS tax returns for the previous year—documents attesting to the fact that she and the deceased *Tracy Emmet Myer* had lived in the same residence in Summit Hill, New Jersey.

To all these items the frowning Capgrass subjected the same assiduous examination, with the pencil-thin light.

"Now, Mrs. Myer: may I see your husband's *Last Will and Testament*."

This was the single document that most unnerved Adrienne. She'd had difficulty locating it in her husband's surprisingly disorganized filing cabinet and she'd been unable to force herself to read more than a small portion of the opening passage—*I, Tracy E. Myer, a domiciliary of New Jersey, declare this to be my Last Will and Testament, and I revoke all my prior Wills and Codicils . . .*

Nervously she said, "I hope this is complete, Mr. Capgrass. It's all that I could find. I'm not sure what 'codicil' means. I'm afraid that . . ."

"Hand it here, please."

Leafing through the document of about twenty pages Capgrass paused midway.

The expression on his face! Adrienne stared uneasily.

"Mrs. Myer, this is—this is not—this is *irregular*."

A crude blush rose into the middle-aged official's face. His eyeglasses glittered in alarm. Rudely he pushed the document toward Adrienne—at first she couldn't comprehend what he wanted her to see, what she was looking at—then she realized it was a page, or several pages, of poorly developed photographs of stunted, broken, naked figures—death camp survivors?—manikins, or dolls?

"I don't understand. What is—"

Numbly Adrienne took up the offensive pages, to stare at them. How could this be? What were these ugly obscene images doing in her husband's will? She was sure she'd looked through the will, or at any rate leafed through it—if barely recognizing what she saw, for she'd been upset at the time, very tired, and the densely printed legal passages had seemed impregnable, taunting. Now she saw that she was staring not at printed passages but at photographs—blurred, not-quite-in-focus photographs as of objects seen underwater—bizarre disfigured manikins, or adult dolls, some of them missing arms, legs—bruised, blood-splattered—several of them hairless, bald—all of them naked—and all of them female.

Adrienne felt a stab of horror, shame. How could this be! How could Tracy Myer who'd been so courteous, so kindly, such a good decent gentlemanly man who'd taken care with every aspect of his work have been, at the same time, so careless, reckless—hiding such obscenities in his study, in his legal files where they would be discovered after his death?

Yet thinking *But they are not real, at least! Not real girls, or women. Real amputees.*

"You may take these back, Mrs. Myer. Please."

"'Take them *back*'? They don't belong to me, or to my husband—I'm sure. I've never seen these before . . ."

Capgrass removed his crooked plastic glasses and polished the lenses vigorously with a strip of chamois. His eyes, exposed, were small, rust-colored and primly disapproving; the crude hot blush had expanded to cover most of his face, and the gleaming-bald dome of his head. Clumsily Adrienne took up the offensive sheets of paper, which were in fact not photographs but Xerox photocopies of photographs, several to a page: not wanting to see she saw nonetheless that the figures were both painfully lifelike and perversely artificial; she had the idea that they were artworks of another era, perhaps "Germanic"; maybe it was possible to interpret the reproductions as a historian's assiduous and uncensored research, and not pornography. Adrienne tried to explain that her husband Tracy Myer—Professor Tracy Myer, who'd taught at Princeton for nearly thirty years—had been a *distinguished historian*, his field of specialization was *post–World War I twentieth-century European history* and this included the notorious—decadent—Weimar era. Though deeply embarrassed Adrienne managed to sound convincing: "By accident my husband must have filed these—documents—in the wrong folder. They seem to be 'art' of some kind—posed manikins or dolls—maybe Surrealist. Or—Dada. Tracy was always fascinated by art—by what art 'reveals' of the culture that gives rise to it, as well as of the artist. They are not . . ." Adrienne couldn't bring herself to utter the ugly word *pornography*.

Capgrass interrupted Adrienne to inform her disdainfully that there appeared to be "irregularities" in her husband's will; he'd had time only to peruse the document in a cursory fashion but had noticed that the first codicil hadn't been properly notarized—the notary public had used a seal with what appeared to be several broken letters which undermined the validity of the transaction, should litigants want to take issue.

Litigants! Adrienne's heart beat in alarm.

"Though it's unambiguous that you've been designated your husband's primary beneficiary, as well as the executrix of his estate, it would appear, from a strictly legal standpoint, that the document is of questionable authenticity. I'm sure that 'Tracy Emmet Myer' was indeed your husband, and that he has indeed died—but, unfortunately, if there is a pre-existing will, either in your possession or elsewhere, it might take precedent over the one we have here."

"But I—don't understand . . . 'Pre-existing'—there is none . . ."

"How many times such a claim has been made, and a pre-existing document turns up, that is *fully legal*. Mrs. Myer, please understand that we can't proceed to 'probate' your husband's will in its present state. There are no legal grounds for the assumption that you are, in fact, the executrix of Tracy Myer's estate."

"But—I am his wife. You've seen my I.D., and the marriage certificate—"

"And if there are claims against the estate—these must be processed."

" 'Claims against the estate' . . ."

Adrienne spoke faintly. What a nightmare this was!

She remembered how several years before—following the unexpected death of one of Tracy's brothers—he'd made arrangements for both their wills to be drawn up. This was a task—a necessity—Tracy had postponed as Adrienne had postponed even considering it and at the signing in the attorney's office she'd so dreaded reading through the dense legal language that she'd signed both wills without reading them assured by the attorney that everything was in order.

It was the future Adrienne had dreaded when one or another of the wills would be consulted. Now, the widow was living in that future, and it was more terrible than she'd anticipated.

"Letters will have to be sent by you, Mrs. Myer, by certified mail, to all of your husband's relatives and business partners, if he had these, as well as to anyone else who might have a legitimate claim upon the estate." Capgrass spoke in a flat perfunctory voice in which there lurked a *frisson* of something insolent, disruptive. "This is standard procedure in probate, and it is very important."

"But—why would anyone make a 'claim' against the estate? Why would this happen?"

"Mrs. Myer, this is *probate*. The court must determine if your husband's estate is 'free and clear' before allowing the estate to be divided among beneficiaries and administered by any executor or executrix."

"But—how would I know how to begin?" Adrienne's voice rose in alarm. "My husband took care of all of our finances—our taxes—insurance—anything 'legal.' He has—had—relatives living in many parts of the country—he didn't have business partners, but—he'd invested in his older brother's roofing business, to help him financially . . ." Adrienne recalled hearing about this, years ago, though Tracy hadn't discussed it with her at any length. And hadn't the brother's business gone bankrupt just the same? A part of Adrienne's mind began to shut down.

Suttee. She'd wakened that morning thinking of *suttee.*

The ancient Hindu custom of burning the widow, alive, on her husband's funeral pyre. A cruel and barbaric custom said to be practiced still in the more remote parts of India and Adrienne thought *There is a cruel logic to this.*

"Your husband was married previously—?"

"'Married previously'? Why do you say that? He was *not*."

"Our records show—"

Capgrass was typing into a computer, hunched forward like a broken-backed vulture peering at the screen. A small thin smile played about his lips. "It seems here—our records show—unless there are two distinct 'Tracy Emmet Myers' . . . Your husband was required by law to inform you of any prior marriages as he was required to inform the individual who performed the wedding ceremony and if he failed to comply with this law, Mrs. Myer, there may be some question about whether your marriage to him was *fully legal*. You may want to retain an attorney as soon as possible to press your claim."

Press your claim. Adrienne sat stunned.

"But—I know my husband. I knew him. It is just *not possible* . . ."

Capgrass continued to type into the computer. In a matter-of-fact voice reading off data to the widow who could not hear what he was saying through a roaring in her ears. *This is wrong. This is not right. You don't know him. None of you knew him.*

Yet, had Adrienne known Tracy? Had she known the man, except as *her husband*? In the hospital an altered personality had emerged from time to time, unexpectedly. Adrienne couldn't forget a curious remark Tracy had made that was wholly unlike the man she knew: one evening he'd muttered in a wistful voice as a cheery Jamaican attendant left his room chattering like a tropical bird—a fleshy girl bearing away soiled linen, the remains of a meal—"If only we could be so simple! It's as if they don't realize they are to die."

Adrienne had objected: "Tracy, you can't judge them by their outward manner. They are spiritual people just like us."

Adrienne's reply had been inadequate, also. Not what she'd meant to say. Not what she *meant*.

It wasn't like her to say *them, they* in this way. As it wasn't like Tracy to speak in such a way. And what had Adrienne meant by *spiritual people just like us*. This was condescending, crude.

Was this how racists talked? How racists thought?

The widow's mistake had been, her husband had been her life. She was a tree whose roots had become entwined with the roots of an adjacent tree, a seemingly taller and stronger tree, and these roots had become entwined inextricably. To free the living tree from the dead tree would require an act of violence that would damage the living tree. It would require an act of imagination. Easier to imagine *suttee*. Easier to imagine swallowing handfuls of barbiturates, old painkiller medications in the medicine cabinet. *I can't do this. I can't be expected to do this. I am not strong enough*

What was mysterious to her was, before Tracy's death she had not ever understood that really *she might lose him*. That really in every sense of the word *he might depart from her, die*.

That there would be a time, a perfectly ordinary morning like this morning in the Mercer County Courthouse, Office of the Surrogate, when the man who'd been Tracy Emmet Myer *no longer existed and could not be found anywhere in the world*.

The very routine of the hospital, to which she'd become almost immediately adjusted, had contributed to this delusion. How capably she'd performed the tasks required of her, bringing Tracy his mail, his work, his professional journals, his laptop—proof that nothing fundamental had changed in their shared life. And the cardiologist was optimistic, the EKGs were showing *stabilization, improvement*. Yet one evening Adrienne had naively approached an older nurse at a computer station in the corridor not far from her husband's room—the woman middle-aged, kindly and intelligent—her name was Shauna O'Neill—you had to love *Shauna O'Neill!*—she'd seemed to like Tracy very much—you had the feeling with Shauna O'Neill that you were a special patient, of special worth—for hadn't Shauna always remembered to call Tracy *Professor Myer* which had seemed to comfort him—and flattered him—but seeing Mrs. Myer about to peer over her shoulder at the computer screen Shauna O'Neill had said sharply, "Mrs. Myer, excuse me I don't think this is a good idea"—even as Adrienne blundered near to see on the screen beneath her husband's name the stark terrible words *conges-tive heart failure*. In that instant Adrienne panicked. She began to choke, to cry. For hadn't they been told that her husband was improving, that he would be discharged soon? Adrienne stumbled back to her husband's room. Tracy had been dozing watching TV news and now he wakened. "Addie? What's wrong, why are you so upset?" Adrienne had never cried so helplessly, like a terrified child. If one of the broken mutilated dolls in the lurid photographs could have cried, the doll would have cried in this way. This was the single great sorrow of which Adrienne Myer was capable—at the time of her husband's death, and in the hours follow-ing, she would not cry like this. She would not have the strength or the capacity to cry like this. Raw emotion swept through her leaving her stunned, hollow. At the time she'd kissed her husband desperately, his cool smooth cheek which the Jamaican attendant had recently shaved; she'd gripped his fingers which were cool also, as if blood had ceased to flow in the veins there. She stammered, "I'm c-crying only because— I love you so much. Only because I love you so much, Tracy. No other reason."

She'd frightened Tracy, crying like this. She'd offended him, violated hospital protocol.

She wondered if he'd forgiven her? If he could forgive her?

She had abandoned him, finally. For that, how could he forgive her?

And yet: she was thinking possibly there was a misunderstanding. A mistake. Possibly she'd been summoned to Probate Court by mistake. As the computer data regarding her husband was mistaken, so the "fact" of his death was mistaken, or premature. Her husband hadn't died after all—maybe. Her husband hadn't died *yet*.

"Ma'am! You will come with me, please *now*."

The interview with Capgrass seemed to have ended with shocking abruptness. Adrienne had been trying to explain the circumstances of her husband's hospitalization and the promises the hospital staff had made or had seemed to be making, she'd begun to speak excitably, but, she was sure, not incoherently, and out of nowhere a security guard—

a dark-skinned woman with hair pressed back so tightly from her face, her head appeared to have shrunken—was tugging at her arm, to urge her from the room. Adrienne was gripping her handbag, in both arms she clutched at documents. She was distraught, disheveled. A pulse beat in her head like a giant worm, writhing. Had Capgrass pressed a secret button, to summon one of the sheriff's deputies? Had the widow said something reckless she hadn't meant to say? She hadn't been *threatening*—had she? The dark-skinned female deputy was escorting Adrienne from the court official's office—Adrienne was perspiring inside her expensive clothes—Oh! she'd forgotten something—she'd left something behind, with Capgrass—but what it was, she couldn't remember. "Ma'am come with me. This way *ma'am*." The deputy spoke forcibly, ushering Adrienne into the hall. Adrienne had had more to tell Capgrass—more to explain—trying now to explain to the deputy that she had to leave the courthouse immediately—her husband was in the Summit Hill Hospital, fifteen miles away. "I have to leave now. I have to see him. His name is Tracy. He can't be left with strangers. He's waiting for me . . . he will be anxious, if I'm not there." Adrienne was thinking how, in the past day or so, for no reason, unfairly, for he'd been sleeping and waking and sleeping and waking and not always knowing where he was, Tracy had squinted at her and said in a hurt accusing voice, "Adrienne? Where the hell have you been? I don't see much of you these days."

Long she would recall the hurt, and the injustice.

Don't see much of you these days.

When he'd loved her, he'd called her *Addie*. The full, formal name *Adrienne* meant something else.

Or maybe—this was another, quite distinct possibility—he'd said, after he'd died, and Adrienne arranged to have his body delivered to a local crematorium, in a voice beyond accusation or even sadness the man who'd been her husband for thirty-two years said *Well! We won't be seeing each other for a while.*

"This way, ma'am. You are not authorized to leave Probate Court just yet."

The deputy handed Adrienne a tissue with which to wipe her inflamed eyes, blow her nose—as she led her back into the waiting room—how vast this room was, Adrienne could only now appreciate—how many were waiting here!—as far as the eye could measure, individuals who'd died, or were waiting to die, or had managed to avoid death temporarily, yes this was Probate Court and all who were here *had not died* but had *survived*.

This was their punishment, that they had *survived*, and that they were *in Probate*.

"Ma'am, slip on one of these."

Without Adrienne's awareness and certainly without Adrienne's consent, the deputy had escorted her through the waiting room and into a corridor, she'd brought Adrienne into a windowless room, and shut the door firmly. What was this? Where was this? Adrienne's tear-blinded eyes could barely make out rows of cubicles—cubicles separated from one another by plywood partitions—the air in this place was close, stale, smelling of the anguish and anxiety of strangers' bodies.

How the gigantic pulse in Adrienne's head throbbed! She'd become confused. It had begun to seem probable to her that her husband was still alive—*not yet dead*—and that Adrienne had come to the hospital herself, to the first-floor radiation unit where women went for mammograms.

She had postponed her yearly mammogram, out of cowardice. Yet somehow she must have made the appointment, for here she was.

"Ma'am? You will please slip on one of these."

A second woman, in a bailiff's uniform—this was made of a drab, dun-colored fabric, while the sheriff's deputies' uniforms were a more attractive gray-blue—had appeared, and was handing Adrienne a paper smock—a paper smock!—which Adrienne had no choice but to accept. If she wanted to be released from this hellish place.

The bailiff instructed Adrienne to step inside one of the cubicles and remove all her clothing—outerwear, underwear—her boots and her stockings and her jewelry—to place her possessions on the bench inside the cubicle—to put on the smock, and a pair of paper slippers—and to come back out when she was ready. Inside the cubicle, Adrienne began to undress like one in a trance. How grateful she was, there was no mirror in the cubicle—she was spared seeing the widow's wan, frightened face.

I love you so much. There is no other reason.

Her husband had told her this, too. He'd loved her so much. Many times he'd told her and yet she could not now recall a single, singular time.

Adrienne was removing her clothing, another time she would have to remove her boots, and this time her stockings. And her beige lace brassiere that fitted her loosely now and her tattered white nylon panties which in fact she'd slept in the previous night beneath a flannel nightgown in terror of being summoned to the hospital another time wakened from her deep stuporous sleep to drive hurriedly to the hospital to be ushered into her husband's hospital room approximately five minutes after a young Asian doctor she'd never seen before had declared him dead—*Mrs. Myer there was nothing to be done your husband's blood pressure plummeted and his heartbeat raced.*

She had loved him, her husband. The man who'd been her husband. But her love had not been enough to save him. Her love had not been enough to save either of them. All that had ended.

Trembling she removed her rings. She was wearing no other jewelry just rings. Hard to remove, these rings. The engagement ring—a beautiful diamond surrounded by a cluster of smaller diamonds—and the engraved white-gold wedding band—though her fingers seemed to have become thinner yet it was hard for her, it made her wince, it made her cry, like a small child or a small hurt bird crying, to remove these rings and to place them carefully beneath her clothing neatly folded on the wooden bench for safekeeping.

Her black cashmere coat, her handbag, briefcase—these she placed carefully on the bench. Thinking *Everything will be safe here. This is Probate Court.*

She put on the ridiculous paper smock, that barely came to her hips. How embarrassing! And the paper slippers! These looked as if they'd been used before, and were scuffed and creased.

The bailiff tugged at the curtain—"Ma'am? Step out here, please."

Adrienne obeyed. No choice except to obey. She hadn't been able to tie the smock behind and the little paper sashes hung loose and ticklish against her bare back.

"Ma'am. You will please remove your garment."

"Remove it? I just put it on."

The bailiff was heavyset, humorless, with a coarse sooty-white skin and no eyebrows. Her dun-colored uniform included a heavy leather holster and—was it a handgun?—a *pistol?*—and on her left breast, a brass badge like a glaring eye.

Awkwardly Adrienne tried to shield her breasts with her arms. The bailiff pulled her arms aside.

"Ma'am! You will submit to the examination. You will cooperate."

" 'Examination'—but—"

"Did you sign a waiver in the Sur'gat office, ma'am? What's that waiver say?"

"I—I don't know. I wasn't aware—"

"You signed a waiver, ma'am. You came to Probate of your own volition. You have entered the Courthouse—you are in the territory of the State."

The territory of the State! The bailiff spoke as if reciting words many times uttered, worn smooth and implacable as stones. Adrienne's mouth was dry with apprehension.

Was it a good sign, or not such a good sign, that there was no one else in the examination room, only just Adrienne? The air was steam-heated, humid and oppressive. A fine film of perspiration already gleamed on the sooty-skinned woman's face. With a flourish she pulled on latex gloves saying, "Ma'am, stand very still. Very still, and you will not be hurt."

With her deft latex fingers the bailiff palpitated Adrienne's armpits—was she looking for lumps, swollen lymph glands? Before Adrienne could steel herself she began to palpitate Adrienne's breasts—the pressure was sudden, vise-like and unbearable,

"Ma'am, you may *breathe*."

Adrienne had been holding her breath, in a trance of terror. Such intimacy, and such *pain*.

"Ma'am. Raise your arms, please."

Frowning, the bailiff cupped Adrienne's breasts in both hands—her hands were large as a man's, and strong—and exerted pressure upward, as if shaping resistant clay. Adrienne cried aloud, tears started from her eyes.

Her breasts were waxy-white, and had shrunken in the past week. The nipples were berry-sized, small and hard, sensitive as exposed nerve endings.

Her stomach too seemed to have shrunk, yet the skin was flaccid, like an ill-fitting body stocking. There were thin white striations in her belly and thighs like stitches in the flesh that had worked loose.

He'd adored her body, at one time. Her forgotten body.

"Ma'am. You will be seated, please."

Adrienne was panting. Her breasts throbbed with pain and her mouth had gone dry as ashes.

"Ma'am. I said *seated*."

In lieu of an examination table, Adrienne was made to sit on a wooden bench and spread her legs.

"I—can't. I can't do this . . ."

"*Ma'am!* You will cooperate or you will be *in contempt of court*."

With a grunt the bailiff stooped to push Adrienne's thighs farther apart, and to poke, and then insert her latex forefinger into the tight, dry, shrunken space between Adrienne's legs. It was one of those moments in a lifetime when one thinks *This is not possible* and then, a moment later *This is what is possible.* Adrienne flinched with pain and bit her lip to keep from crying out.

The bailiff was panting as if she'd run up a flight of stairs. Was the woman taking a swab, of the interior of Adrienne's body? Or was she— a bizarre possibility—checking to see if Adrienne had smuggled anything into the courthouse, in such a lurid way? (On the walls of the courthouse corridors were signs warning against *contraband.*) For next the bailiff inserted her latex finger so deeply into the tight shrunken ring of flesh, of Adrienne's anus, Adrienne was unable to keep from screaming.

"Ma'am! You have not been *hurt.*"

The bailiff spoke in exasperation, as if her professional integrity had been challenged. Yet at last, the examination seemed to be concluded. The bailiff removed her latex gloves and dropped them into a trash basket. Adrienne had a glimpse—no more than a fleeting glimpse—of something rust-colored on the latex forefinger.

"Ma'am, you are free now to clothe yourself. And then you will wait here for the officer to assess your case."

"'Assess my case'—what do you mean?"

"I am not authorized to release you, ma'am. You will be released by the Surrogate."

"But—how can I be 'released'—am I in custody? Am I *arrested?*"

"Ma'am, you are in the custody of the Probate Court. You are not *arrested.*" The bailiff scowled as if Adrienne had tried to be amusing and had failed, lamely.

"But when will this be? When can I go home?"

"Ma'am, I have no way of knowing. *Ma'am* you will wait here."

Adrienne re-entered the cubicle, to put back on her clothes. Her hands were trembling badly. The pain between her legs had begun to throb like fire. A trickle of liquid high on the inside of her thigh, trickling down—blood? She wiped it away quickly not daring to look.

Her clothes—where were her clothes?—on the floor was her black cashmere coat—on the bench, her dark silk shirt and beige sweater she'd worn over it, no longer folded neatly as she'd left them but looking as if they'd been examined and flung down. There, on the floor, partway beneath the partition to an adjacent cubicle, her trousers—fine light cashmere wool, so charcoal-gray as to appear black. But her underwear was gone—no brassiere, no panties—and her rings—*where were her rings?*

On the floor also, as if they'd been examined, pilfered and kicked aside, were Adrienne's handbag and her husband's briefcase. Papers spilled out of the briefcase, Adrienne shoved inside without taking time to sort them. She couldn't recall if her husband's will had been returned to her or if Capgrass had confiscated it . . .

Hurriedly and haphazardly she dressed. She couldn't button the shirt evenly; the zipper of her trousers caught partway, scraping the flesh of her belly; both her dark stockings were tangled beneath the bench, stiff with dirt, but her boots—the expensive black leather boots!—were missing.

In her desperate state Adrienne was grateful for the paper slippers.

How strange it felt, to be naked inside her clothes. How strange her body had become to her, slick with perspiration, exhausted yet aroused like a hunted animal. She thought *He is dead. He is not only dead he is gone. I am alone here.*

In that instant Adrienne felt a thrill of something like elation, triumph. Though she was distraught, and humiliated—though the lower part of her body throbbed with pain—yet she felt this thrill of triumph. She thought *Already I am someone he could not have imagined.*

To escape the Probate Court, and to return home—this would be bliss to her, the most intense relief, happiness.

Nothing more than that!—only just to escape, and to return to the empty house, that had been chill and appalling as a sepulcher to her only hours ago.

When Adrienne stepped out of the cubicle, she saw that the examination room was empty. The sooty-skinned bailiff had left. Anxiously

Adrienne tried the door—the door that led back to the corridor outside the waiting room—but it was locked.

"Hello? Hello? Is anyone there?"

Adrienne rapped on the door hesitantly. She didn't want to incur the wrath of the sooty-skinned bailiff. She stood, then sat—then stood again—ten minutes, fifteen. Her skin had begun to itch, where the bailiff had touched her. And the soft flesh of her breasts, and the soft flesh between her legs, throbbing with pain.

She happened to notice at the farther end of the room a second, smaller door. It was the kind of door that is permanently shut. Even as Adrienne went to try it, thinking *Of course this is locked. I am locked in* the doorknob turned, and the door opened.

Quickly Adrienne stepped outside. She was in a corridor— a familiar-looking corridor—she'd come this way when she'd arrived at the Office of the Surrogate, it seemed like hours ago.

In her overwarm coat and the absurd paper slippers, Adrienne made her stealthy way to the staircase.

No looking back! No glancing to the side! Could the widow leave Probate Court so easily? Was no one going to see her, apprehend her? Her heart was beating deliriously. Her body throbbed with the strange wild exhilaration of the hunted animal.

Descending now the broad baronial staircase. Gripping the railing, steeling herself as in the presence of danger.

"I am exiting the Courthouse. I have been in Probate Court, and now I am released"—Adrienne rehearsed her little speech, should one of the uniformed officers stop her.

And now again on the lower floor was the *Office of the Public Defender*—it seemed that there were fewer young captives in orange jumpsuits seated here at this time—but still there remained the young man with the savage tattooed face and rat-tail at the nape of his dingy neck—Edro Hodge? Adrienne hesitated only a moment before deciding to approach the man—his bleary bloodshot eyes swerved to her face, startled—Adrienne whispered hoarsely, "If you are 'Edro'—'Leisha' has said she retracts her statement. She says—'Don't plead guilty.' "

The young man with the tattooed face stared at Adrienne. Beside him was an older man, in a dark suit, a court-appointed attorney Adrienne supposed, and this man stared at Adrienne, too.

"Don't! Don't 'plead guilty.' "

Before either man could speak to her, Adrienne turned and hurried back to the staircase.

Outside, it appeared to be late afternoon. Hours had passed, the overcast sky had darkened. A chill icy rain continued to fall and the fraught air smelled of the river. Adrienne was disoriented, she hadn't thought so much time had passed in the courthouse though she was exhausted, wrung dry. Calmly she thought *They can find me, they will know where I live. But not just now.*

In her paper slippers she would have to walk in slushy ice, mud. The near-empty parking lot was the size of a city block, its outer perimeter lost in shadow. Adrienne looked around for the snub-faced girl in the *faux*-fox-fur jacket but of course no one was there, where the girl had been standing with the baby in her arms.

Yet, Adrienne heard a cry. A child's cry, faint and plaintive—and to her astonishment she saw, near-hidden between the granite wall of the old courthouse and the parked police vehicle, the toddler in the stroller.

"Lilith?"

Adrienne hurried to the child, who was whimpering, feebly kicking her thin, wasted-looking legs. The little girl had managed to work her arms free of the tight-wrapped blanket and flailed them now in the frantic way of a bird with broken wings.

"Oh—God! This is terrible! What has happened to you! Has your mother left you here?—abandoned you?"

Adrienne could not believe this—yet it seemed to be so. Had the child been left for *her*?

What to do! What was Adrienne to do! She could not bring herself to re-enter the courthouse—which in any case seemed to be shutting down for the evening. Already the higher floors had dimmed their lights, each floor in succession was growing dimmer, like a rotted wedding cake, candles going out.

Adrienne's mind worked rapidly. If the girl who called herself Leisha had abandoned her two-year-old daughter in such a way, clearly she was an *unfit mother*; the child would be taken from her by county welfare authorities, and put into a foster home. In the city of Trenton, what a fate!

"You poor baby! Poor dear—darling—Lilith . . ."

Adrienne picked the child up in her arms. She wasn't accustomed to a child's weight, made heavier by the child's kicking and thrashing. It did seem to comfort the distraught little girl that Adrienne knew her name, and was smiling at her.

"Don't cry! No need to cry, now."

The little girl's eyes were cobalt-blue, very dark; her face was narrow, a sort of feral face, with a look of being hurt, wounded; there was something just discernibly deformed about her. She'd wetted herself, a strong odor of ammonia lifted from her soiled clothing. Yet Adrienne hugged her, Adrienne kissed the chilled little face, murmuring words of comfort. Adrienne thought *This is our only purpose on earth: to give comfort to others.*

The thought was immensely satisfying to Adrienne. She felt her heart swell with warmth, well-being.

In the crude paper slippers, that were already soaked through, and tattered, Adrienne carried the little girl to her car, which was on the far side of the lot. Her stocking feet were freezing but her face was feverish. Happily she whispered to the little girl—she would take care of her, she promised not to turn her over to police, or to welfare—"You can come home with me, Lilith! You will be safe with me. No one will know."

The panicked child bit Adrienne's hand—fortunately her teeth were tiny milk teeth, not strong enough or sharp enough to break Adrienne's skin. Adrienne was shocked but managed to laugh. "Lilith! I'm not your *mommy*. You have no reason to be frightened of *me*."

At her car, which was a new-model Acura her husband had bought less than six months before, Adrienne saw that something unfortunate had happened. A heavy ridge of earth—chunks of broken concrete, ice, and soil—had been plowed against her front wheels, no doubt by one of the earthmoving machines that had been grunting and grinding in the parking lot when she'd arrived. What bad luck, and at such a time! Adrienne had to set the fretting child inside her car, in the passenger's seat, and for several desperate minutes kick, claw, and swipe at the dirt, to free the wheels—"God *help* me. Oh God—*help* me." Her hands were filthy, the front of her coat, her legs—she was laughing, and she was crying—it might have been God who gave her the idea to drag a plank over to her car, and insert it behind the left front wheel, on a patch of ice, to provide traction.

"This will do it, Lilith! Let's try."

Under a New Jersey statute one was obliged to carry a small child in a child-seat in the rear of a vehicle, not in the passenger's seat, but Adrienne had no choice except to buckle Lilith in the front seat beside her, as best she could in the oversized belt. "Please don't cry! You're safe with me—I promise." By this time all floors of the courthouse had gone dark.

By a miracle the motor flared into life. Calmly and deliberately despite her desperation to escape Adrienne maneuvered the Acura out of the lot. No police vehicles on the street! No one was following her! The nighttime city appeared to be less frantic than the daytime city and in a maze of one-way and dead-end streets Adrienne worked her way gradually back to Route 1 which would bear her north and out of accursed Trenton.

"We're safe, Lilith! Almost safe. Please don't cry, darling."

Darling. The word was immensely soothing, familiar somehow. It was not a word available to everyone.

On northbound Route 1 sleet rained from the sky. Tiny bits of ice hammered against the hood and roof of the white Acura. Adrienne's headlights were on bright but she had difficulty seeing the highway. Blindly she drove, happily—she was thinking of how when they were safely home she would give the child a much-needed bath—a hot soaking sudsy bath—she would shampoo the child's fine, fair hair, and comb it free of snarls—she would dry the child in her largest bath towel, in her arms—she would feed the starving child, and herself. She could prepare a thick delicious tomato soup—scrambled eggs—oatmeal? Oatmeal with raisins and honey. Or she would save the oatmeal with raisins for morning. She would spoon food into the child's mouth and put the child to bed in the rarely used bed in her guest room. She would sing the child to sleep if the child continued to fret. She would sit by the child's bedside through the night, to protect her. For there was the child's cruel mother, and there was the child's cruel father, from whom the child must be protected. And in the morning all that was confusing would become clear, she knew. She had faith.

DONOR ORGANS

Must've been a time of contagion somehow he'd picked up like hepatitis C this morbid fear of dying young and his "organs" being "harvested"   rib cage opened up, pried open with giant jaws   you'd hear the cracking of the bones   deftly with surgical instruments the organs spooned out   blood vessels, nerves "snipped" and "tied"   your organs packed in dry ice, in waterproof containers to be carried by messenger to the "donor recipient"   this sick-slipping-helpless sensation in his gut like skidding his car, his parents' new Audi they'd trusted him with, on black ice approaching the Tappan Zee Bridge   deep in the gut, a knowledge of the futility of all human wishes, volition   *This is it, you are fucked*   Only twenty-three years old   not *old*   no reason to worry about the future, his mom can worry for him   moms are

experts at worrying, moms are most useful at worrying   yet moms
should be shielded from knowing too much about their sons   moms
should be protected otherwise you feel guilt   sick-guilt, like sick-
worry about dying young   he wasn't worried really, it's just his mind
        maybe there's a tapeworm burrowed into his brain   it's not
normal to be aware of your "organs"   wakened in the night when he
finally gets to sleep by the rude *thump! thump!* of his heart   dazed
thinking someone was in bed with him?   was it B., she'd just slipped
from bed to use the bathroom and would be back stumbling in the dark,
giggling and collapsing on top of him   the narrow sunk-mattress
bed with smelly sheets of his college dorm room in Mackie Hall but no,
can't be, Jason has graduated, all that's gone   once his brain is fully
awake he has no trouble comprehending   he's in his own bed, in his
own home   he's safe here   Only twenty-three yet he has become obsessed   knows people his age who've already died   that
is, already he knows people his age who've died   "head-on collision"
    "by his own hand" (gun)   "mountain-hiking fall" (Ecuador)
    "drug overdose"   it is morbid to dwell on such things but really
he's kind of anxious   so much time to think   naturally, you become anxious   maybe there *is* a tapeworm in his brain   (can't
suggest this to Mom, Mom would freak)   at the same time he's capable of discussing the issue openly and easily with people, with friends,
as he'd done in his ethics class, saying what you'd expect an intelligent
person to say   Sure I'd want to donate my organs   my eyes
        to some other person in need   *Greater love than this hath no
man, than that he lay down his life for his friends*   he believes this, kind
of   he is a Christian, kind of   being an "organ donor" doesn't
mean that you die for that purpose but that after you die your "organs"
are "harvested"   this is a crucial distinction   this makes him
anxious   you start off in a car, never return alive and your organs
shunted off to be planted in strangers, your eyes inserted in the eye
sockets of a stranger, no wonder he can't sleep   she'd twined her
thin arms around his neck, mashed her hot yearning face in his neck

half the time he hadn't known what the hell was she serious? was she joking? it was some other guy she loved, not him? or was it *him*?

he doesn't sleep with any of them now   it's been seven, eight months   living in his mom's family house in Rye, New York   avoid people   easier to avoid   in August, they'll be on Nantucket   yet he's eager to contact his friends   each morning waking frantic to make contact with as many of his friends as he can   as if in the night might've lost someone   has been lost to someone   checks his e-mail immediately before even rinsing his putrid mouth, washing his face that's a clay mask dried and shrunken

his cell phone he's frantic to call his friends   mostly guys from his eating club, and a scattering of girls   not so much to talk with them, within a few seconds of starting a conversation he's ready to break it off, just to see are they there   are they still there   as he is still here   It makes him laugh to think how there's a final message that will be enshrined, sort of   *Jason's last e-mail! next thing I hear he's dead*

his friends calling one another, excited   flurry of e-mails and attachments, text-messages   his friends thrilled, breathless   he will be pried out of the wreckage by the "Jaws of Life"   he will feel his chest being pried open   the rib cage must be cracked like breaking apart a roasted chicken   the first organ to be "harvested" is the heart   only a few hours after brain death this organ begins to deteriorate   dry ice, an airtight container   sometimes by messenger carried on airplanes   eyes without lids, very carefully wrapped in sleep mode, unseeing   optic nerves and blood vessels snipped, tied   this is microsurgery   he's laughing this is truly so weird   nobody seems to acknowledge how weird   how alone he is, in this knowledge   can't say to Mom you are so fucking afraid of dying, it might be better to die and get it over with   senior year he'd had lots of friends   B. was not Jason's closest friend   B. belonged to Jason's eating club, they'd taken a popular bio-ethics course together   he'd hooked up with B. a few times during their senior year haphazard and casual   by mutual consent (he was certain!)

casual   after graduation drifted apart   B. went to Bangkok to teach in the university's extension program there   B.A., Ivy League university, tuition somewhere beyond $40,000 a year, you're qualified to teach English "as a foreign language"   recently B. has e-mailed Jason out of nowhere   out of cyberspace   must've gotten his address from a mutual friend   *Hi Jason thinking of you & missing you it's challenging here but kind of lonely turns out Bangkok is the Sex Capital of the world & a buyer's market (Germans, American, Japanese males the primary buyers) & at one hundred fifteen pounds I am thirty pounds too heavy & at age twenty-three way too old. Sucks, huh?*   Surprised by B.'s tone, disturbed and not knowing what B. wants, he'd replied a few times   briefly he'd replied   wary of too much confiding, that can happen too quickly in e-mail   anyway not much news at Jason's end, job interviews in the city fizzled out   summer internship in Hartford a fucking disappointment, not what he'd been promised   he'd quit and returned home   at Princeton he'd taken economics courses, did O.K. until the math got too complicated   courses in environmental studies, ecology   played some tennis, soccer   like a dream now, it has faded so swiftly   the guy he'd been, Jason T., faded so swiftly   his friends, too, seem to have changed   scattered across the country   Mike who'd died (it's said) in a suspicious hiking-trail accident in Ecuador at 12,000 feet   B. who's in Bangkok, Thailand   feels sorry for B., but God damn wishes she'd cease writing to him   sends him all kinds of weird attachments maybe meant to be jokes   he's deleting most of these without reading them   it's like B. is stalking him   Christ he's lonely, too   he has his own sick thoughts   quick death, that's the best death, skidding on black ice approaching the mammoth bridge in November sleet S K I D D I N G as if floating, airborne   delicious weightlessness   *This is it, man you are fucked*   he'd been smiling in fact he'd been paralyzed   panicked   black ice is invisible in headlights   hadn't died, though   only just the passenger's side of the elegant silver Audi smashed   mild bruising from the damned air bag   none of this he'd

share with B.   never share anything with anybody you get naked
with   any guy knows that   like a dream now, the girls Jason had
slept with   hopes they remember him better than he remembers
them   smashed out of his mind, some nights   it's O.K., you
won't remember   in bio-ethics they'd discussed   cloning/
euthanasia/"selective breeding"/"selective abortion"/"organ donors"/
"harvesting organs"   in certain countries lacking human rights laws
like China, organs can be ordered by the wealthy and specimens selected from the prison population and their organs "harvested"
      logical development of science their professor said   what sci-
ence can do, science will eventually do   always, science will do
      moral reasons will be found for what brings profit to the market
      "greatest good for the greatest number"   there is no code of
ethics intrinsic in humankind there is only codified   law without
law, no civilization   without civilization, no ethics   thinking of
this he's feeling his heart prepare to *thump!*   sweat breaking out in
his underarms, crotch   his mom has warned him not to "stress"
himself   he's got plenty of time to re-apply to law schools   that
sick-slipping-sensation in the gut at the prospect of returning to school
      any kind of school   a (secret) sensation he can't tell his mom
      anxious that Jason will "stress" himself as his father did   minor
heart attacks then cardiac arrest, aged forty-nine   Jason can't envi-
sion himself beyond forty   even beyond thirty, he feels very tired
      the crucial question is who'd want to live that long   yet, once
you get started, you don't seem to want to stop   freaks him out totally, the prospect of somebody else looking through his eyes   for
wouldn't Jason be there, too? somehow, still? in his eyes?   wakened
in the morning checks his e-mail   anxious to see if he has new messages   always he hopes for new messages   yet anxious to see if
B. has written   B.'s tone has become openly mocking, cruel   B.
had not been like this at Princeton   *Hello Jason it seems that you must
be very busy, don't have time to write to me, what's it require, 20 seconds of your
precious time   about 20 seconds is as long as youre good for you self-important*

white-boy prick   shocked, Jason deletes this message   stung, ashamed   furious   nothing you can do for a disturbed bitter person on the far side of the earth   looks up Thailand on a world atlas   surprised how close it is to Vietnam, Cambodia   not far from the Philippines   a Filipina woman named Maria had worked for Jason's family when Jason had been a boy   very quiet, reserved Maria who'd been like one of the family   Jason's mom had adored Maria so much more reliable than the Hispanic women she's had to hire in recent years   Jason's mom is concerned about her son   you'd think the university would be doing more for its graduates everybody can't be summa cum laude Rhodes scholars   Jason sleeps some-times until noon   heavy dreamless sleep like a stupor   Jason isn't seeing his friends from school   his girlfriend, if that's what she'd been, he'd been seeing in New York for a while, that seems to be over   Jason's mom understands Jason's anxiety, she thinks

Jason's mom is sympathetic   can't explain to his mom he can't be involved, getting naked is repulsive to him   no he is not "doing" drugs   maybe some weekends in New York but now, no   God damn B. continues to send him her vicious messages   should delete without reading yet can't seem to resist in revulsed fascination   sui-cidal hints, Jason isn't going to fall for   *when i am not who will you be? where i am going will you follow?*   what's this supposed to mean, some kind of crap Zen wisdom he isn't going to print it out, maybe it's evi-dence that B. is cracking up, needs psychiatric help fuck he isn't going to get involved   in their bio-ethics class when suicide was discussed B. was vehement saying suicide is wrong   their professor (a world-famous philosopher, a really cool guy they all admired) pointed out that "wrong" is a subjective moral claim and whose claim? by whose authority?   in the discussion, Jason said he thought that suicide was O.K. in certain circumstances   he was a Christian, kind of   not a Muslim! you were pegged as a Christian   his mom's family was Roman Catholic, but not his mom not him   in bio-ethics you could see that most of the students were really getting off on it   suicide's a

favorite topic   an alternative to graduation (joke)   morbid/
compulsive thinking of such things when you're twenty   now
twenty-three   makes him feel dazed and light-headed, the prospect
of living to forty   which you sort of have to do (don't you?) if you
get married, have kids   never make forty-nine   hopes his mom
is gone by that time, a mother should not outlive her son   secretly
Jason has felt it's good, Dad being gone   he hadn't been living with
Jason's mom at that time, temporary separation (Mom said) so when
Dad died it was in another city   out of state   kind of like Dad
to get the last word, bad sport playing tennis when his teenaged son was
starting to beat him   make the old guy run around the court lunging and panting and cursing under his breath, Jason had laughed seeing
his father's flushed-red face thinking *Go for it, Dad! Cardiac arrest*   this
morning there's a new message from B.   God damn that bitch, ruin-
ing Jason's peace of mind   deletes the message without reading
      seven e-mails in a row from B. he has deleted without reading
since last Friday   so pissed maybe this a mistake but Jason decides
to reply   one final time   *Sorry I don't have time for games, I don't
like games, I have my own life, get a life of your own*   on TV that night
there's an interview with Jason's grandfather   Jason has switched on
the TV in his room bored and restless surfing channels   and there
on public TV (which Jason never watches)   his grandfather being
interviewed by Charlie Rose   it has been a while since Grandpa has
been on TV, Jason realizes   Mom's elderly father the only individual among Jason's relatives to have achieved what you'd call prominence
      some notoriety, but "renown"   Grandpa had been a fierce critic
of liberal political and social agendas in the 1960s and 1970s   nobody at Princeton in Jason's circle had heard of him   well maybe the
name   something to do with politics? books?   Jason himself
hasn't read more than a few pages of his grandpa's numerous books
      in a close-up the elegant white-haired old gentleman is peering
into the camera   that look of disdain   handsome ruin of a face
a mask of fine wrinkles   but the pale blue eyes still alert, combative

Jason's famous grandpa enunciating his words with such care, the most slow-witted in the TV audience can't mishear   *I am eighty-two years old   I am not in especially poor health   I don't see much reason to continue to live   it's a debased era but no more debased than previous eras I have lived through   but I would not commit suicide   I am a Roman Catholic and the sacraments are sacred to me*   so calmly speaking, Jason isn't certain he's heard what he has heard   his "famous" grandpa on national TV saying such things!   Jason listens to the remainder of the interview in a daze   as soon as the TV program is over, Jason's mom enters his room   tears glittering in her eyes, she's upset asking if Jason has   happened to see his grandfather interviewed on Charlie Rose just now   Jason is embarrassed saying he saw just the end of the interview   his mom asks what did he hear   he shrugs saying Grandpa was being funny as usual, I guess   funny! his mom says uncertainly oh yes I suppose so   my father is known for his dry sense of humor   Jason says, wishing she'd leave, sure Mom that's about all that anybody knows about Grandpa isn't it? next morning Jason does an unexpected thing, calls his grandpa hasn't been on easy terms with the old man for years but Jason says to him why'd you say what you did last night on Charlie Rose, Grandpa!   you kind of hurt our feelings, Grandpa   especially Mom   the old man is quiet for a moment as if he's surprised by this then laughs saying Jason you must know that I was just joking   my God everybody in the family has been calling me chiding me   just joking for God's sake   wouldn't have thought my own family lacked a sense of humor   Jason isn't going to let the old man off so easily   he's remembering fishing for bluefish off Grandpa's boat, in Nantucket Sound   he's remembering Grandpa hugging him, when his dad died   saying God damn Grandpa you expect grandparents to say things like *Life is precious, and this is the happiest time of your life while you're young*   you don't expect your grandparents to say *life is shit*   Grandpa   is   protesting   now   remorseful-sounding   dear Jason, dear boy it's my pride, I abhor clichés   Jason says

you had a happy life, Grandpa   you have money, you're a famous
man   all my friends have heard of you, ask about you   Grandpa
is quiet again for a moment then says Jason you are correct   my
life has been pretty damned good   and I like being famous it's like
seeing yourself in a room of mirrors   if you're good-looking especially still if I had to live my life over again, I'd swallow poison
Grandpa bursts into laughter   terrifying old-man laughter
Jason is stunned gripping the phone receiver   stammering Grandpa
what? Grandpa you're joking are you? Grandpa *why?*   Grandpa
manages to control his laughter saying   why son, you tell me

DEATH CERTIFICATE

"**G**od *damn.*"

It was more a sob than a curse. Somewhere overhead, deranged bells were ringing. She'd pushed open the heavy door of the county courthouse and descended into a dimly-lit and soupy-aired ground-floor corridor like a tunnel only to discover that the office of the county clerk of records was locked and on the door a snotty notice WILL RETURN AT I P.M.

Noon! She'd arrived at noon.

In exasperation she rattled the doorknob. She wasn't one to resist a gesture only because it is futile.

She had come to receive from the Chautauqua County Office of Records, for a fee of five dollars, a facsimile of a death certificate. She had no personal wish for this document, the very thought of which made her wince, and her eyes shift in the rapid-eye-movement of the deepest phase of sleep, but lawyers were insisting she must have it and so she'd driven three hours, forty minutes halfway across the massive state of New York and now she was herself in a state somewhere between manic and wounded. She was wearing stylish, very dark sunglasses that made her resemble a sleek-sexy insect not entirely steady in the upright position, in high-heeled summer sandals. She was wearing a white cord skirt that showed much of her sleek-sexy thighs and a flame-red top showing, at the midriff, a sliver of creamy skin. Her legs (calves, thighs) were sturdy and supple and her upper arms had a meaty firmness, yet. Beneath her likeness she could see the caption *Would you guess thirty-eight?*

Though since the death, the awful death, eleven days before, that had come at the worst possible time in her life, she'd been in a foul, mean mood. "*Fuck.*"

She'd drifted to the end of the corridor past more locked doors. Frosted glass windows the color of dingy teeth. It had been eight years, seven months since she'd been in this northwest corner of the state. More years than that, since she'd been in this very building with her husband, before he'd been her husband, acquiring a marriage license. She'd been too young to be incensed at the absurdity of such a law, such logic, that legal documents are required for being born, being married, dying.

Mount Olive, New York. A small town south of Lake Erie. When she'd lived here, here had been everywhere. Now she lived elsewhere, here was nowhere.

Noisy and panting, there came another customer to the county clerk's office. Yvonne smiled meanly to see this guy—youngish, big, blundering, in white T-shirt and khaki shorts, bald-blond-fuzz head and what looked like mallet hands—squinting at the notice on the door and tugging, hard, at the doorknob. She heard him curse under his breath, "Shit."

It was Woody Clark. That big beautiful boy Woody who'd broken her heart.

"Woody?"

"Yvonne?"

They greeted and grabbed at each other. They laughed like demented kids. It was lightning flashing! It was pure chance, therefore innocent. Yvonne would recall afterward almost in disbelief how immediate, how without hesitation they'd been, each of them. Each of them equally. Their dazed delight in each other, that had been wholly unplanned.

"Jesus, look at you! Gorgeous."

Woody was staring. His scrutiny of her was beyond rude: her breasts, her rear, her legs (calves, thighs), even the creamy slice of midriff he couldn't resist pinching between his big forefinger and thumb.

Yvonne teetered on her high-heeled sandals, with happiness. She couldn't keep her hands off Woody, either: his brawny forearm dense with sand-colored hairs, his big rounded jaw where she'd smeared scarlet grease from her mouth.

"And *you*. You haven't changed, either."

Woody laughed, this was so hugely untrue. He'd gained weight, he'd lost hair. There was some sort of W-pattern on his sunburnt forehead where wanly curly sand-colored hair was receding. Woody had been vain of his good looks, not that he'd have ever admitted it, and was rubbing his head now with both hands, frantic-funny: "I'm looking like an American dad, which is what I basically *am*."

This remark, seemingly playful, uttered with bared teeth and a goofy grimacing grin, was possibly a warning, Woody would use his kids as human shields in this encounter, or, maybe, it was an unconscious unpremeditated gesture. Yvonne decided not to care. Woody Clark was so luscious! She was so starved! "Woody, my God. I'm crazy for you. I mean, I love you. Just the look of you." She was laughing at the sick scared look in the guy's face, remembering how everything had showed in Woody's face, every quick thought, every fleeting emotion, Woody

Clark was direct and guileless as a dog wagging, or not wagging, its tail, or so she'd wished to think. She'd removed her dark glasses—or maybe Woody had removed them—and she was swiping at her eyes quick and deft, just the edges of her fingers, so that her mascara wouldn't run. Oh, she shouldn't be saying these things to Woody Clark! Her words had come out unbidden, like bats. She had a quick flash of an antiquarian drawing of, what was it, Pandora's box, ugly winged things flying out past horror-stricken Pandora.

Or maybe it was Medusa's head she saw: horror-stricken Medusa with a head of writhing snakes.

"Oh, hey. Yvonne."

Woody was blushing. His entire face went sunburnt. He was glancing around, guilty-like. But no one was likely to be observing them. His reaction was reflexive: he was recalling their seemingly accidental meetings at their kids' soccer games, at the hardware store and the drugstore and Grand Union and Barre Mills, the library, Starbucks, The Ice House Grill on Main Street—they'd grab at hands and arms, brush lips against cheeks, no mouth kisses only just smiles like released springs, the two of them fine physical specimens of a clearly superior species, gleaming and glistening, you might say preening with happiness, on public display and yet, maybe, innocent—it was only when they were alone in their secret places, not by chance but by design, that there might be cause for Woody's guilty look.

"I'm serious, Woody. I miss you."

Woody laughed, uneasy. Because maybe she wasn't serious. (Was she?) It had been a contention between them, like a badminton birdie they'd batted back and forth, that Yvonne said the most extravagant things and didn't, couldn't, mean them; while Boy Scout Woody said only truthful things or at any rate practical/sensible things, and meant them.

Woody was hugging her now, nearly cracking her vertebrae. He was all sudden vehemence hugging to hurt. "Put your mouth where your money is, baby." Woody's dumb jokes, that was what she'd been missing.

Nobody she knew now, not one person in her life, made such dumb-ass jokes and expected you to laugh. Her arms came around Woody with iron-maiden swiftness. She wanted Woody to know, to feel, how strong she was, obviously she worked out at a health club, maybe had a personal trainer, lifted (ten-pound) weights, jogged, fast-walked, panted and puffed on the elliptical stairs. She was gratified to feel love handles at Woody's waist, loose beneath the untucked-in T-shirt and flabbier than she remembered.

She liked it that Woody was feeling, at her waist and back, not an ounce of flab. Her ribs were right there to be grasped, strummed.

"Baby, you've lost weight. What're they doing to you over there in what's-it?"

As if Woody didn't know the name of where Neil had been transferred. Where he'd moved his family eight years before.

"*You're* just right, Woody."

"I mean, you're beautiful. Only just a little thin."

Woody was actually grasping her waist in both hands as if measuring. She saw the worried-dad look in his face and felt a wave of emotion for him that left her weak. She had to remember that Woody Clark had been too much for her. She'd had to give him up. She'd moved away from Mount Olive and had not thought of Woody since and now, somehow here he was. Hair mostly gone but the baldie-fuzz head seemed to soften his features. Woody still looked young, he was three years younger than Yvonne and she hadn't ever felt comfortable with that for always, in the matter of men, certainly in the matter of her husband Neil, she'd been the young one. And Woody's eyes: ridiculous watercolor-blue, Paul Newman–blue, you never saw in actual life, or almost never. These eyes shone with ardor, unabashed.

"Your face, Yvonne. What are you thinking?"

"What am I thinking? You."

"Me? How?" Woody was happy, giving off heat as if he'd been running, panting and stumbling to get to her.

"How, you know, you'd get excited. I mean, you know, turned on.

Like a match tossed into gasoline." Yvonne made an explosive gesture with hands, mouth.

"Yeah, well. I was a kid then, practically. Now, maybe not."

"Don't be *faux*-modest, Woody. It isn't you." She was calculating whether she dared mash the heel of her hand against his groin in the khaki shorts. How Woody would react. He could be unpredictable. Just when you were loving him like one of those big clumsy sheepdogs that want only to lick your face and thump their tails, he'd turn on you and say with wounded dignity *Don't ever patronize me*.

"Now what're you thinking? Your face is fantastically transparent, Yvonne."

"If it's transparent, you tell me what I'm thinking."

Woody flashed his left incisor, a snaggle tooth that looked as if it belonged in someone else's jaw. The laugh-lines around his mouth sharpened like sudden blades. "Is old Woody good for a quick screw? For old times' sake? Or is it, maybe, too much of a hassle? What'll he expect from me, afterward? The poor slob."

Yvonne blushed. She was laughing, but her face flooded with blood. "Woody, come *on*. The last thing I'd ever think of you, for Christ's sake, 'poor slob.' You know better."

"Hey, I am. A slob. I'm fat." Woody clutched at his waist, the fleshy knobs. He was ignoring his stomach, that pushed against the T-shirt in a way Yvonne hadn't seen before, in him. But then, there was his baby-dome of a head. This was new, too.

Woody was saying, "You, you're in your own class. There's only one of you, baby. And maybe I'm wrong, you're not too thin. I guess it's healthy, you read about low-calorie diets, the leanest laboratory rats live longer. I mean, 'way underweight rats, anorexic rats, not that the poor bastards have any choice about being starved, but—" Woody could digress for long interludes. He had a mind like a vacuum cleaner, sucking up miscellaneous information, often "scientific," that was forever on tap. Instead of a post-coital smoke, with Woody Clark you got a post-coital lecture. Yvonne had found this charming and exasperating in about

equal measure. Once, she'd relied on Woody to fill her in on news—
what to think, be incensed by. Movies, music, even who to vote for.
Later, she'd stopped listening. She'd stopped even watching his mouth
move. But now she was watching, and she was listening. And she felt a
sick, sinking sensation. *We could. We could, again.*

"—after this, we could have lunch? There's this terrific new restaurant on the river, I doubt you know. A decent wine list, improbable as
it sounds."

Quickly Yvonne said, "I can't, Woody. I have to get back."

"Fuck you do. You don't."

"Woody, I *do*." She'd come close to calling him *honey*. And her tone,
too, was familiar as if they'd had this conversation before, more than
once. Yvonne was practically in tears, she was so sincere. Her daughter
Jill would be waiting for her back home and already she'd lost time, having failed to factor in a one-hour wait for the damned clerk's office to
open. "I'm a chauffeur for Jill right now. She's had a 'crisis' and I need to
be reliable for her since of course Neil is otherwise engaged."

"God! Jill must be how old?" Woody had heard *Jill* and not *Neil*.

"Fourteen. But a young fourteen."

Woody shuddered. He had two sons, Yvonne calculated they were
still in middle school. Jill, fourteen going on twelve, was over her head
in ninth grade.

Woody asked about Jill, as he always had. He'd been sweet that
way, and seemingly sincere. Yvonne, asking about Woody's boys, had
not always been sincere for she'd been jealous of anyone, even Woody's
children, making emotional demands on him. Only rarely had Yvonne
asked after Woody's wife and yet more rarely, out of tact Yvonne had
thought, had Woody asked after Neil.

Now Woody was asking, as if he'd only just thought of it, why
Yvonne was in Mount Olive waiting for the county clerk, and Yvonne
hesitated, and said evasively that she had to pick up a death certificate.
And Woody's blue eyes widened. "You *do*? Jesus, so do I."

"*You?*"

They stared at each other. This was too strange! There had to be something ominous about it, such a coincidence.

Woody was frowning and shaking his head muttering he didn't want to "go into it," the circumstances of his death certificate. Yvonne felt a clutch of fear, also distaste. Woody (who could read minds, when it suited him) would know that she didn't want to know who in his life had died, and that annoyed her. Always he'd known more about her than she felt comfortable with his knowing while at the same time, for this was Woody Clark, he'd behaved as if he was the naive one of the two of them, innocent because three years younger.

"Oh, Woody. Is it—family?" She paused, biting her lower lip. "Not your—father?" In a moment of panic she couldn't remember whether Woody's father had died years ago, and she'd heard the news second- or third-hand, or whether—well, she couldn't remember. In the eight years, seven months since she'd lived in the large white Colonial on Washburn Street her thoughts of Woody Clark had become comfortingly tattered and smudged as a poster on a billboard. Maybe you could see a face on that billboard, and maybe the face was smiling, but you couldn't recognize the face.

"No." Woody was frowning, not very attractive now.

Yvonne drew back. She could see herself in the very short very white cord skirt and high-heeled sandals stepping backward in her own imprudent footsteps. In damp sand. *Don't go farther, you'll regret it.*

She said, awkwardly, for her tongue seemed to twist when she lied, "I'm here to pick up a document for tax purposes. My mother's mother who was, maybe you remember, her stepmom? Not a blood relative of hers, or mine. Oh, she was a nice woman, she was a sweet old lady, but—" Yvonne spoke quickly and carelessly to indicate that her reason for being in Mount Olive on such a mission was not important. It was sad, someone had died, an elderly woman not a blood relative had died, but it wasn't interesting. Woody's death certificate was much more interesting, obviously. But they wouldn't go there.

"—Caroline? Is it—?"

The words leapt out. Again it was winged things out of Pandora's box. Yvonne wanted to clamp her hands over her mouth like a comic-strip character but Woody wasn't in a mood to be entertained.

Staring at his feet, enormous silver-gray Nikes with bands of rotting black reflector tape, Woody said nothing. Veins and tendons in his muscled neck visibly pulsed.

Suddenly Yvonne was remembering, she'd been hearing about Woody's wife. They'd been separated, and they'd reconciled. And maybe they'd been separated again. And there was some medical problem. Probably breast cancer, for that was the cancer everyone had, everyone female who had cancer, as prostate cancer was male, and for this reason Yvonne who had long resented, been jealous of, hated, disdained and envied Woody Clark's wife couldn't be certain now if she'd heard such grim news about the woman because if she had she'd have blanked it out, blocked it like the kind of caller ID Neil had bought for their phones, where you're spared even knowing who is trying to call you.

Yvonne swallowed hard. She was frightened suddenly. If Caroline had actually died, was that, somehow, though years later, *her fault?* Would Woody, unfairly, or fairly, blame *her?* Or, blaming himself, in his clumsy-blundering-belated way, inadvertently stumble, like a drunk careening across a dance floor, and bring her down with him? Where a minute before he'd been grinning like a high school athlete who's scored the winning point now Woody was glowering. His mouth was downturned at both corners. Yvonne thought in dismay *Why'd I go there?* She could have bitten her lower lip until it bled.

Instead, she took Woody's hands in hers. He wasn't responding, so she squeezed harder. "I'm sorry, Woody. I won't pursue it. I know, well—how you take things. How hard."

Woody mumbled something that sounded like *sure.* It was adolescent-boy sarcasm, clumsily disguised hurt.

Yvonne slid her arms around his muscled neck and pressed her face against his muscled-fatty chest. His heart beat beneath her cheek like a fist. She drew a deep, deep breath. If Woody's arms closed around her, or even if they didn't, she was feeling good now, she was feeling somehow justified. She had been the one to blurt out to Woody Clark that she missed him, she loved him, and she was sincere, she'd opened herself to him, to be wounded, as he wasn't opening himself to her. So, she was the naive one, in her heart she was the younger of the two of them. The strange thing was, she hadn't actually thought much about Woody Clark in years. Not that she'd repudiated him but that, the way she shoved older clothes back into the corners of her walk-in closets, to make way for newer clothes, not a cyclical but a chronological progression, and the older clothes faded from memory as from sight, so she'd ceased thinking urgent thoughts about Woody. There'd been an actor on *Seinfeld* who resembled Woody to a degree. And sometimes in public she'd find herself watching a tall burly crew cut guy, ex-athlete beginning to go to fat, one of the baby-face bandits as she and her women friends called them: guys that, well into their forties and fifties, and, who knows, into their sixties and beyond, could get away with every kind of bullshit because they had baby faces and you had to love them.

Yvonne said, in a suddenly husky, choked voice, "I think of you all the time, Woody. I just want to tell you." If the lie came so easily, maybe it wasn't a lie? "And I don't mean sexual, Woody. Not just that."

Pinched-glowering, yet Woody managed to laugh.

"'Not just that'? I doubt it, honey. There isn't all that much outside sex. I mean, to take seriously."

"Well, maybe. But it's more than that, for me." Yvonne spoke vehemently. She gave his chest a thump with her fist, as if to push him away. "I miss you, I mean as an individual. As a unique person. You're the only man practically to make me laugh." Yvonne was so serious now, she had to speak lightly. Her eyes were welling with ridiculous tears.

"You miss my dick. Good old good old. Reliable." Woody made a snorting noise. "Or anyway, mostly."

"Stop talking like an asshole, Woody, when you're not. It's like calling yourself a slob when you're not. What you have is style, a natural kind of style. If you wear slovenly old clothes, rotting old shoes, if your jaws are covered in stubble, it doesn't matter because you're you. While other men, no matter what they wear, what car they drive, how their hair is styled, it's irrelevant. You must know that, God damn. I hate it when you put yourself down."

Suddenly she was hurt, sulky. He hadn't moved a step backward when she'd thumped his chest. Now she pushed at his stomach that was perceptibly harder than she'd expected: he must be doing some kind of stomach exercises, from a prone position. His upper arms were thick as hams. And his neck!—she couldn't have closed her two hands around it, even if she'd wanted to strangle him. The primitive part of her female brain was impressed but the rest was pissed by the dumb-dead weight, the obdurate bulk of the guy. And him protesting, "'Put myself *down*'? Like, you're saying it's some kind of *suicide*? When I'm trying to be up front, honest? To you it's 'talking like an asshole'? That's what it is, to you?"

Woody was pretending to be hurt. Woody was wanting Yvonne to remember how, when she'd lost it and screamed at him, really screamed at him those several times, like a crazed woman, stammering and choking and spitting out the most vicious words, he'd never lost control and insulted her. The most agitated he'd been, he'd stammered red-faced, "You—you better stop! You better not say anything more!" He'd let her burn herself out, like a flash fire. Somehow, even at such times, as if knowing he'd provoked her, Woody had been *on her side*.

That was the remarkable thing about Woody Clark, Yvonne was remembering now. Essentially, unlike anybody else she knew, Woody had been *on her side*.

She was saying, "It's just, I do miss you. I wouldn't be crazy, the way I was. I wouldn't be, you know, jealous." Here was a sudden swerve into the subjunctive. *Wouldn't. Would.* No wonder Woody Clark was suddenly very still. A damp stain like wings, if you could have wings on your chest, had materialized on the front of Woody's T-shirt, Yvonne was tracing with her fingers.

"It wasn't good, Vonnie. You know that. Not just for you, it made you into somebody you basically aren't, but for me, too. I hated what I, well—was responsible for."

Vonnie! She wasn't hearing what Woody was saying but she heard *Vonnie* which meant their old intimacy. When they were naked together, vulnerable. *Vonnie* meant a time when they would never, never hurt each other.

"I know! But I could change. I mean, I have changed. I'm older— I'm not so emotional. I wouldn't be so frantic about you, Woody. So— watchful." Christ she was hearing herself sound like a defense attorney pleading a cause in which he wants you to believe he believes.

"But—see, honey—we don't love each other, now. We don't actually know each other, do we? We're different people. I know I am." Woody was pleading, too. Not exactly pushing Yvonne back but holding her at bay, palms of his meaty hands against her shoulders while she was clutching at his forearms.

"I could love you, Woody. I never stopped, it just went underground. You know that, come *on*."

"Fuck this, Vonnie. This is bullshit."

"I'm serious! You know I am."

She'd begun to cry. The tears were spontaneous, hot as acid. Did this mean they were sincere? The way she was feeling, a sensation like a rag being twisted inside her chest, and something inky running down her face, she felt sincere, like the outermost layer of her skin was being peeled off, but Woody was being weird and not-himself repeating it hadn't been good, it hadn't been any kind of life for either of them, and there was Yvonne's husband Neil, and her daughter, and Yvonne interrupted saying he wasn't listening! wasn't hearing her!—"I've just been explaining, Woody, I would not be so crazy now. I've been telling you and you don't *hear*." Her voice was lifting dangerously. But why did Woody provoke her! "I think I panicked, then. I had to get out. I was going to pieces, and Neil was close to finding out, and you know Neil, I mean you knew Neil, he isn't like us, he isn't the kind to *forgive*. So he was ready to leave Mount Olive, things were falling into place for him,

a transfer, a new job, he's fine, we're like people digging in different parts
of a garden, we're in the garden together but, you know, not *together*.
Not like you and me. I mean, maybe Neil did know something, the way
Caroline knew something, without exactly knowing what it was"—
speaking quickly now not wanting to see in Woody's face how he was
feeling about this, that possibly Caroline had known more than she,
Yvonne, had wished to believe she'd known—"but it was me, my fault,
I understood even then but I couldn't seem to stop it, I had a hard time
not being with you all the time, Woody. I never saw you sleep, for Christ's
sake." There came the note of reproach, the old indignation, something
prim and punitive like a glass struck at a banquet, the heart sinks to
hear a glass struck at a banquet meaning toasts, speeches, soul-killing
and tedious, and so practically in mid-syllable Yvonne quick-changed
her tone, before (she hoped!) Woody could register it, like recognizing
an old melody in some scrambled jazz improvisation. She said, lowering
her voice, "There were things I stopped, after you, sweetie. I mean, forever. Smoking dope, and drinking vodka, and masturbating. After *you*."

Woody blinked and stared. Woody decided to laugh, this was meant
to be funny was it? "You're kidding, right? You aren't serious."

"I am! I am serious."

For it was true. Dope, vodka, masturbating. All that was tied up
with Woody Clark for no one else in Mount Olive had smoked dope
with her except Woody, no one else in Mount Olive had offered her
dope except Woody, and the vodka had been some kind of flashy fad,
Dostoyevskian-dangerous to one like Yvonne with dipsomaniac genes
and in fact she'd had a little problem with that, with the drinking, after
moving across the state from Mount Olive, but she didn't intend to tell
Woody Clark that. And the masturbating: not exactly something she
was proud of but why not tell Woody, spill her guts to Woody as she
hadn't been able to spill her guts to any therapist, ever. The masturba-
tion was something she'd done compulsively, fierce and insatiable and
(maybe) slightly deranged, after afternoons with Woody when she'd
had to fantasize the man back with her and so vividly she could not

cease thinking of him, seeing him, smelling his sweet-funky sexy-sweaty odor, feeling him inside her, and out; and to call such frantic sexual need *pleasure, pleasurable* let alone *self-pleasuring* was some kind of crude joke. Seeming to see from a distance of about ten feet a woman scream-ing and tearing at a pillow cover with her teeth, moaning, sobbing as if her heart was being broken, her desperate fingers inadequate trying to contain the muscular convulsions between her chafed legs, and there was a mad wish to pry up inside herself with, what?—a knife-blade, a pair of scissors. Those months she'd been in a fever, this had been sick-ness, and trying then to sleepwalk through her life as a man's wife and a (needy) girl's mother with dilated eyes, swollen mouth and thoroughly fucked-up head—she had no idea how she'd managed, it was a wonder to her like sending a man to Mars, or wherever. No possible way you could comprehend it except to assume it had happened, somehow.

Flush-faced Woody was saying, "Ohhhh fuck. Just fuck, Yvonne. Why'd you tell me this shit?" and Yvonne was saying, wiping at her eyes, speaking eagerly now, "Because, well—I thought we told each other everything." And Woody was saying, "*Everything?* We told each other *noth*ing" and Yvonne was saying, "We did? I mean—we didn't? I mean, I did—" and Woody was saying, in the voice of an aggrieved twelve-year-old, "Here I thought we were so terrific together. We were fantastic, I thought. You were so classy-cool and ice-blond not what anybody'd think from seeing you which was a terrific turn-on, for me I mean, you were always, like, 'I'll try anything,' like I was some kind of native safari guide, leading the white lady into the jungle. And now you're telling me, you're actually telling me that all that time you—" Woody shook his head as if to dislodge something inside it. He could not bring himself to enunciate just what it was, Yvonne had been doing.

She protested, "But that's why, Woody. I was crazy for you. I couldn't get enough of the actual you. It's the way women are, I think. I mean, when it's like a sickness. When love is, well—like a sickness. The fantasy."

"What fantasy? I was there, wasn't I real? *I* thought I was plenty real."

How to make Woody, or any man, know, the more real he is in actual life, the more real in fantasy? Yvonne began to stammer, "But you, you must have fantasies, too? Don't men? I mean, sometimes? Come on, Woody, you must have masturbated, too—"

Woody said, appalled, "No! Why'd I do that! I wasn't thirteen for Christ's sake. This is really sick, Yvonne. This is so *you*. Telling me now, eight years later like a delayed kick in the groin."

Yvonne laughed. Woody was so hot-eyed and excited, the blond fuzz covering his flushed scalp looked radioactive. You'd have thought she had insulted his lineage, his dignity. "Oh, Woody. Come on. I'm only just telling you how it was with me, it's a compliment to *you*. How many female residents of Mount Olive, all ages, are fantasizing about Woody Clark any given time of the day, or night? Live with it."

Woody was sulky-mouthed, skeptical. "I suppose now you're going to tell me, jacking-off was better." Better than what, Woody left unsaid.

Yvonne said, hurt, " 'Jacking-off' isn't what women do. With women it isn't so crude, it's more fantasy, romantic. I mean, it isn't all that physical." Yvonne paused, not knowing what she meant. For certainly it had been physical. And yes, often it had been better than the seemingly real thing, with the man. She began to laugh, a little short of breath. The courthouse was nominally air-conditioned, but you'd hardly have known it in this submerged corridor that smelled like the interior of an old refrigerator.

Woody said, frowning, "Baby, cut the bullshit. You're breaking my heart. My balls, you're breaking. *Was* it better? 'Mas-tur-bating' some secret place where Neil wouldn't be likely to find you?"

Yvonne laughed. Ohhh no she wouldn't say one word more on the subject. Almost, she'd think that she and Woody had been smoking dope in the basement of the old courthouse, he'd been passing her one of his "fantastic" joints (he'd acquired, he said, from the same high school dropout kid who supplied the local teenagers) and laughing at the dazed-silly expression on her face, hilarious when she coughed, choked, wheezed and couldn't seem to keep her mouth closed.

There were footsteps at the farther end of the corridor, on the stairs.

Someone else was coming to the county clerk's office? A man in what appeared to be a rumpled seersucker suit, looking like a courthouse lawyer. Thank God, no one Yvonne recognized. He bypassed the clerk's door to unlock another door, and disappeared inside.

During this exchange, Woody had been looming over Yvonne. She remembered with a thrill his air of menace, the way sometimes he'd use his big body aggressively, in the guise of seeming-playful so you'd think *He's kidding, but this is the real thing.* In their circle, Woody Clark's reputation was up-from-blue-collar, therefore frank-talking, cut-through-bullshit, straight-Democratic ticket, though in fact (not that Woody would talk about this, much) his father ran a family-owned business, Woody had gone to one of the small, good colleges in New York State (maybe Colgate? Hamilton?), had a business degree from Cornell and was a partner in Mount Olive's preeminent accounting firm. "Let's get some fresh air, Yvonne. It's badly needed." He'd been herding her in the direction of a rear door marked EXIT.

Unexpected bright air! After the dim-lit corridor, it felt like TV exposure.

The asphalt lot was shimmering with heat. A surprising number of vehicles were parked there. Woody inquired which car was Yvonne's and she explained she'd parked on the street, her car was a metallic-green Acura; Woody pointed out his massive black Land Rover, parked close by in a way to take up two spaces. Yvonne said, "Why am I not surprised, Woody? The Land Rover was invented for guys like you."

Woody took this as a compliment. He offered her a cigarette, some low-tar filter brand Yvonne didn't even recognize, and she declined, though with regret. (Yes she'd stopped smoking. Was trying to. Like the personal trainer, the Atkins diet. Other things that made the navigation of a single day like a voyage in a kayak in white-water rapids.) Woody was talking about cars, or maybe he was talking about the economy, looking over her head now restless-eyed, smoking his cigarette with zest. It was sharp as pain, how badly Yvonne wanted to ask about Caroline, or anyway who'd just recently died in Woody's family, for surely it had to be family, to upset Woody the way it had seemed to upset him, unless she was misreading him but no: she was sure she'd read Woody just right, a few minutes ago. But she couldn't ask, and he wasn't going to volunteer, though Woody was asking, circumspectly, politely, about Neil, Neil's work, for he'd heard Neil was "doing really well" and, you could see that Woody sincerely meant it, he was "happy" for them both.

He said, sucking in smoke, "Everybody always said, Neil wouldn't stay in Mount Olive long. That seemed evident."

Yvonne took this as a compliment, and not a backhanded one. She'd been wiping at her smudged mascara with a tissue, trying not to be too obvious. In the acid-bright air her eyes ached but she didn't want to retrieve her sunglasses from her handbag, the lenses were so dark-tinted as to seem opaque. She wanted to see Woody Clark clearly, and she wanted him to see her clearly. She heard herself say, in a casual, seemingly retrospective voice, not at all an accusing voice but soft-sounding as she could manage, "I really did want you to know, Woody: I think of you often. You were the love of my life." She paused. Her mouth twitched. Each was waiting for some further remark, a comic one-liner perhaps. But Yvonne couldn't think of anything funny enough to risk.

(Oh, they'd joked so much together! Yvonne was remembering that now. Every assignation was a conversation and every conversation was packed with laughs. Her laughter with Woody Clark had been like hyperventilating: once you start, it's hard to stop.)

Woody said, exhaling smoke like punctuation, "Bullshit! You haven't thought of me in years. Why'd you think of *me*?" It was a sincere question, Woody meant it. "You have your family. You have your 'corporate attorney' husband and your 'Tudor mansion'—yeah, I heard about that—and your 'social life' in—wherever."

"Averill Park."

"Upscale suburb of Albany? I've heard."

Yvonne smiled. She was embarrassed, just slightly, but she liked it that Woody had heard. Meaning he'd been asking after her, maybe. Or that, hearing of the departed Wertenbakers, Yvonne and Neil, mutual friends naturally passed on the word to Woody Clark as if, in retrospect, their secret liaison hadn't been so secret after all but a matter of public record like the Police Blotter column in the *Mount Olive Weekly*.

Yvonne said carelessly, " 'Social life' is a hobby. It's for spare time. It isn't, you know, *real*." Though she recalled how Woody had loved parties, Woody Clark glowing and glistening and loud-laughing so people were drawn to him, how people awaited Woody's arrival, how a light seemed to go out if Woody Clark had to leave early. "Neil and I, when we go out, don't even talk together, it's like we just arrive together then drift away. Some parties, they're just blurs to me. I feel like some kind of amateur porn actress, smiling and smiling, so-happy smiling, Neil Wertenbaker's wife, and the sad thing is, if Neil and I just met at one of these parties, for instance seated next to each other at dinner, we wouldn't be drawn together, at all. One time we were, I guess. But that time is past. Now we're like"—Yvonne was becoming vague now—"opposite ends of a magnet? That repel."

" 'Diamagnetic.' " Woody sounded interested. For a moment he brooded, as if considering what to reveal of himself, his marriage. "Weird thing, I'm getting that way with my older brother Steve. You know, Steve? In fact, with lots of people. I mean, people I can't reasonably avoid. You start out attracted, sort of, then somehow the poles get switched and you end up repelled. It actually feels physical." Woody thumped the edge of his fist against his torso, in the region of his heart. It was a strange, oddly poignant gesture Yvonne could recall afterward with no idea what it meant.

But Yvonne didn't want Woody to digress. Not now, when time was running out. (She'd been glancing, wincing, at her watch. At noon, when she'd first arrived at the courthouse, she'd had a yawning abyss of time to get through, now precious minutes were rapidly passing, the minute hand was on its upward swath moving inexorably toward 1 P.M.) She said, almost petulantly, as if they'd been arguing, "Social life is like buzzing insects. I can 'do' it but so what? The only things that have ever meant anything to me have happened in private. When I'm alone, I'm—well, you know what I'm like."

"I never did. Frankly."

"You did, Woody! You saw into my heart."

Woody laughed. He was feeling good now, in even the shimmering-hot air of the asphalt parking lot. "Fuck I did. Your 'heart.' I never saw you without makeup, for Christ's sake."

"Come on, you did! Lots of times, you did. It all got rubbed off, be-lieve me. My skin was raw after you. I mean, raw." She laughed, sound-ing like hyperventilation. "I'm covered in scar tissue."

"Oh, man. Are you. That's what it is, huh?"

Woody took hold of Yvonne's chin to tilt it upward. She knew that she looked reasonably good, and her scissor-cut ashy-blond hair looked more than reasonably good, so she didn't flinch, though that was her instinct. She knew that Woody, joker that he was, yet wouldn't joke about anything so personal/private as cosmetic surgery, which she had not had, yet, or laser wrinkle removal, Botox, collagen injections which she had. Yvonne poked him in his belly, that felt softer now, like foam rubber. She thought that he would kiss her, at least lightly on the lips, but he didn't. She said, "You just refuse to acknowledge it, don't you? What we had, for a while, together."

The *for a while* was subtle, poetic. Yvonne wondered where it had come from.

Woody was backing off. The cigarette was some sort of protective shield he'd been using, Yvonne saw that now. He said, "Talk of being 'alone'—you were never alone, when you were with me. So how'd I know what you were truly like, when you're 'alone'?" He laughed, in a whirl of smoke. He was delighted to be tripping her up. Despite the baby face, Woody was a sharp, shrewd guy. In their circle, some of the men had played poker occasionally, including Neil, and Woody Clark was the one to beat. Despite his relative youth, or because of it, he'd been the one to master home computers early on. When your computer crashed, when you couldn't retrieve a disk, you went to Woody Clark for help. Even Neil Wertenbaker, for all his pride. And more than once.

By the time the county clerk returned, at 1:08 P.M., two other disgruntled citizens were waiting. Yvonne was processed first, then Woody. She waited for him out back, at the Land Rover. She had the death certificate in a manila envelope, in her handbag. She'd only just glanced at it in the clerk's office, her eyes damp with moisture. Quickly she'd put it away. And now her car keys were in her hand. Her heart kicked with the sudden impulse to escape, before Woody Clark joined her. How surprised he'd be, how he'd been taking her for granted! The surprise on the baby-bandit face, when he saw she'd gone.

If she waited for him, if she lingered, very likely he would invite her to lunch another time, but she'd have to refuse. (Unless she called her housekeeper on her cell phone. Just maybe, Lucia could drive Jill to her tennis lesson, and swing around afterward to pick her up. Though Yvonne hated to ask. Chauffeuring wasn't Lucia's usual task. And Jill would be sulky and sarcastic for the remainder of the day.) She was thinking how, if she slipped away, Woody wouldn't try to contact her. He hadn't tried to contact her in more than eight years. She hadn't tried to contact him. (A few postcards, sent from exotic places like Belize, Costa Brava. Nothing too personal, just for fun.) That had meant something final, and sensible. That had meant something profound, hadn't it?

"Yvonne? Hey."

Woody came at her, eager and frowning. His big sunburnt face looked as if it must hurt. His impossibly-blue eyes, too, appeared excessively moist. He was clutching a manila envelope identical to the one in Yvonne's handbag, return address COUNTY OFFICE OF RECORDS, CHAUTAUQUA COUNTY COURTHOUSE, CHAUTAUQUA, NEW YORK. Except now Woody was looking like a man in a hurry who wouldn't be inviting Yvonne to lunch after all. More, he was looking like a guilty man who needs to make a quick call on his cell phone even as he drives hurriedly through Main Street traffic.

Of course, Woody would have another woman by now. Women. That was obvious.

He fumbled in his pocket, gave Yvonne his business card. He brushed his lips, that felt parched, against her cheek. Like a man out of breath he said, "O.K. look, what we said—if you want to, you know, pursue it." This was a new business card of Woodrow Clark, Jr.'s, made of a stiffer material than the old. It would have e-mail, cell phone information on it, as the old card had not.

She didn't watch Woody maneuver the Land Rover out of the parking lot. She knew he expected it, but no. She was in a hurry, too.

By 1:35 P.M., Yvonne was driving east on the Thruway. She'd slipped Woody's business card into the envelope with the death certificate, for safekeeping. What was worrying her immediately was, the adrenaline charge she'd felt, first seeing Woody, that had lit her up like a Christmas tree, was rapidly receding now. You could practically see the brave little glitter-lights going out one by one. If she wasn't careful she'd have one of her blinding migraines on the drive to Albany. This feeling of fatigue, a taste of something sour and brackish like panic. Sometimes all that was required to set off a migraine was a sudden sharp knife-blade of light reflected off the hood, windshield, chrome of another vehicle. A pulse beat in her head, behind her eyes, in warning. Not even the dark glasses could spare her, if a migraine was imminent.

"Yes, maybe." Her lips moved, in answer to a question. But what was the question?

She stopped the car on the Thruway shoulder, impulsively. Woody's card—what had she done with Woody's card? Anxiously she checked the manila envelope containing the death certificate—yes, it was there.

URANUS

T he party was in *full swing*—like a cruise ship that has left the dock and is plying its way through choppy waves out of the harbor—glittering with lights and giddy with voices, laughter, music. The party was her party—hers and her husband's—in fact, today was her husband's birthday—at the farther end of the living room Harris was in a fever-pitch of conversation surrounded by his oldest friends who'd been post-docs with him at MIT in Noam Chomsky's lab, 1963–64—he wouldn't detect her absence she was sure.

Seven-fifty P.M.—near-dusk—a strategic moment for the hostess to slip away between the swell of arrivals, greetings, cocktails and appetizers and the (large, informal) buffet supper that would scatter guests through the downstairs rooms of the sprawling old Tudor house at 49 Foxcroft Circle, University Heights.

How many years the Zalks had hosted this party, or its variants! Leah Zalk took a childlike pleasure seeing her house through the eyes of others—how the rented tables were covered in dusky-pink tablecloths—not the usual utilitarian white—how the forsythia sprigs she'd cut the previous day from shrubs alongside the house were blossoming dazzling-yellow in tall vases against the walls—how beautiful, flickering candlelight in all the rooms—track lighting illuminating a wall of Harris's remarkable photographs taken on his travels into the wilder parts of the earth—in a farther corner of the living room a guest who was clearly a trained pianist was playing cheery show-tunes, dance tunes of another era—"Begin the Beguine"—"Heart and Soul"—alternating with flamboyant passages of Liszt—the rapid nervous rippling notes of the *Transcendental Etudes* that Leah had once tried to play as a girl pianist long ago.

A party in *full swing*. What a relief, to escape.

Between her eyes was a steely-cold throb of pain. Quickly it came and went like flashing neon she had no wish to acknowledge.

Leah made her way through the crowded dining room and into the kitchen where the caterer's assistants were working—made her way through the back hall to the rear of the house—pushed open a door that opened onto a rarely used back porch—and was astonished—disconcerted—to see someone leaning against the railing, smoking—a guest?—a friend?—this individual would have to be an old friend of the Zalks, who'd had the nerve to make his way into the rear of the house to the back porch—yet Leah didn't recognize him when he turned with a startled smile, cigarette smoke lifting from his mouth like a curving tusk.

"Mrs. Zalk? Hey—h'lo."

The young man's greeting was bright, ebullient, slightly over-loud.

Leah smiled a bright-hostess smile: "Hello! Do I know you?"

He was no one she knew—no one she recognized—in his mid- or late twenties—somewhat heavy, fattish-faced—yet boyish—looming above her at six foot three or four—with bleached-looking pale blond hair curling over his shirt collar—moist and slightly protuberant pale-blue eyes behind stylish wire-rimmed glasses—an edgy air of familiar-ity or intimacy. Was Leah supposed to know this young man? Clearly he knew *her*.

He bore little resemblance to Harris's graduate and post-doc stu-dents and could hardly have been one of Harris's colleagues at the Institute—he had a foppish air of entitlement and clearly thought well of himself. He wore an expensive-looking camel's hair sport jacket and a black silk shirt with a pleated front—open at the throat, with no necktie—his trousers were dark, sharp-pressed—his shoes were black Italian loafers. In his left earlobe a gold stud glittered and on his left wrist—a thick-boned wrist, covered in coarse hairs—a white gold stretch-band watch gleamed. A cavalier slouch of his broad shoulders made him look as if, beneath the sport jacket that fitted him tightly, small wings were folded against his upper back.

A coarse sort of angel, Leah thought, with stubby nicotine-stained fingers and a smile just this side of insolent.

"Certainly you know me, Mrs. Zalk—'Leah.' Though it's been a while."

How embarrassing! Leah had no doubt that she knew, or should have known, the young blond man. As she'd pushed out blindly onto the porch she'd been rubbing the bridge of her nose where the alarming pain had sprung—she wouldn't have wanted anyone to see her with anything other than a hostess's calmly smiling face—if Harris knew he'd have been surprised, and concerned for her.

Leah could not have told Harris how early that morning—in the chill dark of 4 A.M.—she'd wakened with a headache—a sensation of dread for this party they'd hosted every spring, at about the time of Harris's birthday. Somehow over the years the Zalks' party in May had become a custom, or a tradition in the Institute community: their friends, colleagues, and neighbors had come to expect it. Through the long day Leah had felt stress, mounting anxiety. She was sure that Har-ris had been inviting guests by phone and e-mail, far-flung colleagues of his, former students of whom there were so many, without remembering to tell her, and that far more than sixty guests would arrive at the house . . .

"Yes. A while . . ."

"How long, I wonder? Five, six years . . ."

"Well. That might be . . ."

"*You're* looking well, Mrs. Zalk!"

Now Leah remembered: this emphatic young man was the son of friends whom she and Harris saw only a few times a year, though the Gottschalks, like the Zalks, lived in the older, west-end neighborhood of University Heights. The young man had an odd first name—and he'd matured alarmingly—Leah was sure that the last time she'd seen him he'd been an adolescent of twelve or thirteen with a pudgy child's face, a shy manner, hardly Leah's height. Now he carried his excess weight well, bursting with health and vigor and an air of scarcely suppressed elation like an athlete eager to confront his competition.

He was smiling toothily, the smile of a child of whom much has been made by adoring elders. Leah felt herself resistant to his charms—wary of his attention. In a lowered voice he said, "Remember me?—'Woods'? 'Woods Gottschalk'? Dr. Zalk and my father used to play squash together at the gym."

Squash! Leah was sure that Harris hadn't played that ridiculous frantic game in years.

"Of course—'Woods.' Yes—I remember you—of course."

In fact Leah vaguely recalled that something had happened to the Gottschalks' only son—he'd been stricken with a terrible debilitating nerve-illness, or a brain tumor—or was she confusing him with the son of other friends in University Heights? What was most disconcerting, Woods had grown so *large*, and so *mature*. So *swaggering*. She was sure she hadn't seen the Gottschalks enter her house—she wondered if Woods had dared to come alone to the party.

Woods murmured, with an air of deep sympathy: "Yes, it's been a while, Mrs. Zalk. You can be sure—I've been thinking of you."

The blandly glowing face assumed, for a moment, a studied look of gravity. The eyes behind wire-rimmed glasses moisted over. Woods reached out for Leah—for Leah's hands—suddenly her hands were being gripped in Woods's hands—a handshake that quivered with such feeling, the rings on Leah's left hand were pressed painfully into her flesh. As if a blinding light had been turned rudely onto her face, Leah's eyes puckered at the corners.

"You've been so *brave*."

How uneasy "Woods" was making her!—his very name obtrusive, pretentious—staring at her so avidly, hungrily—as if awaiting a response Leah couldn't provide. *Brave?* What did this brash young man mean by *brave?*

Leah didn't like it that he was smoking. That he hadn't offered to put out his cigarette. Nor had he made even a courteous gesture of shielding her from the smoke as another person might have done in similar circumstances. *She* had never smoked—had never been drawn to smoking—though her college friends had all smoked, and of course Harris had smoked, both cigarettes and a pipe, for years.

At last, Harris had given up smoking when he was in his early thirties. Proud of his *willpower*—for he'd loved his pipe—he'd smoked as many as two packs of cigarettes a day—and had done so since the age of sixteen. Giving up such a considerable habit hadn't been easy for Harris for he'd been involved in a major federal-grant project in his Institute lab that frequently required as many as one hundred work-hours a week and smoking had helped relieve the stress of those years—but Harris had done it and Leah had been proud of her husband's *willpower*.

"It's wonderful to see you smile, Mrs. Zalk! You are well—are you?"

"Yes. Of course I'm 'well.' And you?"

Leah spoke with an edge of impatience. How annoying this young man was!

As Woods talked—chattered—Leah stared at a swath of pale blond hair falling onto Woods's forehead—yes, his hair did seem to be bleached, the roots were dark, shadowy. Yet his eyebrows appeared to have been bleached, too. A sweetish scent of cologne wafted from his skin. Woods Gottschalk was a stocky perspiring young man yet oddly attractive, self-assured and commanding. His face was an actor's face, Leah thought—unless she meant the mask-face of a Greek actor of antiquity—as if a face of ordinary dimensions had been stretched upon a large bust of a head. The effect was brightly bland as a coin, or a moon. Lines from Santayana came to Leah—a beautiful poetic text she'd read as a graduate student decades before: *Masks are arrested expressions and admirable echoes of feelings once faithful, discreet and—.*

"As you see I've stepped outside—outside 'time'—and slipped away from your party, Mrs. Zalk. In one of my incarnations—speaking metaphorically, of course!—I'm an emissary from Uranus—I'm a visitor *here*. People of your generation— my parents' generation—and my grandparents' generation—are so touching to me. I so admire how you carry on—you *persevere*. Well into the 'new century,' you *persevere*."

Leah laughed nervously. "I'm not sure what option we have, Woods."

"Look, I know I'm being rude—circumlocution has never been my strong point. My mother used to warn me—you knew my mother, I think—you were 'faculty wives' together—'Take care what you say, dear, it can never be unsaid.'" Woods paused. He was breathing deeply, audibly as if he'd been running. "Just, I admire you. I'm just kidding— sort of kidding—about 'Uranus'—being an 'emissary.' See, I did a research project in an undergraduate course—'History of Science'—a log of the NASA ship *Voyager* that was launched in 1977 and didn't 'visit' Uranus until 1986—one of the 'Ice Giants'—composed of ice and rocks—the very soul of Uranus *is* ice and rocks—but such beautiful moon-rings—twenty-seven moons, at a minimum! Uranus ate into my soul, it was a porous time in my life. Now—I am over it, I think! Mrs. Zalk—Leah?—you are looking at me so strangely, as if you don't know me! Would you care for a—cigarette?"

"Would I care for a—cigarette?" Leah stared at the blandly smiling young man as if he'd invited her to take heroin with him. "No. I would not."

She was thinking, not only had she not seen the Gottschalks that evening in her house, she hadn't seen either Caroline or Byron—was it Byron, or Brian?—in a long time. In fact hadn't she heard that Caroline had been ill the previous spring . . .

"It doesn't matter, Mrs. Zalk. Really."

"What doesn't matter?"

"Cigarettes. Smoking. If you smoke, or not. Our fates are genetic—determined at birth." Woods paused, frowning. "Or do I mean—*conception*. Determined at *conception*."

"Not entirely," Leah said. "Nothing is determined *entirely*."

"Not *entirely*. But then, Mrs. Zalk, nothing is *entire*."

Leah wasn't sure what they were talking about and she wasn't sure she liked it. The disingenuous blue eyes gleamed at her behind round glasses. Woods was saying, with a downward glance, both self-deprecatory and self-displaying, "My case—I'm an 'endomorph.' I had no choice about it, my fate lay in my genes. My father, and my father's father—stocky, big, with big wrists, thick stubby arms. Now Dr. Zalk, for instance—"

"'Dr. Zalk'? What of him?"

Dr. Zalk was Leah's husband. It made her uneasy to be speaking of him in such formal terms. Woods, oblivious of his companion, plunged on as if confiding in Leah: "My grandfather, too. You know—'Hans Gottschalk.' He was on that team that won the Nobel Prize—or it was said, he should have been on the team. I mean, he *was* on the team—molecular biologists—Rockefeller U.—who won the prize, and he should have won a prize, too. Anyway—Hans had ceased smoking by the age of forty but it made no difference. We'd hear all about Grandfather's 'willpower'—as if what was ordinary in another was extraordinary in him, since he was an 'extraordinary' man—but already it was too late. Not that he knew—no one could know. Grandfather for all his genius had a genetic predisposition to—whatever invaded his lungs. So with us all—it's in the *stars*."

"Is it!" Leah tasted cold. She had no idea what Woods was talking about except she knew that Harris would be scornful. *Stars!*

"*I* think you're brave, Leah. Giving this party you give every May at about now—opening this house—that shouldn't become a mausoleum . . ."

And now—Woods was offering her a drink?—he'd slipped away from her party with not one but two wineglasses and a bottle of red wine? "If not a cigarette—you're right, Leah, it's a filthy habit—'genetics' or not—how's about a drink? This Burgundy is excellent."

Leah was offended but heard herself laugh. When she told Harris about this encounter, Harris would laugh. It was not to be believed, this young man's arrogance: "I have an extra glass here, Leah. I had a hunch that someone would come out here to join me—at large parties, that's usually the case. Like I say, I'm an 'emissary.' I'm a 'Uranian.' I bring news, bulletins. I'd hoped you would step out here voluntarily, Mrs. Zalk—I mean, as if 'of your own free will.' So—let's drink, shall we? A toast to—"

Leah had no intention of drinking with Woods Gottschalk. But there was the glass held out to her—one of their very old wedding-present wineglasses—crystal, sparkling-clean—just washed that morning by Leah, by hand. Unable to sleep she'd risen early—anxious that the house wasn't clean, glasses and china and silverware weren't clean, though the Filipina cleaning woman had come just the day before.

Woods held his wineglass aloft. Leah lifted hers, reluctantly, as Woods intoned:

"'The universe culminates in the present moment and will never be more perfect.' Emerson, I think—or Thoreau. And who was it said—'Who has seen the past? The past is a mist, a mirage—no one can breathe in the past.'" Woods paused, drinking. "From the perspective of Uranus—though 'Uranus' is just the word, the actual planet is unfathomable—as all planets, all moons and stars and galaxies, are unfathomable—even the present isn't exactly *here*. We behave as if it is, but that's just expediency."

Leah laughed. What was Woods saying! All that she could re-member of Uranus is that it was—*is?*—unless it had been demoted, like Pluto—one of the remote ice-planets about which no romance had been spun, unlike Mars, Jupiter, and Venus. Or was she think-ing of—Neptune? She lifted the wineglass, and drank. The wine was tart, darkly delicious. It had to be the last of the Burgundy wines her husband had purchased. Woods was saying, "These people—your friends—Dr. Zalk's friends—and my parents' friends—are wonderful people. Many of them—the men, at least—I mean, at the Institute—'extraordinary,' like Hans Gottschalk and Harris Zalk. You're very lucky to have one another. To 'define' one another in your Institute community. And the food, Leah—this isn't the Institute catering service, is it?—but much, much better. What I've sampled is excellent."

"The food is excellent. Yes."

"*I* could be a caterer, I think. The hell with being an 'emissary.' If things had gone otherwise."

Leah was distracted by the deep back half-acre lawn that was more ragged, seedier than she remembered. Along the sagging redwood fence were lilac bushes grown leggy and spindly and clumps of sinewy-looking grasses, tall savage wildflowers with clusters of tough little bloodred berry-blossoms that had to be poisonous. And a sizable part of the enormous old oak tree in the back had fallen as if in a storm. This past winter, there had been such fierce storms! But Leah was sure that Harris had made arrangements for their annual spring cleanup . . . She felt a stab of hurt, as well as chagrin, that the beautiful old oak had been so badly wounded without her knowing.

"What do you do, Woods, since you're not a caterer? I mean—what does an 'emissary' actually *do* for a living?"

"Oh, I do what I am doing—and when I'm not, I'm doing something else."

Woods's tone was enigmatic, teasing. His eyes, on Leah's face, flitted about lightly as a bee, with a threat of stinging.

"I don't understand. What is it you *do.*"

"Strictly speaking, I'm a 'dropout.' I've 'dropped out' of time. Make that a capital letter *T*—'Time.' I've 'dropped out' of Time to monitor eternity." Woods laughed, and drank. "The crucial fact is—*I am sober*—these past eleven months—eleven months, nine days. I am not a caterer—not an 'emissary'—I just 'bear witness'—it's this that propelled me here, to deliver to *you*."

Was he drunk? Deranged? High on drugs? (Halfway Leah remembered, she'd heard that the Gottschalks' brilliant but unstable son had had a chronic drug problem—unless that was the Richters' son, who'd dropped out of Yale and disappeared somewhere in northern Maine.)

"My news is—the Apocalypse has happened—in an eye-blink, it was accomplished." Woods spoke excitedly, yet calmly. "Still we persevere as if we were alive, that's the *get* of our species."

"Really? And when was this 'Apocalypse'?"

"For some, it was just yesterday. For others, tomorrow. There isn't just a single Apocalypse of course, but many—as many as there are individuals. There is no way to speak of such things adequately. There is simply not the vocabulary. But make no mistake"—Woods shook his head gravely, with a pained little smile—"you will be punished."

Now it was *you*. Leah shivered, she'd been thinking that Woods was speaking with cavalier magnanimity of *we*.

"But why?—'punished'?"

" 'Why'?" Woods bared big chunky damp teeth in a semblance of a grin. "Are you kidding, Mrs. Zalk?"

"I—I don't think so. I'm asking you seriously."

A rush of feeling came over her. Guilty excitement, apprehension. For Woods was right: why should *she* escape punishment? A Caucasian woman of a privileged class, the wife of a prominent scientist—long the youngest and one of the more attractive wives in any gathering—a *loved woman*—a *cherished woman*—how vain, to imagine that this condition could persevere!

"Global warming is just one of the imminent catastrophes. The seas will rise, the rivers will flood—the seashores will be washed away. Cities like New Orleans will be washed away. History itself will be washed away, into oblivion. It happened to the other planets—the 'Ice Giants,' long ago. No one laments the passing of those life-forms—none remain, to lament or to rejoice. In our soupy-warm Earth atmosphere there will arise super-bugs for which 'medical science' can devise no vaccines or antibiotics. There will arise genetic mutations, malformations. These are the 'Devil's frolicks'—as it used to be said. Entire species will vanish—not just minuscule subspecies but major, mammalian species like our own. There will be as many catastrophes as there are individuals—for each is an individual 'fate.' But you will all be punished—when the knowledge catches up with you."

"You've said that but—why? Why 'punished'? By whom?"

Leah spoke with an uneasy lightness. This was the way of Harris—Harris and his scientist-friends—when confronted with the quasi-profound proclamations of non-scientists.

The pain between her eyes was throbbing now and her eyes blinked away tears. A kind of scrim separating her from the world—from the *otherness* of the world—and from invasive personalities like Woods's—had seemed to be failing her, frayed and tearing. She'd been susceptible to headaches all her life but now pain came more readily, you could say intimately. Harris—who rarely had headaches—tried to be sympathetic with her stooping to brush his lips against her forehead. *Poor Leah! Is it all better now?*

Yes she told him. *Oh yes much better thank you!*

Though in fact *no.* Except in fairy tales no true pain is mitigated by a kiss.

"Because you'd had the knowledge, and hadn't acted upon it. Your generation—your predecessors—and now mine. Human greed, corruption—indifference. Humankind has always known what the 'good life' is—except it's fucking *bor-ing.*"

Woods spoke cheerily and as if by rote. There was a curious—chilling—disjunction between the accusation of his words and the playful banter of his voice and again Leah was reminded of an actor's face—a mask-face—fitted on the young man's head like something wrapped in place. Defensively she said: "Evolution—that means change—'evolving.' Species have always passed away into extinction, and been replaced by other species. But no species can replace *us*."

"Wrong again, Mrs. Zalk! I hope your distinguished-scientist husband didn't tell you something so foolish. *Homo sapiens* will certainly be replaced. Nature will not miss us."

Woods laughed baring his big chunky teeth. Leah stared at him in dislike, repugnance. This arrogant young man had so rattled her, she couldn't seem to think coherently. Badly she'd been wanting to leave him—to return to the comforting din of the party—by now Harris would have noticed her absence, and would be concerned—but she couldn't seem to move her legs. In a festive gesture Woods poured more wine into Leah's glass and into his own but quickly Leah set her glass aside, on the slightly rotted porch railing. Woods lifted his glass in a mock-salute, and drank.

"Yes—we will miss one another, Mrs. Zalk—but nature will not miss *us*. That's our tragedy!"

"How old are you, Woods?"

"Forty-three."

"'Forty-*three*'!"

Leah wanted to protest *But you were a boy just yesterday—last year. What has happened to you . . .*

Woods's face was unlined, unblemished, yet the eyes were not a young man's eyes. Through the wire-rimmed glasses you could see these eyes, with disturbing clarity.

He's mad Leah thought. *Something has destroyed his brain—his soul.*

"Well. I—I think I should be getting back to my party—people will be wondering where I am. And you should come, too, Woods—it's cold out here."

This was so: the balmy May afternoon had darkened by degrees into a chilly windblown dusk. Dead leaves on the broken oak limbs rattled irritably in the wind as if trying to speak. Quickly Leah retreated before Woods could clasp her hand again in his crushing grip.

She would leave her unsettling companion gazing after her, leaning against the porch railing that sagged beneath his weight. Cigarette in one hand, wineglass in the other, and the purloined bottle of Burgundy near-empty on the porch floor at his feet.

How warm—unpleasantly warm—the interior of the house was, after the fresh air of outdoors.

At the threshold of the crowded living room Leah paused. Her vision was blurred as if she'd just stepped inside out of a bright glaring place and her eyes hadn't yet adjusted to the darker interior. In a panic Leah looked for Harris, to appeal to him. She looked for Harris, to make things right. He would slip his arm around her, to comfort her. Gravely he would ask her what was wrong, why was she so upset, gently he would laugh at her and assure her that there was nothing to be upset about, what did it matter if a drunken young man had spoken foolishly to her—what did any of that matter when the birthday party Leah had planned for him was a great success, all their parties in this marvelous old house were great successes, and he loved her.

Harris didn't seem to be in the living room talking with his friends— they must have moved into another room. The party seemed to have become noisier. Everyone was shouting. From all directions came a harsh tearing laughter. The pianist who'd been playing Liszt so beautifully had departed, it seemed—now there was a harsher species of music—a tape perhaps—what sounded like electronic music—German industrial rock music?—primitive and percussive, deafening. Who *were* these people? Was Leah expected to know these people? A few of the faces were familiar—vaguely familiar—others were certainly strangers. Someone had dared to take down Harris's wonderful photographs from his world travels—in their place were ugly splotched canvases, crookedly hung. The dazzling-yellow sprigs of forsythia had been replaced by vases of artificial flowers with slick red plastic stamens—birds of paradise? The rental tables were larger than Leah had wished and covered with garish red-striped tablecloths—who had ordered these? Without asking her permission the caterers' assistants had rearranged furniture, Harris's handsome old Steinway grand piano had been shoved rudely into an alcove of the living room and folding chairs had been set up in place of Leah's rattan chairs in the sunroom. The buffet service had begun, guests were crowding eagerly forward. In a panic Leah pushed blindly through the line of strangers looking for—someone—whom she was desperate to find—a person, a man, from whom she'd been separated— in the confusion and peril of the moment she could not have named who it was, but she would know him, when she saw him, or he saw her.

LOST DADDY

The mommy was at the University Medical Center Clinic where she worked—the mommy's work was *anesthesiology* which made your tongue twist like a corkscrew—one of those words that make you laugh and cringe—you could hear it, and recognize it, as a dog recognizes his name, but could not ever pronounce it.

Mommy puts people to sleep the daddy said. *Mommy is paid very handsomely to put people to sleep and to wake them up again—if Mommy can.* The daddy laughed saying such things like riddles—the daddy often laughed saying things like riddles which made Tod uneasy and provoked him to say in a whining voice *Why'd you pay to sleep?—why'd anybody pay to sleep?—you can just go to bed to sleep can't you? Daddy's being silly*—because really you never knew if the daddy was being silly or serious or something in-between and not-knowing was scary.

This day was a special day. At breakfast, Tod knew.

The daddy waited until the mommy left for work then pushed aside the bright yellow Cheerios box and the daddy whistled loudly preparing French toast pouring maple syrup lavishly onto slabs of egg-soggy toast so the toast floated in the syrup and spilled out onto the Formica-top breakfast nook table. Some of the toast burnt in the frying pan and the daddy scraped it out with a sharp knife and the smell of scorch filled the kitchen, the daddy grunted opening a window and fresh air rushed in making Tod sneeze. It was one of those fierce bright mornings the daddy loved *little dude* so, hugged him so hard Tod shrieked with laughter anxious the daddy would crack his ribs or drop him onto the hardwood floor.

Love you li'l dude! One day, you'll know how much.

The *change in our schedules*—this was what the mommy called it speaking in a lowered voice on her cell phone when the daddy wasn't near—began so soon after Tod's birthday—which was March 11—when Tod was four years old—that sometimes it seemed maybe his birthday had something to do with it. Tod knew better but sometimes he felt that the daddy blamed *him*—for it was just a few days later that the daddy was *downsized*.

What this meant wasn't clear for if Tod asked his father what was *downsized* his father just joked waving his hands in the harassed-daddy way as if brushing away flies *Some kind of shrink-wrap it's the principle of mummization* which Tod didn't understand—for the daddy said such things, to make you realize you didn't understand—not just to Tod but to everyone including the mommy and Tod's grandparents—and once—this was in the park, the daddy was talking with a friend—*Miniaturized is what it is, each day I shrink a little till my kid and I will be twins and fit in each other's clothes.*

This was scary too but Tod knew, the way the daddy laughed, and the other man laughed with him though not so loudly as the daddy laughed, it was meant to be a joke, and meant to be funny.

Now it was, in the weeks following Tod's fourth birthday in March, the daddy was home much of the time. This was so strange!—for as long as Tod could remember the daddy had always been *away at work* all day and returned in time for supper at 7 P.M. or sometimes later after the mommy had put Tod to bed. Now the daddy was *always home*. The daddy was home in the morning after the mommy left for the medical center. The daddy was the one to make Tod's breakfast and walk Tod six blocks to nursery school and return at noon to bring Tod back home.

No longer was there any need for the nice Filipina lady to take care of Tod after school. Suddenly it happened that Magdalena was gone for *the change in our schedule* came abruptly and seemingly irrevocably and within days Tod was forgetting that there'd ever been Magdalena for now there was just the daddy in the house when the mommy wasn't there. There was just the daddy to rouse Tod from bed, bathe him and hug him hard in the bath towel and feed him. And sometimes it was the daddy who put Tod to bed if the mommy came home late. All this because the daddy had been *downsized*—which was a word the daddy pronounced like it was something sharp inside his mouth cutting it or a red-hot coal the daddy would have liked to spit out except it was making him laugh, too—or was the daddy trying not to laugh?—you had to look at the daddy closely like somebody on TV to see if he was serious or not-serious but if you looked too close at the daddy the daddy became angry suddenly because the daddy was like *Canis familiaris* he said he *did not like* to be stared at at close quarters *Got that, little dude?*

There was a threat in this—a threat of a sudden backhand slap—not a slap to hurt but a slap to sting—and it was risky, if you smiled when you shouldn't smile or failed to smile when you should. But Tod was *little dude* and this was a good sign. Tod liked being *little dude*. Tod was thrilled being *little dude* for this suggested that the daddy wasn't mad at Tod just then.

Li'l dude just you and me. Love ya!

Most times when the daddy took Tod to nursery school in the morning and to the park in the afternoon, the daddy would make sure that Tod wore his Yankees cap and a warm-enough sweater or jacket and the daddy would tie his sneakers the right way—*tight!*—so the laces wouldn't come loose and cause Tod to trip over them. If the daddy whistled tying Tod's shoelaces this was a good sign though if the daddy hadn't remembered to wash Tod's face and hands after breakfast this might be a not-good sign like if the daddy's jaws were covered in scratchy stubble and if the daddy's breath was sour-smelling from cigarettes the mommy was not supposed to know that the daddy had started smoking again. Nor was it a good sign if when they were walking together the daddy made calls on his cell phone cursing when all he could get was *fucking voice mail.*

Tod's nursery school was just a few blocks away from their house and Terwilliger Park just slightly farther so there was no need for the daddy to drive. There was no need for a second car. In the park the daddy smoked his cigarettes—*This is our secret, kid*—*Mommy doesn't need to know got it?*—and read the *New York Times*—or a paperback book—(the daddy had been reading a heavy book titled *The World as Will and Idea* for a long time)—or scribbled into a notebook—or stared off frowning into the distance. At such times the daddy's mouth twitched as if the daddy was talking—arguing—with someone invisible as Tod played by himself or with one or two other young children in a little playground consisting of a single set of swings and monkey-bars and a rusted slide. Sometimes the daddy fell into conversations with people he met in the park—there were young mothers and nannies who brought children to the playground—and women walked dogs in the park—or jogged—or walked alone—and often Tod saw his father talking and laughing with one of these women not knowing if she was someone his father knew or had just met; once, Tod overheard his father tell a flame-haired young woman that he was a married man which was *one kind of thing* and simultaneously he was the father of a four-year-old which was *another kind of thing.*

Whatever these words meant, the woman laughed sharply as if something had stung her. *Well that's upfront, at least. I appreciate that.*

This was a time when they'd begun going to the park every day. This was a time when the mommy's work-hours were longer at the medical center. This was a time when there was just one car for the mommy and the daddy which was the Saab, that had become the mommy's car. Before the *downsizing* there had been a Toyota station wagon which the daddy had driven but this vehicle seemed to have vanished suddenly, like Magdalena.

Turnpike. Totaled. Towed-away. End of tale! the daddy reported with terse good humor of the kind Tod knew not to question.

"Let's surprise Mommy at work. D'you think 'Dr. Falmouth' would like that?"

This day in Terwilliger Park the daddy snapped shut his cell phone in disgust—shoved it into a pocket of his rumpled khakis that drooped from his waist beltless and a size too large—and spoke in a bright-daddy voice as Tod trotted beside him trying to keep up. Tod was thinking—somber *li'l dude* as the four-year-old was—that the river was miles away, where Mommy worked at the University Medical Center was miles away and he and the daddy had never walked so far before.

But Tod was *little dude* and any idea of the daddy's was an exciting idea. Like a man on TV the daddy was rubbing his hands briskly saying here was their plan to discover whether "Dr. Falmouth" was really where she claimed she was—"We will see with our own eyes like Galileo looking through his telescope."

Tod laughed—Tod laughed not knowing who "Galileo" was—though something in the daddy's voice sounding like gravel being shoveled made Tod uneasy—anxious—wasn't Mommy where Mommy was supposed to be?—*where was* Mommy?—and the daddy gripped Tod's skinny little shoulder reprimanding him—"Don't be so literal. Christ sake! If 'Dr. Falmouth' is there she will give us a ride back home. If 'Dr. Falmouth' is not there, we will take the fucking bus back home."

The daddy spoke matter-of-factly. Tod swallowed hard trying to comprehend. It seemed to be that, if Mommy was somewhere they couldn't find her, they would have a way to get back home as if *getting back home* was the crucial thing.

"Has your daddy ever misled you, li'l dude? Yet? Have faith!"

The daddy was tugging at Tod's hand jerking him along like a clumsy little puppy. Sometimes you saw such puppies—or older, stiff-limbed dogs—jerked along on leashes by their impatient masters. Sometimes it happened, the daddy was seized by an idea and had to walk fast. Since the lavish French toast breakfast that morning the daddy had been in an excitable mood. The daddy's eyes were glistening and red-rimmed and the sharp-looking little quills in the daddy's jaws glinted like mica. Though often on these walks the daddy wore a fur-lined cap now the daddy was bare-headed and his dust-colored hair disheveled in the wind that was cold and tasted of something wet-rotted like desiccated leaves—the daddy had crookedly buttoned both Tod's corduroy jacket and his own suede jacket—the daddy was wearing his rumpled khakis and on his feet water-stained running shoes. Tod wasn't sure if the daddy was talking to him—often in the park the daddy was talking to himself—the daddy was whistling—just pausing to shake a cigarette out of a near-depleted pack when there came hurtling at them— almost you'd think the boy was on a bicycle, he came so fast—a tall skinny spike-haired boy with a chalky-pale face, whiskers like scribbles on his chin—a purple leather jacket unzipped to the waist and on his black T-shirt a glaring-white skull-and-crossbones like a second face. What was strangest about the boy was his lacquered-looking hair in two-inch spikes lifting from his head like snakes—Todd turned to stare after him, as he passed on the woodchip path without a backward glance.

It must have been that the daddy recognized the spike-haired boy—or the spike-haired boy recognized the daddy—some kind of look passed quickly between them—and the daddy stopped dead in his tracks.

The daddy told Tod go play on the swings—there was a playground close by—the daddy had to use the restroom.

The daddy was talking to Tod but not looking at him. There'd come into the daddy's voice a faraway tone that was excited but calm, almost gentle. Tod saw how the daddy had not turned to look after the spike-haired boy who'd strode away and disappeared.

Close by the woodchip path—on a narrower path forking into a stand of scrubby pines—was a small squat ugly cinder block build-ing with twin doors: MEN, WOMEN. Both doors were covered in graffiti like the squat little building itself. The daddy had taken Tod into this restroom once or twice—Tod recalled a dark dank smell that made his nose crinkle just thinking of it—but now the daddy just pushed Tod in the direction of the playground saying, "Go hang out with those kids, Tod-die—Daddy will be right back."

Tod-die was a good sign too. Usually.

Tod drifted off alone. It felt strange, to be alone in the park. At first it felt exciting then it felt scary. The daddy had never left him before even for a few minutes. The mommy had never left him in any public place nor did the mommy leave him alone at home, always there had been Magdalena, or another lady to watch him if the daddy was not home. Because it was not a warm day but chilly and gusty for late April there were only a few children in the playground and a few young mothers or nannies. Tod found a swing low enough to sit on with his short stubby legs but it was strange and unnerving to be alone—it was no fun with-out the mommy or the daddy pushing him, praising him or warning him to hang on tight. No one was aware of him—no one was watching him—no one cared how high he swung, or if he fell and hurt himself—except—maybe!—there was some other child's mother a few feet away looking at Tod—staring at Tod, frowning—a pinch-faced woman in a down parka with a hood, half her face hidden by curved tinted glasses.

Was this someone who knew him, Tod wondered. Someone who knew his mother, the way she was staring at him, but the woman didn't smile and call out his name, the woman didn't smile at all but just stared in a way that would be rude if Tod had been an adult and made him self-conscious and uneasy now and before he knew it, he'd lost his bal-

ance and fell from the swing—tried to scramble up immediately, to
show he wasn't hurt.

Tod wasn't alone in the park or lost—the daddy was close by—he
wasn't hurt and he wasn't going to cry like some little baby with a runny
snot-nose but there was the pinch-faced woman in the glasses right beside him—"Oh! Let me help you, little boy! Did you hurt yourself?"
With quick strong hands the woman lifted Tod—steadied Tod—you
could tell these were *mommy-hands* by their quickness and deftness—
the woman brushed his hair out of Tod's eyes peering at him as if there
was some secret in his eyes she had a right to know.

The woman was asking Tod if he'd been left alone in the park—if
that had been his father she'd seen with him, a few minutes ago—Tod
was too shy to look at the woman or to reply to her except in a near-
inaudible mumble that gave the woman an excuse to lean closer to him
squatting beside him with the disconcerting intimacy with which adult
strangers approach children as if in some way children are common
property; she'd lifted the tinted glasses to peer yet more directly into
his face so that her eyes were revealed stone-colored and serious like
Tod's mother's eyes—the kind of eyes you couldn't look away from.
In his confusion Tod was moved to ask the woman if she knew his
mother—his mother worked at the University Medical Center over
by the river and she *put people to sleep*—did she know his mother? Tod
couldn't think of his mother's name, the name that the daddy called her
sometimes, the name she was called at the medical center—the woman
said she was afraid she didn't know Tod's mother—"Tell me what is
your name, little boy?"—Tod mumbled a reply but the woman couldn't
hear—asked him to repeat what he'd said—Tod was silent feeling resentful, obstinate—if he'd been a little dog, he'd have bitten this pushy
woman right on the nose. Again she was asking where Tod's father had
gone—"That man who was walking with you just now on the path—is
that man your father?" Tod made a sniggering noise and twisted from
the woman's grip—"He's Dad-dy—that's who. Dad-dy. And you're ugly
like some nasty old witch."

This was surprising! The woman was surprised, and Tod was surprised. Like a feisty little dog Tod pushed free of the woman and ran away—ran as the woman called after him—out of the playground and in the direction of the cinder block restroom—he'd sighted a tall man who resembled his father coming out of the restroom—though as he drew nearer he was embarrassed to see that the man wasn't his father but a stranger—for a moment he felt panic thinking the daddy had left him—how close he came to breaking down and bawling like a baby—a silly little snot-nose baby like certain of the children at nursery school—but now the daddy did appear—there was the daddy emerging from the restroom blinking in the light frowning and distracted and his suede jacket unbuttoned, he was tucking his shirt into the beltless waist of his khakis as Tod called, "Dad-dy!" and ran at him headlong.

The way the daddy stared at Tod, the child was made to think *He doesn't remember me! He doesn't know who I am.*

That was silly of course. The daddy knew who Tod was!

"Christ sake your nose is running. Here, c'mon—*blow*."

Out of a pocket the daddy extracted a fistful of wadded tissue, that looked as if it had been used already. Dutifully Tod blew his nose as bidden.

"This place is depressing. Let's get the hell out of this place."

The daddy was edgy, alert. The daddy's eyes were alert and dilated and darting-about like a wild animal's eyes. Some change had taken place in the daddy, Tod sensed. Tod was anxious, the pinch-face woman was still watching him, seeing him now with his father, she was the kind to ask a sharp question of Tod's father, that was none of her business. Badly Tod wanted to turn to stick his tongue out at the woman—nasty ugly *witch*—but then the daddy would see the woman and Tod didn't want that. The daddy would discover how Tod had fallen and scraped his hand because the daddy had forgotten Tod's mittens and Tod didn't want the daddy to discover *that*.

"C'mon, li'l dude. Circumstances compel us."

Often the daddy made such statements, that were utterly mysterious to the child. Like, "D'you recall Ingmar Bergman—that's 'Ing-mar Bergman'—famed Swedish filmmaker, deceased 2007—*Always keep a project between you and your death*"—which the daddy had made more than once on these urgent park outings.

So the walk was resumed. The hike of at least two miles through Terwilliger Park to the river, that was farther than the daddy and Tod had ever hiked before. In his edgy-cheery mood the daddy smiled frequently, or maybe it was just the daddy's mouth that smiled; the daddy's face must have felt itchy for the daddy was rubbing at it vigorously, eyes, nose, mouth as if wanting to erase his features the way a TV cartoon character might erase his face. The daddy had not asked Tod about the playground but Tod was boasting how he'd gone *way high* on the swing—higher than the other children—so high, he'd gone *over the top*—like the child-gymnasts they'd seen on TV, that had won Olympic gold medals. The daddy made no reply to the child's boastfulness not even to chide him or to laugh at him. The daddy was clearly thinking of other things. In his face a look as if the daddy was listening to something in the distance for always in this park on damp chilly days especially there was a background murmur of something like voices—muffled laughter—traffic on the interstate, or wind high in the trees—gusts of wind like knives cutting into the slate-colored river in which human cries were mixed. *Listen closely* the wide-eyed daddy once said *that is the dark underside of the world you are hearing, son. Souls in Hades.*

After a half-mile or so the woodchip path ended. Now the path was mud-rutted and treacherous. This was a hiking trail but only sporadically marked. Or maybe real hikers knew how to use the trail, as the daddy did not. For several times the daddy lost the trail, Tod had to point out to him the little blue triangles on trees that let you know where the trail was. Tod hoped his father would become discouraged and turn back with one of his harassed-daddy jokes but he said only, "Your mother will be damned impressed by us! Taking the back way like Che in the jungle."

Tod asked who was *Che in the jungle?* but the daddy ignored him.

Ever deeper the daddy and Tod hiked into the woods. Though the air was chilly and the trail overgrown with brambles the daddy walked with his suede jacket open and his face was flushed, ruddy. Still the daddy's eyes were quick-darting like an animal's and Tod wondered if the daddy was looking for someone, or if someone was looking for the daddy. Since he'd passed Tod and his father on the woodchip path the spike-haired boy had not reappeared so far as Tod knew.

The daddy was saying this was a *shortcut*. The daddy was saying *things wear out, wear down*. The daddy was saying that *the human will is a pitiful vessel to withstand the tidal waves of the non-human will*. Tod had no idea what the daddy meant but he was grateful that the daddy's tone wasn't angry or accusing, it was more as if the daddy was reciting facts commonplace and banal and of the sort the daddy might be expected to confer onto the son as in an ancient ritual of enlightenment, erasure. Tod remembered how before his birthday a few weeks ago—before the *downsizing* and before the *change in our schedules*—even the daddy had been restless and distracted watching TV news with the remote control in his hand switching among three or four channels—sometimes too the daddy prowled through the house in the night while the mommy slept and Tod slept and Tod was wakened to see the daddy leaning over his bed—at first thinking it was a scary thing in a dream then it was the daddy's face dark in the shadows—the daddy's face was soft-crinkling with pain so exquisite it couldn't have been named and the daddy whispered *Love you! Whoever you are, whoever sent you to us*.

By *us* the child knew that the daddy was referring not just to himself but to the mommy as well. But it was rare, the daddy spoke of *us*.

They were passing overturned trash cans. Sad to see here in the woods trash spilled across the trail. Beer cans, Styrofoam containers. There was a single rotted jogging shoe, that scared Tod making him think there was a human foot inside. There was a smell as of something dead and rotted. The daddy must have smelled this smell for he shuddered and laughed saying, "All shortcuts entail risks. Have faith, son!"

The thought came to Tod like a tiny bird pecking at his skull *He will leave you here. He is taking you here to leave you.*

In the sky—that they could see, for only part of the sky was visible now—clouds had turned heavy and sullen like a face suffused with blood. Steadily the day was becoming colder—it didn't seem like April now. Tod was tired trying to keep up with the daddy pulling him along the path but didn't dare try to pull his hand free. The daddy seemed not to know how hard and how tight he was gripping Tod and in such a way that the child's arm felt as if it might be pulled out of its socket.

Not-knowing was the scary thing. At four years of age so much is *not-knowing* like crossing a stream of rushing water on just rocks—this, Tod had seen on TV—a boy only a little older than Tod fleeing a black bear—in Alaska—having to put his trust in these rocks, to save him— a desperate boy—Tod had shut his eyes not wanting to see the boy fall into the stream and the black bear catching and devouring him . . . Magdalena had quickly switched channels.

"Here! Here we are."

In triumph the daddy pulled Tod into a clearing—it was a large open space, in the forest—they were entering the open space from the rear—an outdoor amphitheater with a crude stone stage and six rows of stone benches lifting in a semi-circle. The daddy had seemed to know that this was here, he was very pleased to have found it. On the stone benches moss grew in leprous patches and here and there were ugly red graffiti-scrawls like those on the restroom walls. On the stage lay broken tree limbs and other debris. The outdoor theater was in poor repair as if it were centuries old and long abandoned yet still the daddy seemed pleased and excited and in a burst of sudden energy bounded up onto the stage as if his name had been called.

"Hello—hello—hel-*lo*! Thank you *thank you!*"

Quivering with gratitude—unless it was in mockery of gratitude— the daddy smiled out at the (invisible) audience lifting his hands as if to quell a wave of deafening applause.

"I hope I have not made you good people wait impatiently."

More applause!—the daddy lifted his hands as if overcome with emotion. His expression was both apologetic and eager.

"You say you want—who? *Li'l dude?* My son Tod Falmouth—you're awaiting *him?*"

Tod giggled wildly, this was so silly! Empty stone benches in the ruin of an outdoor theater and the daddy's loud voice echoing. Out of shyness Tod hadn't followed his father out onto the stage. In public places the son did not entirely trust the daddy for the daddy frequently teased the son, exposed him to the eyes of strangers as the butt of jokes the son did not comprehend. Strange and disconcerting to Tod to hear his name uttered in this way. No one in sight—empty stone benches—yet Tod felt embarrassed, the daddy spoke in that bright loud TV voice.

The daddy turned to Tod now, beckoning.

"Son! Come join Daddy onstage! These good people demand it."

Tod shook his head *no.* How silly this was!—yet a sickish sensation stirred in the pit of his belly as if in the ruin of the old theater there was yet an audience, staring at him. They were not so welcoming as the daddy seemed to think. Their blurred eyes sought him out where he was hiding amid rubble at the foot of the stage.

In his sparkly mood the daddy wasn't at all intimidated by the buzzing audience. As Tod stared in astonishment the daddy began to dance—tap-dance—flailing his arms in a comical fashion. The daddy continued to address the audience in a familiar way as if they were all old friends. The daddy's silky thinning dust-colored hair was disheveled in the wind and his face was unusually warm, ruddy. The daddy looked so eager, and so happy!—as Tod hadn't seen his father in a long time.

After a few minutes the tap-dancing ceased. The daddy stopped to catch his breath—a new mood was summoned. Advancing to the very edge of the stage the daddy clasped his hands to his chest and spoke in a grave voice: "'Thou, Nature, art my goddess; to thy law / My services are bound; . . . / I grow. I prosper: / Now, gods, stand up for bastards!'"

Tod laughed as if he'd been roughly tickled—*bastard* was one of the bad words. Yet the daddy pronounced *bastard* happily, like the words of a song.

Another time the daddy paused to wait out the applause of the audience. Then with a dramatic flourish the daddy rubbed his face as if erasing its features to begin again, with a look now of grief. His voice thickened as if he were about to cry. "'All my pretty ones? / Did you say all? O hell-kite! All? / What, all my pretty chickens, and their dam, / At one fell swoop?'"

Hearing these utterly perplexing words Tod became frightened. He had no idea why his father was speaking of chickens but by the tone of his father's voice he understood that something very bad had happened to the chickens.

The daddy's voice trailed off. The daddy seemed less pleased with this recitation. Perhaps the applause was less enthusiastic—the daddy waved it away negligently as if brushing away flies.

Now the daddy repositioned himself on the stage, as if beginning again. He kicked aside several broken tree limbs then thought to pick up one of the smaller branches which he broke in two. Across the daddy's flushed face came a look of something furtive and eager.

"Tod—come up here. I will need you for this, Tod. Daddy insists."

Quickly Tod shook his head *no*. Between his legs he felt a pinching sensation, a sudden need to pee. The daddy onstage regarding him expectantly and the blurred faces of the invisible audience turned to him were making Tod very nervous though he knew that no one was seated on the stone benches—of course. It was what the mommy called *All in your head.*

"Tod! Don't you hear me? Come."

The daddy had been brandishing the stick which now he hid behind his back in a playful manner. Tod had seen that the broken-off end looked sharp as a knife. He felt a thrill of childish fear, the daddy meant to hurt him.

Like a large predator bird the daddy paced about the stage flapping his arms. In his right hand he held the sharp-ended stick. His voice was deep and quavering like a voice out of a well.

"'And it came to pass that God did tempt Abraham, and said unto him, "Take now thy son, thine only son Isaac, whom thou lovest, and get thee into the land of Moriah; and offer him there for a burnt offering upon one of the mountains which I will tell you of" . . . And Abraham rose up early in the morning, and clave the wood for the burnt offering, and laid it onto Isaac his son; and he took the fire in his hand, and a knife; and they went both of them together. And Abraham stretched forth his hand and took the knife to slay his son . . . '" Gripping the sharp-ended stick in both hands and in a crouched-over posture like a wicked old man Tod's father approached the edge of the stage where Tod was cowering. Tod scrambled away, tripped and fell amid rubble but managed to scramble to his feet like a panicked rat.

At the edge of the stage the daddy squatted glaring at Tod. "What God has decreed isn't for us to countermand. Daddy is telling you, Tod—*come up here.*"

Still Tod held back. Still Tod dared to disobey. That look in the daddy's eyes was scary to him.

For a long moment the daddy glared at Tod. Tod saw the daddy's mouth working as if something had gotten inside his mouth he had to chew, chew, chew in order to swallow.

At last the daddy straightened out of his strained squatting position. His knees ached, he made a blowing noise with his lips. "Christ! You don't trust your own father! This is unacceptable."

Tod jammed his thumb in his mouth. Tod was ready to giggle, if the daddy relented.

Still the daddy said, in disgust: "Tod, for Christ sake this is just a *stick.* It is not a knife and I am not the Biblical Abraham—far from it. And this crummy setting is just a stage, you must have noticed—a ruin of a stage. None of this is real. Did you think that Daddy was real?—or you? *You* are just some ejaculate that got lucky."

Some ejaculate. Tod understood that it was something nasty. The daddy's face was red-flushed and creased and the daddy's eyes shone with indignation.

"Which brings us to—'destiny.' Humankind is the only species besotted and beset, beguiled and bespoiled by its own destiny. Long ago—before you were born—your daddy was not your daddy but a student—a graduate student in biology—your daddy immersed himself in studying 'the teeming life of multitudes'—in a lab, we were studying a species of cuttlefish—not a fish but 'most intelligent invertebrate'—a fist-sized thing the shape of a clam with tentacles— slimy—sharp-eyed- -color-blind yet camouflages itself in coral reefs of the most exquisite colors. It was our task to try to comprehend how the cuttlefish can 'instruct' its body to change color when its eyes can't see color. *Why* we knew, but not *how*—never any mystery about *why* in animal/plant camouflaging—but *how* eluded us. Such design, such complexity in something of such little consequence as a cuttlefish means that for higher primates like *Homo sapiens* a more meaningful destiny might not be utterly absurd . . ."

Yet another time the daddy's voice trailed off. Tod could not fail to note how, as soon as his father ceased speaking, the silence returned.

In the distance were muffled voices, or wind—far distant. Here in the ruin of the outdoor theater there was a sudden terrible silence. As soon as you ceased speaking this terrible silence oozed back.

Then, suddenly, unexpectedly—"Bra-*vo*! En-*core*!"

There was someone in the audience after all. Suddenly now a sound of clapping—loud frantic clapping—coming from the rear, right-hand side of the stone benches. About forty feet away on the ground beside one of the benches was what appeared to be a bundle of rags—a bundle of rags that had stirred into life.

"Bravo! Bravo!"—the bundle of rags clapped and whistled.

The daddy was taken utterly by surprise. The daddy blinked and shaded his eyes to stare though there was no sun to obscure his vision. At last with a wry, rueful smile the daddy said, "Well—thank you, sir. We didn't see you over there. We appreciate your applause."

The clapping man was old, or old-seeming—of that category of individual the mommy called *homeless*. If Tod had been alone, he'd have run from such a person. The man had very dirty matted white hair and his jaws sprouted whiskers like a dirty broom. He had wrapped himself in what appeared to be an old blanket or tarpaulin. In his face there was something livid and pitted like the skin of a fricasseed chicken.

The daddy thanked the wild-white-haired man for his applause and "good taste"—the daddy said he'd had an "aborted career in the theater"—his "destiny" had derailed him in other less rewarding directions. The daddy said that he had a "very bad" child in his keeping—and wondered if the white-haired man wanted him?—"His name is Tod. He's four years old. He'd been a reasonably good baby, a promising toddler, now he's a very spoiled little boy who believes he can disobey his father with impunity for his father *is not of God's Hebrew chosen*."

Stricken with shame Tod heard these words of his father's flung out carelessly and with a strange sort of daddy-elation. The white-haired old man laughed heartily. In horror Tod saw the old man wriggle erect, like some sort of nasty big insect out of a cocoon. His eyes shone with merriment in the fricassee-face. In his hand was a grimy paper bag he lifted to his mouth, to take a swig from a bottle inside.

"Yah? Y'say so, mister? Shit how much you askin for him?"

"One hundred dollars and ninety-nine cents."

"One *hunnert*! So why'd I want to pay so much for a brat like that, that nobody wants?"

"Sir, this boy may be bad but he's a bargain. He's been discounted for the month of April, forty percent off his usual price. Do I have a bid?"

The wild-white-haired old man took another swig from the bottle inside the paper bag. Wiped his whiskery mouth on the edge of a filthy sleeve. "Nineteen dollars and ninety-nine cents. *That's* a bargain."

As Tod listened in disbelief the daddy and the old man shouted back and forth like TV characters. You could almost hear the audience laughing—you could almost see the ugly contorted faces. Tod was crying, he'd become so frightened. He knew—he believed he knew—that his father was only joking yet there was something so terrible—so final-sounding—in the daddy's words and the wild-white-haired old man's rejoinders that Tod couldn't stop his tears. To his distress, his nose was running. He no longer had the big wad of tissue the daddy had given him and so had to wipe his nose on the sleeve of his jacket and the daddy looked at him in disgust.

"Christ son it's a joke, why are you so *literal*. Like your prig of a mother is so fucking *literal*. Can't think outside the fucking *box*."

The daddy had the power to make you cry and when you cried the daddy was disgusted and angry with you so that you cried harder which was really upsetting to the daddy.

Even a child of four felt this injustice. As his father and the old white-haired man hurtled jokes at each other like lightning bolts Tod crept away like a wounded dog. As soon as he was out of his father's sight he began to run along the trail—wasn't sure in which direction he was going, ahead or back the way they'd come—the trail was overgrown, brambles tore at his clothes and scratched his face—the little blue triangles on trees were nowhere to be seen.

Very bad. Spoiled. Brat!

Was that the daddy calling after him? Tod stopped to listen—the daddy's voice was so faint, Tod couldn't tell if the daddy was angry with him or sorry. Tod was frightened of the daddy and did not ever want to see the daddy again! He ran, until his breath was ragged. He ran, until his heart beat like a crazed little toad inside his rib cage. He ran, until he came to another clearing, that looked as if part of a hill had slid down in a heap. Here the earth was pocked with stones—you couldn't run here, you would turn your ankle and hurt yourself. It was a place of rust-colored rocks and boulders and a deep ravine inside which, some thirty feet below, Tod saw something slithery and gleaming that might have been a shiny snake, or trickling water.

He was so tired! He'd been sobbing and was so tired, he could only just crawl now. Amid the rust-colored boulders was a fallen tree sprawling in all directions and Tod hid behind the trunk, panting and shiver-

ing and anxious that the daddy would find him and give him to the
wild-white-haired old man.

The daddy was calling faintly and fearfully—"Tod? Christ sake son
where are you?"

The daddy could not see Tod, evidently. For a long time it had
seemed that both the daddy and the mommy could see Tod even if he
was hiding as they could hear his thoughts inside his head but recently
Tod had come to believe that this was not so. The way the daddy called
"Tod? Tod?"—you could tell that the daddy didn't know how close
Tod was.

In surprise Tod saw a smear of blood on his hand—a smear of blood
on his jacket. There must have been blood on his face—he'd struck his
nose, falling. He'd slipped on the rocks, and fallen. Sometimes when he
stuck a furtive forefinger into his nose his nose began to bleed as if in
derision or accusation and so now Tod's nose began to bleed, he would
be terribly shamed if the daddy saw.

"Tod? Where are you? You've gotten us both *lost.*"

Tod peeked through the desiccated old leaves of the fallen tree and
saw his father making his way along the trail slowly. And now in the
rock-strewn clearing. The daddy was climbing the hill—there was a hill
here—slowly and wincing as if his legs hurt. The daddy was yet ruddy-
faced like something skinned. Looking for Tod—where he thought Tod
might be hiding—the daddy blinked in frustration and helplessness as
if peering into a bright blinding sun.

"Tod? We're *lost,* son. That's what you've done—you're to blame—
we are fucking *lost.*"

The daddy's voice was petulant, furious. The daddy's voice sounded
as if it might break into sobs. Tod believed it must be true—the daddy
was *lost*—the little blue triangles on the trees had vanished utterly.

Such disgust he felt for the daddy!—he rocked back on his heels.
He was thinking he would not go back to the daddy—he would not
show the daddy where he was—not ever! He would find the river by
himself if it took the remainder of the day and all of the next. He would

find the river and he would find the medical center, he would find his mother though he wasn't sure of her name—her doctor-name, that would be in a clip-thing on her white jacket.

The mommy would smile at him in surprise. The mommy would not ask *Where is your father? How on earth did you get here?* The mommy would drive them home just the two of them, in the mommy's car.

At home the house would be empty, awaiting them.

The kitchen where the Formica counters were yet sticky, and the air smelled of egg-batter scorch. This room like the others empty and yet Tod's mother would not say *Oh but where is your father? What have you done with Daddy?*

In the quiet of the house they would laugh together. Tod would tell his mother about swinging on the swing—in the park—swinging so high, he'd swung *over the top*—and she would want to hear, every word. She would feed him, and she would bathe him, and she would read to him out of his favorite storybook until he fell asleep in his bed.

So clearly Tod knew this would happen, it was as if it had already happened. Not once but many times.

Here was danger!—the daddy was approaching Tod's hiding place behind the fallen tree. The daddy could have no idea where his son was hiding yet blindly tramping along the overgrown trail the daddy was blundering near—Tod could hear him panting, cursing under his breath.

"Christ sake son where are you! Your daddy never meant to scare you! God damn *obey me.*"

The daddy must have fallen, his khaki pants were muddy and torn at the knees. The daddy's mouth was the mouth of a panting dog that is furious but baffled where to attack.

With the desperation of a wounded snake Tod crawled behind the fallen tree, to the very tip of the tree where limbs and branches were spread out in all directions and where he couldn't make his way any farther. The desiccated leaves through which Tod crawled made a harsh rattling noise but the daddy who was only a few yards away seemed not to hear. How labored the daddy's breathing, and how distraught the daddy was! Nearby was one of the huge rust-colored boulders and beneath the boulder was a hollow place into which Tod could force himself—like a rabbit hole it was, a burrow, a small creature could crawl into, where a larger predator could not follow.

The daddy was pleading, half-sobbing they were *lost*. For God's sake where was Tod, where was the son, the daddy had to rescue them from *this fucking place before dark*.

Tod took a deep breath—crawled beneath the boulder—slipping sideways inside—the hardest part was to force his head inside, and under—into a kind of carved-seeming cavity—here was a smell of the dark, dank earth—a smell of rock—the danger was, the immense boulder might loosen, fall and crush the child but this was a risk worth taking.

Here was a strange thing: the daddy couldn't know that Tod had crawled beneath the rust-colored boulder yet as if by instinct the daddy was drawn to the boulder—"Tod? Are you under this? Tod for Christ sake—where are you?" The daddy was begging. The daddy was very angry. The daddy made grunting noises sprawling flat on his stomach pressing his length against the boulder, that he might grope beneath it with his right hand. The daddy thrust his arm as far beneath the boulder as he could, spreading his fingers that were scratched now, and bleeding. The daddy's fingernails were broken and bleeding. The daddy tried to peer beneath the boulder but could see nothing—only just shadowy shapes that appeared to be inanimate. For here was a rock-cemetery, here was the end of all life. The daddy's breath came quickly and shallowly hurting him like knife-blades in his lungs. If his son was beneath the terrible boulder, if his son was alive yet, and breathing, the daddy could not hear him, in the exigency of his distress. By this time the son had crawled halfway beneath the boulder, that measured approximately nine feet at its widest point. Now the son's way was blocked, he could crawl no farther. Nor had the son who was only four years old begun to calculate how he would turn his small body to crawl out again.

In his burrow-space, the son was safe. In the cunning of animal panic the son lay very still. Like a dazed creature that has been injured but knows not to move, scarcely to breathe, to preserve its life. As if far distant on the surface of the earth the daddy lay pressed against the boulder, the daddy's arm extended beneath the boulder to the shoulder-socket. In tight, constricted circles the daddy's hand moved clumsily. If there was futility in the daddy's gesture yet there was determination, zeal. There was the wish *not to give up—not ever*. For as long as his strength remained the daddy would persevere uttering the son's name until the name lost all meaning. Like words in a foreign language or nonsense-words the syllables *Tod, son, li'l dude* became shorn of meaning as rock is shorn of meaning, implacable, unnameable. Beneath the great boulder the child lay very still. The child's small heart still beat, the child's lungs still pumped, the child would never return to the daddy again, not ever.

SOURLAND

1.

Hardly aware of them she began to see them. Or maybe she sensed them without exactly seeing them. At first singular, isolated spiders, solitary in their shimmering webs—in a high corner of the bedroom in which she now spent so much time, in the musty space beneath the kitchen sink, in the glassed-in porch at the rear of the house where tiny desiccated husks of insects were scattered underfoot. It was the onset of winter, this had to be the explanation. Though she didn't recall an infestation of spiders from other winters, this had to be the explanation.

In a fury of housekeeping she destroyed the webs, killed the spiders and wiped away all evidence. Her hands moved jerkily, there was much emotion in her fingers. Sometimes her fingers clenched like claws, transfixed with rage.

Surviving spouse, she'd become. The one of whom it's said by observers *How well she's taking it! She's stronger than she thinks.*

Or *She's braver than we expected.*

Or *Now she knows.*

That first week after he'd died. First days after death, cremation, burial. Frequently she was but part-dressed, part-awake and staggering somewhere—desperate to answer a ringing phone for instance—or a doorbell rung by yet another delivery man bearing floral displays, hefty potted plants, "gift" boxes of fruits, gourmet foods as for a lavish if macabre celebration—unless it was a woman friend concerned not to have been able to reach her on the phone—and of course there was the trash to be hauled to the curb if only she knew the dates for trash pickup and mornings she found herself outdoors—one morning in particular the day following probate court and here was cold pelting rain and wind whipping her hair—where was she, and why?—telling herself she had no choice, this was her duty as the *sole survivor* of the wreckage at 299 Valley Drive—the task was to retrieve mail from the mailbox— days of accumulated—unwanted—mail and thus dazed and staggering in November rain on the cusp of sleet, a trench coat thrown over her sweated-through flannel nightgown and raw-skinned bare feet thrust into inappropriate shoes she was making her unsteady way up the long driveway careening with manic rivulets of rainwater soaking the soles of these shoes. And thinking *I will not slip and fall here, alone. I will not fall to one knee. I will not shatter any bones in a sudden faint.* For almost at probate court she'd fainted. And twice in the house alone and the horror of her new, posthumous life washed over her like dirty water in her mouth and almost she'd fainted—maybe in fact she had fainted striking her head against the hard unyielding surface of the dining room table. And now blindly she was reaching into the mailbox—not a box precisely but a tubular aluminum vessel impracticably narrow for the quantity of mail she was now receiving as the *surviving spouse* of a man who'd had numerous friends, business acquaintances, and associates—into which for the past several days the increasingly impatient mailman had thrust, pushed, stuffed mail so that brute strength was required to remove it— and trying to extract a mangled envelope at the rear she thrust her hand into something strangely feathery—gauzy—a spiders' nest—a cluster of alert, antic brown-speckled spiders—of which one—not-large, the size of a housefly—scurried swiftly up her groping hand, up her arm, and nearly reached her shoulder with seeming demonic intent before it was flung away with a breathless cry—even as the mail Sophie clutched in the crook of her arm slipped and fell to the wet grasses at her feet.

O God help me. This is the rest of my life.

2 . K .

Approximately three weeks after her husband's death the first of the odd-shaped envelopes arrived.

Amid a welter of belated sympathy cards, ordinary mail, and trash-mail an oblong manila envelope postmarked Sourland, MINN— return address **K.**

Just that single initial—**K.**

This was mysterious, ominous. Sophie knew no one who lived in Sourland, Minnesota. She could not imagine who **K.** was.

She knew that her husband had had friends—professional associates—in Minneapolis. For sometimes he'd flown to Minneapolis, for meetings. But never had he mentioned Sourland.

They'd been married so long—in December, they would have been married twenty-six years—it was reasonable to assume that neither knew anyone of whom the other wasn't aware, to some degree. If the *surviving spouse* was unsure of many things she was sure of this.

The clutch of fear, the *surviving spouse* feels at such moments. The prospect—the impossibility of the prospect—that the deceased had secrets of which the *surviving spouse* had not a clue.

Though stacks of mail had been left unopened on the dining room table—sympathy cards from friends, heartfelt handwritten letters she couldn't bring herself to read—quickly Sophie opened the envelope

from the mysterious K. postmarked Sourland, MINN. There appeared to be no letter inside, just photographs—wilderness scenes—a
steep grassless hill strewn with large boulders, mountains covered in
dense pine woods, a broad river bordered by tall deciduous trees and
splotches of color like a Matisse painting. There was a steeply-plunging
mountain stream, there was a ravine strewn with fallen trees, fallen
rocks—an obscure shape in the near distance that might have been a
crouching animal, or a person—or oddly shaped exposed tree roots.
Was Sophie supposed to recognize these scenes? Was something here
familiar? There was no identification on the backs of the photos which
seemed to her to have been taken without regard to form, composition,
"beauty"—as if for a utilitarian purpose—but what was the purpose?
She was annoyed, uneasy. Her heart beat rapidly as if she were in the
presence of danger. *Why have these been sent to me? Why now? Who would
do such a thing?*

She saw that the envelope from the mysterious K. had been addressed to *Sophie Quinn.* Not *Mrs. Sophie Quinn,* or *Mrs. Matthew Quinn.*
The address was hand-printed, in a black felt-tip pen. She thought *He
wants to disguise his handwriting. He doesn't want to be identified.*

Badly she wanted to tear up the photographs. This was some sort of
prank, a trick, something cruel, sent to her at a vulnerable time in her
life.

The husband might have advised *Give them to me Sophie. Don't give
this another thought.*

The husband might have advised *Be very careful now Sophie. You will
make mistakes in your posthumous life, I won't be at hand to correct.*

Sophie laid the photographs on the dining room table. Like dealing
out cards this was, in a kind of riddle. It seemed to her—unless her
heightened nerves were causing her to imagine this—that some of the
wilderness scenes overlapped.

A steep rock-strewn mountainside, a basin-like terrain covered in
immense boulders of the shape and hue of eggs, harsh bright autumn
sunlight so dazzling that the colors it touched were bleached out . . .

Most beautiful was a narrow mountain stream falling almost vertically, amid sharp-looking rocks like teeth.

A strange dreaminess overcame her, like a sedative. She was seeing these stark beautiful scenes through the photographer's eyes—it had to be **K.** who held the camera—it was **K.** who'd sent her the photographs.

Is this where I will be taken? Why?

She realized—her forefinger was stinging. A tiny paper cut near her cuticle leaked blood.

She saw—her fingers were covered in such tiny cuts. The furnace-heated air in the house was so dry, her skin had become sensitive and susceptible to cuts. Opening mail, unwanted packages, "gift" boxes from the well-intentioned who imagined that a widow craves useless items as compensation perhaps for having lost her husband . . .

In the following days as she passed through the dining room she paused to examine the photographs. Very like a visual riddle they were—pieces of a jigsaw puzzle like the puzzles she'd patiently pieced together as a child—of wilderness scenes, or landscape paintings. Shaking herself awake then as out of a narcotic stupor.

Those days! Grief, very like dirty water splashed into her mouth. Yet she had no choice, she must swallow.

Not wanting to accuse the husband *Why did you abandon me! I'd trusted you with my life.*

It was a posthumous life, you would have to concede. Though no one wishes to acknowledge the fact. Though there is every reason to wish not to acknowledge the fact. Long stretches of time—vast as the Sahara—she was the *surviving spouse* and thus never fully awake—and yet she was never fully asleep. Never was she *deeply, refreshingly* asleep. When it became "day"—after the winter solstice, at ever-earlier hours—she could not bear to remain in bed. And once up, she had to keep in motion. She could walk, walk, walk for as many as forty, fifty—sixty—minutes at a time, in a kind of spell of self-laceration. Fierce with energy she cleaned out closets, cleaned the basement, on her hands and knees cleaned the hardwood floors with paper towels and polish. Never did she find herself in the right room—invariably she'd forgotten something, that was in another room. It was becoming impossible—physically impossible—for her to remain in one place for more than a few seconds. Such rooms she'd shared with her husband in their daily lives—dining room, living room, a glassed-in porch at the rear of the house—she could not now occupy for long.

Ghost-rooms, these were. Except for the bedroom and the kitchen—rooms she couldn't reasonably avoid—and the room she considered her study, that the husband had not often entered—the rooms of the house were becoming uninhabitable.

The *surviving spouse* inhabits a space not much larger than a grave.

Hard not to think, the husband had abandoned her to this space. Hadn't he promised when they'd first fallen in love *I will protect you forever dear Sophie!*—in an extravagance of speech meant to be playful and amusing and yet at the same time serious, sincere. And so—he'd abandoned her.

This season of grief, when her mind wasn't right.

At about the time when she'd become accustomed to—inured to—the photographs on the dining room table—it might have been several weeks, or months—the second envelope from K. arrived.

How curious the envelope! The paper was thick and grainy, oatmeal-colored, as you'd imagine papyrus. The hand-printed letters in black felt-tip pen were stark and impersonal as before.

Sophie's heart leapt. At once she snatched the envelope out of the jammed mailbox.

No danger of spiders in the mailbox now—she'd destroyed the feathery nest and all its inhabitants. In any case it was winter, and too cold for spiders to survive outdoors.

In the interval Sophie had looked up Sourland, Minnesota, in a book of maps: it was a small town, probably no more than a village, about one hundred miles north and west of Grand Rapids in what appeared to be a wilderness area of lakes, rivers, and dense forests. In addition to

Sourland there was Sourland Falls, and there was Sourland Junction, and there was the vast Sourland Mountain State Preserve which consisted of more than four million acres. All these places were in Sourland County east of romantically named Lake of the Woods County and west of the Red Lake Indian Reservation in Koochiching County.

And this time too the manila envelope contained no letter, just photographs—a sparsely wooded mountainside, the interior of a pine forest permeated by shafts of sunshine, a lake of dark-glistening water surrounded by trees as the water of a deep well is surrounded by rock. In the background of another photo you could just make out a structure of some kind—a small house, or a cabin. Sophie thought *Is this where he lives?*

She knew, this had to be. K. was teasing her, like one dealing out cards in a specific order, to tell the story he wants told.

In the final photo, you could see that this structure was a cabin, of coarse-hewn logs. The roof was steep, covered in weathered tar paper; there was a stovepipe chimney; there were strips of unsightly plastic, to keep out the cold. In this photo there was snow on the ground, snow crusted against the cabin as if it had been blown there with tremendous force. Close by the cabin was a small clearing, stacks of firewood, an ax embedded in a tree stump.

In a rutted and mud-puddled driveway was a steel-colored vehicle with monster-tires, for the most rugged terrain. And beside this vehicle stood a bewhiskered man in a parka and khaki shorts, the hood of the parka drawn over his head; his legs were dark-tanned, ropey with muscle. Though his face was partly obscured by dark-tinted glasses, the parka hood and the bristling beard, you could see that the man's features were severe, unsmiling though he had lifted his right hand as if in greeting.

Sophie took the photo to a window, to examine. She couldn't make out the man's face, that seemed to melt away in a patch of shadow.

Nor could she determine if the man was lifting his hand in a gesture of welcome, or of warning.

Hello. Go away. Come closer. Did I invite you?

So this was **K.** Sophie was certain she'd never seen him before.

Yet he'd addressed the envelope boldly to *Sophie Quinn.* If he'd known her husband, and through her husband had known of her, it was strange that he didn't include a letter or a note in reference to Matt. For he must have known that Matt had died.

Your loss. Sorry for your loss. My condolences Sophie!

There was little that anyone could say, to assuage the fact of death. Sophie understood that people must speak to her, address her, in the rawness of her grief, who could not quite grasp what she was feeling. For she, too, had many times spoken to others distraught by grief—not able to know what it was they felt. Now, she knew. At any rate, she knew better than she'd known.

But **K.** wasn't offering condolences, or solace. Sophie didn't think so.

She remembered how, when she'd first met him, Matthew Quinn had been something of an outdoorsman. Not a hunter—no one in Matt's family had ever hunted—but a serious hiker and camper, as a graduate student at the University of Wisconsin, at Madison. He'd never taken Sophie with him—by the time they met Matt was nearly thirty and impatient to finish his Ph.D. in American constitutional law, and leave school. He'd been impatient to begin what he called adult life.

He'd made up his mind to marry Sophie, he told her afterward, at their first meeting. Sophie had asked was this *love at first sight* and Matt said *Something better, and more durable.*

In Madison, Sophie had heard tales from Matt and his friends of their wilderness adventures, their camping trips to northern Wisconsin and on Drummond Island and in the Canadian wilds south of Elliot Lake, Ontario. Matt had belonged to the university sailing club, that sailed on Lake Mendota in the most turbulent winds. But these outdoor activities had begun to lose their appeal to Matt, at about the time Sophie entered his life.

She'd been twenty-two. Matt had been nearly thirty. In all ways he'd been older than Sophie: intellectually, politically, sexually.

Matt's friends were older, as well—Ph.D. candidates in such fields as history, politics, Russian studies. Most of them were political activists engaged in protesting the Vietnam War. For this was the late 1960s when the war had finally spread its poison everywhere. To be young was to be aroused, outraged. The university at Madison, Wisconsin, was a center of socialist dissent and political activism; there were highly vocal chapters here of SDS, Weathermen, and other left-wing organizations agitating for the overthrow of the hopelessly corrupt U.S. government. Matt had close friends in these organizations but whether he himself belonged, Sophie wasn't certain.

Not that Matt had secrets from her, exactly. But he was taciturn, reserved. To question him too directly was to risk offending him as Sophie had instinctively known, upon meeting him.

She had not been very political. Of course she'd protested the Vietnam War in large campus marches with hundreds—thousands?—of others. She'd been disgusted by the official American politics of the time, like everyone else she knew. But the radical-left counterculture— was alien to her, temperamentally. She'd come to Madison to study nineteenth-century American literature, from Wells College in upstate New York; her father was a public school administrator, and her background was Protestant/secular. She'd been intimidated by other, older students in the graduate school as she'd been intimidated by the sprawling size and tempo of the university itself.

Just once, Matt had taken her along on a march to the state capitol building in downtown Madison, a risky venture since the leaders of the march had no permit and the National Guard shootings at Kent State had occurred the previous week. In the wake of young protestors' deaths in Ohio emblazoned in headlines across the country and in that single, iconic photograph they'd marched—two or three hundred protestors of varying ages—as uniformed Madison police officers and Wisconsin National Guard soldiers lined State Street brandishing billy clubs and Mace, their faces obscured by tinted visors. Matt had instructed Sophie that if the police charged, to try to get behind him; if they began shooting, to get beneath him. He would shield her, he said. He'd spoken earnestly, sincerely. He'd been excited and frightened and exhilarated. Sophie had no doubt that they were in imminent danger, and that Matt would protect her from all harm. A strange reckless elation flooded her veins, a conviction of immortality she would never again feel in her life.

It happened that the protestors were greeted with sympathy by a sizable number of Wisconsin legislators—the demonstrators were made to feel placated and respected and the dangerous situation was defused. They didn't die! They didn't even get struck by billy clubs, their heads and faces bloodied. This was the first time—as it would be the last time—that Sophie would find herself in such a situation, in a crowded, public place without any knowledge of what might happen to her within the next half-hour.

Sophie checked the envelope from K. a second time—a folded sheet of yellow lined paper slipped out.

> Sophie—
> Come see me here. We need to meet.
> Now you are prepared.
>   KOLK

Next thing Sophie knew, she was lying on the floor.

It had seemed that the floor—hardwood, and very hard—swung up to strike her, on the side of the head. Like a billy club the floor struck her, with vehemence, malice. She'd had no time to put out her hand, to mitigate the force of the blow. How many minutes she lay there, part-conscious, she had no idea. Perhaps no time had passed. Perhaps a very long time had passed. By the time her strength returned, she'd forgotten where she was. She could not have said what day this was. Or where Matt was, that he hadn't heard her fall, and call out for him.

Hairs on the back of her neck stirred in fear. Something seemed to be crawling over her skin. Feathery-light these tiny things were, and very quick. She brushed at them, blindly. Her skin was clammy-cold, covered in sweat that had partly dried. And so some time must have passed, the panic-sweat had partly dried. *No! no!*—she brushed at the crawling things. She was on her elbows now, lifting her head. Her dazed eyes saw that the hand-printed letter signed **KOLK** had fallen to the floor beside her.

3.

Matt? Where are you . . .

Waking in the dark, frightened and disoriented.

How many times, like one afflicted with a fairy-tale curse. Waking in the dark—calling for her husband—the absent husband—the *no longer existing* husband.

Sophie would confide in no one.

Nor would Sophie confide in anyone how on that November day when Matt had been hospitalized he'd wakened early to prepare IRS forms to send to their accountant in Hackensack.

He'd known that he was ill, and would need to be hospitalized. He had not known when he'd be back home, to complete the forms.

Sophie had wakened at their usual time—7 A.M.—and still dark—knowing that something was wrong. *His side* of the bed was empty. Carefully the bedclothes had been turned back, Matt had slipped away without her knowledge.

He had not confided in her. Of course Matt would say, in his maddening way of brushing aside her concern, her anxiety—*Look. I didn't want to upset you.*

And so barefoot and curious but not yet alarmed Sophie sought out her husband downstairs—she guessed he'd be in his study, working at his desk—as she approached the room on the first floor of the darkened house there was Matt just emerging in T-shirt and shorts which was his nighttime attire—his expression was strangely intense, a small fixed smile, a smile of a kind Sophie had not seen before—in his hands that were trembling—Sophie saw this, took note of this, with a part of her brain that had become immediately alert, aroused, yet inarticulate—was a large FedEx envelope. (So Sophie told herself *This is all it is! Something for the IRS.*)

Thinking how like her husband to be so zealous, to behave so responsibly. Determined to send their joint financial papers off well before the deadline to their accountant in Hackensack who would include them with other documents and send everything on to the U.S. Treasury. *Sophie I will protect you! I promise.* It was an ordinary morning Sophie wished to think and yet with that preternaturally alert and aroused part of her brain she saw unmistakably that her husband was looking exhausted, his face was ashen, his lips so pale as to appear blue and his movements tentative like those of a man uncertain whether he can trust the floor beneath his feet. And that strange rasping sound—a sound Sophie would long recall, as the *surviving spouse*—of his labored breathing.

Yet calmly he spoke her name:"Sophie."

And calmly he told her, in Matt's way of giving precise instructions that Sophie must not misunderstand or misconstrue, no matter how emotional she was to become:"Call FedEx to have a driver pick this up. I'm sorry, I need you to drive me to the hospital."

Or had Matt said,"I'm sorry I need you to drive me to the hospital."

Each way Sophie would hear. Like one entranced she would hear, and rehear. The *surviving spouse* would exhaust herself with just these two possibilities.

I'm sorry, I need you to drive me to the hospital.

I'm sorry I need you to drive me to the hospital.

No ambiguity about the word *hospital*!

Immediately Sophie knew, this had to be serious. Her husband wasn't a man who went willingly to the doctor. Through his adult life he'd been indifferent, even careless of his health, as if there were something unmanly in taking caution. And now, that bravado had vanished.

Sophie asked him what was wrong. He said,"I think—my heart."

I think—my heart. This too Sophie would hear, and rehear. A curious phraseology. *My heart, I think* would have been a more natural way of speaking but there was nothing natural about her husband's behavior on that morning.

There would be other mornings in Matthew Quinn's life. Several more mornings in Matthew Quinn's life. But this was the final morning, of the life Sophie would share with him.

His heart! The previous summer Matt had had a bout of fibrillation—was that what the condition was called, *fibrillation?*—after protracted physical exertion in the New Jersey heat. Stubbornly he'd been mending their eroded flagstone terrace at the rear of the house and this time too he'd come to Sophie—rapped on the kitchen window to get her attention and said apologetically that his heart was behaving "weirdly" and he couldn't seem to "catch his breath" and would she drive him to their doctor?—which of course Sophie did, calling the doctor's office on her cell phone from the car; and from his doctor's office she'd driven him to the ER of the hospital which was less than a mile away and he'd been given an intravenous drug and sedated and in the morning successfully treated for his rapid and erratic heartbeat and by midday he'd been discharged, Sophie had driven him back home. And so now Sophie had every reason to think that the same thing would happen again. Telling herself *It's a routine procedure. We have gone through this before.*

Hurriedly she'd dressed. That last morning of their lives together in haste assembling a traveling bag for Matt—underwear, toiletries—a clean shirt, socks—for possibly he'd be in the hospital overnight as he'd been the previous time. Sophie was chattering brightly, nervously. Sophie could not have said what she was telling Matt nor did Matt appear to be listening to her. He was fumbling to put on his trench coat—quickly Sophie came to help him. Strange to her, and disconcerting, that her husband was breathing as if he'd run up a flight of stairs.

Matt was fifty-six. Not a tall man but giving that impression. He'd become soft-bodied in the torso and midriff, he was overweight by perhaps fifteen pounds, the young lean husband she'd married in Madison, Wisconsin, had vanished. His dark hair had become sand-colored and was thinning at the crown of his head. His somewhat small gray-brown eyes were creased at the corners with a fierce inward concentration.

Sophie saw that Matt had washed his face and damp-combed his hair but hadn't shaved. Metallic stubble shadowed his soft-jowled lower face like an encroaching shadow. She felt a stab of love for him—a stab of terror—for in love there is terror, at such times. She knew that if she went to kiss him he'd have stiffened, this wasn't a gesture he would have welcomed right now. He wouldn't have pushed her away but in his dis-tracted state he'd have stiffened, drawn back. On his ghastly pale-blue lips a small fixed smile.

Worse yet: he'd have relented and kissed her to humor her. His lips would be icy, against her skin.

This had not happened. Yet Sophie felt the impress of the icy lips against her overheated cheek.

Still the wave of love for him flowed into her, like an electric current. She could not bear it, how she loved this man: the connection between them, that was in danger of breaking. Suddenly it was a possibility, the connection might be broken. Such desperate love Sophie felt for her doomed husband yearning and insubstantial as a tiny flame buffeted by wind. Such desperate love, she had to hide her face from him, that he wouldn't see, and chide her.

She slid her arm through his—he didn't resist, but leaned against her—surprising to Sophie, they were almost of a height as if the man who'd once been inches taller than she had become diminished over-night, aged.

She led him through the darkened downstairs of the house and to the door that led into the garage. Telling herself *Exactly as it was last time. So it will be this time.*

In the car driving to the hospital she spoke calmly asking Matt how he felt, if his condition was the same or if he felt worse. She asked him please to fasten his seat belt but he seemed scarcely to hear. In subse-quent days, weeks, months the *surviving spouse* would see herself behind the wheel of the car which was not her accustomed place when she was with her husband for always her husband drove their car, not Sophie; she saw herself beside her stricken and distracted husband in their gleaming-white vehicle propelled forward by momentum as irresistible as the lunar tide or the sway of galaxies with not the slightest comprehension of where they were going or that their desperate journey was in one direction only, and could never be reversed. As time cannot be reversed. She would see herself as the bearer of Matthew Quinn to his grave. She would see herself as the person who betrayed him for never would he return again to their house. Never would he return to the life he'd so loved, in that house.

If she'd known: that Matt had slipped out of bed in the middle of the night. That he'd spent hours on the tax forms, instead of waking her and asking her to take him to the hospital.

Had he known how serious the *fibrillation* was? Or had it steadily worsened, while he'd worked on the tax forms?

She couldn't bear to think *He risked his life for something so trivial! For our financial well-being. For me.*

Now he was gone from the house. The husband was gone, the husband would not return. Yet a dozen times a day she heard his voice—not as it had been on the morning of his departure but as it had been, before—nor did she hear his labored arrhythmic breath that had so terrified her—though the house was empty, deserted.

Except for the *surviving spouse*, the house was deserted.

The husband had vanished utterly in the way of the incinerated. Made not into soft powdery ashes but into coarse-grained ashes and bone-chunks "buried" in an aluminum container in a cemetery several miles from their house where for years they'd walked—for they were frequent walkers, hikers, bicyclists—they'd loved the outdoors in its more benign weathers—admiring the older, eighteenth-century gravestones and giant aged oak trees buttressed by iron rods like the fanciful drawings of invading Martians on the paperback cover of H. G. Wells's

The War of the Worlds. How innocent they'd been in those days! You could say how blind, how stupid. How utterly oblivious. Walking in the cemetery with no regard for what lay moldering beneath their feet.

Now, they'd been punished for their blindness. The *deceased husband*, the *surviving spouse.*

In a haze of anesthetized grief she'd purchased a plot in the quaint "historic" cemetery. At the open grassy area at the rear, where new graves were dug. Fresh graves, unrelenting. Matt's "remains" were set beneath a small rectangular grave marker the crematorium provided. Set in frozen grass in what was called a *double plot* for which she barely recalled writing a check. In a kindly avuncular voice the funeral director had urged *You might as well secure a double plot, Mrs. Quinn This is a practical step.*

The widow wished above all to be practical. You don't want to embarrass, upset, or annoy others. You don't want to become a spectacle of pathos, pity. The widow resolved that grief itself might become practical, routine. Though at the present time her grief was slovenly and smelly as something leaking through a cracked cellar wall.

Also her grief was demented. For often in the night she heard her husband. He'd risen from their bed in the dark, he'd slipped from the room. Possibly he was using his bathroom in the hall just outside their bedroom. Every sound of that bathroom was known to her, they'd lived together in this house for so long. In her bed on *her side* of the bed her heart began to pound in apprehension waiting for him to return to bed with a murmured apology *Hey! Sorry if I woke you.*

Maybe, he'd have called her *Sophie. Dear Sophie!*

Maybe, he'd have brushed her cheek with his lips. His stubbled cheek against her skin. Or maybe—this was more frequent—he'd have settled back heavily into bed wordless, into *his side* of the bed sinking into sleep like one sinking into a pool of dark water that receives him silently and without agitation on its surface.

Often in the night she smelled him: the sweat-soaked T-shirt, shorts he'd worn on that last night.

4 .

Soon then **Kolk** entered her dreams. Like the rapid percussive dripping of thawing icicles against the roof of the house. As she was vulnerable to these nighttime sounds so she was vulnerable to **Kolk** by night.

In her dreams he was a shadowy figure lacking a face. The figure in the photograph, hand uplifted.

A greeting, or a warning.

She had believed that the man was dead. The actual man, Kolk.

In their few encounters in Madison, Wisconsin, many years before they'd spoken little to each other. Kolk—was his first name Jeremiah?— had been one of Matt's political-minded friends but not one of his closest friends and Sophie had never felt comfortable in his presence. There was something monkish and intolerant in Kolk's manner. His soot-colored eyes behind glinting wire-rimmed glasses had seemed to crawl on her with an ascetic disdain. *Who are you? Why should I care for you?* He'd never cared enough to learn her name, Sophie was sure.

It was said of Kolk that he was a farm-boy fellowship student from Wisconsin's northern peninsula who'd enrolled in the university's Ph.D. program to study something otherworldly and impractical like classics but had soon ceased attending classes to devote time to political matters exclusively. It was said that Kolk had an older brother who'd been a "war hero" killed in World War II. Among others in Matt's circle who spoke readily and assertively Kolk spoke quietly and succinctly and never of himself. He had a way of blushing fiercely when he was made self-conscious or angry and often in Sophie's memory Kolk was angry, incensed.

He'd quarreled with most of his friends. He'd insulted Matt Quinn who'd been his close friend.

He'd called Matt *fink, scab*. These ugly words uttered in Kolk's raw accusing voice had been shocking to Sophie's ears. Matt had been very angry but had said *We have a difference of opinion* and Kolk said sneering *I think you're a fink and you think you aren't a fink. That's our difference of opinion.*

Sophie recalled this exchange. And Sophie recalled a single incident involving her and Kolk, long-forgotten by her as one might forget a bad dream, or a mouthful of something with a very bad taste.

Or maybe it was excitement Sophie felt. And the dread, that accompanies such excitement.

Matt hadn't known. Sophie was reasonably sure that none of their friends had known. For Kolk wouldn't have spoken of it.

They'd been on a stairway landing—the two of them alone together—the first time they'd been alone together for possibly Sophie had followed Kolk out onto the stairs for some reason long forgotten but recalled as urgent, crucial. And Sophie had reached out to touch Kolk's arm—Kolk's arm in a sleeve of his denim jacket—for Kolk was upset, to the point of tears—his face flushed and contorted in the effort not to succumb to tears—and so Sophie who wasn't yet Matt Quinn's young wife but the girl who lived in a graduate women's residence but spent most of her time with Matt Quinn in his apartment on Henry Street reached out impulsively to touch Jeremiah Kolk—meaning to comfort him, that was all—and quickly Kolk pushed Sophie away, threw off her hand and turned and rapidly descended the stairs without a backward glance and that was the last time she'd seen him.

So long ago. Who would remember. No one!

Sophie had been conscious of having made a mistake, a blunder—following after Matt's friend, who was no longer Matt's friend. Why she'd behaved so recklessly, out of character—why she'd risked being rebuffed or insulted by Kolk—she could not have said.

Of course, it was Matthew Quinn she'd loved. It was Matt she'd always loved. For the other, she'd felt no more than a fleeting/disquieting attraction.

Not sexual. Or maybe sexual.

Who would remember . . .

After they were married and moved away from Madison, Wisconsin, and were living in New Haven, Connecticut, in the early 1970s—Matt was enrolled in the Yale Law School, Sophie was working on a master's degree in art history—rumors came to them that Jeremiah Kolk had been badly injured in an accidental detonation of a "nail bomb" in a Milwaukee warehouse.

Or had Kolk been killed. He and two others had managed to escape the devastated warehouse but Kolk died of his injuries, in hiding in northern Wisconsin.

No arrests were ever made. Kolk's name was never publicly linked to the explosion.

All that was known with certainty was that Jeremiah Kolk had never returned to study classics at the University of Wisconsin at Madison, after he'd dropped out in 1969. Long before the bombing incident he'd broken off relations with his family. He'd broken off relations with his friends in Madison. He'd disappeared.

Years later when they were living in New Jersey, one morning at breakfast Sophie saw Matt staring at a photograph in the *New York Times* and when Sophie came to peer at it over his shoulder saying, with a faint intake of breath, "Oh that looks like—who was it?—'Kolk'— 'Jeremiah Kolk'—" Matt said absently, without looking up at her, "Who?"

The photograph hadn't been of Kolk of course but of a stranger years younger than the living Kolk would have been, in 1989.

◆ ◆ ◆

> SOPHIE—
> PLEASE will you come to me Sophie this is the most alone
> of my life.
> KOLK
> P.O. Box 71
> Sourland Falls MINN

5. APRIL

Her April plans! Now the *surviving spouse* was sleepless for very different reasons.

Thinking *It will be spring there, or almost. The worst of the ice will have thawed.*

These were reasonable thoughts. There was the wish to believe that these were reasonable thoughts.

From Newark Airport she would fly to Minneapolis and from Minneapolis she would take a small commuter plane to Grand Rapids and there Kolk would meet her and drive her to his place—not *home* but *place* was the word Kolk used—in the foothills of the Sourland Mountains. By his reckoning Kolk's *place* was one hundred eighty miles north and west of the small Grand Rapids airport.

By his reckoning it would take no more than three hours to drive this distance. If weather conditions were good.

Sophie asked if weather conditions there were frequently *not-good* in that part of Minnesota.

Kolk said guardedly that there was a "range" of weather. His jeep had four-wheel drive. There wouldn't be a problem.

Several letters had been exchanged. Sophie had covered pages in handwriting, baring her heart to Jeremiah Kolk as she'd never done to another person. For never had she written to her husband, always they'd been together. *The person I am is being born only now, in these words to you, Jeremiah.*

Kolk had been more circumspect. Kolk's hand-printed letters were brief, taciturn yet not unfriendly. He wanted Sophie to know, he said, that he lived a *subsistence life, in American terms.* He would not present himself as anything he was not only what he'd become—*A pilgrim in perpetual quest.*

In practical terms, Kolk worked for the Sourland Mountain State Preserve. He'd lived on a nine-acre property adjacent to the Preserve for the past seven years.

Speaking with Kolk over the phone was another matter. Sophie heard herself laughing nervously. For Kolk's voice didn't sound at all familiar—it was raw, guttural, oddly accented as if from disuse. Yet he'd said to her—he had tried to speak enthusiastically—"Sophie? That sounds like you."

Sophie laughed nervously.

"Well. That sounds like *you*."

After years of estrangement, when each had ceased to exist for the other, what comfort there was in the most banal speech.

They fell silent. They began to speak at the same time. Sophie shut her eyes as she'd done as a young girl jumping—not diving, she'd never had the courage to dive—from a high board, into a pool of dark-glistening lake water. Thinking *If this is happening, this is what is meant to be. I will be whoever it is, to whom it happens.*

Kolk had invited Sophie to visit him and to stay for a week at least and quickly Sophie said three days might be more practical. Kolk was silent for a long moment and Sophie worried that she'd offended him but then Kolk laughed as if Sophie had said something clever and riddlesome—"Three days is a start. Bring hiking clothes. If you like it here, you will want to stay longer."

Sophie's eyes were still shut. Sophie drew a deep breath.

"Well. Maybe."

They would fall in love, Sophie reasoned. She would never leave Sourland.

She wanted to ask Kolk if he lived alone. (She assumed that he lived alone.) She wanted to ask if he'd been married. (She assumed that he'd never been married.) She wanted to ask how far his *place* was from the nearest neighbor. And what he meant by saying he was a *pilgrim in perpetual quest.*

Instead—boldly—impulsively as she'd reached out to touch Kolk years ago when they'd both been young—Sophie asked Kolk what she might bring him.

Quickly Kolk's voice became wary, defensive.

"'Bring me'—? What do you mean?"

She'd blundered. She'd said the wrong thing. With a stab of dismay she saw Kolk—the figure that was Kolk—at the other end of the line in remote northern Minnesota—a man with a shadowy half-hidden face and soot-colored eyes behind dark glasses watching her as if she were the enemy.

"I meant—only—if you needed anything, Jeremiah. I could bring it."

Jeremiah. Sophie had never called Kolk by this name, in Madison. The very sound—multi-syllabic, Biblical and archaic—was clumsy in her mouth like a pebble on the tongue. But Kolk laughed again—after a moment—as if Sophie had said something witty.

"Bring yourself, Sophie. That's all I want."

Sophie's eyes flooded with tears. To this remark she could think of no adequate reply.

Of course she would tell no one—not her closest friends, nor those relatives who called her frequently because they were worried about her—of her plans to fly a thousand miles to visit a man she had not seen in a quarter-century. A man whom she'd never known. A political-radical outlaw believed to be dead, who had died twenty years before in the clandestine preparation of a bomb intended to kill innocent people.

In the cemetery amid the damp grasses she stood before the small rectangular grave marker, she had not visited in months.

MATTHEW GIDEON QUINN

On this misty-cool and sunless April morning she was the only visitor in the cemetery.

The air was so stark! So sharp! Her eyes stung with tears like tiny icicles. She felt a flutter of panic, at all that she'd lost that was reduced to ashes, buried in the frozen ground at her feet.

Waiting for a revelation. Waiting for a voice. Of release, or condemnation.

I will protect you forever dear Sophie!

Was this Matt's voice? Had she heard correctly? Had he ever made such an extravagant promise to her, he could never have kept?

Sophie was feeling light-headed, feverish. She hadn't slept well the previous night. Her brain was livid with plans, what she would pack to take with her, what she would say to Jeremiah Kolk when they were alone together. Early the next morning she was flying out from Newark, west to Sourland, Minnesota.

"Matt? I will be back, I promise. I won't be gone long."

Plaintively adding, "I need to do this. Kolk needs me."

How silent the cemetery was! Sophie felt the rebuke of the dead, their resentment of the living.

Sophie are you so desperate? Maybe you should kill yourself, instead.

6 .

And then, in the small grim airport at Grand Rapids, she didn't see Kolk.

In a shifting crowd of people, most of them men, not one seemed to bear much resemblance to Jeremiah Kolk.

The flight from Minneapolis to Grand Rapids had been turbulent and noisy. For the past forty minutes which were the most protracted forty minutes of Sophie's life the small commuter plane had shuddered and lurched as if propelled through churning water and as the plane descended at last to land Sophie felt her heart beating hard, in primitive terror. Of course, this was a mistake. Anyone could have told her, this was a mistake. Grief had made her a desperate woman.

Yet chiding herself with a sort of dazed elation *No turning back! You have brought yourself to this place, where a man wants you.*

The commuter plane disembarked not at a gate but on the tarmac in a lightly falling snow. One by one passengers made their perilous way down steep metal steps, that had been wheeled to the plane. There was an elderly woman with a cane, who had to be assisted. There was a heavyset Indian-looking man with a splotched face, whose wheezing breath was frightening to Sophie, who had to be assisted. Sophie had the idea—it was a comforting idea—or should have been a comforting idea—that her friend must be just inside the terminal watching—watching for her—and so she made her way down the metal steps calmly if in a haze of anticipation, a small mysterious smile on her lips.

No turning back!

And then inside the terminal—her deranged girl's heart was beating very hard now—she didn't see him. At the lone baggage carousel she didn't see him. No one? No Kolk? After their letter-exchanges, their telephone conversations? Sophie stared, at a loss. Several men who might have been Kolk—of Kolk's age, or approximately—passed her by without a glance. A rat-faced youngish man with ragged whiskers and hair tied back in a ponytail passed so closely by Sophie that she could smell his body, without glancing at her.

Sophie thought *My punishment has begun. This, I have brought on myself.*

Kolk had provided her with a single telephone number, in case of emergency—not his home or cell phone number but that of the auto repair in Sourland Junction. Useless to her, now!

And then, she saw a man approaching her. He was walking with a curious limp. Sophie stared, and began to feel faint.

This man was middle-aged, bulky-bodied. For one who limped with a shuffling-sliding motion of his left foot he moved quite readily. He would have been a tall man of over six feet but his back appeared to be bent like a coat hanger wantonly twisted. His face glared like something hard-polished with a rag. His head looked as if it had been shaved with an ax blade. There were the schoolboy wire-rimmed glasses but the lenses were dark-tinted, hiding the eyes. From the lower part of his face metallic-gray whiskers sprang bristling yet as he drew closer Sophie could see that the left side of his face was badly scarred, disfigured—a part of the lower jaw was missing, a double row of teeth exposed as in a ghastly fixed smile. The right side of his face was relatively untouched, unlined. As he made his shuffling-sliding way forward people glanced at him—turned to stare after him—but he ignored them. Perhaps in fact he didn't see them. Having sighted Sophie standing very still staring at him as he approached he smiled exposing stubby teeth that glistened, of the color of old piano keys.

"Sophie. You came."

It was a blunt statement of triumph, elation. It was a statement of masculine appropriation.

Sophie stammered hello. There was a deafening roar in her ears. She thought—they were in a public place, he could not harm her if she ran away. If she ran into the women's room, and did not reappear. He would have to let her go.

Seeing the look in Sophie's face, Kolk smiled harder. "Am I the person you expected to see, Sophie? No? Or maybe—yes? If you are 'Sophie.'"

Sophie had no idea what this meant. She was staring at Kolk's eyes—the dark-tinted lenses of his glasses, that hid his eyes—to avoid looking at his mutilated jaw. Weakly she said:

"Are you—'Jeremiah'? Is that what people call you—'Jeremiah'?"

"No. 'Kolk.'"

It was a blunt ugly name. It had not seemed to suit Jeremiah Kolk as a young man in Madison, Wisconsin, but it had come to suit him now in this middle-aged ravaged state.

As Sophie hesitated, not knowing what to say, Kolk took her hand in greeting, squeezed her fingers hard as if claiming her. Now, could she run away? Could she hide from him? She was smiling confusedly, trying not to wince in pain. Though his spine seemed to be twisted, yet Kolk was taller than Sophie by several inches and loomed over her. He wore fingerless gloves, his exposed fingers were nicked with small cuts, scars and burns, Sophie was remembering how years ago she'd dared to touch Kolk's arm and he'd thrown off her hand. Rudely he'd turned from her as if her touch had repelled him but now Sophie wondered if this strange awkward disfigured man expected her to embrace him in the way of people greeting one another in airports—to throw her arms around him, and brush her lips against the side of his face.

But which side of Kolk's face—the shiny-scarred melted-away side, or the more normal side—would Sophie kiss? She guessed that Kolk would be keenly aware of such a choice.

Kolk asked if Sophie had anything more than the single suitcase at which she was clutching and Sophie said no she had not. Kolk frowned.

"Let's go, then. It's good to get back before dark."

Something had disappointed him. The single suitcase, maybe.

This lightweight suitcase, Kolk insisted on taking from Sophie. It was on rollers, but Kolk carried it.

The roaring in Sophie's ears had only slightly abated. Was she going with this man, then? This disfigured man? At a first glance you might imagine that he was wearing animal hides. And on his feet, hobnailed boots. Before Sophie could pull away Kolk took her arm, and linked her arm through his. He said nothing as they walked through the terminal together. Sophie had no choice but to accompany him. She dared not pull away from him, such a gesture would offend him terribly.

How likely it seemed to her, the disfigured must be vainer than the rest of us.

Awkward to walk with Kolk who limped so markedly. And how self-conscious Sophie was made to feel, walking with a man at whom people—wide-eyed children, rude adults—stared openly.

"S'reebi! Quiet. *Sit*."

In the rear of Kolk's vehicle was a lunging barking dog—a bulldog mix—with splotched steel-colored fur, a milky right eye, quivering jowls and small flattened torn ears. Sophie felt her blood freeze, she feared and disliked such dogs.

Kolk struck the lunging dog on its skull, so sharply you could hear the impact.

"I said *sit*."

Sophie said, "He's—handsome." With forced warmth Sophie addressed the frantic barking dog, that was throwing itself against the back of the seat. His slobber shook in frothy droplets from his mouth— surreptitiously she wiped it from her face with a tissue.

Kolk laughed. It wasn't clear why Kolk laughed.

Kolk said not to worry, *S'reebi* would not dare attack her.

In swirling snow the drive from Grand Rapids north and west into the foothills of the Sourland Mountains took longer than Kolk had anticipated. Though it was early April yet the air was blustery and wintry, and tasted of metal. During the more than three-hour drive Kolk said little as if he were chagrined or resentful or possibly he'd forgotten his guest in the passenger's seat beside him. Sophie could have wept. How miserable she was shivering in her attractive and inappropriate clothing—cream-colored cashmere coat, light woolen slacks, leather shoe-boots that came only to her ankles. It was clear that Kolk was accustomed to being alone in the jeep—driving long distances with a sort of stoic fortitude—punching in radio stations that came to life, prevailed for a while then faded into static—in the interstices of which Sophie chattered nervously, to fill the silence. The female instinct: to fill up silence. The (female) fear of (masculine) silence. Sophie heard her anxious voice like the palpitations of a butterfly's wings, throwing itself against a screen.

Kolk said: "You don't need to talk."

In profile, seen from the right, Kolk did not appear obviously disfigured. His face was strong-boned, his skin ruddy, weathered. The untrimmed whiskers looked charged with static electricity like those of a mad sea captain in a nineteenth-century engraving. His eyebrows, in profile, stood straight out, gunmetal-gray. His shaved head was stubbled with steel-colored quills. The scalp was discolored, blemished and bumpy as a lunar terrain. In the fingerless gloves his hands were twice the size of Sophie's, the hands of a manual laborer, or a strangler. The short-cut nails were edged with the kind of grime that could never be removed.

There was little of the young Jeremiah Kolk remaining. This was a fact, Sophie had to concede. Yet the old intimacy between them persisted, unmistakably. *Though we are changed we are not different people. He knows this!*

Sophie saw that in the rear of the jeep there were miscellaneous articles of clothing—a lightweight jacket, a mangled-looking sweater, a single hiking boot, dirt-stiffened gray wool socks. There were advertising flyers, newspapers that had never been unfurled, unopened envelopes as if Kolk had grabbed his mail out of his P.O. and dumped it into the jeep without taking time to sort it. The frothy-mouthed bulldog lay atop the jacket panting as if he'd been running and had just collapsed in a partial doze. Sensing Sophie looking at him he began to pant more loudly and his pink-rimmed eyes opened wider, glistening.

No!—no! Sophie looked quickly away before the dog began barking.

They'd made their way through the despoiled suburban landscape outside Grand Rapids—mini-malls and shopping centers, motels, gas stations, fast-food restaurants, discount outlets. Beyond were desolate winter fields not yet stirred into life. Still the snow continued in lightly swirling white flakes like mica-chips, much of it melting on the pavement.

Kolk gave Sophie a sidelong glance. The exposed teeth were hidden from her, she could see only the unmutilated side of the man's face, his mouth barely visible amid the bristling beard. The dark-tinted glasses were all but opaque.

If you will be kind to me. Please promise me!

If you will not hurt me. I am the person who has come to you, whom you have summoned.

"How did you learn about—my husband's death?"

Sophie spoke hesitantly. In her letters to Kolk she had never asked him this crucial question nor had he volunteered to answer it.

Kolk's reply was an enigmatic shrug of his shoulders. He was staring straight ahead, at the highway.

Sophie persisted: "Did you keep in contact with Matt, over the years? Or with mutual friends? Was that how you knew?"

"I kept contact, yes. With some part of the past."

Sophie wondered what this meant. Some part of the past?

"But you never called Matt. When we were all still in Madison, you might have called him. Matt had been your friend, he'd been badly hurt when you . . ."

Was this true? In some way, Sophie thought it had to be.

Kolk hadn't called Matt, and Matt hadn't called Kolk. Matt had said stiffly *He's not my friend. We're out of each other's life.*

All that Sophie could remember with any degree of clarity was following Kolk out of an apartment—not the one in which she and Matt were living at the time, but someone else's apartment—and into a drafty stairwell. There'd been a smell of cooking odors—curry? A man's stripped-down bicycle on a stairway landing, leaning against a wall? The circumstances of that incident had almost entirely faded from her mind. Yet vividly she recalled the need to touch Kolk, and the way he'd thrown off her hand.

She wondered if that memory had lodged deeply in Kolk, as it had in her.

Or is it a false memory. Like so many posthumous memories.

A willed hallucination whetted by loneliness and desperation as parched grass whets the wildfire that ravages and destroys it.

By degrees the despoiled landscape had dropped away. In the drafty rattling jeep they were traveling on a less populated state highway. Passing farmland, or what had been farmland—abandoned and boarded-up houses and outbuildings of a bygone era—amid vast swatches of acreage belonging to corporate farms. But all the land lay fallow in the late-winter chill as if in a suspended animation.

Ever more they were ascending into the foothills of the Sourland Mountains. Ever more, the highway was becoming less traveled and houses were farther apart and set back farther from the road. There was no radio reception here—Kolk had given up his radio music in a blaze of static. In the distance was a dramatic landscape of steep hills, small mountains covered in pine woods, a pearlescent-marbled sky through which shafts of sunshine pierced like flames.

Leaving Koochiching County. Entering Sourland County.

Here were signs for small quaintly named settlements: Mizpah—Shooks—Boy River—Elk Hunt—Grygle—Bowstring—Black Duck—Squaw Lake—Leech Lake. Then came Sourland Junction, and Sourland Falls.

Soon then they were passing the vast tract of the Sourland Mountain State Preserve on their right. Kolk asked Sophie if she could guess how large the Preserve was and Sophie said she had no idea—five thousand acres?

More like four million, Kolk said.

Four million! Sophie's voice registered astonishment.

Kolk must have smiled, his visitor spoke so naively.

Sophie thought *He could not imagine that I would know. His idea of me is that I could not possibly know.*

At last in the waning light of early evening Kolk turned off a gravel road onto a narrow lane leading into the wooded interior and bounded by hostile signs—NO TRESPASSING PRIVATE PROPERTY—NO TRESPASSING PRIVATE PROPERTY—which Sophie supposed to be signs posted by Kolk himself. In the backseat the bulldog began to whimper excitedly as if in anticipation of home. Sophie's teeth rattled in her jaws, the lane was so bumpy. Kolk took them hurtling deeper into the woods—they were descending a steep hill, toward a creek at a perpendicular angle before them—a narrow creek rushing with water—it was the aftermath of the winter thaw, the creek was unusually high—Sophie steeled herself waiting for a bridge to materialize—waiting for the jeep to clatter over a crude plank bridge—but there was no bridge—to Sophie's astonishment Kolk aimed his vehicle into the rushing water at a speed of twenty miles an hour—water lifted in flaring wings beside the jeep even as the jeep catapulted up the farther bank.

He'd shifted gears, the four-wheel drive held firm. Sophie gave a little cry of surprise—it had happened too quickly for her to be frightened.

Sophie asked why wasn't there a bridge across the creek. Kolk said what was the need of a bridge—most of the summer the creek was dry, in the winter it was frozen over.

"The trick is to take it fast, when the water's high. Slow, you get your feet wet."

It was clear that Kolk took pride in his wilderness *place*. Sophie saw how beyond the clearing in which Kolk parked the jeep were mountains, a view of a valley, miles of pine forest she would have found beautiful but for her fatigue from hours of travel.

There was the log cabin, Sophie recognized from the photographs. A crude plank addition had been built onto it, unpainted, with a single small window. Close by was a storage shed, a chicken coop/rabbit hutch, what appeared to be a kennel, stacks of traps or cages. At the edge of the clearing were old, abandoned vehicles—a car stripped of everything but its chassis, a rusted pickup truck, a tractor missing its tires. A layer of gritty snow lay over everything, the air here was very cold piercing Sophie's lungs as she opened the jeep door. Her attention was drawn to one of the cages stacked against the storage shed, some twenty feet away. She had a vague vertiginous sense that something—some small creature—had been trapped in this cage and made to starve to death and become mummified.

A thrill of dismay coursed through her *Why have I come here, am I mad!*

Quickly before Kolk could come around to her side of the jeep to help her down, as he'd helped her up into the cab, Sophie climbed down from the jeep. The cab was so high, she nearly turned her ankle.

The bulldog leapt out, panting and barking. Kolk was telling her something—about the cabin, or the Preserve—Sophie wasn't able to concentrate—Kolk hauled out Sophie's suitcase, beneath his arm. She was feeling dazed, light-headed. She was feeling *unreal* and could not have explained to her companion that she had not felt anything other than *unreal* since the morning she'd driven her husband to the hospital which had been the final morning of their life together.

Kolk broke off what he was saying. Sophie was staring at the mummified thing in the trap—she'd imagined that it had moved, quivered—not a creature but a dirt-stiffened rag. That was all.

The bulldog followed at their heels, quivering with excitement. A small barrel of a creature with brindle markings like splattered paint drops, a single sighted eye, the other milky and glaring. How like a pig the dog was, with its flattened snout, wriggling hairless bottom and piglet tail.

"S'reebi, get the hell away. *Sit.*"

Sophie laughed uneasily, the dog had a way of nipping surreptitiously at her ankles and feet. A trail of slobber shone on her leather shoe-boots. She perceived that the dog was her enemy, he would wait until Kolk was away, or inattentive, to seriously attack her.

Sophie asked what was the dog's name?—she couldn't quite make out what Kolk called him.

"'S'reebi'—'Cerberus.'"

Cerberus!—the three-headed dog of Hades.

Sophie remembered, Jeremiah Kolk had once studied classics,

Kolk took Sophie's arm, to lead her in the direction of the cabin. Again this sudden intimacy between them, as in the airport when he'd taken her arm without a word and linked it through his own in a husbandly/proprietary manner.

The touch of his hand—his hands—was like static electricity, coursing through Sophie's body.

Sophie heard herself stammer how beautiful it was in this place—"But so remote."

She couldn't bear to look at the man—the melted-away jaw, the exposed stubby teeth.

Flatly Kolk said: "No. A place isn't 'remote' except in relationship to another place, or places. The longer you remain here, you will see it is just *here*. There is nothing 'remote' about it."

Kolk led Sophie into the chilly cabin, carrying her suitcase. The thought came to her—a ridiculous thought—utterly unwarranted—

that if she'd balked at the threshold of the cabin like a panicked animal resisting confinement, the man would have forced her into the
cabin.

Here, a prevailing odor struck her—grease, scorch—cooking
smells—the sweetish-yeasty smell of unlaundered clothes, bedsheets.
The interior of the log cabin was a single large room with a low ceiling
and few windows, like a cave; there was both a stone fireplace and an
antiquated wood-burning stove; scattered on the floor by the fireplace
were piles of crudely hewn logs with dried cobwebby bark still attached.
A breeding place for spiders Sophie thought, appalled.

Yet the interior of Kolk's cabin was attractive, in its way. Cozy, comfortable. A kind of nest. The bare-plank floor was uneven, and haphazardly covered with small woven grime-saturated rugs—one felt
hidden here, protected. In a corner was a brass bed with a sunken
mattress—Kolk's bachelor bed?—heaped with blankets and bedclothes; in a narrow alcove, a small kitchen with open shelves to the
ceiling, a two-burner stove and a dwarf-refrigerator.

She would be preparing meals in that kitchen—would she? Sophie
smiled to think so.

Kolk's furniture was mostly of brown leather—a massive sofa,
matching chairs—furniture of the kind one might expect to see in an
old-fashioned gentlemen's club—once of excellent quality but now so
badly worn its color had nearly vanished. There was a tarnished brass
floor lamp with a parchment-colored lampshade, there were mismatched
tables. These were items Kolk had purchased in a used-furniture store,
Sophie supposed. Or rescued from a dump. Prominent on the wall beside the fireplace were unframed photographs of Kolk's—wilderness
scenes of the kind he'd sent her. Sophie saw how haphazardly they'd
been mounted—tacked in place, or taped, as if the photographer had
no wish to take time, to display his work as art.

She would do that, if things worked out between them.

Most of the wall-space was taken up with bookshelves. These were
makeshift shelves of bricks and planks. So many books!—Kolk saw

Sophie peering at one of the shelves—a complete set of *Encyclopedia Britannica*. Other shelves were waterstained Modern Library classics—Plato, Euripides, Homer, Catullus, Augustine's *City of God*, Marx's *Das Kapital*, Darwin's *Origin of Species* and *The Descent of Man*. There was an entire shelf of Latin titles. Seeing Sophie peer at these books Kolk said he'd bought the discards from the Latin Academy, a private school in St. Paul where he'd taught briefly—"and not very happily"—in the 1980s.

All these books, Kolk said. And more, in the next room. And journals in boxes, he'd never unpacked. All for ninety dollars.

In fact there was an addition to the cabin, at the rear—a "guest room" as Kolk called it—which, he said, he tried to keep in better condition than the room in which he and S'reebi lived. It was into this addition that Kolk led Sophie, switching on a light.

This was a small room, quite narrow, with a single small square window looking out into the woods. Beside the bed—a girl's bed, less than adult-sized, built low to the floor—there was a space heater, which Kolk switched on. The bed was covered with an attractive blue-striped goose-down comforter—Sophie believed it was goose-down, testing it with her fingers—she wondered if Kolk had made this purchase especially for her, at a secondhand store? The comforter did not appear to be very soiled, nor did it appear to be worn. Even secondhand goose-down comforters were not cheap, Sophie knew. She felt a touch of vertigo, like sickness.

He will come here. He will make love to me here.

On the plank floor in this room was a handwoven Indian carpet of red, beige, and black patterns like lightning bolts. Here too the floor was tilted, just slightly, as in a fun house. There was a bureau of old cedar wood, badly scarred but with a subtle, beautiful smell—Kolk pulled one of the drawers open an inch, as if to encourage his reluctant visitor to unpack.

The crude plank wall was insulated in panels. On one of the panels was a row of pegs for clothes to be hung on. Sophie saw that a woman's robe, of some dark-green satin material, with a peacock-tail appliqué on the back, was hanging here.

He wants me to know. There have been others. His life is an entirety, I will never realize.

"Here. This is new, this summer."

It was a tiny bathroom—a lavatory—in an alcove behind the cedar bureau. It was hardly the size of a telephone booth. Sophie wondered how she was to bathe, if there was a shower elsewhere in the cabin. She could not bring herself to ask. Enough that there was a tiny sink in the room, and faucets; a toilet. On a towel rack, towels! Sophie heard herself thanking Kolk—how grateful she was sounding!

The towels appeared to be clean, she saw. There were only two of them and they were not very thick but for this, she was grateful.

In the corner of her eye she'd seen—something moving— quivering—the impress of a body on the blue-striped comforter— a female body—slender, girl-sized.

Sophie Quinn was herself a slender woman. Since her husband's death she'd lost fifteen pounds. She felt her bones thinning like the bones of a sparrow.

Kolk said why didn't she sleep, for a while. Kolk said she was look- ing tired.

"I'll make supper. I'll wake you for supper."

Sophie was having a difficult time remembering—for the moment—where she was, and why she was in this place. Kolk? Jere- miah Kolk? Her frantic smiling eyes were fastened to the man's upper face, she dared not look elsewhere.

Her companion too was tired from the drive—a six-hour round- trip in the jeep. But he was a stoic, he would not complain. With half his bewhiskered face he smiled at her—that was what it was meant to be, a smile—Sophie believed. Sophie wondered if one of the man's legs was shorter than the other, a portion of muscle and cartilage blown away in the detonation. She thought *He will sleep with me. He knows I can't refuse him.*

She wondered how it would be—to hold a man so mutilated, disfigured. There would be much more scar tissue than you could see, hidden beneath his clothes. Waves and rivulets of scar tissue, terrible to the touch.

Kolk left the room limping, without a backward glance.

Quickly Sophie shut the door. It had no lock! At least, not from the inside.

How exhausted she was, as Kolk had perceived. The touch of vertigo that had seemed to her sexual was sheer exhaustion, on the cusp of nausea.

Beyond the door she could hear Kolk talking to the bulldog, in a cheery-chiding manner. Having a guest in this remote place—a female guest—seemed to please and excite Kolk even as it provoked him to feeling, like his guest, edgy and apprehensive. Sophie listened closely but could hear no distinct words through the door. She wondered how soon—if ever—Kolk would speak to her in the intimate way in which he spoke to the barrel-shaped little bulldog.

As if nothing were yet at stake, all had been decided between them.

You summoned me. I came to you. It has been decided!

Hesitantly Sophie pulled back the blue-striped comforter. She saw with a stab of dismay that the comforter was more badly worn than she'd believed, though it had been—hadn't it?—recently laundered; Kolk had washed it by hand—had he?—and hung it up to dry outdoors, which would have required days.

Beneath the comforter, bedsheets worn almost transparent from laundering. The sagging mattress beneath, and no mattress cover. Sophie snatched up the single pillow on the bed to fluff it out—tiny bits of down exploded into the air. Out of the bedclothes wafted a musty odor, that pinched her nostrils. She thought *She has died here. My predecessor. Allowed to starve to death, to die and become mummified.*

Sophie saw that the single window in the room was too small for an adult to push her way out—no more than two square feet.

So tired! She had no choice but to stretch out warily on the bed.

No choice but to sink into the bed. This musty-yeasty-smelling bed. In her clothes and socks—she'd removed only the shoe-boots. It was terrible to be sleeping fully dressed but she could not risk undressing nor had she the strength to remove her clothing. She had not the strength to open her suitcase and hang up her things—she'd forgotten the suitcase entirely. The satin robe on the peg was hers to wear, she supposed. Though she would have to be naked beneath it, she supposed. She'd begun to pant, her eyeballs felt seared as if she'd been staring into the sun. She could never sleep in this terrible place! A grave-smell, wetted ashes, grit. If you breathed in too deeply you breathed in microscopic bits of skin, cell-particles. You breathed in the death of another. Her skin crawled with this knowledge. Hairs at the tender nape of her neck stirred. She felt an almost sexual yearning—the dark pit was opening beneath her, the tar pit, beneath the low-slung bed. In her haste to sleep she'd neglected to switch off the light, from a bedside lamp with a milk-glass base, an attractive little girl's-room sort of lamp which Kolk had switched on: the bulb couldn't have been more than sixty watts, not enough to keep Sophie from sinking into the tar pit which was the identical tar-pit that was beneath her bed back home . . . Gratefully she shut her eyes. Something black washed over her brain. Almost immediately she began to sleep. She was sobbing in her sleep, in relief. Her limbs twitched, she was gripping herself in a tight embrace, arms crossed over her chest and fingers at her rib cage. *O hold me! help me! I am so alone and I don't want to die please help me!* She saw the man approach her—the man with the melted-away face, the exposed and grinning teeth—whose name she could not recall, at the moment. It was a name she knew, but she could not speak it. He had removed his tinted glasses, his soot-colored eyes were glassy, dilated. His soot-colored eyes moved over her caressingly. She saw the mouth inside the bristling beard. It was a scarred mouth and a mutilated mouth but it was a mouth she wanted to kiss, to comfort. Yet she could not move, exhaustion so gripped her in all the cells of her being.

· · ·

"Sophie?"

There came a man's voice, at a little distance. Someone was speaking her name through a shut door.

Now he opened the door, just slightly. Not wanting to upset or offend her he spoke through the crack, that mutilated mouth she couldn't see from where she lay.

"Sophie? Can you wake up? It's almost nine."

In a daze Sophie opened her eyes. The lashes were crusted together with dried mucus. Her mouth was parched, aflame. In her stuporous sleep she'd been breathing through an opened mouth, for hours. How long? Nine o'clock? The wicked little two-foot-square window framed a tarry-black night.

Asprawl she lay in tangled bedclothes smelling of her body. At first she couldn't recognize her surroundings, this cave-like interior she was certain she'd never seen before. The ceiling overhead was low like heavy clouds pressing near to the earth. Tendrils of cobweb trailed from the ceiling. Something wispy crawled across her forehead—Sophie brushed it away with panicked fingers.

"Sophie—hey? You must be starving. We should eat soon. I've made us something to eat. D'you need anything?"

Quickly Sophie said *No! No* she didn't need anything. She was awake, she would join him in five minutes.

Her joints ached. Her neck ached. Her upper lip itched, badly. Beneath the rumpled linen shirt and sweater, a flaming sort of rash across her belly.

In a rush it returned to her—memory of where she was, and with whom. Who had summoned her.

The heavy down comforter had slid partway onto the floor. Sophie's shoe-boots were tangled in it—she fumbled to put them on. She dreaded walking on this floor, without shoes.

In the tiny lavatory that smelled of drains and disinfectant she peered at her reflection in a mirror so cheap it appeared to have warped. Its lead backing had begun to poke through, like leprosy. She saw that her eyes were bloodshot and swollen and her mouth—her upper lip—was terribly swollen, enflamed.

Something had bitten her, in that bed.

"My God! A spider bite . . ."

She shuddered, in revulsion. She ran cold water into the sink, and wetted her swollen lip. How it throbbed, and burned! In the mirror she saw with dismay her dazed and sallow face, the bloodshot eyes with deep shadows beneath, the shiny-swollen upper lip.

The man would not find her attractive, sexually. Yet that morning early when she'd set out on her journey—her pilgrimage?—she'd been an attractive dark-haired woman with a ready if unfocused smile of whom it was said by those who wished her well *How rested you're beginning to look, Sophie! How young.*

How rested was a sort of code, Sophie supposed. Such words were only pronounced to widows, convalescents, survivors of terrible disasters. *How rested* and not rather *how devastated.*

How rested and not rather *how dead.*

Hurriedly Sophie combed her hair, that was snarled at the nape of her neck. She fumbled to put on makeup squinting into the leprous mirror. Her fingers were oddly clumsy, she dropped the tube of lipstick not once but twice onto the grimy linoleum floor.

Blood rushed into her face as she stooped to retrieve the lipstick. Groping in the cobwebby corner of the tiny lavatory. *So it has come to this, Sophie! Such desperation.*

No time to unpack her suitcase. Kolk was waiting for her. She could hear the panting little pig-dog snuffling and clawing at the base of the door she had no choice but to force open.

"*S'reebi!* Come over here, damn you *sit.*"

Kolk growled at the dog, that reluctantly obeyed him. How like a TV sitcom this was—was it? Sophie's mouth smiled, hopeful.

Kolk had lighted a fire in the fireplace. He'd laid cutlery, plates, swaths of paper towels on a crude wood-plank table in front of the fireplace. Not a TV sitcom but a romantic scene, this was. In the Sourland Mountain Preserve, in snowy April.

Sophie would have thought that the prospect of eating would nauseate her. In fact, the aroma of something meaty and gamey stewing on the stove made her mouth water.

Kolk said, with forced exuberance: "Soph-ie! How d'you feel?"

"I—I—I feel—wonderful."

Was this so? Light-headed with hunger Sophie leaned against the table smiling. Wonderful! Wonderful. Wonder-ful.

Her joints still ached, she felt as if she'd been hiking for hours in her sleep. But she would betray no weakness to the man. Glancing about for something useful to do, some task to which she might be put—setting the table. And there were stubby candles she located on a shelf, to set on the table and light with trembling fingers.

How romantic, candlelight! Sophie was thinking how, at home, a thousand miles away, she and Matt had eaten their evening meals by candlelight.

Maybe at this very moment—was this possible?—the Quinns were sitting down to dinner, in that house in Summit, New Jersey. There was Sophie, and there was her husband Matthew Quinn. Could this be?

"What happened to your face?"

Kolk was staring at Sophie. He'd removed his dark glasses.

"A spider bit me—I think."

"A spider? Where?"

Where do you think? Where have I been?

"While I was sleeping, I think."

Kolk came closer, peering at Sophie's face. He was embarrassed, chagrined. His eyes were dark, puckered at the corners, deep-set and bruised-looking. It was something of a shock to Sophie, to see Kolk's eyes, without his glasses. The man's eyes fixed on her face. "Christ! I'm sorry."

"Oh no, no—it's nothing. Really it's nothing."

Sophie laughed, certainly it was nothing. She touched her lip that had swollen to twice its size. Beneath her clothes other bites itched violently, she dared not scratch for fear Kolk would be embarrassed further.

Muttering to himself Kolk stomped into the other room, Sophie saw him on hands and knees peering beneath the bed, cursing and grunting. With a rolled-up newspaper he swatted at something beneath the bed.

When he returned Kolk was flush-faced, frowning. He said that Sophie could sleep in his bed that night—he would sleep in the "guest room."

Now it was supper! A romantic supper by firelight.

Kolk brought the stew-pan to the table. Self-consciously he ladled the rich dark liquid into bowls. There was also multigrain bread, he'd baked the previous day. And dark red wine, Kolk served in jam-glasses. Sophie thought *I won't drink, that would be dangerous.*

The stew contained chunks of fibrous root vegetables, onions and pieces of a chewy meat, a dank-flavored meat Sophie couldn't identify. Hesitantly she asked Kolk if it was—venison?—and Kolk said no, it was not venison; she asked if it was—rabbit?—and Kolk said no, it was not rabbit.

Other possibilities Sophie could think of—raccoon?—ground-hog?—she did not want to ask about.

Still, she was hungry. Her hand trembled, holding a spoon—Kolk reached out to steady it.

Kolk said they could go hiking in the morning. Or snowshoeing, if the snow didn't melt.

"Snowshoeing! In April."

"This is northern Minnesota. We're in the mountains."

Sophie laughed a little too loudly. Sophie saw that her jam-glass was in her hand, she'd been drinking after all. Thinking of her husband in his grave, reduced to ashes. *She* had done that—she'd signed the document, for the cremation. And yet, she'd gone unpunished. No one seemed to realize.

On the drive from the airport Sophie had asked Kolk about his life since Madison, since he'd dropped out of school, and Kolk had answered in monosyllables, briefly. Discreetly she'd made no reference to the alleged bomb accident. She'd made no reference to Kolk's anti-war activism, that had frequently crossed the line into civil disobedience. Now, Kolk began to speak. He told her about his father—who'd "disowned" him. He told her about his older brother—who'd been shot to pieces in Vietnam. He told her how he'd incurred the wrath of Sourland residents when he'd volunteered to speak at local high schools, explaining the "imperialist designs" fueling the Gulf War. He'd been arrested, "roughed up" by Grand Rapids cops, for picketing the army enlistment office there.

"And then—?"

" 'And then—' what?"

"What happened then?"

"Nothing happened then. As much as I'd expected."

Sophie had finished the wine in her glass. Sophie felt her swollen lip throb with heat. Inside her clothes, the spider's-bite rash pulsed and flamed.

He will touch me now. Now, it will happen.

Beneath the table the fat panting dog, that had been clambering about their feet through the meal, gave a sigh like a grunt and fell asleep.

Kolk poured the remainder of the wine into their glasses. He'd eaten twice as much as Sophie had eaten, and drunk even more. His skin exuded a ruddy heat, like the heat of Sophie's swollen lip. She found that she'd been looking at the disfigured flesh of his jaw, the exposed teeth, without feeling repelled. Suddenly she wanted very badly to touch Kolk's jaw—the soft melted-away scar tissue.

Kolk stiffened as if sensing Sophie's thoughts.

The yearning between them. Like molten wax, dripping and shapeless.

Gently Sophie said, "Your—injury. It was an accident—?"

Kolk shrugged. Kolk's face was flushed still, stiff.

Sophie said, uncertainly: "We'd heard about it—an accident. An explosion. We'd heard that you had been—killed."

Kolk laughed. Possibly, Sophie had taken him by surprise.

"It was good, 'believed dead.' Nobody follows you there."

Kolk lurched from the table to fetch a bottle of whiskey—Canadian Club. Without asking Sophie if she wanted any he poured the amber liquid into their emptied wineglasses. Not what Sophie's fastidious husband would have done, this was an act of barbarism. Sophie laughed, and tasted the liquid. So strong! Sophie was not a drinker of whiskey, Scotch or gin; she was not a drinker at all; a single, small glass of wine was her limit.

In the shifting firelight Kolk's ravaged face looked like the face of a devil reflecting flames. Sophie thought *This is what the surviving spouse deserves. A demon missing half his face.*

She wondered what it would be like to be kissed by a demon missing half his face. The teeth!—if only the teeth would not touch her.

Kolk drank, and Sophie drank. Kolk began to speak in a confiding manner. Sophie was curious, and moved. Sophie was eager to hear of Kolk's life, that had been hidden from her. With an air of aggrieved irony Kolk spoke of the "accident"—the "explosion"—except there are "no accidents" in the universe. He spoke of the "logic" of history. Or was it the "illogic" of history—what has happened once, cannot happen again in quite that way. Yet, it cannot happen again in any way that is very different. Kolk spoke of the "great vision" of the 1960s and of the "betrayal of the vision"—the "revolution"—by its most fervent believers. He spoke of having sacrificed a "personal life" for—what?—so many years after the wreckage, it wasn't clear what.

Sophie said, "But I had a personal life. And that, too, is gone."

Kolk was leaning on his elbows, on the table. His forearms were dense with muscle, covered in wiry black hairs like an animal's pelt. Yet his beard was a bristly steel-color, and the short tough quills on his scalp had no color at all. The young Jeremiah was trapped inside the older man, only his eyes were untouched, baffled and wary.

Kolk was confiding in Sophie, he'd never been arrested. He'd left the state of Wisconsin within hours of the explosion and he'd never returned. He'd broken off contact with his friends—not "friends" but "comrades"—yet not "comrades" either—really. For years he'd moved about the country working with his hands. Learning skills with his hands: carpentry, plastering, roofing. He drove trucks, he learned to operate bulldozers. He used chain saws. He'd lived in Alaska, and in Alberta; he'd worked in New Orleans, and Galveston; he'd never returned to his family's farm but he'd returned to the Midwest, to northern Minnesota, which was very like his home, yet isolated. And no one knew where he was. Only Sophie knew where he was, and who he was. In the Sourland Preserve he helped maintain the trails, kept roads open in winter. He was a forest ranger on the lookout for fires, in times of drought. He helped search for lost hikers. He brought back the injured, he knew CPR. He could go days—weeks—at a stretch in this place of utter solitude without encountering anyone or speaking with anyone. More than once he'd found bodies on the trails, in high ground where hikers weren't likely to go in the winter. After the start of the spring thaw, he found them. Men—all had been young men, in their twenties or thirties—who'd gone out deliberately into the wilderness, into the snow, to lose themselves, to lie down and sleep in the numbing cold. He'd found them, lying motionless on the ground, so utterly still, peaceful as statuary, their faces strangely beautiful—for no decomposition had yet set in.

Sophie shuddered. "But—that's terrible. Finding someone like that—must be very upsetting."

Kolk shrugged. "Why? Whatever was rotten in them is gone—'cauterized.' That's the point of killing yourself."

Sophie was thinking: Matt had liked—loved—hiking in the wilderness, before she'd known him. Then abruptly he'd ceased. That part of his life had ended. Rarely would he talk about it, he hadn't been one to reminisce. The walks they'd taken together—the "hikes"—hadn't been very arduous, challenging. After law school, Matt had gone into corporate law. He'd been a brilliant and ambitious student at Yale and he'd gone into a corporate law firm immediately after law school, in Summit, New Jersey. Initially he'd been successful—always he'd been moderately successful—always competent, reliable. Always he'd been well paid. But he'd been disappointed with the nature of his work and with his associates—never would he have called them "friends," still less "comrades"—and by degrees he'd lost all passion for his work. Servicing the rich, aiding the rich in their obsession to increase their wealth while giving away as little as possible to others. Sophie had no wish to confide in Kolk that her husband had never been happy in his work—possibly, in his life. By his late thirties he was becoming a middle-aged man, his body had gone slack, fleshy. He'd lost his youth though he had always loved Sophie—it was his wish, that they not have children. They'd lived a life of bourgeois comfort of the sort Kolk would find contemptible, Sophie thought.

Strangely Kolk was looking at her now. Almost, a kind of merriment shone in his soot-colored eyes. In a voice that might have been teasing, or accusing, he said: "You're a widow, are you! So, you must have money."

Or maybe he'd said—"You're a widow. So, you must be lonely."

Money, lonely. It was logic, these fitted together.

Sophie said yes, Matt had left her money—and their house of course—but she worked, also—she'd worked for years at a university press that specialized in academic/scientific books—though she was now on a leave of absence.

Warmed by whiskey, Sophie told Kolk that she'd just finished copy-editing a manuscript for the press by an anthropologist/linguist on the subject of twins. Most fascinating was a decades-long study of twins through their lives, twins who'd cultivated "private languages," twin-survivors after the death of a twin, iconic and symbolic meanings of twins, that varied greatly from culture to culture. Kolk listened in silence, drinking. Sophie heard herself say that grief too was a "private language"—when your twin has left you.

Has anyone written about the "private language" of grief, Sophie wondered.

It was then that Kolk said in a halting voice that he'd lost his father—that is, his father had lost *him*. His father had disowned him, after Madison. More recently, his father had died—not that it mattered to Kolk, belatedly.

He'd lost his brother, that had been more painful. He'd been nineteen at the time. But a consolation to think that if his Vietnam War-hero-brother had lived, his brother, too, would have disowned him.

"Why?" Sophie asked..

"Because he was a *war hero*. I was the enemy."

"I mean—why is it a 'consolation'? I don't understand."

"Because he'd have 'lost' me—eventually. When, doesn't matter."

Kolk fell silent then, for some minutes. Beneath the table the bulldog snored wetly. The candles were burning down, luminous wax dripped onto the table like lava. Sophie saw that Kolk's mouth moved as if he were arguing with someone. At last he said: "Friends I had here in Sourland, or thought I had—by degrees I lost them, too."

"And why?" Sophie asked. Her veins coursed with something warm, reckless. "Why did you 'lose' them?"

Kolk shrugged. Who knew!

Sophie thought *You need a woman in your life. To give your life direction, meaning.*

You need a woman in your life to give you—your life.

In his slow halting voice Kolk was saying that he'd been waiting for—wanting—someone here in Sourland with him. He'd had some involvements with women, that had not worked out. This past winter especially—he'd been the most alone he had ever been, in his life. And when he'd thought of someone he wanted—when he lay awake plagued by such thoughts—it was she—Sophie—who came to him.

Sophie, whose face he saw.

But which face? Sophie wondered. Kolk had not seen her face in twenty-five years.

"You look the same. You haven't changed. You . . ."

Sophie stared at Kolk's fingers, gripping the jam-glass. She could not bring herself to look up at him, at his eyes. Was he drunk? Did it require drunkenness, for Kolk to speak in such a way? Was what he said true?—how could it be true? Sophie could think of no reply that would not be facile, coy, clumsy—her heart had begun to beat absurdly, rapidly.

Wanted. Was it good to be *wanted* by a man, or not so good?

Kolk confessed, he hadn't been sure if he remembered her name. But he'd remembered Matt Quinn's name.

Kolk was easing closer to Sophie. Hairs on the nape of her neck—hairs on her arms, beneath her linen shirt and sweater—began to stir, in apprehension. Unless it was sexual anticipation, excitement. For it had to be a good thing, to be *wanted*. Kolk said that when he'd "lost his way"—his "faith"—he'd "wanted to die"—he'd "come close to dying." He'd hiked out into the wilderness—in Alaska, in Alberta, here in Minnesota—thinking how sweet, how beautiful just to lie down in the snow and sleep, shut his eyes. It would not be a painful death once you got over the initial shock and pain of the cold.

Sophie shuddered. Another time she wanted to touch Kolk, to comfort him.

"And what about you, Sophie? D'you ever think about such things, too?"

"No."

"Yes. I think you do. I have a feeling, you do."

The sudden interrogation made Sophie uneasy. Her swollen lip was throbbing, she saw how the man stared at it, as if fascinated. Elsewhere on her body the lurid little bites itched, throbbed with heat.

To be *wanted* was the reward, as it would be the punishment. To be *wanted* was not to stumble out into the snow and die, just yet.

Sophie conceded, yes she might have had such thoughts. But she hadn't meant them.

Kolk said yes. All thoughts we have, we mean. No escaping this fact.

Fact? Fact? Sophie's head spun, she had no idea what they were talking about.

In a lowered voice like one suggesting an obscene or unthinkable act, that dared not be articulated openly, Kolk said they could do it now— together. This night, in Sourland . . .

Kolk splashed more whiskey into their glasses. Crude jam-glasses these were, clumsy in the hand. Their commingled breaths smelled of whiskey. A *twin-language*, Sophie thought. No language more intimate than *twin-language*.

That was why she was here: her twin had summoned her.

This night. Together. Love me!

Then, Kolk surprised her. Saying—this was in a murmur, a mumble:"See, I saved his life. That was why."

His life? Whose?

Sophie smiled quizzically. Was she expected to know this? What exactly was she expected to know?

In an aggrieved voice Kolk was saying that that was why he'd hated him—why Matt Quinn had hated him. Why he'd turned against him. His brother.

His *brother?*

He, Kolk, had known Matt Quinn long before Sophie had. Their connection was deeper, more permanent. On the canoe trip to Elliot Lake when Matt had almost drowned. Afterward, they'd never talked about it.

In a wistful voice Sophie said,"You loved him!—did you."

Kolk spoke haltingly, not entirely coherently. He said that the canoe had overturned in white-water rapids, on a river south of Elliot Lake. It was their second day of canoeing. There were two canoes, his and Matt's was in the lead. In the rock-strewn stream the canoe had plunged downward much faster than they'd expected, and had overturned— both men were thrown into the water—Matt struck his head on a rock—his clothes were soaked at once—except that Kolk had been able to grab hold of Matt, he'd have been swept downstream and drowned.

So fast it happened, like all accidents. A matter of seconds and the rest of your life might be required to figure it out.

Matt had thanked Kolk for saving his life. He'd been deeply moved, he'd been badly frightened, some sense of himself had passed from him in the white-water rapids in the Ontario wilderness, and was gone. Never would Matt Quinn regain whatever it was he'd lost.

"We never talked about it afterward," Kolk said.

Sophie said, "Why did you cut yourself off from us! You could have seen us, all those years." Quickly Sophie spoke, a little drunkenly. Saying that Matt would have wanted to see him—he'd have forgiven him, for their political quarrel. For whatever it was, he'd called Matt. An ugly word—*fink*. Sophie had never heard that word uttered, before or since. Whatever those old quarrels had been—"escalated resistance"—the Viet Cong, Cambodia, Kissinger, war criminals. . . .

She was wounded, hurt. She was very angry. Fumbling for the jam-glass. She was very drunk now. If she were to stand up—the room would tilt, lurch, spin, collapse. This was funny to anticipate—she had to be cautious, not to succumb. For she was angry, and not wanting to laugh. And when the man moved closer, she bit at her lip—her freaky swollen lip—and did not move away. Seeing her hand reach out to Kolk—to Kolk's stiff-raised shoulder—to Kolk's face—daring to touch the melted-away flesh at Kolk's jawline, that was like hardened wax, serrated scar tissue.

She felt a sick-swooning sensation, vertigo. Badly she wanted to kiss the man's mouth, that was mutilated. Kolk grabbed her hand, twisting the fingers to make Sophie wince.

Was he angry? Repelled by her? He touched her swollen lip, that seemed to fascinate him. Another time he murmured *Sorry!* Leaning close to Sophie and suddenly he was looming over her, upon her, seizing her face in his hands, kissing her. Sophie's instinct was to shrink away but Kolk held her tight, unmoving. There came then a strange sort of kissing, mauling—the way a large cat would kiss—a panther, mountain lion—the man's mouth was wet, hungry, groping—the man smelled of whiskey, and of his body—a sweaty-yeasty smell—a smell of unwashed clothes, bed linens, flesh—Kolk might have tried to bathe or in some way cleanse himself but dirt was embedded in his skin, beneath his fingernails. The most thorough soaking could not cleanse this man. Kolk had become a mountain-man, in a few years Kolk would be a crazed old mountain-man, beyond reclamation. No woman could live with such a man, it was folly for Sophie to have thought she might live with such a man. Wildly she began to laugh, she could not breathe for his tongue in her mouth, his hot panther-mouth pressed against hers and sucking all the oxygen from her. With the years Kolk's whiskers would sprout more wildly from his jaws, like jimsonweed. His soot-colored eyes would grow crooked and glaring in his bald hard head like rock. His stubby-yellow teeth would grow into tusks. Winters Kolk would hibernate, in bedclothes stiffened with dirt. He and Cerberus the guard-dog of Hades, pig-pitbull with a milky eye, a freak like his master in a stuporous winter sleep, in their own filth wallowing, no woman would consent to such a life—had Sophie come here to Sourland, to this life, of her own volition?

Yet Sophie was kissing the man—out of schoolgirl politeness, good manners—out of schoolgirl terror—Sophie dared not resist, as the man hungrily kissed her—he was a predator, ravenous for prey—he kissed and bit at her lips—he sucked into his mouth the swollen lip—this lip that beat and throbbed with venomous heat was delicious to him—and there was the taste of the man, in Sophie's mouth—a whiskey-taste, an acrid-taste, a taste as of ashes—the man's gigantic tongue protruding into her mouth—snaky, damp, not warm but oddly cool. *He will strangle me. Choke me like this.* For she could not breathe, she could not move her head away from the man's mouth, the man's tongue. She could not free her head from the grip of the man's fingers. She did not want to offend the man. She knew, a woman dares not offend a man, at such a time. In the throes of desire. In the throes of a ravenous appetite. A woman who has touched a man as Sophie had touched this man, dares not then retract the touch. She did not dare to enflame him. She did not dare to provoke him. She did not dare to insult him. She did not wish him to cease liking her. She did not wish him to cease *wanting* her. It was essential for her survival in Sourland, as in all of the world, that the man not cease *wanting* her. Sophie knew this—she had been a wife, and she was now a widow—and so she knew this—with a part of her mind, calmly—yet she was losing control, her limbs seemed to be going numb—along the pathways of her nerves, eerie rippling flames. The spider bite throbbed in her lip. In other parts of her body spider bites throbbed. Like any besotted lover Kolk was saying her name—a name—*Soph-ie*—*Soph-ie*—she felt a thrill of triumph, at last the man knew her name. She had made him know her name, finally. She felt a thrill of triumph, the man was *wanting* her. Now *wanting* began, it could not be made to stop.

Soph-ie! Won't hurt you Soph-ie—Kolk was urging her to come with him—pulling at her, impatiently—his strong-muscled arms lifted her to her feet—he was half-carrying her somewhere—not to the brass bed in a corner of the warm firelit room but into the other, smaller room—back to the room with the girl-sized bed, the blue-striped comforter in a tangle on the floor. Now Sophie was resisting, or trying to resist—the man was pulling at her clothes—Sophie had the option to help the man undress her, or risk the man tearing her clothes—he was laughing in delight, or moaning—he was very excited—Sophie did not want to impede his excitement—Sophie did not want to antagonize him—he was breathing heavily, arduously—still he was kissing her, hunched over her—this was a kind of kissing—the bulldog had been wakened rudely and was rushing about barking, clicking his toenails against the plank floor—Kolk cursed the dog, and kicked the dog out of his way—as one might kick a child's toy dog out of the way, as if the fat little dog weighed no more than a child's toy dog Kolk kicked S'reebi aside—pushed Sophie onto the bed and with his foot shut the door behind them, as the dog yipped and whined like one bereft.

Kolk was telling Sophie that he loved her—he loved her and he

wanted her—he loved her, that she had come to him—in Sourland, where he'd dreamt of her—for so long he'd dreamt of her in
Sourland—mistaking the woman's agitation for passion, for a sexual need ravenous as his own—was this it?—was this what was
happening?—for it was true, Sophie clutched at the man—as a drunken
dancer clutches at her partner, so Sophie clutched at the man, to keep
from falling—each was only part-dressed now—the man's shirt was
open, the man's trousers were open—he'd pulled the cashmere sweater
over her head—the linen shirt he'd unbuttoned hurriedly, tearing off
a button—on the bed amid the rumpled bedclothes the lovers were
lying asprawl—like lovers drowning together they were clutching at
each other's bodies—Kolk pushed Sophie's legs apart—Kolk pushed
Sophie's thighs apart with his knees—he'd pulled down her fine-
woolen trousers, he'd torn at her white silk panties—his fingers were
inside her suddenly—Sophie screamed, Sophie gripped his shoulders
with her fingernails *Oh oh oh!* the man's fist was rubbing against her,
hard between her legs, her crinkly pubic hair, her tender vagina—with
his knuckles the man was rubbing against her—in a rhythmic beat the
man was rubbing against her—he was breathing hotly, crudely into
her face—in terror of drowning Sophie clutched at him, his back, his
shoulders, his muscled upper arms—in terror she was kissing him,
trying to kiss him—this was a way of placating the man, kissing the
man—hoping to control the man or at least to accommodate him,
she feared the man's roughness, she feared the man's superior strength,
she feared the man's impatience and his abruptness and his waywardness which was the waywardness of a runaway vehicle on a steep grade
and she feared the pain he could inflict if he wished to inflict pain—she
felt a quivering sort of sensation, a sudden desire for him—a desire delicate as the fluttering of a candle flame—if the man was rough with her
in an instant all sensation would vanish, her sense of herself that was
her bodily self would vanish, a net of sheer sensation, the slightest mis-
touch tore the net, she would feel nothing except discomfort, pain. His

knee between her legs, the man was moaning, angry-sounding the man was moaning for possibly he believed that Sophie liked this, a woman would like this, the woman's response was passionate and not fearful, the woman's response was ardent and not panicked, it was sexual yearning that made her cry, pant, half-sob, now the man was mashing his hot scarred face against her thigh, the soft skin of her thighs, and between her legs where she was open to him, split open like a nut—she gave a cry, a sharp startled cry, the man had touched the very quick of her, with his mouth, his tongue—as if he'd reached inside her—as if in his fingers he held her quivering heart.

Trying to speak but she could not speak. Her throat was shut up tight, her eyeballs turned in their sockets. Trying to protest *No!* Trying to tell him *No* she did not want this not like this, she was frightened of him, she was terrified of such sensation, now truly she was resisting him, trying to push him off. The whiskers like steel wool scratched her skin. The rough serrated skin like an animal's hide was wearing her skin raw. She had never kissed a man with such a beard before, the sensation was so very strange. She had never kissed a man with a mutilated face, a ruin of a mouth, the sensation was so very strange. The man lay with his full weight on her, as a wrestler might lie on his opponent, naked, sweating, determined to triumph. Like some bare smooth-skinned creature she squirmed and thrashed beneath him, she could not breathe, another time he was smothering her, his hungry-sucking mouth on hers was suffocating her, his penis was immense and terrible as a club, she could not believe the size and hardness of this club sprouting from the man, such a thing thrust against her blindly, stupidly, a blind brute thing, that had no idea where to enter her, by sheer force pushing inside her as she gasped for breath her eyes flung open *Oh! oh oh* in the girl-sized bed that creaked and jangled beneath their struggling bodies she was being pounded—hammered—beaten into submission—beaten into unconsciousness—she was clutching at the man's heaving sweat-slick shoulders, her nails tore and broke on the man's back, she felt scar tissue like Braille beneath her fingertips as between her legs she was torn open, eviscerated as darkness rushed at her, into her, in the bliss of utter extinction.

Waking then, later. How many hours later. In the tangled and smelly bedsheets. And the man was gone from her. Rising painfully— she was naked, barefoot—her hair in her face and her eyelashes stuck together—she began to pull on her clothing—what she could find of her clothing—the fine-woolen trousers, the linen shirt, the sweater— quickly and clumsily she dressed—she stumbled to the door, that was shut—she turned the knob, and the door opened—she had not expected the door to open.

In the other room the man turned to her, startled—in waning firelight his face was a demon's face, she could not bear to see it.

Sophie told him she wanted to leave. She was desperate to leave this place. She would leave now, he must drive her back to Grand Rapids now, she'd been very sick, her head pounded. She'd been very drunk. She was certain, she was not drunk now. Except she'd been sleeping with her mouth agape, the interior of her mouth was parched as sand.

Kolk came to Sophie, to touch her—to calm her. Sophie threw off his hand, like a snake. Sophie could not have said what was wrong, why she was so furious with the man. She began to scream—*Take me away from here. I hate it here take me away from here.* The man seized her arms, her elbows. The man was speaking harshly to her. The man was shouting at her. Sophie kicked at him, or tried to. Sophie wrenched her arms free and beat at him with her fists—his head, shoulders. He cursed her, and pushed her back into the room. He pushed her back onto the bed. In the doorway, the little pig-dog was barking hysterically. Flames rippled in Sophie's brain, blue-rippling flames of madness. With furious strength she struggled with the man, like a panicked cat, trying to claw him, trying to bite but the man was too quick for her. He left her—he shut the door—she heard the door being locked from the outside and knew that it had happened now.

All that she had dreaded in Sourland, had happened.

◆ ◆ ◆

What happened next, Sophie would not fully recall.

She'd been furious with her captor—she'd been hysterical—she shook and turned the doorknob, to no effect—she pounded her fists against the door, to no effect—the door was solid planks, it would not yield. In the other room the fierce little dog continued to bark, there was a hysterical elation in the dog's barking. The man stood close outside the door and spoke to Sophie—he was telling her to be still, to be quiet, to lie down and try to sleep, he would not hurt her, he would not touch her, but she could not leave.

In a voice of forced calm the man spoke to Sophie but she knew, the man was furious, shaken. His manhood had been insulted, he would never forgive her. He would keep her captive forever, he would murder her. He was not to be trusted. The mock-calm of his speech, the "logic" of his manner—he was not to be trusted. Between her legs Sophie was raw, luminous with pain. Something liquid-hot ran down the insides of her thighs, revolting to her. She smelled of her body, and of the man's body. She could not bear it, she'd been violated by him. She would never forgive him. The man was saying she couldn't leave by herself—it was the middle of the night—and he wasn't about to drive her. He had driven more than six hours that day, he was not going to drive her any-where now. In the morning, maybe—if she still wanted to leave. In the morning—maybe—he would drive her to the airport at Grand Rapids.

This, he told her: but she paid no heed to him. She did not trust him, she detested him. Her body crawled with the memory of hav-ing been touched by him, there was no part of her that had not been violated by him. She was screaming until her throat was raw, she was pounding at the door with both her fists. Everywhere, her body was covered in bruises. Her fists throbbed with pain, her knuckles were skinned, bruised. She could not bear it, the man had locked the door and would not open it. The man had locked her in the room, and would not release her. She was his captive now, he had triumphed over her and would not release her until she was broken by him, annihilated. In a faint she stumbled back to the bed. All her senses were alert, spinning. Her brain was so alert, so alive the nerve-endings pained her. She was so distraught she'd begun to hyperventilate, she could not breathe normally. She crawled onto the bed, she burrowed beneath the blue-striped comforter that was a soft-down comforter, and kept her warm.

She woke later, it was very quiet. The air in the cave-like room was close and stale and chilly but beneath the comforter, she'd been warm. She stood now, shakily. She was not so furious now. The hysteria had subsided. Her quick sharp vaulting breath had subsided. She breathed more normally, her thoughts came more normally. The door—she tried the door—was still locked. She was at the man's mercy—was she? He would wait for her to beg him—would he? Through the single window she saw a bright moon. Half the moon's face had been battered, there were bruises, creases. Yet the moon was cunning, glaring light into the clearing. Snow had ceased falling hours ago, now the sky was clear. The air was very cold, a scrim of snow remained on the ground, unmelted. She tasted vomit at the back of her mouth—she'd been very drunk—but no longer. With frantic fingers she managed to loosen the window—it was opened by a crank. Her heart beat quickly, in astonishment. It was not possible, what she was doing!—while the man slept in the other room drunk and oblivious.

She managed to open the window, that was no more than two-foot-square. She pushed her coat through it—she pushed her gloves, her scarf. Her shoe-boots, that fell with a thud. She pulled a chair to the window and climbed onto it trembling with excitement, she forced herself through the window as a cat would force itself through a small space, squirming, writhing. She forced herself through the window like one giving birth, the creature to which she was giving birth was herself.

The night air was very cold. She was panting, her breath steamed. Where she would go, how she would find her way to a road, or to another house—she had no idea. She could not think coherently, the circuits of her brain were jammed. Enough for her to escape. Enough for her to escape the spiders' nest. The man's crude groping hands, the thing he had jammed up inside her. The man's hungry mouth, so like her own—she had escaped it. She was sick with disgust, to recall what she'd escaped. On the snowy ground she groped for her coat, she shoved her arms into the sleeves. She had lost the gloves—she couldn't find the gloves. She would tie the wool scarf around her head, her face. She would protect her face, that smarted from the man's hateful beard, against the cold. Her swollen lip was not so swollen now yet ached, throbbed. The man had gnawed at her mouth like a ravenous animal. She set off behind the cabin, in the direction of a trail she'd seen the previous day. How long ago that had been—a lifetime ago!

She was too clever to follow the driveway out to the road for the man would simply follow her in the jeep, he would bring her back and lock her in the cabin. And so she set out into the Preserve, ascending the hill behind the cabin. When she looked back she saw that the cabin was darkened, or semi-darkened. Smoke drifted upward in languid white streams like dreaming thoughts. The man was asleep—was he? She had escaped him—had she? What a fool he was, to imagine he could keep her captive—she laughed to think of how surprised he would be, in the morning. She did not want to think that the man would track her in the morning, like an animal. He would set the ugly little dog after her. He could follow her footprints in the snow, the dog would follow her scent. She did not want to think this, she was desperate not to think this. Though knowing better she began to run. The trail was slippery from fresh snow, the exposed rock-strata were slippery, a fall in the woods could be fatal to her, she dared not risk it. Yet she couldn't bring herself to walk at a normal pace, she was desperate to escape the man. By moonlight she could see the ground, not clearly but as in a dream, just enough to make out her footing. She saw a faint trail, rotted leaves covered with snow. With childish gloating as she thought *He won't find me. By the time he looks for me I will be a hundred miles away.*

How surprised she was then—within a few minutes the man was calling after her—*Soph-ie! Soph-ie!* She was shocked, and she was frightened. Truly she had thought she could escape the man, in the wilderness. Though she had no idea where she was going she understood that she was going away from *him*. Yet he'd wakened, and discovered her missing—that must have happened. And now he was outside, and following her. She began to run, desperate and panting. It was hopeless to run from the man yet she could not help herself. She had no wish except to escape the man. To punish the man by escaping from him, even if she injured herself. Thinking *If I am lost, I will die. I will die in these millions of acres of wilderness. That will be his revenge.*

Behind her then she heard his voice sharp in the cold air, like knife-blades. "Soph-ie! *Soph-ie!*" He was in pursuit of her, and he was walking—hiking—fast. He knew the trail, he had hiked this trail hundreds of times. She was in terror that he would set the dog after her—but she didn't hear the dog. Behind a tree, she hid. She hid, and tried to rest. She'd been ascending the trail—this was a mountainside trail, strewn with boulders—an ancient volcanic upheaval, the Sourlands of north central Minnesota—she was badly short of breath, climbing the trail. Also she was very cold, trembling. Her eyelashes were stuck together as if frozen. Her eyes spilled frozen tears. Her husband had died and abandoned her and this now was her fate, in Sourland. Even the spider bites on her body throbbed with the heat of accusation. There was a hot ribaldry to these itches. She fumbled to pick something up with which to protect herself—a broken tree limb. She would strike the man with it, if he came too close. If he set the dog after her, she would murder the dog. She was running, hunched-over. Her limbs ached, her head ached, she tasted vomit. She slipped on an icy rock, fell and cut her hand. She forced herself to her feet. She was talking to herself, whispering. She'd become a hunted creature. The man shouted after her knowing exactly where she was. From the first, he'd known. She could not hide from him, her footprints were revealed to him. He carried a flashlight in one hand and in the other hand he gripped a walking-stick like a figure in a Grimm's fairy tale. He would seize her and drag her back to the cabin by her hair. She would be cleaved in two, the man would jam his fist into her, his penis hard as a club deep inside her body. She would be cleaved in two, she would die. She could not survive another assault, she would die.

Something screamed nearby—a screech owl. There was a blurred frenzy of wings not twenty feet away overhead in the pine boughs, an owl striking its prey in the shadow of a boulder, a rabbit's shriek, the tiny death was over in an instant.

All this while the moon hung crooked in the sky. The man was hunting her, swiftly yet not in haste. His movements were never careless, he knew the trail by night. In his left hand he held a flashlight and in his right hand he gripped a five-foot walking-stick. It is a terrible thing, to be pursued in the night by a man with a five-foot walking-stick. Sophie tried to hide, she'd crawled behind one of the great white boulders like the eggs of a giant prehistoric bird. *Soph-ie! Come here! You'll hurt yourself for Christ sake.*

She heard the *click!* of the walking-stick. The stick against the frozen earth. Striking the rocks, deflected from the rocks. By now it was well past midnight. By now the moon was careening across the sky, toward a distant horizon. Sophie scrambled to her feet, stumbling into the wild for she'd lost the trail. Yet telling herself *I want to live. This is proof, I want to live and I will live.* She slipped, she fell. She fell hard, injuring her wrist. And her ankle—she'd turned her ankle. Oh! her ankle had twisted beneath her, she cried with pain, disappointment. She was sure she'd heard the bone crack. She was sick with loathing for herself. For now the man was close behind her, closing the distance between them. The light of the flashlight swarmed onto her, blinding her. How he'd known that she'd left the cabin, she could not imagine. She'd been so quiet, so circumspect! Now the man loomed above her. He'd put away the flashlight, he had no need of the flashlight now. And there was moonlight, that came splotched and strangely glowing through the trees. Like a cornered animal she struck out at him, a small vicious creature, a mink, a ferret, she had only her claws to protect her, and her teeth. But the man was too quick for her, and wary. She could only flail with her hands, that were numb as with frostbite. She was on the snowy ground now, amid the rocks, sprawled, helpless. She was crying softly, all passion had drained from her. The man had triumphed, he was lifting her, grunting as he lifted her, in triumph, gloating. She knew, he had to be gloating. He had to be laughing at her. She had not the strength to scream at him to tell him how she hated him, she despised him, all that he'd done to her and would do to her, he was repulsive to her. In silence he lifted her, his arm around her waist. He was a man who would say little, Sophie knew. She would have to communicate with such a man in a way more primitive than words.

He held her, standing. She could not have stood, on her own. Her right ankle throbbed with pain. Her clothes were torn, her hair was wild as tangled briars. Still he held her steady. She was sobbing, pushing at him, yet weakly now. There was no hope, she could not escape him. She'd gotten less than a mile from the cabin, for all her cunning and desperation. By daylight you would be able to see how far. By daylight he would laugh at her. The pig-bulldog would laugh at her. Footprints in the snow, her prints and his prints in pursuit, until he'd caught up with her, hauled her to her feet, he would half-carry her back down the trail to the cabin where a fire still smoldered in the fireplace, where the bulldog had been confined and yipped frantically as they approached. Bitterly she was saying she didn't want to be with him, she didn't want this. She had made a mistake, she didn't want this nor did she want him. She was sobbing with pain, frustration. She leaned against him, with great difficulty she walked, her right ankle was near-useless. Still the man held her, walked with her bearing the brunt of her weight as they made their way cautiously in slow downhill skids, on the icy rock. His was a perverse and unyielding strength, she understood would not fail them. She could feel the heat pulsing from his body, through the nylon parka. She asked how much farther it was back to the cabin and the man said, "Not far."